SECRETS BEHIND THE BILLIONAIRE'S RETURN

RACHAEL STEWART

SECOND CHANCE IN SRI LANKA

NINA MILNE

KT-164-717

MILLS & BOON

First Published in Great Britain 2022
by Mills & Boon, an imprint of HarperCollins*Publishers* Ltd,
1 London Bridge Street, London, SE1 9GF

www.harpercollins.co.uk

HarperCollins*Publishers*
1st Floor, Watermarque Building,
Ringsend Road, Dublin 4, Ireland

Secrets Behind the Billionaire's Return © 2022 Rachael Stewart

Second Chance in Sri Lanka © 2022 Nina Milne

ISBN: 978-0-263-30216-5

04/22

MIX
Paper from
responsible sources
FSC® C007454

This book is produced from independently certified FSC™ paper
to ensure responsible forest management.
For more information visit www.harpercollins.co.uk/green.

Printed and Bound in Spain using 100% Renewable Electricity
at CPI Black Print, Barcelona

SECRETS BEHIND THE BILLIONAIRE'S RETURN

RACHAEL STEWART

MILLS & BOON

For our besties, the Watkins!
And the beautiful market town of Leyburn, North Yorkshire,
their home and the inspirational setting for this tale…
Much love xxx

CHAPTER ONE

SEBASTIAN DUBOIS STARED at the gates ahead and wished himself a world away.

They seemed no less hostile than he remembered— the wrought iron looming high, lording it over visitors and family alike. The stone walls with their run of spikes feeding off in either direction communicated with ease the silent message: Outsiders Are Not Welcome.

Hell, insiders weren't either...

He clutched the key fob in his hand, the hard edges cutting into his palm as he wrestled with an alien unease. Sixteen years had gone by. He'd been barely a man the day he'd left, fearing a future he had no control over. Fearing the dawning responsibility, too.

Never mind the realisation that everything he'd believed about his family—himself, even—had been a lie.

Well...not quite everything.

The unforgiving Yorkshire rain lashed at the windscreen of his idle Range Rover, mocking his frozen state. The rapid beat of the wipers contending with the throbbing in his skull.

You're not a scared sixteen-year-old any more. You're beholden to no one. Afraid of no one. So, press the damn button and drive.

He hissed a breath between his teeth, fisted his hands tighter. 'For God's sake!'

It was bricks and mortar. Empty. Soulless.

The estate had been that way for at least a year. There was nothing to fear—*no one* to fear. Given another year, it would be transformed. Reborn under the elite Dubois hotel chain.

His hotel chain.

This visit was about facing up to the past and laying it to rest. A short stay within its walls, time to re-envisage it before obliterating its legacy. Simple. Or so it should be.

He swiped a forearm over his clammy brow, glared up at the dark sky above. His arrival was later than planned thanks to freak weather stateside delaying his private jet's flight from New York, but it was still only six-thirty. It was the damp and dreary Yorkshire weather making it feel so much later.

That and the fact he'd been country hopping for the past week and jet lag was setting in. He was tired, tetchy, and on edge. Just as Theo had warned him he would be. His younger brother and business partner advising him with a rare show of gravity to get a hotel, take a break and then face it. And he'd dared to laugh him down, telling him it was a waste of money, completely unnecessary, ridiculous even.

'Argh!' He punched the steering wheel—angry at himself for his hesitancy, angry at the past for still having such a hold over him. But nothing could detract from the power of the words twisted in the iron gates before him: The Ferrington Estate.

Ferrington. The name he'd once borne before he'd fled to France. Escaping both it and the family's patriarch, his grandfather.

And here he was letting the old man get the better of him again.

Cursing, he yanked open the glove compartment and tossed the fob inside, hating his own weakness but hating the estate and his past more.

He slammed the car into reverse, feeling his chest ease as darkness swallowed the gates once again but his relief was short lived as the in-car system announced an incoming message from his brother.

So how is the old place?

He grimaced and set his sights on the road.
Not answering you, bro.
Especially when he'd gone against his brother's advice and had the place fully stocked for his arrival, a bed made up, food brought in, staff primed… He'd made all the preparations—save for his own mental capacity to face it.

Ignoring the little voice in his head calling him out for being a fool, he pulled into the winding country road, his headlamps lighting it up and enshrouding the bordering countryside in darkness.

Now what?

Ahead, the tiny lights of Elmdale flickered and the smallest of smiles touched his lips, a melancholic warmth unfurling within and taking out some of the chill. Another blast from the past, another step to take…only he wasn't about to back away from this one.

He urged the car on, bolstering courage from the misery he was leaving behind. The car wipers beat harder, faster, his heart pounding in tune, the thud ever more pronounced as he hit the base of the hill in the heart of the village and squinted through the rain-smeared windscreen.

It looked the same. The cluster of pubs on either side of

the road. The red phone box outside the post office. The bakery next door. The greengrocer's opposite the market square, the war memorial, and the village hall. The potted flowers and bunting from a recent event lifting the darkness of the age-blackened Yorkshire building stone. The streets devoid of life as the rain kept everyone tucked up indoors.

And there, straight ahead, standing proud at the peak— Gardner Guest House.

Her home. His refuge once upon a time, too.

He leaned forward, hungry to see more, to spy all that was familiar…all that had changed.

The blossom tree in the garden out front was taller, broader, and in full bloom. The wooden front door and gate were still duck egg blue. The same sign still swayed out front: a Yorkshire tree of life with the 'Vacancies Available' sign beneath, lit up and dripping with rain.

Was it still owned by the Gardner family?

Would *she* still be there?

He followed the signs for the car park out back and pulled up alongside a very familiar, very old VW Beetle. He took in the yellow paintwork that had seen better days and realised he had his answer. If the car was here, surely she must be, too.

And you're sure you want to go on in?

He eyed the three-storey building, the warm glow from its windows far more welcoming than the Ferrington gates had been.

They had vacancies; he needed a bed.

There was no need to debate it.

Nothing like jumping out of the frying pan and into the fire…

He ignored the inner jibe and accepted the truth. He wanted to see her.

Call it curiosity, unfinished business, distraction…
whatever.

Thrusting his coat on, he stepped out into the torren-
tial rain and yanked up his hood, zipping the collar. He
certainly hadn't missed the Yorkshire weather.

As for the girl that had lived within these walls… He
ignored the way his stomach rolled and legged it around
to the front. Swinging open the gate, he made sure it
caught on the latch before racing for the door. He could
already smell the fire burning within, hear the low rumble of laughter from the patrons, but as he pushed open
the door silence descended and all heads turned his way.

He breathed through the unease that threatened to return and closed the door, shoving his hood back as he
scanned the room.

A pair of elderly men sat before the fire drinking pints;
they gave a brief nod before going back to their conversation. A couple in the window alcove quickly went back to
their bottle of wine and cosy embrace. And the parents of
a family of five, who were enjoying a board game, smiled
at him as he dipped his head in greeting.

The welcome desk was notably deserted.

'She won't be long,' the mother at the table explained,
spying his focus. 'She's just making hot chocolate for
this lot.'

She gestured to her kids and he smiled, or at least tried
for a smile, but it was tight with the increasing churn in
his gut. Who was 'she'? Would it be Flick or her grandmother?

In either case, would they turn him away?

He raked a hand through his hair. What had he been
thinking? Turning up after sixteen years, unannounced
and seeking a room. Craving the warmth this building

had once provided. The shelter, the love, the kindness, the feeling of belonging.

This was a mistake. He shouldn't have come. He started to turn, ready to take his chances on the iron gates when the door that led off to the kitchen swung open.

'Three hot chocolates with all the trimmings at your—'

Startled blue eyes met his and his brain emptied, his mouth opening to speak as the tray in her hands tilted and the mugs slid. He rushed forward but it was too late. The mugs hit the wooden floor with a crash that had everyone leaping to their feet.

'Goodness, Felicity, you okay?' One of the old chaps made to help her but she dropped to her knees and waved him back.

'I'm fine, Bill.' She spoke to the floor, shutting Sebastian out as he joined her, his hands picking out broken china but his attention wholly on her. 'I'll be right with you, sir, if you can wait at the desk.'

Sir? He frowned, her name rasping past his lips. 'Flick?'

Her eyes shot to his, her tone harsh. 'At the desk, please, I—'

She winced and lifted her hand. A fresh prick of blood welled on one finger, and he couldn't stop himself from reaching out—guilt, blame and regret all clamouring for dominance as he sought to help her.

'I said I've got it.' Her eyes flared, her body recoiling from his touch, and he felt something within him shrivel, snuffing out the emotional torrent.

'Okay.' He tossed a piece of china on the tray and backed away. 'I'll wait.'

She sucked the tip of her finger, her cheeks flushing pink. She sent a moment's glare in his direction and then her lashes lowered, blocking him out again.

Relegating him to no one. A stranger.

Exactly as he deserved.

Felicity hurried back to the kitchen, shoving the door open with her hip and flinching as the handle dug into her flesh. *Sebastian.* Sebastian was here. In her home.

Not a dream, or a figment of her overactive imagination.

'*Sebastian.*' His name left her lips with a rush of air, her hands shaking as she emptied the tray into the bin and shoved it on the side. She checked her finger; the bleeding had already stopped, but his near touch, his voice… still, they resonated through her.

Flick? She hadn't been called Flick in for ever. Not since her school friends had upped and left, chasing their dreams all over the world.

She pressed her hands to her cheeks, clamped her eyes shut and sucked in a breath. She couldn't believe it was him. Not after all this time.

But standing here wasn't going to change what was so unbelievably true.

And she had a mess to clean up. Guests to look after.

She yanked open the broom cupboard, took out the mop and bucket and froze as she recalled those steely grey eyes, so close moments before, the way they made her belly flip; the way his sandy hair, swept slightly to the right, made her fingers tingle, the dimples in his cheeks—

'Mum, is everything okay? I thought I heard a crash.'

She spun around, clutching the mop to her chest as she took in her daughter's sudden presence. Angel's blue eyes widened over the state of her—*flustered* was probably an understatement. 'What's happened?'

'*Nothing.* I—I dropped a tray.'

Her daughter frowned as she lowered the textbook she'd been carrying. 'You want me to help clean up?'

'No!' She winced—*way to go in acting normal*—and swiftly softened her tone. 'I want you to go back to your revision. You've helped out enough this week.'

'It's fine, I'm due a break anyway.'

'I said, no.'

Softly, it's not her fault you don't want her in the same room as...him.

She forced a smile over her gulp. 'Sorry, love. All's okay, I promise.'

Angel eyed her a second longer. 'Okay, so long as you're sure... I'm going to grab a hot chocolate to take up with me.'

'In that case, would you mind making three more? Fully loaded?'

'Is that what hit the deck? The O'Briens' supper treat?'

'Yup.' She eyed the door, pins and needles spreading over her skin as she thought of him out there, waiting. Waiting for what, exactly? Why would he come here after all this time? *Why?*

'You sure you're okay, Mum?'

She swallowed and plastered on her smile. 'Of course. Just tired, it's been a busy week.'

'Don't worry.' Her daughter smiled back. 'Another week and the Easter rush will be over, it'll be back to just you and me.'

Or not... Felicity's gaze returned to the door, her mind on him. 'Leave the drinks on the side, won't you, love? I'll take them out when I've cleaned up.'

'Sure.' Her daughter went back to her book as she navigated the kitchen without looking, blissfully ignorant of the situation brewing on the other side of the door.

Felicity wanted to keep it that way. Wanted to pretend it wasn't happening.

Oh, God, how was she going to tell her…tell him, even?

It had never been a secret of her choosing. Sebastian had taken away the choice when he'd vanished without a trace.

But now he was back. It didn't matter why he was here; now that he was, she had no choice. She had to tell him.

Him *and* Angel.

She hurried to the door and tugged it open. She didn't need to look to know his eyes were on her and her skin tingled top to toe, alive on his presence as her heart and mind raced. She wanted to yell as she mopped up the mess. Yell as she demanded where the hell he'd vanished to sixteen years ago when she'd needed him most. And why, why, why, did he have to come back *now*? Just when the pressure was on for Angel at school—her daughter didn't need this. Neither of them did.

Her head continued to spin as she tried to fight the panic and form sentences that worked. How to tell him, to tell them both, in a way that would cause the least amount of chaos. But there was no way of saying it without turning all of their lives upside down.

The only thing she knew for sure was that she needed to do it without an audience.

'Right, kids…'

Felicity's heart launched into her throat as she spun on her heel. Angel was in the kitchen doorway, a tray of drinks before her and an indulgent smile on her face.

'Three fully loaded hot chocs!'

She gaped at her daughter, felt the colour draining from her face as she approached. *Why do kids never listen?*

Angel's eyes shifted to her, a little crease teasing between her brows, but years of working in service had her smile staying in place.

'Here we go.' She placed the drinks on the table to a chorus of thank-yous and then she was turning to face Felicity, who still hadn't moved. Her eyes narrowed and quickly shifted to the right. To…*him.*

'Hey, Mr, I'll be with you in a second.' She was talking to Sebastian but approaching her mother, her beaming smile at odds with the speculation in her eyes. 'You want to go and put the mop away? I'll sort out the new customer.'

'He's not—he's…but…' Words failed her. She needed to get a grip. She needed to get a handle on the situation. But Sebastian. Angel. In the same room.

'Okay.' A spark entered her daughter's eyes. 'Why don't I take these, then, and you deal with the not customer?'

'I…you…'

'Oh, my God, Mum!' she said between her teeth. 'He may be hot but there's no need to look so terrified. He won't bite.'

'That's not…'

Not what? How could she explain to Angel the reason she was scared had nothing to do with his looks and everything to do with who he was?

Angel took the items from her limp grasp, her eyes dancing as she added under her breath, 'You never know, maybe he'll do you some good.'

She gave a wink and then pranced away, leaving Felicity bracing herself.

She'd never planned it this way. In her head it had always been her going to him, her getting hold of him *because* she had this news, this confession, this revelation.

None of those situations factored in him reappearing out of nowhere, him coming to her, and it was that which had her floundering, that which had her turning to face him and wishing herself a million miles away.

How did you even tell someone who was now a stranger that he was a father?

CHAPTER TWO

EVERY INSTINCT URGED him to help her clean up, to apologise, but he gritted his teeth and stayed put, reminding himself that regret was futile. It changed nothing. Helped no one.

He would apologise, explain and then they could move on.

Just as he would take over the Ferrington Estate, bury its legacy, and move on.

Only, as he watched her, there was the prickle of something else making his pulse race…and it wasn't unease.

'So…' She walked towards him, strands of her long brown hair falling loose from her ponytail and brushing against her pale cheeks. 'You're back.'

'I am.'

'Why?' She placed the mahogany reception desk between them, a defensive move he couldn't miss.

He breathed deeply. What was it about smells that could transport you back in time? To the boy he'd once been, standing in this very room, running from the latest hiding courtesy of his grandfather, and wishing he had a different life.

A life far more akin to Flick's…

'Well?' she pressed, tugging him back to the present, to those eyes so big and curious, drawing him in.

He cleared his throat. 'You have some vacancies and I need a room.'

Her eyes widened. 'You want...*you want to stay here*?'

He ran a hand through his hair, felt his throat threaten to close again. 'For a couple of nights, if possible?'

She gave a soft scoff, a shake of the head.

'I also owe you an explanation.'

'An explanation?' she repeated dumbly, her eyes going to the others in the room, his doing the same. No one seemed to be paying them any attention. Thankfully. She leaned closer anyway. 'Are you *kidding* me? After sixteen years you want to *explain*?'

'I want to tell you why I left.'

'Right. Okay.' She gave a disbelieving laugh, shook her head some more as she looked to her computer and woke it up. 'Double or single?'

'Either.'

'Double it is.' She didn't spare him a glance as she held out her hand. 'I'll need a card to secure the booking.'

He reached into his chest pocket, took out his wallet. 'Here.'

She eyed the card he presented as if it were an unexploded bomb, careful not to touch him as she took it. He saw the moment the name on the card registered, saw her eyes widen a second before they lifted to his.

'Dubois?'

He nodded.

A flurry of questions flickered across her face before she blinked and the shutter fell, her attention back on her computer screen as the crease between her brows furrowed deeper.

She processed his booking in silence, her bottom lip trapped in her teeth, and he found himself entranced.

They were the same age and yet she seemed younger,

fresher, more vibrant…aside from the colour she'd lost the second she'd set eyes on him.

Time had been kind to her, enhancing her English rose complexion, which she'd left make-up free. Her rich brown hair was longer than he remembered. Her lashes, still thick and long, framed eyes so blue they reminded him of the sky on the sunniest of days. Her skin-tight jeans were off-set by an oversized baby-pink sweater, so fluffy it gave him the obscene urge to reach out and pull her to him— to *hug* her.

'I'll show you to your room.'

It took him a moment to back out of his mental musings, another to dampen the foreign heat in his veins, and another to realise she was holding out a key.

He took it, grateful that his fingers were steady, his voice, too, as he thanked her.

What was wrong with him? First, he couldn't get past the gates, and now this.

Jet lag. It was all down to the jet lag.

She led him through to the back where the staircase rose to the gallery landing from which the first-floor rooms branched off. He wondered if she still lived in the attic quarters. He wondered where her grandmother was. Question after question building as the memories forced their way in. Weekends, evenings, and holidays helping in the B & B with Flick. It had been worth every trek up and down the stairs when, at the end of the day, they were paid in her grandmother's homemade shortbread or scones.

'How's Annie?'

She faltered over the next step, her delayed response sending an icy trickle down his spine.

'She passed away two years ago.'

She didn't look back as she quickened up the stairs and he cursed, hurrying after her.

'I'm sorry, Flick.'

She chanced him a glance, the sadness dulling the blue of her eyes. 'She was sick for a while…' She was moving again. 'It was almost a relief by the end that she wasn't in pain any more.'

His mother had been the same. He remembered watching her waste away and wishing her pain would just stop. 'What happened?'

'Cancer.' She took a breath as she reached the top step. 'Gran was never one for seeing the doctor. Didn't matter how much pain she was in, she kept on going until…well, anyway…' She paused beside the first room to the right, clearly shutting the conversation down. 'This is yours.'

She pushed open the door and waited for him to enter.

'Breakfast is served eight 'til ten. We offer picnic baskets for lunch. If you want somewhere to eat in the evening, I can recommend The Black Bull over the road, or if you want something a little finer…' her eyes trailed over him and he sensed her pricing up his outfit, which had him wanting to loosen his collar '… Adam and Eve's, on your right as you enter the village, comes highly recommended, though this time of year it gets fairly booked up so I'd ring to ensure you get a table.'

'Adam and Eve's?' He couldn't help the amused quirk to his lips and was grateful to see her mirror it.

'You remember Nadine from school?'

'The one obsessed with books and poetry?'

'The very same. She's a renowned chef now who ploughs all of her romantic energy into her food.'

'I'm surprised she didn't call it Romeo and Juliet.'

'She did. That's in the next town along.'

He gave a soft huff. 'Well, I'll be…'

She shifted from one foot to the other, her eyes on anything but him. 'Right…well, I'll leave you to settle in.'

She turned to go and he reached out to stall her, his hand gentle on her arm. His gaze fell to where he touched her, to where the heat came alive beneath his fingers, swept through his arm, his core…

'Sebastian?'

His eyes shot to her face—did she feel it, too?

He swallowed the foolish question, the even more foolish reaction. 'Can we talk?'

'We serve drinks until ten. The older folk prefer to come here, as it's quieter than the pubs these days, but they tend to leave soon after.'

'I'll come downstairs then, wait for it to quieten down.'

She hesitated on the threshold; her lip caught in her teeth.

'Please, Flick, I'd like to explain.'

'You don't—'

'Mum!'

Her body tensed beneath his touch as the call came from the bottom of the stairs. It sounded like the girl he'd seen delivering the hot chocolates earlier and he frowned at Flick—*Mum?*

Her eyes were wide, fearful. 'I have to go.'

She was racing down the stairs before he had chance to say anything more.

'What's up?' he heard her ask.

'Bree's here, she's asking about tomorrow's order.'

Flick was a mum. A mum to a *teenager*. Shock numbed him to the core.

Maybe the girl wasn't as old as she looked. Didn't girls always look older, especially when they were wearing make-up as she had been? Or had Flick jumped from him to another guy so quickly and if so, was the father here, too?

Had he unknowingly fled the hostile estate and waltzed

straight into her family home, an outsider who truly didn't belong?

He swung the door closed, pressed his palm into the solid surface as he sucked in a breath. And if that was the case, why did it bother him so much?

They were ancient history.

Weren't they?

Felicity raced down the stairs in a panicked daze, the past colliding with the present in such timely fashion and she felt…*guilty*.

As if it was somehow her fault that he didn't know.

'Are you sure you're feeling okay, Mum?'

She gave Angel a semi-smile. Her ears ringing with the unspoken, the nausea swelling in her gut. She needed to tell him. Or should she tell Angel? Who deserved to *know* first?

Him. Because he was the adult.

Her. Because Angel was her daughter and the most important person in her world.

No. It had to be him. She had to understand the lie of the land, of the future and what role he wanted to play in it before she could breathe a word to Angel.

'I'm fine, it's just been a long day.'

'Long week more like. Bree's out front, chatting to Bill and Frank. You okay if I head over to Iona's? I want to go over a couple of things with her. This Chemistry revision is blowing my mind.'

'Sure, of course.' She mustered a more convincing smile, pulling her daughter in for a quick hug and finding she couldn't let her go. Here she was, the grown adult, and yet she needed to absorb the strength from her daughter. The innocent in all of this.

'You can let me go now,' Angel murmured into her chest. 'I'll be back, you know, in an hour or two.'

She gave a soft laugh, cupping her face and kissing her forehead. 'Have fun.'

'It's revision, Mum, it's hardly fun.'

'Well, why don't you kip over with her, get an early start on it tomorrow, too? I can handle things here.'

Angel frowned. 'You sure?'

'Absolutely. Iona's mum was asking only yesterday if you wanted to sleep over.'

'I know and you said all hands were needed on deck.'

'And I was wrong.'

'But—'

'No buts, now go. I'll be fine.'

'Okay…' But Angel didn't budge.

'Go!' she urged, turning her around and giving her a nudge. 'Pack your stuff and have a productive study session.'

'Okay, okay…but call me if you need me though, yeah?'

'Promise.'

She watched her fly up the stairs before taking a deep, steadying breath and smiling wide. If Angel knew something was up, Bree surely would. And if her friend caught even the slightest whiff of unease, she'd have her confessing all before she could even say the word 'father'.

'Hey, honey!' The woman herself appeared in the hall then, all flamboyant colour against her deep brown skin, luscious curves, and ebony hair in flouncy waves. 'You ready with the breakfast order?'

'Sure am.' She didn't meet her friend's eye as she headed to the front desk and pulled her notepad out, tearing off the top sheet and keeping the carbon copy for her record.

'Everything okay?' The proximity of Bree's cheery voice made her jump.

'Yup, everything's fine.' She wanted to wince at the pitch to her voice. 'Why?'

'Oh, nothing. Bill just mentioned you'd dropped a tray and Angel said you had…' she lowered her voice as she leaned in close, a wicked gleam in her chestnut eyes '…some hot guy check in and now you're looking a little flushed…so…?'

She could feel the colour rising in her cheeks. Hot was an understatement. Not that she wanted to dwell on it. He was already a whole heap of trouble to her status quo.

'Here's the order, same time as usual.' She shoved the sheet into Bree's palm, hoping she would get the message.

'No problem.' She didn't back away though. 'Come on, you need to give me…' The hot guy in question chose that moment to walk in and Bree's words trailed off.

'I'm just going to unload the car…' He pointed in the direction of the door as though Felicity needed the added visual and she nodded dumbly, watching him go.

Bree turned to lean back on the desk, her eyes shamelessly taking in his rear as she murmured, 'Oh, *my*, come to Mamma.'

'Bree!' She swiped her friend's shoulder as the door swung shut. *'Behave.'*

'What? It's not like he heard me.' Bree turned to face her, her grin alive with mischief. 'And he *is* the hottest thing to walk into this village in… In fact, I can't remember anyone looking that hot.'

She swallowed, trying to calm her body, which had gone into overdrive the second he'd reappeared. 'Yes… well…he's a guest, so leave well alone.'

'Hey, Felicity.' Bill wandered up behind Bree. 'Isn't that the Ferrington boy?'

Oh, dear God. She made a non-committal sound that could be taken either way.

'The Ferrington boy?' Bree's ears visually pricked up. 'You know him?'

'My sight isn't what it used to be, but he sure looks familiar.'

Both Bree and Bill were looking at her expectantly and she wished the ground would open and swallow her. She loved Elmdale, the community, the support, but right now she could happily live in the middle of nowhere, where no one knew anybody, and her dirty laundry wasn't at threat of being outed to all.

'Well?' Bree pushed.

'Yes.' She cleared her throat. 'He's the Ferrington boy.'

'I knew it! Frank, you owe me a tenner!' Bill grinned over his shoulder as Frank waved him down. 'Bet he's back now that no good grandfather of his has kicked the bucket.'

Her eyes widened. 'Bill!'

'What?' He gave a shrug. 'The man was an arse. Couldn't even see fit to help mend the church spire last year. Not like it would have made the slightest dent in his bank balance.'

'I'm sure it's bad form to speak ill of the dead,' she murmured, Bill's words making the questions race faster, harder. *Was* he back? Like *properly* back? Did he intend to live at the estate? Right on her doorstep? And if he did, why was he here instead of there?

'Not when you speak ill of them when they're alive, too.' He gave a wink. 'We'll have the same again when you're ready, love.'

'I'll bring them over.'

She felt Bree's narrowed gaze on her and knew she sounded distracted, but…

'A penny for them?'

'Nothing to tell.'

She hated lying to Bree, the closest friend she had, but it didn't feel right to tell her when the people it concerned didn't know. Bree didn't know her history with Sebastian. She'd only moved to the village three years ago, when Bree's aunt, the owner of the local bakery, had fallen ill and they'd needed someone to chip in. Bree had come for a few months, fallen in love with the village and never left.

Now she was as much a local as Bill, and just as inquisitive too, her probing gaze still trying to do its thing.

Felicity was saved by the return of the man in question and this time she averted her gaze, her computer screen far more interesting than his swanky shirt now soaked through and clinging to his impressively broad and toned chest.

'Hubba-hubba.' Bree dragged her eyes from his exiting form. 'Now I understand *everything.*'

She feigned a laugh. 'Whatever you say, just quit lusting after my guests.'

'Says you! You might as well have had heart eyes popping out of your head.'

She refused to rise to it, her cheeks giving away enough of her guilt as she crossed the room to the bar.

She was filling a fresh pint glass when Bree joined her and started pouring the other. 'Why do I feel like this is about more than having a hottie in our midst?'

She kept her lips tightly sealed, her eyes on the pint.

'I didn't even know Ferrington had grandkids. The idea of that particular man procreating makes me shudder.'

'They left a long time ago—' *sixteen years, to be precise* '—a few years after their father passed.'

'He must have died young?'

She swallowed, the tragic story catching up with her. 'A car accident.'

'How awful!' Bree went quiet for a moment. 'Is that what happened to Ferrington senior?'

'Hmm?'

'Is that how he became the infamous grump we all knew and loved?'

'Hardly.' She snorted. 'He was already a difficult man to deal with. Nothing was ever good enough…more so after he lost his wife. I think she was the happy to his misery, the necessary balance. But after she died, he shut himself away and would only attend events if he was lauded as the special guest. Then he lost his son and he retreated altogether.'

'So much grief… Poor guy.'

So much grief, yes, but did it justify his behaviour, the way he treated his family, the way he treated her sixteen years ago? No. And she wouldn't forgive him for that, dead or not.

'And so, his grandson is back because…?'

She shrugged as they stepped out from behind the bar. 'Beats me.'

'Interesting,' Bree drawled. 'And he's staying here, rather than at the estate?'

Felicity sent her a look. Her friend had that gleam back in her eye. 'Stop it.'

'There's a story there, I reckon.'

'And it's none of our business.'

Except it was, kind of…

'Whatever you say, honey. Whatever you say.'

CHAPTER THREE

FRESHLY SHOWERED AND ready to face Flick, Sebastian returned to the bar.

The visiting family had retired for the evening, something he'd already surmised as he'd heard the laughter and footsteps pass his room over an hour ago. The couple had also left, leaving the two gentlemen at the fire, who were standing as he came into the room.

'We're going to call it a night, Felicity, love,' the one donning his flat cap said and that was when Sebastian spied her straightening up from behind the bar. Her smile for the men was warm and friendly—it took his breath away—until she saw him.

She averted her gaze then, her fingers fluttering over her hair as she crossed the room and pulled open the door. 'Make sure you're careful on those cobbles. The rain has turned the square into a waterfall.'

'You don't need to worry about us, love,' the same guy said, buttoning his coat as he walked towards her. 'We were navigating this village long before you were born.'

'You love that she cares really, Bill,' the other said.

'Aye, that I do. I'll be back first thing to look at that boiler, okay? Angel mentioned it was on the blink again.'

She grimaced as she placed a hand on Bill's shoulder. 'Thanks. I don't know what I'd do without you.'

'Likewise. I'd have nowhere to drink in peace.' He dipped her a wink. 'Mabel doesn't understand that a man needs quiet to enjoy a good beer.'

Her expression lifted with her laugh and it kickstarted a weird dance inside Sebastian's chest. 'I think you and Frank give Mabel and her knitting circle a run for their money on the talking front.'

'And speaking of Mabel…' Frank nudged Bill towards the door '…she'll have my head if I don't have you home in the next fifteen minutes.'

She watched them go, a frown building as she closed the door. They were alone. If she did have a partner, he was nowhere to be seen. Sebastian looked to her left hand as she reached to bolt the door—no ring. Though that didn't mean there wasn't one and he had the burning need to ask her even though it wasn't any of his business.

'Can we talk now?'

Her shoulders lifted with her breath, and she gave the faintest of nods as she crossed the room to pick up the empty glasses on the recently vacated table. 'Can I get you a drink?'

'So long as I'm not keeping you from anything, or…?'

Anyone. He found his hand lifting aimlessly as he followed her to the bar, and she gave a short laugh.

'If you mean, do I have a man waiting for me to finish up… No, I don't. So, drink?'

She eyed him over the bar, the spark in her blue depths momentarily flooring him. It also made him want to reach over the divide and relive the chemistry they'd once shared. A chemistry that seemed all the stronger for their age, the time apart…it was the only thing that explained away his curiosity and his inability to keep his cool.

'I'll have whatever you're having.'

'Fair enough.'

She spun away, plucking a bottle off the shelf before turning back to face him. He quirked a brow at her selection.

'What?' A smile teased the corners of her mouth. 'Whiskey too strong for you?'

'For me, no.' He slid onto a bar stool as she lifted two glasses from beneath the counter. 'I wouldn't think it your drink of choice though.'

'You know nothing about me any more.' She uncorked the bottle as she stated the simple fact…a fact that stung far more than it should 'And right now, this is the only drink capable of taking the edge off your arrival.'

If he hadn't felt the knife before, he sure did now.

He forced himself to smile. 'That bad, hey?'

She sloshed the drink into the glasses, corking the bottle and placing it down with a thud. 'What do you think?'

'In that case…' He took up a glass and raised it to her in mock salute. 'Cheers.'

She gave a choked sound that could have been a laugh, a scoff, or a note of disgust. 'Cheers.'

They drank and warmth spread through his gut, a warmth that had nothing to do with the settling whiskey and everything to do with her. The way her lips glistened from the drink, the way she swept away the remnants with the slightest sweep of her tongue, her delicate throat bobbing as she swallowed…

He dragged his eyes back to hers, tried to suppress every urge that had no place in the now, and yet he swore the same burn was there, firing back at him. She might not appreciate his homecoming, but her body was singing a different tune…a tune very similar to his own.

'I guess I should start with my explanation.'

'What for?' She nipped her lip, colour flushing her

cheeks and enhancing the blue of her eyes. 'Why you're here now? Or why you abandoned me sixteen years ago?'

'I didn't… That wasn't…' He raked his fingers through his hair, took a breath. 'At least come sit with me and let me explain.'

He could read people well enough to know she was keeping the bar as a barrier between them, just as she had the desk earlier, and he didn't like it.

Turning on his stool, he gestured to the one beside him. 'Please?'

Slowly, she slid her glass across the bar and did as he asked, tugging the stool back a foot before perching herself on it. She folded her arms and crossed her legs as she faced him. 'Okay, spill.'

Spill. Like it was that easy. He took another breath, another sip of the harsh amber liquid as he held her eye and felt the continued stirring deep inside.

How could she still have this hold over him after so long?

How could her eyes, her mannerisms, even her voice with its rich Yorkshire twang get to him so readily, so profoundly?

'Well?' she prompted, a steel façade descending as her knee started to bob with her impatience.

He clutched his glass tighter. 'Do you remember the last night I saw you?'

The pain flickered to life behind her eyes, the façade slipping as she lowered her gaze and took up her drink. 'Yes.'

'It was the end of school party…'

'I said I remember,' she bit out, her knuckles around her glass turning white, and his jaw pulsed. He didn't want to face her pain, any more than he wanted to relive the past and explain it, but he knew he owed it to her.

'Everyone was high on the rush of exams being over, buzzing with the thrill of the summer ahead, all of their plans, *our* plans…' He swallowed. 'We were supposed to meet the next morning, take a ride down to the river with the horses, we had a picnic planned…'

Her eyes were on her drink as her lips gave the hint of a smile. 'Cheese and pickle sandwiches.'

A melancholic laugh. '*That's* what you remember?'

'They were your favourite, those and Gran's scones…' She lifted her lashes, her eyes reaching his for a second's connection, a second where the bad never happened. And then she went back to her glass, moment gone. 'You never came to meet me. I stood on the square, picnic at the ready, but no you.'

He reached for her on impulse, a gentle touch to her knee though his whole body stiffened against the unwelcome zip of heat it triggered. 'I'm sorry, Flick. I didn't want to leave you like that.'

She removed herself from his touch, turning away to face the bar and plant her forearms on the surface. 'So why did you?'

He dragged in a slow breath, blocked the painful memories threatening to overcome the fore. 'I returned from the party that night, just gone ten and my curfew was—'

'Ten. I remember. Set by your grandfather and one you would never break.'

'I wouldn't but Theo…' He shook his head. 'My grandfather was a hard man. I don't think my brother and I realised how hard until Dad was gone. Or maybe he got worse.'

'He was always cold.'

'He was *more* than cold.' His vehemence caught her eye, his laugh devoid of humour. 'He was cruel. To Mum, to us. After Dad died, Mum tried to move off the estate.

She couldn't cope with his autocracy, nor the punishments he sought to inflict on Theo and me.'

Her eyes wavered over his face. 'He—he hurt you?'

'Me, not so much.' He threw back a swig of his drink. 'I'd learned to keep a low profile, stay off his radar. But Theo… He went off the rails after Dad died, acting out, rebelling against anyone who tried to tell him what to do.'

He tried to roll his shoulders back, ease the tension between his blades. 'Our grandfather was ready to have us shipped off to boarding school and Theo…well, you can imagine.'

She didn't speak, but she was listening and that was all he needed.

'Mum was angry, too. Distraught at the idea of us being sent away and when Theo didn't come home that night and my grandfather declared it as the final straw, they had a huge fight.'

Her cheeks paled as her eyes widened. 'He hurt your mum?'

His throat closed over as the scene played out, quick-fire, so much worse than anything Flick could imagine.

'Not intentionally. He was aiming for Theo and Mum came between them. All hell broke loose. One minute she was standing, the next she was on the floor with a bloodied lip.'

'Oh, my God, Sebastian.'

It was her hand on his knee now, her sympathy, but he didn't deserve it. And he couldn't tell her the rest. He'd buried those demons long ago and wasn't prepared to let them rise again. Another swallow, another blacking out of the scene trying to play to completion in his head as he squeezed his eyes shut.

When he opened them again, her hand was still there, her eyes still soft. 'What happened?'

'We packed our bags and were gone before morning,' he said, skipping over the worst of it. It wasn't a lie, it was an omission, he told himself. 'Mum bought an old banger from a friend and, car loaded, we headed for the Euro-tunnel. Mum had a childhood friend who owned a B & B on the outskirts of Paris. She put us up and we never came back.'

'You moved to *France*?'

'Escaped, more like. My grandfather tried to track us down, but my mother changed our names, removed any trace…'

Her eyes widened with realisation. 'Hence the Dubois?'

He nodded. 'Mum knew our grandfather had the re-sources to find us, she also knew he'd stop at nothing to make our lives and those of anyone who tried to help us very difficult. He'd do whatever it took to ensure we came back with our tail between our legs. We were his heirs after all, he wanted to shape us into the same mould as him, have the place kept just so, the name preserved, the reputation…' He scoffed. 'Being feared was the same as revered in his book.'

'It was a miracle your father turned out like he did.'

His gut turned over, bile rising so quickly he had to throw back his drink to keep it down. Of course, that was how she would see it. That was how he'd seen it until that night. Until his grandfather had told him otherwise, until he himself had *proved* otherwise.

And so, he deflected. 'Mum had no family of her own. It was important to her that we keep our heritage, our leg-acy, but not like that.'

'So that's why you left and never looked back?'

A beat of silence, the chilling sickness of what he hadn't divulged making his skin prickle, words difficult to form.

'Something like that. It wasn't planned, Flick. I didn't

set out to hurt you. My focus was on them. My brother. My mum. I was sixteen and suddenly the man of the family… I had to keep them safe.'

'I'm so sorry.' It choked out of her, her eyes searching his as her hand lifted to his arm. 'I wish I could have been there for you.'

'There was nothing you could have done. Money made him powerful and dangerous.'

'How could he be so hateful?'

'He was a Ferrington.'

Her eyes narrowed. 'But so are you.'

She was trying to be encouraging, reassuring, telling him one didn't necessarily follow the other.

He knew better.

Looking away, he sipped at his whiskey, the demons within making themselves known. He knew he was damaged and broken, and, regardless of the pain his disappearance had inflicted, Flick had been better off without him.

He didn't doubt it. Not for a second.

'Your mum must have been so scared he would find you.'

He recalled his mum back then, their early days in Paris. Used them to warm away the chill as a smile played about his lips. 'She was, but she didn't let it show. She was strong, driven—*amazing*. She worked long hours as a cleaner, a waitress, whatever she could find, and in turn, we studied hard, worked harder. Made sure she never regretted walking away from the Ferrington name and the privilege and wealth that came with it. We made sure we made something of ourselves and did her proud.'

Felicity watched him closely, watched every fleeting expression and felt the enormity of what he was telling her. She nodded softly, dumbly, her eyes lost in the sincerity of his. Everything about him spoke of the success he had achieved…save for the shadows persisting in his depths.

'You've certainly done that.'

'What? Made something of ourselves?'

'Yes.' She looked to where her fingers still rested on his arm and pulled away, her cheeks warming as she realised how long they'd remained there…and how much they tingled from the simple touch. 'And your mother? How's she doing now?'

'Dead.'

Her eyes shot to his as the air rushed from her lungs. *'Sebastian.'*

His mother could only have been… She did the maths and placed her in her fifties. Felicity might have lost her mother in childbirth, her father unknown, but to hear he'd lost his mum, after everything they'd been through…

'I'm so sorry.'

He barely looked her way. 'Breast cancer. Stage four by the time she sought help.'

She swallowed the pain rising within, its force magnified by her own experience, her own loss. *'Blasted* disease.'

His eyes found hers. 'The same with Annie?'

She shook her head, her throat tight. 'Pancreatic.'

'Blasted disease indeed.' He covered the hand that had found its way to his arm once more, warming her, soothing her. 'We paid for the best the country could offer, of course, Theo and I. Flew in specialists, tried to get different answers, better ones…'

'Some things money can't buy.'

His fingers flexed over hers. 'No and I wouldn't wish that feeling of helplessness on anyone, not even my worst enemy.' He looked at her, his haunted gaze stealing her breath. 'I'm sorry I wasn't there for you.'

She wanted to say she was sorry she hadn't been there for him, too, but he was the one who had left, the one who had taken away the chance for her to be there…and left her with a secret she hadn't wanted to bear.

Gently, he squeezed her fingers. 'Forgive me?'

Forgive him.

If only it were that simple. Forgive and forget.

If only there weren't this secret between them.

Her chest spasmed, her heart pulsing as she pulled away from his touch. 'It's not that simple.'

'I know…more than you can possibly know.'

She shook her head, took up her drink. 'No, you don't.'

He frowned and she had to look away, sip her whiskey as she found enough courage to ask, 'Why have you come home? Now, after all this time?'

She felt his gaze on her, burning into her, and for one silly moment, she wondered: was he going to tell her he was here for her?

Like some fairy-tale romance where the hero made his fortune and returned to sweep the heroine off her feet…

As if. She almost laughed aloud at the ridiculous notion and choked on her drink in the process.

'Steady.' He placed a hand on her back, the innocent touch reverberating right through her. 'You okay?'

She hurried to recover, to break the electrifying contact. 'You avoiding the question?'

He gave her a slight smile. 'No. Truth is, now my grandfather's gone, Theo and I can do what we like with the estate. We toyed with letting it go but I figure the old man will turn in his grave to see us return to it.'

She could hear the bitterness, see the smile still playing about his lips adding to the chill of his hatred, and fought back a shudder. She'd never known Sebastian to be cold, stripped of his good humour, his care, his passion.

Was this more the man he was now? A cold-hearted business mogul? Did he have a woman on the scene, multiple women, even, or was it just him and his brother? There was no ring on his finger but that didn't mean...

And what about friends? What about—she swallowed—*other* children?

She wanted to ask, she wanted to know it all. But she was only putting off the inevitable, the all-important conversation that they had to have and that wasn't fair...on any of them.

'Sebastian?'

His eyes wavered over her face, his brows drawing together. 'Yes.'

'There's something I need to tell you...'

'I figured as much.'

She wet her lips. 'You did?'

'You look like you're about to confess to some heinous crime.'

'No.' She gave a tight laugh. 'No crime. Only...'

'Only?'

'I'm—I'm a mum.'

'I know.' His smile softened, his eyes, too, something akin to regret lingering there. 'I gathered that earlier. Is—is her father around? I notice you don't wear a...'

He gestured to her ring finger and she snatched it back self-consciously, twisting her hands together. 'No, he is—wasn't.'

Oh, God, why couldn't she just say it? Why was it so hard?

'Can't have been easy bringing her up alone, looking after your gran, especially when she got sick, and then there's this place...' He gestured around him and she couldn't even nod, couldn't even blink.

His eyes narrowed as the silence extended…a beat, two, three. 'Flick?'

'She's yours,' she blurted, her lips pressing together as her heart threatened to escape her chest. 'She's…she's ours.'

CHAPTER FOUR

HAD SOMEONE TURNED on a faulty appliance or were his ears genuinely ringing?

He stared at the grooves in the wooden bar top until his eyes stung, trying to string a sentence together, a thought even, and nothing would come.

'Sebastian?'

He flinched.

'I'm sorry.' Tears welled in her eyes; her voice was barely above a whisper. 'I'm sorry you didn't know sooner, but I couldn't—I couldn't reach you. I tried. I did.'

The boulder in his throat expanded.

'Please, Sebastian, say something—*anything*.'

His lashes fluttered as he tried to draw breath. Say what? Where did he even start?

'How old is she?' *Damn stupid question!*

'Sixteen.' She wet her lips. 'She was sixteen on Boxing Day.'

'Boxing Day,' he repeated numbly. *Sixteen*. He'd had a daughter for sixteen years and knew nothing of her. His head spun as he shoved himself away from the bar, strode to the fire, his fingers tugging at his hair. This couldn't be happening. It couldn't be real.

But why would she lie? She wouldn't...

It had to be the truth, only...

'*Sixteen*—the age you must have been when you…had *her*.' He choked on the last, a heavy silence following that crackled with his frenzied thoughts, the image of her young, pregnant and alone. Far too young to have a child. Far, far too young. His gut rolled. How could he have been so foolish? So ignorant? So stupid?

'But *how*?' They'd never been reckless. *Never.*

'I don't know, the condom must have split, I wasn't on the pill…'

He could feel her eyes boring into his back as he stared at the dying embers in the grate. How could he not have known? How could he have left her pregnant with *his* child?

He was a father. He had a daughter. A daughter who was almost an adult.

A curse erupted from his lips, the pads of his fingers pressing into his forehead as if he could somehow push the news out. 'Where—where is she now?'

She didn't answer and he turned his head enough to see her on his periphery. 'Is she upstairs?'

'No, she's at her friend's for the night.'

'Because I'm here.'

'Yes.'

'Does she know?'

'No.'

He looked back at the embers, his skin buzzing and tight. He'd spent his entire adult life avoiding meaningful relationships, anything close to a family of his own and she'd been here all this time. Her and Flick.

The lost years mounted in his mind's eye. The birth, her first words, her first steps, birthdays—*so many birthdays…*

Had Flick known before he'd left? Could she have told him? Damn it, if she'd told him, he wouldn't have gone.

Liar. How could you stay when the damage had already been done?

He fisted his hands, fought it all back. 'When did you find out?'

'A few weeks after you vanished. I didn't… I didn't want to believe it at first…and then there was no denying it. I didn't tell anyone. Not until Gran caught me crying one night. I was supposed to be at Nadine's birthday party, but I couldn't face it. I could barely face anyone by then. I was so scared of how I would be seen. You know what this place is like; everyone knows everyone's business—the gossip, the looks…'

'So, you kept it to yourself, you struggled alone?' Bile stripped the back of his throat—the guilt, the anger, the surrealness of it all urging the whiskey to make a reappearance.

'To begin with. But then I had Gran and she was incredible. She did everything she could, buying what I needed, attending every appointment—'

'But I *should* have been here.' The anger won out as he spun to face her.

'In hindsight, I'm not sure what good it would have done, other than to prevent this situation now.'

He blinked and blinked again. Was she trying to make him feel better?

'You were as much a child as I was.'

He shook his head, denying it even as he recognised it for the truth. 'Children don't make a baby.'

She coloured. 'You know what I mean.'

He did. He also knew that he wasn't fit to be a partner, let alone a father. He knew that and still those lost years mounted, the not knowing…

'We were *always* careful! I never would have—I would never have risked…' His fingers were shaking as he raked them through his hair, scouring his brain for the moment it could have happened.

'There's always a risk, even with protection, but I never thought it would happen to us. I was so caught up with you leaving it took me a long time to realise I was late and by then...' A sad smile, a shrug. 'But you know what? Even if I could go back in time, I wouldn't change it. Not for the world. Not now.'

He narrowed his gaze. 'Are you *serious*?'

'I'd change the fact I couldn't reach you, of course I would, but...' The smile still teased at her lips, the emotions chasing over her face with whatever private thought she entertained. 'She's wonderful, Sebastian. She's clever, funny, supportive.'

The boulder was back in his chest, his throat. *Wonderful. Clever. Funny. Supportive.* All things he would know if he'd been here to see her grow up.

A thousand butterflies seemed to take off inside his chest, the war of emotion impossible to contain as he stressed again, 'I should have been here.'

'But you weren't.' Her gaze remained level, unfazed. 'And I tried to track you down, I even...'

She blinked and looked away.

'You even?'

Her eyes flitted back to him. 'I went to the estate. I spoke to your grandfather.'

'He *knew*?'

'No—God, no.' She shook her head, her hands rising. 'I wasn't going to tell him. I just wanted to find out where you were, talk to you. I was hurt when you vanished, but I told myself you must have had a reason.'

'And what did he say?'

'I couldn't even get past the gates. When he refused to see me, Gran tried and when that failed, she managed to collar one of his staff in the market square one day. Scared the life out of him by all accounts…'

A smile trembled on her lips, a burst of nostalgia catching up with him too. 'I bet she did.'

Annie had been fierce. Fiercely loyal and loving and everything his grandfather hadn't been.

'She discovered that you'd left—you, your brother and your mother—with no forwarding address, nothing. That's when I had to accept…' she swallowed, her knuckles white as she gripped her knees '…that you were gone, and I wouldn't be able to tell you.'

He stared at her long and hard, his head starting to pound. 'You had your life ahead of you, dreams of going to university, of moving to the city, of becoming a lawyer…'

'And I chose Angel.'

'But the life you envisaged?'

'What about it?'

'I'm sorry, Flick, I'm just…' He shook his head. 'I'm struggling.'

'You're struggling!' She launched herself off the stool, stomped towards him all fire and grace, animated and passionate and everything he'd missed in his life these past sixteen years. Her scent reached him first—floral, soft, subtly sweet—and then her forefinger was pressing into his ribs as her presence engulfed him. 'You don't get to struggle, Sebastian Ferrington—*Dubois*—whatever you want to call yourself now.'

He opened his mouth, closed it again and she bit into her lip.

'Sorry, I didn't mean…it's just, when you said that… I was sixteen again, young, lost, my heart torn in two. People judging me, advising me…'

She drew away and he dragged her hand back to his

chest, craving to keep the contact and all the warmth it brought.

'I'm sorry.' He felt her fingers flex beneath his, felt her body tremble, or was that him? 'I didn't mean to hurt you, Flick.'

'Stop calling me that.'

'Flick?' He frowned. 'Why?'

'Because it makes me feel… It makes all those years fall away…' Her eyes swam with emotion as she gazed at him. 'She's the best thing that's ever happened to me, Sebastian. Don't you see? Back then she was my last link to you, and I naively thought that one day you would return, one day you'd come for me and discover her and we'd— we'd…' She shook her head, looked to their hands locked upon his chest and gave the smallest of laughs.

'What? What did you naively think?'

Another shake of her head. 'It doesn't matter. It was just the foolish dream of a foolish teen who couldn't let you go.'

'It matters to me.'

She tried to pull away, but he wasn't ready to let her go. His body vibrated with her proximity, more alive than he had felt in so long, her presence beating back the chill as the future she hinted at painted an image too painful in its perfection.

Because maybe it would have been possible, before he'd been so broken, before that fateful night…

'Flick?' He touched a finger to her chin, tilted her head back, his body urging him to taste those soft pink lips, his long-forgotten heart hammering to hear her confirm what she hadn't yet admitted.

His eyes were dark, his finger beneath her chin soft, her name on his lips softer still and the yearning swelled within her. The need to forget the years apart, the pain, the loss, the pressures of reality…all in the heat of his kiss.

Because he wanted to kiss her. She could feel it in the thrum of his heart beneath her palm, see it in the fire behind his eyes…but where would that leave them?

In an even greater mess than you are now.

'Tell me what you dreamed of, Flick.'

'Why?'

'Just…humour me.'

He didn't want to tell her why, and she didn't want to put words to a foolish teenage fantasy, but out they came. Well remembered. Well versed.

'I dreamt of you walking through those doors, your life in a bag on your back asking for a room… Gran would give you that special smile she had, the one that made everything feel possible, and welcome you in.' She took a breath, taking in his alluring scent, his real-life presence. 'She'd call out to me and I'd walk in, Angel in my arms, and you'd know, without me saying a word…you'd know.'

His eyes trailed over her face as his palm brushed against her cheek. 'And then what?'

'And then you would say you were sorry.' She took a short breath, a pant, incapable of more when trapped under the spell he had effortlessly wove. The delicate touch of his palm sparking every nerve ending to life. 'You were sorry for not being there for me, for us. Sorry for running away.'

His eyes flashed. 'And?'

'I'd tell you it was fine, and you'd say it wasn't. You'd wrap me up in your arms, promising me that you were back for good…'

He stepped closer—or did she move towards him?—and raised his other hand to cup her face, his eyes holding hers captive. His body, too, as she felt the subtle brush of his sweater against hers, the hardness of his chest against her softness.

'And then?'

'And then you'd kiss me.'

Her words were distant, as though spoken by someone else a whole lifetime ago, and as he bowed his head her lashes closed, her lips parting under the gentle sweep of his. A shiver ran through her, a hunger unlike any other clawing its way through her middle as her hands lifted to his shoulders, his neck, his hair, pulling him closer as she angled her head to deepen the kiss.

'Sebastian.' His name rose on a whimper she couldn't control. His hungry growl a reciprocal beat as he palmed her back, pulling her closer.

'Flick?'

It sounded like a plea, begging permission to seek more, and she nodded, careless, reckless.

When was the last time she'd been reckless? Had she ever been reckless?

The day you got pregnant...

No. She hadn't been reckless then. They'd been in love. They'd been careful...but fate had stepped in.

Are you going to blame this crazy coming together on fate, too? And what about when you're breaking this news to Angel?

Her eyes flared open, the warning sudden, jarring and so very timely.

She's who you should be thinking of...she's who you should be talking about, making plans for, not this!

She shoved at his chest. 'Stop! Stop! We can't do this.'

'I'm sorry.' He cursed, broke away. 'I didn't mean...'

He dragged a hand over his face, his eyes wide with surprise, shock, disbelief.

She pressed her fingers to her thrumming lips, shook her head to try and empty out the haze. 'That was…'

'A mistake?' He sucked in a breath, gripped his sides as he stared at the exit as if it would somehow anchor him, save him. 'I just…'

His eyes came back to hers; he looked as confused as she felt. 'It's been so long since I've felt… Since I've… I got carried away on your dream.'

'We *both* got carried away.'

She smoothed her palms down her jeans, her fingers shaking, her body burning, still eager, still wanting.

God, how she wanted…

She'd thought herself immune, disinterested in men altogether after Angel had been born. She'd dated, mainly to put Gran's mind at rest that she wasn't going to die a spinster, but it had always been so forced.

That wasn't though…that had been electric, coaxing her entire body to life after sixteen years as though it had been waiting for him to come back.

'Yes, well, not to worry…' She ran her teeth over her bottom lip, wishing it would stop thrumming. 'I'm not the naive teen I was when I dreamed it up and I'm sure if we focus on the practical, we can hopefully make this as painless as possible.'

'Practical and painless.' He frowned. 'Right. I assume we're talking about breaking the news to A-Angel.'

She didn't miss the way he stumbled over their daughter's name and her stomach lurched. He was her father and yet he'd had no say in naming her. He was her father and yet he didn't even know her.

Guilt twisted inside her. A guilt she shouldn't feel but couldn't quite suppress.

'Now isn't the best time for her.' If she wanted to feel

any worse, she'd just succeeded. His eyes lanced her as her meaning hit home.

'Now isn't the best time for what?' He folded his arms, his eyes refusing to release her from their pain. 'Telling her?'

She nodded, unable to shift the aching wedge in her chest.

'Will there ever be a good time?'

'There'll be a better one. She has her exams coming up, and she's studying so hard. I'm worried that if we…' She swallowed, lifted her chin. 'If we tell her now it will unsettle her, and I'm worried about the impact it will have on her results. She's been doing so well, Sebastian. After Gran passed away, she struggled, we both did. She's not had it easy and to see her so focused again is great, but I'm not sure she could cope with this right now. You understand, don't you? Please tell me you understand?'

She pressed her lips together, couldn't breathe as she waited for him to speak. She knew she'd rambled, but she was desperate to make him see, to make him understand.

'I don't want to hurt you any more than this already has, Sebastian, and we will tell her, of course we will…' Then a thought struck her. 'Unless you don't want to tell her?'

A mobile started to ring and for a heart-stopping second, they just stared at one another.

Had she misread his reaction so completely? Was he horrified at the prospect of this getting out? Did he *want* to pack up and run?

And then he moved, pulling the chiming device from his trouser pocket. He checked the screen and cursed.

'I have to get this.' She could see the hesitation in his eyes, the fight in his body. 'But mark my words, Flick…' His eyes hardened, his stance, too. 'We're telling her.'

Relief battled with fear as she nodded. 'Only, not yet—okay?'

His nod was curt, grave. 'We'll talk about it. Tomorrow. Can you get someone to cover the B & B after breakfast?'

'Yes.' She'd have to. Somehow. She had to speak to him away from the B & B and prying eyes…or rather, ears. Particularly those of her—*their*—daughter. She couldn't run the risk of their secret getting out before they were ready; before Angel herself knew all there was to know.

And with that he was gone, like a whirlwind stirring up her entire life and leaving everything hanging mid-air.

Being around him again…losing herself in him again… she could feel it happening already. He wasn't the boy running from his horrific grandfather any more, he was a grown man capable of ripping apart her life, and she needed to keep her wits about her…and her lustful thoughts well clamped.

She took a long, slow breath and focused on the positive.

Sebastian was back and Angel had a father. No matter how rocky the path ahead, ultimately that had to be a good thing.

Wasn't it?

CHAPTER FIVE

SEBASTIAN'S HEAD THROBBED. He'd slept an hour, two at most.

The rest of the time he'd stared up at the ceiling, coming to terms with it all. Even Theo had known something was up. He'd been too distracted on their call, his brother's assumption that it was down to the roof over his head forcing him to admit he hadn't got past the estate gates.

Much like Flick when she'd tried to see his grandfather all those years ago.

His stomach lurched as the scenario played out, far too clear as he thought of her, young and scared, desperate as she pleaded with the old man for his whereabouts.

He pressed his forefinger and thumb into his temples as if it would somehow force the painful image out, change reality, change the way he'd stripped Flick of her dreams for a future and broken her heart in one.

No regrets.

Already the old mantra was wearing thin and staring up at the B & B in the morning light didn't help either. The rain had stopped. It was bright and crisp, the sun unforgiving as it revealed what the dark had concealed the night before.

Yes, it was picturesque—the flowers in the window boxes, the vintage bistro tables either side of the front door, the cherry blossom tree with an old yellow bicycle leaning up against it, flowers flourishing in its front basket—but the building itself needed work. The duck egg paint was starting to peel at the windows, the slate tiles on the roof looked precarious in parts, the guttering was sprouting greenery…

As for the inside, it was as expected—comfortably chic and cosy throughout. But it was also tired, especially in the high traffic areas. And though the splashes of colour, the fresh flowers, the scent of bread baking and fresh coffee went some way to averting attention, his critical hotelier eye couldn't help noticing the work required.

He'd left Flick with Bill, who, good to his word, had arrived to check the boiler. He got the distinct impression that, as Annie had before her, Flick depended on the locals to keep the B & B ticking along. Ageing locals at that.

It hardly made for a secure future, for the B & B, or for her…or his daughter.

He knew all about running costs and even a B & B on this small scale would require a hefty income to keep itself going to an acceptable standard.

The pressing need to do something weighed heavy on his chest, but what? Would she accept his financial aid? Unlikely. But then, he owed her sixteen years of child maintenance and that would be a start. Money he could readily provide.

And focusing on the practical was far easier than thinking on the emotional repercussions. How his daughter would react to the news. To his presence. Would she *want* to know him? Would she hate him for leaving? Would she resent him for coming back now? Would they *both* resent him?

He rubbed his neck, trying to massage out the tension as the frown between his brows deepened. Money he could fix. Time, on the other hand. There was no getting that back. And even if he could, it didn't change what had happened that night, it didn't change him…

A tingling sensation ran down his back, an awareness rippling through him that had nothing to do with the unease within. He was…he was being watched.

Hand still on his neck, he turned. There, outside the post office, were two elderly women, eyes brazenly on him as they talked. It was the same across the way, a man and woman chatting outside the bakery. His attempt at a polite nod was greeted with a widening of the eye and a swift turnabout.

So much for being polite.

He was rescued by Flick opening the door to the B & B, her presence a very welcome breath of fresh air…and hammering home the way she made him feel. He smiled over the unwanted thought, burying it deep.

'All set?'

'Yup.' Her ponytail swung behind her as she walked towards him, her tan boots clipping the cobbles, her blue eyes bright and cheeks flushing pink in the sun. 'Sorry to keep you waiting.'

'No problem at all.'

She wore a cream cable-knit jumper with stone-washed jeans, everything about her relaxed…save for the dark smudges beneath her eyes that he could now make out as she paused before him, the fine lines marring her brow betraying a far too frequent frown.

'Did you get it sorted?'

'It will be soon enough,' she said, though her smile was strained. 'Bill's a man of many talents.'

He nodded, but her obvious stress had his hotelier brain working overtime, his concerns too.

'What?' The lines deepened as she squinted at him,

her hands sweeping over her cheeks. 'Do I have something on my face?'

'No, no, not at all. You look fine, just…tired.'

She gave a soft huff. 'Charming.'

'Not in a bad way,' he was quick to say.

'Since when does looking tired come across in a good
way?'

Since he was looking at the most beautiful woman he
had ever known—*and that's another thought to bury deep.*

It wasn't as if she were a classic beauty, her eyes were
too big, her button nose too small, she was too tall and
slender, and her hair refused to stay tame in her ponytail,
but he was enraptured by it all. Her very presence seemed
to breathe life into his otherwise stale existence.

And now he was still staring, and she was looking even
more uncertain.

He cleared his throat. 'Did you not sleep well?'

'Did you?' She pursed her soft pink lips and immediately he was transported back to the evening before. To
their kiss. Their explosive, mind-blowing, knee-buck-
ling kiss.

He ran a finger under his collar, his eyes lifting to hers,
and she cocked a brow, her blues sparking with something
akin to amusement. 'It's okay, you can admit it. I won't
take offence that the bed was— *Oh, God.*'

She looked past him and smiled wide, her teeth gritted
as she raised her hand and gave a flutter of her fingers.
'Morning, Maggie, Miss Jones!'

He turned to take in the same two women he'd caught
eyeballing him earlier. '*That's* Miss Jones?'

'The one with the hat and sunglasses.' She spoke under
her breath. 'And if you don't want to be the subject of the
ever-efficient Elmdale rumour mill we'd best move. She

may not work in the school any more, but her network is as efficient as ever.'

'Sounds great. I'll drive.'

He pulled his car keys from his jeans pocket and she fell into step beside him. 'Where are we heading?'

Good question.

He thought of the estate. Guaranteed privacy, even if it meant facing off the past. But somehow the idea of doing it with Flick felt...easier.

'What do you say we pay the estate a visit?'

She sent him a look. 'Really?'

'I figure we both have ghosts to put to rest and we'll be free of an audience there.'

'Okay.' She pulled her sunglasses from a denim bag slung over her shoulder and slid them on. 'The Ferrington Estate it is.'

He didn't even react to the name, so casually said. And if it bothered her, she didn't show it. She was confident. Composed.

And utterly captivating.

Already he could feel his wits dispersing in her presence. They had things to discuss. A plan of action to put in place. A plan that saw Flick and his daughter in his life from this day forth and the idea had his head in a spin. Because other than his brother, a few trusted employees, and his housekeeper, he didn't share his life with anyone.

He was a loner, regularly labelled a recluse by the media, and did he care? No. He *was* a recluse, and he was happy that way. He had no interest in the schmoozing, the social niceties, the public role—Theo gladly took on that mantle. It gave Sebastian time to focus on what was important: the business.

And it meant his life was his own, just the way he liked it.

Only now it wasn't, and he had no idea how to deal with it.

And he hated the not knowing, he hated the uncertainty, almost as much as he hated the events of that night sixteen years ago.

She'd known it was his car when she'd taken the rubbish out that morning. The black muscle vehicle screamed Ferrington—*you mean Dubois.*

No, she couldn't get her head around the whole Dubois. Too French, too foreign…not Sebastian, who was English aristocracy whether he'd fled that life or not.

And now he was back—all sexy and intriguing and coming to terms with her news.

With his eyes on the road and hers hidden behind her shades, she was free to sneak her fill and just like the night before he had her mouth drying up, her heart pattering to an entirely different beat. He was all hard angles in the face—chiselled jaw, defined cheekbones, strong nose. And muscle. So much muscle in his tall frame, perfectly enhanced by the slim fit of his designer shirt and dark jeans.

She took a breath and looked to the road, seeking distraction from the heat within. 'Have you been to the estate since you returned?' She couldn't deny she was curious about the place. For over a decade, no one had been granted access save for the staff. Certainly not the British press, who had arrived in their masses to cover the news of the disappearing heirs to one of England's finest country homes…

'No.' He grimaced, his fingers flexing around the wheel. 'I drove there last night but couldn't get through the gates.'

'Oh. Do you not have the key?' How did he expect them to get in today?

'I have the key. I just…' A soft laugh. 'I drove up to the gates, stared up at the name and…' a shrug '…couldn't go in.'

She opened her mouth but was lost for words. Sebastian had always been brave, strong, older than his years. Seeing him now, in his fancy car, his even fancier clothing and yet anxious—fearful, even—it made her ache for the boy he'd once been and the man he'd become.

I figure we both have ghosts to put to rest.

It was what he'd said…but did it truly haunt him so very much now as an independent adult with his grandfather long gone?

Well, he stayed at your B & B, didn't he? If that's not desperation, what is?

'You can say it.'

She started. 'Say what?'

'That it's ridiculous. It's just a building. It has no hold over me. I've told myself the same repeatedly.'

'So that's why you came to me—*I mean the B & B*—last night? You couldn't face it?'

'That and…' Another quick look.

Silence.

'And?' she pressed before she could stop herself.

'I did want to see you, Flick.' His shoulders eased with his confession, his words raw and honest and making him less formidable again, more reminiscent of the boy she'd loved.

Her heart fluttered even as she told herself it meant nothing. 'How did you know I'd be there?'

'I didn't.'

She pulled her eyes from him, from the danger he represented when he opened himself up to her. It wasn't safe to get carried away with him, to let him in again, not when he'd hurt her so much and she still had no clue as to his intentions.

But she couldn't control her heart, her body…it wasn't as if she *wanted* to be so susceptible to him. The whole situation would be far easier if she could keep her distance, separate what they'd shared in the past from how the future would be.

The only emotions she should care about were Angel's.

Last night, as she'd lain in bed, her body still alive on that kiss, her head had been a mess of what ifs. Of how Angel would take the news, of how their lives would change and not knowing to what extent. It terrified her.

They were inseparable. While other mothers complained that their daughters were spending too much time with their friends, she'd been the opposite, worrying that her daughter spent more time in the B & B, helping and being by her side than she did socialising. And she knew that wasn't normal, not for any teen.

But what now? It wasn't just her and Angel any more.

She was so preoccupied by her thoughts that she jumped when he reached across her to open the glovebox a short while later, the car suddenly idle, the infamous gates now before them.

'Sorry.' He took out a little fob and she gave him a small smile of encouragement, praying he'd attribute her blush to surprise rather than the heat from the near brush of his arm.

'Well, here goes…' He pressed his lips together, his mouth pulling off to one side as he hit the button and the gates eased back.

'Are there many staff still here?' she asked, curious and desperate to distract herself from the last time she'd been here, pregnant and alone, her heart in two.

'A few. It doesn't take long for a place like this to go to

ruin if it's not properly maintained and I called ahead to have the kitchen stocked and a bedroom made up.'

A bedroom he decided against using...

She tried to ignore the returning ache in her chest, throwing her focus into their surroundings as he drove. Only she couldn't stop her thoughts racing. If he didn't want to be here, why return? Why not sell and forget?

Or did he want to overcome his past by setting up home here?

Gravel crunched beneath the wheels, filling the silence in the car, and birds flitted between the cherry blossom trees lining the long winding driveway, their branches in full bloom. 'I'd forgotten how stunning the trees were this time of year.'

He gave a non-committal shrug. 'They were my grandmother's favourite. I think my grandfather would've sooner had it lined with evergreens. He saw the fallen blossom as a maintenance nightmare, not that it ever stayed on the ground long. His men were too efficient for that.'

'Well, I think it's breathtaking.'

His eyes found hers briefly, his expression unreadable, and she went back to the view, uncaring if he thought her sentimental, romantic or, worse, foolish, for letting such feelings in where the estate was concerned.

It *was* beautiful—beautiful and peaceful. The grounds stretched as far as the eye could see, rolling green pastures with deer grazing, pheasants roaming, a fishing lake reflecting the bright blue sky and surrounding hills…picture perfect.

Even the house was more impressive than she remembered, its grand stone walls and turrets in all four corners lending it a fairy-tale charm. The magic enhanced by the rectangular pond out front with its cupid statue shooting water from its bow and the scattering of topiary art…

'The old man didn't let his standards slip.' He sounded cold, hard, detached. 'He cared more for this place than he did his own flesh and blood.'

'On the bright side,' she tried for some cheer, 'it shouldn't be too much of a maintenance headache for you now.'

'True...'

She couldn't imagine the cost of rescuing such a building if his grandfather hadn't been so careful. Not that Sebastian seemed short of cash, but still.

He parked in front of the sprawling steps and she undid her seat belt, peering up through the windscreen at the stone-pillared portico and heavy oak doors. 'I keep expecting your grandfather's butler to appear.'

'Ha. Old Higgins. He was almost as grumpy as the old man.'

'We did make his life a nightmare.'

They shared a look, a sparkle of humour. 'Well, not today. Higgins is six feet under and the house is deserted.'

'I thought you said there were staff.'

'There are, but they've vacated for a couple of days.'

'Oh.' She frowned, looked back to the house and then it struck her. 'You didn't want them to witness your reaction?'

He didn't confirm it; he didn't deny it either.

'And yet...' she turned to him, confusion deepening '...you've brought me.'

'I have.' His mouth lifted into another almost smile, his eyes glimmering and making him more boyish and bashful and...and there was that ache again.

'You always kept me grounded, Flick.'

She gave a choked laugh.

That's it; laugh it off. Because he can't be serious, not after all this time. Back then, yes, but not now...

He was strong, successful, he oozed wealth and charisma. He had an air of affluence that had nothing to do with what he was born into and everything to do with his self-made stature.

But he kept doing this…giving her glimpses of his vulnerability, making her feel needed.

'Has your brother been to see it?' It squeaked out of her, but it was a fair point to make. Surely his brother would have been a better source of support?

'Not yet. He'll be joining me soon, though. We need to assess the work it's going to need if we're to realise its full potential.'

'Work? It looks pretty sound to me.'

She peered back up at the entrance and thought of her own B & B, the work it truly did need, compared it to the scale of this place…the daunting responsibility of it too. He didn't sound daunted though, in fact there'd even been the hint of excitement in his tone.

Did that mean that underneath the unease he was excited to return? To restart his life here. A life that would now include their daughter…

She thought of Angel in the B & B, she thought of Angel here—would her daughter want to *live* here with him…to live her life unrestrained by money or the pressures of the B & B?

'Right!'

She started at his sudden exclamation.

'Let's get this over with and then we can talk.'

She nodded, trying to ease her sudden panic. 'Okay.'

Though nothing felt okay in that moment. Not the location. Not the situation. Not the years he could never get back with Angel and vice versa.

And now the future was so uncertain…

Her fingers trembled as she reached to open her door,

needing to get out of the car, needing to breathe fresh air and stabilise her thoughts. There was no denying that he had the money to make Angel's life so different, so easy—less work, more free time to make up for her childhood cut short. More time to follow her dreams as Flick hadn't been able to.

She shoved open her door and stepped out—the sooner they talked, the sooner she'd know what was going through that seriously attractive head of his and could quit with the second-guessing.

CHAPTER SIX

SEBASTIAN EYED THE sweeping stone steps leading up to the main entrance.

They looked sound. No cracks or loose stone. No weeds breaking through. The sandy colour to the Yorkshire stone gleamed in the sunshine, the windows sparkled, and the turrets stood proud.

Everything polished, everything flawless, just the way the old man would've liked it.

A chill ran through him despite the sun high in the sky, the heat uncharacteristic for spring—or was it the afterglow of Flick's proximity in the car…? So close and yet he'd sensed the moment she'd withdrawn, her mood shifting with their conversation.

Was she as haunted by his grandfather's treatment of her? Had he made a mistake in bringing her here? A selfish one?

He cursed under his breath as the gravel crunched behind him, and he fought the urge to turn. Sixteen years ago, he would've held out his hand, squeezed her fingers softly but he'd already overstepped when he'd crossed the line so spectacularly the night before. Kissing her as if all those years had never happened.

But he'd been driven on instinct, an instinct he needed to

keep under control if they were to navigate the road ahead without further hurt, confusion or, worse, resentment.

Resentment that he'd been gone for so long. Resentment that he was back.

She came up alongside him, lifting her shades and sweeping away a few escaped strands of hair. His fingers thrummed. He wanted to loosen the lot, comb his fingers through it and have it tumble around her shoulders, relaxed and carefree…as she'd been before he'd upended her life.

His throat tightened, the visceral turmoil inside impossible to quell. Was he so unaccustomed to feeling anything that he didn't know where to start in dealing with it now? Theo would rib him without mercy if he could see what he was going through, and take great delight in it, too, happy to see his unfeeling brother *feel something*.

And though his return to the estate had triggered the emotional torrent, it paled into insignificance when presented with Flick and the family he'd never known he had.

Family. Was that what they were now?

He watched her closely. No, they were far from it.

Family wasn't simply blood. His grandfather had taught him that well. Family required a bond nurtured over time. It required trust, an ease, a dependency… *Love.*

'It's as impressive as ever.'

His jaw was locked so tight it took him a second to release it, another to trust his voice to reply. 'It needs work.'

Her eyes had been on the house, but he got the impression she hadn't been seeing it. Like him, she'd been distracted by her thoughts. She flicked him a quick look and he knew the bitterness had crept into his voice.

'Nothing that can't be fixed though.' He attempted a smile as he gestured ahead. 'Shall we?'

He wasn't lying. Work *would* be needed to meet health and safety standards, to adjust the interior layout to create the right zones, bedrooms, en suite bathrooms. To add the luxury features Dubois guests were accustomed to. And he tried to focus on that as they approached the entrance and he took the key from his pocket, slid it into the lock.

His hand stilled over the unwelcome shiver that ran through his fingers, and he forced himself to turn the key, twist the knob, and push.

It's just a building.

The door opened, the well-oiled hinges silent as the vast entrance hall stretched out before them, the shafts of sunlight from the tall windows filling the place with a visual warmth that contended with the rolling chill inside.

White sheets hung over the paintings, the furnishings, the ornaments—veiled items that he could see as clearly as yesterday. The twin armchairs before the fire that were never used, the grand piano beneath the sweeping staircase that his grandmother had once played, the twin busts to the left and right of the archway leading towards the living areas.

He felt his collar tighten, itched to run his finger through it and clenched his fists, refusing to look so weak in front of Flick. He'd already looked weak enough. But then her fingers were there, teasing apart his fist as she took his hand and gave it a squeeze.

Of course, she knew. Of course, she got it. She always got *him*.

'A quick tour,' she said softly, 'and then we'll talk.'

He nodded. A tour to face off the memories, have it done with and then he could focus on what mattered—Flick, Angel, the future. The estate would be absorbed by his corporation soon enough. Not quite unrecognisable, but he wouldn't have to come here again. Not if he didn't want to.

They wandered aimlessly through the house, their

footsteps echoing in the quiet, the high ceilings and the dark wood floors doing nothing to ease their stark resonance. Or maybe it was the echoes of the past catching up with them…?

'Nothing's changed.' Her fingers were still wrapped in his, their presence soothing even as he acknowledged how alien it was. To take support from anyone…let alone the woman he had torn apart by his actions.

'My grandfather always did like things kept just so… after Gran died, he hated even the slightest adjustment.' He felt her eyes on him as they walked through the living room into the connecting library, its double height making the floor-to-ceiling books even more impressive. 'I remember when her dried flowers were taken from the great hall for cleaning, he went into a huge rage that could be heard through the house. They weren't to be touched; nothing was. As though any change would in some way deplete her memory.'

'He really loved her.'

'He loved her at the expense of all else.' He released Flick's fingers, unable to keep the bond when the cold inside him was on the rise.

'It's kind of tragic.'

'It's kind of selfish.'

She eyed him tentatively. 'I remember when they would open the house up for the summer gala and the entire village would descend. It was the event of the year.'

His lips twitched with the memories. The noise, the competitions, the baking entries… 'I think it's more the food you remember.'

She laughed, her eyes sparkling as happier memories took over. 'It *was* good food.'

'And we ate far too much of it.'

'We did.' She covered her belly, her cheeks a delectable shade of pink.

He smiled, resisting the urge to get lost in her joyous expression and take her hand once more. 'They were good times.'

'Yes.' Her smile wavered. 'It was a shame the galas came to an end.'

And just like that the chill was back. 'Heaven forbid the village continued to have fun, hey?'

'I think everyone understood why your grandfather didn't want to do it any more. It had been your grandmother's passion, she loved organising it, taking part in it—' She pressed her lips together, cutting off her words as she must have realised where they were heading. It was the taking part in it that had killed her. If his grandmother hadn't been showjumping, taking an active role in the day's entertainment, maybe she wouldn't have died, maybe his grandfather wouldn't have lost himself in his grief.

Maybe he wouldn't have had to flee.

Maybe he could have been…a father?

His chest spasmed, his mind quick to back away. 'I'm guessing they never started up again?'

'No.' She tilted her head, a sparkle in her eye. 'But maybe it's something you could look at doing again…in the future.'

Never. He wanted no part of the estate and its pain. First, losing Gran in such a spectacular and newsworthy fashion that they hadn't been able to avoid the press for months, and then his father's car accident… The years that had followed…the discovery that his happy childhood had been a lie, that he was capable of—

No. His fists clenched. He would see the past and his grandfather's island of misery obliterated by the hotel transformation and be done with it. It would represent everything Dubois stood for and excel at it. No more Ferrington.

'Hey…' Those warm fingers were back, taking hold of his. 'Let's get a drink and take it outside. I think we've done enough walking through the past for one day.'

He pulled away, raked his hand through his hair and blew out a breath. 'You're right.'

'I always am.'

He choked out a laugh. How could she do this? Make him laugh in the space that had haunted him for so long… pull him back from the edge when the anger threatened to engulf him.

He led the way to the kitchen at the back of the house, which, aside from a state-of-the-art coffee machine he'd had installed ready for his arrival, hadn't changed in all the years he'd been gone.

Smoothing his palm over the familiar centre island that ran the length of the room, he took in the traditional wooden cupboards and marble surfaces. He'd spent so much time here with the kitchen staff, getting underfoot but doing his best to learn what truly made a good meal. Hospitality had always fascinated him.

'This was your favourite room in the house.'

He turned and managed a smile. 'You remember?'

'Of course, I remember…' Her gaze connected with his, the air charged with the simple confession, her cheeks flooded with warmth. Time was falling away again, the distance between them closing in…and then she jolted. 'I'll make us a coffee.'

'No.' He caught her up, pulled her back. 'It's my turn to take care of you.'

He'd meant it in relation to the B & B, to her looking after him with his breakfast that morning, not in the sense that had her eyes widening, his sixteen years of absence and her single parenthood a gulf between them.

He released her hand before he tugged her against his chest fully and kissed away that look, the lost years too, busying himself with the coffee machine instead. Far safer. Far simpler.

When he turned back, she was standing in front of the arched glass doors that led out to the veranda and the Olympic-sized swimming pool that had been his grandfather's pride and joy. Every day had started and ended with a swim. A strict ritual for a strict man. A man who had taken away his grandson's chance to know his own daughter…

But you're here now…you have the power to change that.

He leaned back against the countertop and folded his arms, the empowering thought driving the question, 'Tell me about her?'

Her head snapped around. 'Now?'

The smallest of smiles. 'Yes.'

She gave a soft huff, a sweet smile. 'Where do I even start?'

'Try the beginning. The pregnancy, the birth, the early days… I want to know it all, Flick.'

It was hard recalling the most important moments Sebastian had missed without also acknowledging that she too had missed out in the very early years: Angel's first words that had been spoken with her gran while she'd been at school; her first steps that had been much the same; getting to know what food she liked and didn't…

In the end, the pain of missing out had been too much to bear and she'd jacked it all in. The B & B, Gran and Angel had been all that mattered. She didn't need the degree, the career…seeing Angel grow up had been everything.

Everything Sebastian wouldn't get to see…and the pain of it speared her as his brow furrowed further, the shadows in his grey eyes deepening, the increasing tension in his body…every tale deepening the wound.

'Do you regret it?' he asked gruffly.

She breathed in the coffee he'd made her, its aroma settling the churn to her gut as she held his eye across the small poolside table.

'Quitting school?'

He nodded and lifted his own mug to his lips.

'No. I have no regrets, Sebastian. She was my everything after you left. In truth, if it wasn't for her, I'm not sure how I would've got through losing Gran. The villagers are great. Everyone is so supportive, chipping in when I need it, making sure I keep on my feet, but emotionally…'

Her voice cracked and he lowered his mug, leaning forward, those eyes searching hers…eyes that were far too quick to disarm her and she looked away, waved a hand over her face to rid herself of the tears.

'Angel got me through. Being focused on her and keeping the B & B ticking along…she truly is my rock and so very wonderful.' She smiled, her love for their daughter shining through. 'She's clever, caring, studious. She's as happy with her friends as she is sat before the fire in Gardner Guest House chatting away with Bill and Frank or entertaining the knitting circle with her stories from school. She's like a surrogate granddaughter to them all.'

He returned her smile. 'She sounds amazing, Flick. An absolute credit to you.'

Her chest flooded with warmth, tears spiking once more and stealing her voice.

'Very sensible, too.' His eyes danced. 'Not sure where she gets that from.'

Her laugh caught in her throat. 'What are you trying to say?'

'That we were hardly sensible.'

'I'll have you know that until I met you, there wasn't a single *un*sensible thing about me.'

'So, you don't remember sneaking down to the park with a bottle of cider and hiding in the mini helter-skelter?'

She laughed some more, remembering the tight space, the graffiti, the thrilling company... 'Like I said, I was Little Miss Sensible right up until the point I met you.'

Met you, kissed you, fell in love with you...

Her body fluttered to life and she tried to tamp it down...his blazing greys making the effort futile.

'So, what you're saying is, I led you astray?'

'Are you going to deny it?'

'No.'

And she knew he could lead her anywhere all over again, straight back to Brokenheartsville without a backwards glance if she wasn't careful.

She swallowed down the panic, broke away from the dangerous look in his eye to sip her coffee and take the conversation back to safer territory. 'She has a good crowd around her.'

'And an entire village to look out for her.'

'Pretty much,' she murmured against the rim of her cup.

'I'm glad you have that. The support network, people you can call on, depend on, it's important...'

There was an edge to his voice, a gravity that suggested he lacked the same. Did he not have people he could depend on? His brother? Friends? What about the women she'd pondered over?

'What about you? You have your brother, what about

others? Friends? Is there a lady out there I should know about?' It bumbled out of her as his eyes narrowed, the mental jibe quick to follow—*There's no 'should' about it... it's none of your business.* The heat soared to her cheeks as she tried to hide behind her mug. 'I'm just curious. It's important for me to know, what with Angel and...and...'

The more flapped she became, the more his eyes danced. 'It's okay, Flick, you can ask. The answer is no, there's no lady friend.' And then his expression changed, his eyes lowering to her mouth... 'Do you think I would have kissed you last night if there was?'

She gulped. 'No.'

He took a long breath and lifted his eyes back to hers. 'The truth is, between looking after Mum over the years, getting Theo on the straight and narrow, and then the business, there's not been much time for dating...nor the inclination.'

'So, what?' She gave an uneasy laugh. 'You're a sworn bachelor?'

'Something like that.'

'And...friends?'

'I have a few trusted employees.'

'That are friends?'

He gave a shrug. 'I don't really socialise. I have my brother and a housekeeper that treats me more like a grandson than my grandfather ever did.'

'No insatiable gossip for you, then...' She was hunting for something to say, anything to distract from her mounting concern. Did he really have no friends? He used to be the heart of every party, every crowd...but as she looked at him now, there was something undeniably lonely about him.

'Lucky for me, hey? Especially if the looks I was being sent by Miss Jones and her friend this morning are anything to go by. I'm not sure how you cope with it on a regular basis.'

'Their hearts are in a good place.' She screwed her face up. 'They just don't forget easily, I'm afraid, and they all had front row seats to my heartbreak back then.'

The past, the bad came between them, drained the spark from his eye. 'Do they all know?'

'That you're Angel's father?' She smoothed a hand through her hair, tilted her chin. 'No one asked and no one confirmed it. But… Elmdale's Elmdale; you can't stop people talking or speculating.'

'True.'

The simple syllable sounded so much worse for the remorse in his eye, the life she now knew he led, and she couldn't get her head around the loneliness of it. Especially when compared with her own. She wasn't wealthy by any means, but she was surrounded by love. She was lucky.

Sebastian, on the other hand…

'Don't you ever…don't you ever get lonely?'

His body stiffened and she wished she'd kept her mouth shut.

'My life is what it is. I choose to live it like I do, Flick. It's a personal choice.'

She nodded, swallowed past the sudden rawness in her throat and focused on what he did have—*who* he had. 'So, your brother, how is he these days?'

'Better.' Her chest eased at the glimmer of affection in his eyes. 'Much better. He was a loose cannon when we left. Freed from our grandfather's control he certainly made the most of it.'

'For ever the rebel.'

'That he was.' He shifted in his seat, relaxed back. 'When Mum got sick, I feared it would push him further away, but it had the opposite effect. Sobered him up.'

'A changed man?'

'I wouldn't go that far.' He laughed gently. 'Let's just say, he has my back and I have his. Professionally, I can't fault him either. Our success is as much down to him as it is me. But when it comes to the ladies, he more than makes up for my…inactivity.'

She laughed at his honesty, giddy on his confession. *Too* giddy. She shouldn't care that he wasn't a ladies' man. 'I still can't get my head around that.'

'What? That I'm not hot on the dating scene?'

Her cheeks were so warm she feared she looked sunburnt.

'You don't believe me?'

'It's not that I don't believe you, it's that…' She couldn't hold his gaze any more—her cheeks were too pink, her belly too warm, not to mention the heat returning in his gaze. 'I find it *hard* to believe.'

'And why's that, Flick?'

'Are you really going to make me spell it out for you?'

'I am if it means you're about to pay me a compliment.'

She dared a quick look and wished she hadn't. His eyes seared her, the way he ran his finger beneath his lip as he considered her.

'You don't need me to tell you how attractive you are, Sebastian.' She sounded breathless. 'I'm sure plenty of women have told you it over the years.'

'None that I cared for.'

His eyes flashed with the truth of it and it electrified the air, made her breath catch—he'd only cared for her… was that what he meant?

'Forgive me?'

His plea was raw, his change in focus making her frown. 'Forgive you?'

'For leaving.'

'Oh, Sebastian!' She was reaching across the table before she could stop herself, her palm covering his hand, needing that contact, needing to reassure him.

Hadn't he suffered enough already, learning he had a daughter and could never get back all those years that had been lost?

'I do.'

He turned his hand over, so they were palm to palm. 'I'm sorry you had to do it alone.'

'I wasn't alone; I had Gran.'

His fingers closed around hers. 'You know what I mean.'

'I do.' She swallowed. 'And I'm sorry, too.'

'Don't.' His grip pulsed. 'Don't you say you're sorry. Not to me. Not after what I did.'

'Shh.' Her heart ached to hear his pain, to feel it shudder through him in the grip around her hand. 'We can't change the past, only the future, and you're back, that's all that matters now.'

'Is it though?'

'Of course, it is.' Why couldn't he see that?

'I—I fear she'll hate me.'

'Angel?' She shook her head, wanting to pull him to her and hold him until his pain eased but *she* was scared too. Scared that the intimacy would take them back to that kiss, crack her open, destroy the walls around her heart that were already weak.

'She could never hate you.' She chose her words carefully. 'You didn't know. She knows you didn't know. I never once spoke against you. I didn't doubt your love for me back then, and she knows enough to know that she wasn't a one-night mistake. She knows we loved each other, even if the timing had been all wrong.'

He pressed his lips together, his dimples deepening. Did he not believe her?

'*Trust me*, she won't hate you.'

'We'll soon find out.'

She pulled away, folded her hands in her lap as she sought strength away from his judgement-clouding aura. 'We will, but not yet.'

'When?'

She wet her lips. 'End of May?'

His brows drew together and she hurried on. 'She needs to get her exams out of the way first. They're important if she's to achieve what she wants—she has big dreams, a plan…'

His eyes clouded over. 'Like you once did.'

She twisted her hands together, refusing to get sucked down that road. 'Yes, but we're talking about Angel now.'

'And what she stands to lose because of me.' The guilt was back in his face, his clenched fist upon the table. 'Just as you once did.'

'No! I don't blame you for how my life panned out, Sebastian.' She gripped her fingers to stop herself from taking his hand again. 'It's different from what I planned but no less fulfilling. I'm glad I had her, I'm *lucky* to have her. I won't—I don't blame you or hate you for it.'

He was so still, his eyes unmoving on hers. 'You don't?'

She shook her head, her confirmation whisper-soft but no less adamant. 'No.'

I could never, her heart added for her, and she sought refuge behind her coffee mug as she lifted it to her lips and wished it were something stronger. 'I could murder a wine.'

A surprising laugh burst out of him as he looked to the heavens, the tension lifting so spectacularly. 'You and me both.'

He got to his feet and held out his hand. 'Come on. I know a place that has a well-stocked wine cellar.'

'You can't be serious, it's not even…' She checked her watch—wow, they'd been talking a long time. 'Okay, so it's gone lunch, but still…'

'A tour of the place wouldn't be complete without checking it out…especially since we hid there often enough.'

'We did.' Her voice was husky with the memories, with the heat of his palm as she accepted his aid. 'But you're driving.'

'I can indulge in a glass.'

The problem was she wanted to indulge in so much more than a glass of wine and that was the problem. *He* was the problem, in a huge, huge way.

But he was back. Angel would have her father, and Flick and Sebastian would…

They would what? Have some sort of a relationship? A platonic one? Or something more?

It was hard not to read more into all he had told her. All he had implied. That she was the only woman he had ever cared for in that way…

She hadn't lied when she'd told him that her life was different but no less fulfilling. Could he claim the same? She doubted it…no matter what success he'd achieved professionally. Something else she had yet to learn about.

There would be time for it though. Time for it all.

But now he was back, wasn't he highlighting the one missing piece in her so-called full life?

She pulled her hand from his and tried to smile, tried to stay calm even as his eyes held hers captive.

'End of May it is, Flick.'

Relief swept through her—Angel, the news, of course.

She pressed a hand into the table, fearing her knees would buckle. 'Thank you.'

'Now, let's go choose a bottle.'

She nodded.

She should have refused.

Alcohol mixed in with the intoxicating thoughts of him wasn't sensible by any stretch of the imagination...but it seemed her body had other ideas.

CHAPTER SEVEN

WHAT WERE YOU THINKING?

He was grateful she couldn't see his face; she'd probably change her mind about accompanying him.

And that would be a good thing, you fool!

Going down to the cellar together with *all* the X-rated memories it would conjure and the chemistry so quick to spark…even the bad hadn't snuffed out the fire of it. A fire he wanted more and more to act on. To hell with getting burned.

He yanked open the door from the kitchen to the cellar and only just managed to stop it hitting the wall.

She gave a laugh that sounded as edgy as he felt. 'I can almost imagine Cook giving us the side eye.'

He cocked a brow at her. 'Or hear the clip of my grandfather's cane approaching on the stone floor…'

'Seconds before we scarpered.'

He held the door open while she stepped past him, her scent catching him unawares and making him take a moment before he followed, clearing his throat. 'It was the best hiding place when the weather turned.'

The air around them cooled with their descent. His core temperature though…that was on the up no matter how much he tried to douse it. And he knew it was bad.

Remaining cool and detached was how he'd survived

over the years. How he'd kept his passion in check, his head clear and his body on a tight leash. Nothing like the events sixteen years ago would ever happen again.

It took discipline. Focus. Self-restraint.

All things that had served him well, personally and professionally.

Only he didn't *feel* cool and detached around Flick. He didn't feel in control. And that was a problem. A problem he had no idea how to fix.

He paused in the tunnel of rooms all protected by glass and carefully controlled thermostats, so many memories pressing to the fore as his senses took everything in: the exposed stone, rustic oak and low light, intimate and inviting, the scent earth-like and strangely comforting.

'If these walls could talk…'

She'd meant to say it to herself, the widening of her eyes and slight stain to her cheeks telling him as much and he smiled.

'Indeed…'

He touched a hand to the long oak bench that acted as a tasting table, the action bringing with it a rush as illicit as the memory it evoked. 'Red or white?'

He watched her throat bob, her eyes on his fingers. 'You choose.'

He knew she was right there with him, replaying it. Her legs around his hips, her body reclined back over the bench, her mouth open and begging for his kiss. God, he could taste her now.

And it's wine you should be tasting—just the wine!

He dragged his gaze away to browse the well-stocked rows, finally deciding on a chilled white that he recognised.

Refined. Crisp. Easy drinking.

Though he was no fool, he knew it wouldn't taste as good as— *Focus!*

He felt himself shaking his head.

'Problem?'

He looked up to find her frowning at him. 'Not at all.'

Unless he counted the way she made him feel.

He pulled a corkscrew from the drawer beneath the bench and she slid onto a bar stool opposite, resting her elbows on the wood and her chin in her hands. 'It's as though you've never been away.'

'Like I said, the old man was never one for change.'

The set-up was indeed as it always had been. The stone and oak a neutral backdrop to the star of the show—his grandfather's drinks collection that extended almost the entire length of the house itself. *His* drinks collection now.

He uncorked the bottle with a pop and she reached beneath for two glasses, sliding them towards him.

'I'm not the only one at home here.'

Her smile was veering towards shy. 'Call it evidence of our misspent youth.'

More memories arose, flickering to life…

Their first kiss. An accidental brush up against one another when she'd been taking down a bottle, the giggle that had run through her and into him as she'd almost fallen from the ladder he'd been holding onto. The giggle that had morphed into a whimper as he'd tasted her sweet cherry lips that had taunted him for so long. When she'd gone from being his mischief-maker chum, his best friend, to something more. Much, much more.

She licked her lips, her lashes fluttering over her blue eyes, which were closer to black now and fired with flecks of gold from the low-hanging copper lights…though he fancied it came more from the fire within.

'You going to pour?' she murmured. 'Or shall I?'

'You never were one for patience.'

'And you always acted like you had all the time in the world,' she sparked back.

If only they'd had more time though.

If only he'd known what he'd be walking in on that night and could have forewarned her, prepared himself better, done anything but run.

'Why didn't you try and get word to me?'

They were so in tune her question jarred him, sending wine sloshing outside the glass.

'You could have told me where you were going. *Why* you were going.'

'We didn't have time. And even if we had…' He shook his head—he'd gone over it a thousand times. 'No one could know. If my grandfather had found us…who knows what he would have done to get us back? He knew people. His money and his contacts could buy favour. My mother had already been diagnosed as mentally vulnerable; it wouldn't take much to twist that and gain what he wanted.'

Not to mention what he would have done to you…

'You think he'd have sunk so low as to take you from your mother?'

'I don't know.' He couldn't look at her, not when he knew he was holding back. The truth a lead weight in his gut. 'Probably. That night he was raging, I'd never seen him so blinkered.' *He wasn't the only one.* 'There was no reasoning with him.' *Or you.*

She took the bottle from him, and he realised he was trembling, his body vibrating with the effort to keep back the memories he hadn't divulged, his true nature with them.

'It's okay,' she whispered, giving him a reassuring smile. 'I understand.'

No, you don't, he wanted to scream. Confess. But he

knew it would break him. To see the change in her eye, the look of horror so sure to follow. He couldn't.

She topped up the wine and offered him a glass, her eyes falling to the Rolex on his wrist as he took it, a reminder of how far he'd come on his own terms.

'To you.' She raised her glass to him. 'To breaking free of your grandfather and making your own success.'

His shoulders hunched, his chest tightening. He didn't deserve her toast, her kindness. There wasn't a chance the wine would make it down either.

'I'm sorry.' The glass wavered in her hand, her frown returning. 'I didn't mean to make you feel uncomfortable.'

He rolled his shoulders, ran a finger under his collar. 'I didn't do it all myself, my brother played his part, too.'

'So you say.'

'It's true, we make quite a team.' He tried to relax, to bury the past, to keep this moment easy. 'To use his words—I'm the brains, he's the brawn.'

'Really?' Her lips quivered; her eyes started to dance. '*He's* the brawn?'

A flicker of something came alive in his gut, easing the tension holding his body taut. 'Are you doubting my brains?'

She pressed her lips together—she wasn't laughing, she was blushing.

'Hang on...' the warmth inside him spread '...another compliment?'

'Maybe.'

He shook his head, his chuckle low.

'He's a pro at the schmoozing. I say it how it is, no filter. Doesn't matter who you are, your level of influence, what you have to offer.'

Her smile grew wistful. 'You always did. It was one of the—'

She bit her lip.

'One of the…?'

She hesitated, her colour deepening. 'It was one of the reasons I fell for you. But *anyway*, cheers to brains and brawn!'

She practically threw her glass up, but he was slower, his body too busy reacting to her confession.

'Cheers to you too.' He clinked his glass against hers, held her eye as he told her his heartfelt truth. 'You've done amazing yourself, Flick.'

Her lashes fluttered and she shrank back into herself, sipped her drink.

'You have.' His eyes narrowed on her. 'You know that, right?'

She frowned, vulnerable, unsure and shock threw him so completely.

'Seriously, Flick! You've kept the guest house running single-handedly, a twenty-four-seven job, while also being a single mum. Not to mention you had to do it all while caring and grieving for your grandmother. None of which could have been easy. And from what you've told me Angel is growing up into a fine young woman. That's all down to you.'

She looked away, her laugh unsteady. 'I'm sure I pale in comparison to the females moving in your circles these days.'

'None that I would ever choose over you.'

It was out before he could stop it, and he didn't want to stop it. He wanted her to acknowledge her own worth. Hated seeing her so dismissive.

'Laying it on a bit thick, aren't you?' Her gaze speared his. Did she think he was lying? Saying things just to make her feel good?

He leaned back, giving her more space without him in

it as he assured her, 'I never lay it on thick, Flick. You ask my brother when he gets here if you don't believe me. I still say it as I find it—no more, no less.'

'Right…' She took a large swig of wine, her nod disbelieving. Her swallow was practically a gulp that he could hear across the table and then she was straightening up, composing herself, and he knew a shift in topic was coming…a shift he should be grateful for, only he wasn't.

'So where is your brother now?'

'He had a charity gala to attend in Paris. He should be arriving any day now.'

'A charity gala?'

'Yes.' He took a sip from his glass, appreciating the wine's perfection and acknowledging it was the one thing on which he could've agreed with his grandfather. Still… it wasn't as good as she would t—

'Is the charity a joint interest?'

He gulped another mouthful of the chilled drink. 'It is.'

'What does it do?'

His eyes narrowed and he realised it was more than shifting focus, she was genuinely interested. In him, in them, in their work. Readying himself for her reaction, he folded his arms and leaned into the table.

'It provides sheltered housing for people who need to escape domestic abuse.'

Her eyes widened. 'The kind of place you once needed?'

He nodded; as raw as it felt to admit it, he was proud of it.

On the one hand, the Dubois hotel chain provided the standard of accommodation *only* money could buy, and on the other it provided a place of stability and security to those who had none. Vulnerable men, women and children who had no one else to turn to. 'If it hadn't been for my mother's friend when we fled, I don't know what we would have done. There wasn't a place you could simply turn up to and plead sanctuary, to have a roof put over your head and feel safe.'

'No,' she said quietly, her hands slipping beneath her thighs, making him wonder whether it was to stop herself reaching for him. Something they both seemed susceptible to doing.

Not just reaching out but a whole lot more. Like pulling her to him and reliving one of the wild and uninhibited scenes this room conjured up from the banks of his memory.

'So…' His voice trailed off as she nipped her bottom lip, fuelling the memories, the desire.

He forced his eyes to hers. 'Angel works with you in the B & B, then?'

'Yes.'

'A lot?'

She crossed her legs and lifted her wine to her lips. 'Like I said, she's a good kid, she chips in, she works hard.'

'And her friends, does she get to see them much?'

Her eyes narrowed, her shoulders hunching. 'What are you trying to say, Sebastian?'

'Nothing.' He frowned over her defensive posture. 'Only that it must be hard finding time to do it all— studying, working, socialising…'

He hated that he'd put her on edge, but he cared too much not to say it. Cared that their daughter's life, living and working in the B & B, didn't leave her much room to act her age.

She was silent, her eyes doing all the talking for her as they blazed, their silent message clear: *You don't have a right to comment. You've not been here.*

'Sorry. Forget it. I was thinking aloud. I didn't have

much freedom when I was her age, and neither did you, and I... Well, anyway, I'm sorry. Forget I said anything.'

He looked away from the anger still simmering in her gaze. She'd always had a fire to her. A fire he'd once loved to stoke and then... *No, not helping!*

'How about we take this bottle back out to the garden?' He was trying to rescue the situation. 'Seems a shame to miss out on the sun.'

Seems a shame to be down here and not doing the one hundred and one other things you want to be doing, none of which are advisable, sensible...or involve talking. Much.

He was already starting to rise but she didn't move. 'Let's be clear about something, Sebastian.'

He stilled, forcing himself to hold her gaze and whatever punishment she was about to dish out.

Slowly, she unfolded from her stool and took one step forward, close enough he could feel her body warm his own, could see the flecks of gold in her blue eyes as she looked up at him.

'You might be her father and you might be back, but you don't get to judge my parenting. I've been her mum for sixteen years and you have no idea how hard it's been.'

She pressed her forefinger into his chest and his lungs contracted, every nerve-ending straining towards her touch—*you're not supposed to find it sexy, you fool*.

'You don't get to judge me or the way we live our life now, understood?'

He lifted his hand to cover hers. 'Understood, Flick.'

He bit the inside of his cheek as he fought the urge to kiss her again.

Her breath shuddered out of her, her 'thank you' a whisper as her eyes lowered and she registered their closeness, her step back swift and cutting the connection so completely. 'I did the best I could, Sebastian. She may not have had the perfect childhood, and I sure as hell wasn't the perfect mum, but I tried, and I love her with my all.'

Taking up her wine glass, she strode for the stairs, leaving him to watch her controlled exit as her words teased at the very heart of him. He wasn't jealous of his daughter, of course he wasn't, but he couldn't deny the impulsive beat of his ignorant heart pleading for the same passion, the same care, the same love.

'I know you do, Flick,' he said, too soft for her to hear. 'I know you do.'

Felicity sucked in the fresh air, grateful to be back at the table outside.

The cellar was too cosy, too chock-full of heated memories that had her craving a repeat of one.

And then he'd made her angry.

Bringing her parenting into question, looking at her with sympathy in his greys that had been dark as flint and full of desire moments before. She'd wanted the latter back. That was the problem.

That combined with her defensive shackles had sent her surging forward, naively prodding at that hard muscular chest, no thought given to the inevitable sparks that would fly.

And fly they did.

She wanted him more now than ever.

And it had nothing to do with his money and all it could buy—though she adored his charity work and learning of it had turned her to hapless mush inside. But the rest— the wealth, the success—it only served to highlight how inadequate and unworthy she was.

Even with his aristocratic roots, he'd never made her feel that way when they were younger, but now…now she was definitely Cinderella to his Prince Charming and it scared her, put her on edge, not to mention the fact that her heart wasn't listening to her head.

And Angel was her girl, her baby…the idea of being open to his opinion as her father was terrifying, antagonising even. Though it was only fair and right.

'I forgot how lovely it was here.'

She turned to look at him as he spoke, but his eyes were on the pool and the view beyond.

Did he have to look so darn good *all* the time?

With the sun glinting off his hair and highlighting the bronze of his skin, he looked as if he belonged in some fancy aftershave ad. And she already knew his scent was worthy of one.

'It really is,' she forced herself to say, pleased when her voice sounded level.

'I guess I've avoided thinking about it over the years, but there's something special about the ripple of the pool with the forest in the background, deer grazing, the birds of prey…it's easy to forget such beauty exists.'

She looked back to the view, but her mind was already returning to the memories, to the many amazing experiences they'd shared.

'And I guess it must be hard to remember when you've experienced all that the world has to offer.'

It wasn't as if she knew he had, but she felt it.

He turned to eye her, and she refused to look.

Did she sound like a petulant child? She didn't want to, but it was hard. Hard to acknowledge that he'd managed to achieve so much, that this jet-set lifestyle was all him and she…she was what? A bone-tired B & B owner who didn't know whether she was coming or going most days, chasing her tail and never quite on top of everything.

But you have the community around you, and you

*have Angel...think of all he doesn't have, all that he's
missed out on.*

Rather belatedly she reached for her denim bag and
pulled out the photo album she'd brought with her. 'Most
people use an electronic one these days, but Gran was a
stickler for tradition and so, I've carried it on.'

She slid it towards him, his eyes tracking it with trepi-
dation.

'It's what I call my Mum Diary. It has everything. From
me being pregnant, right up until the present day.' She
sat back as he picked it up. 'Angel doesn't like her picture being taken but she tends to oblige when I tell her
it's for this.'

He didn't move for a second as he stared down at it, his
hand resting on the cover revealing a slight tremor that
she felt right through her—the power of a photo diary,
who knew?

But hadn't she always known deep down that this might
happen, that she would need to fill in the blanks for the
father who had never been around to witness it all?

'I don't know what to say.' It choked out of him, the
sound stealing her breath, extinguishing the anger, the
fear, and the pain.

'You don't need to say anything,' she whispered. 'Simply look...that's the beauty of photos.'

His eyes lifted to hers, a second's hesitation before
turning the page and losing himself in the image before
him, his fingers slowly trailing over it. 'Wow, you were...
you were the picture of health?'

'Yes. A healthy textbook pregnancy.'

He nodded, his throat bobbing as he went back to the
album, turning page after page. 'You look beautiful, glowing and... Oh, my God, she's...she's tiny. Such small fists.'

She choked on a laugh. 'She loved making that boxer pose, used to have me and Gran in stitches.'

'With that look of attitude in her eyes, I can see why.'

Felicity tried not to react to the rawness in his voice, but it was hard to shut off the emotions so desperate to claw their way through.

He gave a laugh and she leaned over. It was a picture of Angel in Gran's lap, sucking on Gran's finger as though her life depended on it.

'She was a hungry monster, too; I'll give her that.'

His eyes lifted to hers, bright, full of…love? 'Takes after her mother.'

Her heart stuttered in her chest as she tried to laugh and feign hurt. 'Woah, woah, woah! You were the one mopping up the leftovers when we were younger.'

'Only to bring them to you before you got hangry!'

Now she did laugh, and it was light, breezy, because he remembered, genuinely remembered. 'Yeah, well, there's plenty like that one.'

'You mean, like this one?' He angled the open book to her and there was Angel in her highchair, her empty bowl of spaghetti bolognese on her head, sauce smeared across her cheeks, her hair, and the happiest grin there ever was.

'Yup. That's our girl.'

He laughed. The sound joyous, happy, free of any tension and she relished it, along with every tremor it sent through her. Telling herself it was okay to take pleasure from it. He was Angel's father, and it was good that he could look at the pictures and find joy in the past.

She couldn't gift him the time lost, but she could gift him this.

'She would have had you wrapped around her little finger, you know.' She held his eye, determined to share, determined not to shy away because she feared getting attached all over again. 'She will do, even.'

'You reckon?'

'Oh, yeah, she has the entire village at her beck and call. You won't escape.'

He chuckled, the sound more to himself as his eyes went back to the book.

He asked her questions and she filled in the blanks as best she could. And she enjoyed it…until he reached the last photo taken just before Gran died.

'This is the last one?' His eyes lifted to hers.

She sipped at her wine, her eyes on the book but her thoughts were on the dull ache in her chest. 'Time seemed to stand still after Gran died… I haven't…'

She broke off, lowering her glass to the table as her hand became unsteady.

'You haven't wanted to add any without Annie?'

'No.'

Her voice cracked and he reached over, cupped her hands in his.

'It just doesn't feel right.' She sucked in a breath. 'She was such a huge part of our life, to add photos now without her, it makes it so much more…final.'

'Real?' he said, simultaneously.

She nodded, feeling the tears overflow, tears she'd thought she was done with.

'Oh, Flick.' He reached up, palmed her cheek, his thumb sweeping up the tears. 'She lives on, just as my mother does in me. In our memories, our thoughts, our hearts.'

She nodded, treasuring his caress, surprised at the accuracy of his words. 'I know.'

'It's the price of loving someone.'

She lifted her gaze to his. 'Better to have loved and lost…'

'So they say.'

That wasn't quite what she'd expected him to say. Was it his way of telling her that he didn't agree? That he'd endured enough loss to last a lifetime? Did he count her as a loss, not something to be gained again?

'What do you—?'

A buzzing cut her off. Then it buzzed and buzzed again. It was coming from his pocket—messages arriving in quick succession. He shifted and tugged his phone from his pocket, eyed the screen with a curse.

'We need to go.'

She frowned. 'Where? Why?'

'The B & B.' He shot to his feet, passing her back the album so he could type in a swift response. 'I'll explain on the way.'

CHAPTER EIGHT

EVEN THOUGH HIS brother had warned him, Sebastian wasn't prepared for the sight as they drove up Elmdale hill.

Straight ahead was Flick's B & B.

Flick's B & B and a swarm of jostling people.

Cameras, giant microphones, and noise. So much noise.

He had to honk to get the crowd to part so they could get through to the car park and even then, they followed them like bees around a honeypot.

'You ready for this?'

He forced the words through gritted teeth, his fists clenched around the steering wheel. Being a recluse had its perks and avoiding scenes like this was one of the biggest.

Beside him, Flick was pale and wide-eyed, her bag clutched to her lap.

Both guilt and anger gnawed at him. Guilt that he'd brought this media frenzy to her door, anger that the press was even here at all.

Maybe a taxi would have been better, at least then she could have returned without him. Avoided rumours he wasn't so sure she would be ready to face—*hell*, he wasn't. Especially when there was Angel to consider. And heaven forbid, the press found out he had a daughter before she'd even learned of it.

But leaving Flick to face the wolves alone hadn't felt right.

Well, not quite alone—Theo was here. Back earlier than anticipated and currently holding the fort.

'This is insane.' Flick flinched from the camera flashes, her head angled towards him as her wide eyes stayed fixed on the story-hungry faces. 'Elmdale hasn't had this kind of media attention in years, in fact the last time…'

She bit her lip.

'Yeah, I saw the footage when news of our disappearance broke.'

'I guess you'd hope to be old news now.'

No, he knew he was far from old news, but…

'I should have anticipated it. I just didn't expect them to catch on so quick.'

'News travels fast in Elmdale—you know that.'

'Aye.' He remembered the eyes on him that morning, the whisperings of the village already spreading news of his return. It wouldn't take much for someone to put two and two together and realise who he was. Not merely the missing Ferrington heir, but the reclusive Dubois out of hiding. He cursed as he saw the bold headline in his mind's eye.

He *should* have expected it. He *should* have prepared her for it.

But what did he know? He'd kept himself locked away for years. 'I'm sorry to get you caught up in this.'

'You don't need to apologise; this isn't your fault.'

He sent her a look as he pulled the car into the same space it had occupied earlier that day. Only now the car park was teeming with other vehicles, his brother's low-slung Porsche among them, engine likely still warm from its long journey.

Why his brother hadn't taken the private jet from Paris was beyond him but that was a question for later…much, much later.

'It is my fault, Flick.' He cut the engine as his eyes reached hers. 'They're here for me and…'

His voice trailed off as the door to the B & B opened and Theo caught his eye—it was time to move.

She followed his line of sight, her mouth falling open. 'Is that…?'

'Yes. Give him a second and he'll clear the way.'

'But he's…he's *huge*.'

A laugh caught in his throat. 'He's only two inches taller than me.'

'But all that muscle?'

He laughed some more.

'And that grin…'

'Okay, okay, that's my baby brother you're ogling.'

She snapped her mouth shut and turned to look at him. 'I was *not ogling*.'

'Of course, you weren't.'

'But he was so…so *small* when you left.'

'All the more reason for him to beef up.'

She looked back to his brother, watched as he expertly cleared a path to the car.

Sebastian shifted in his seat. 'I *did* tell you he was the brawn.'

'I know but I couldn't imagine anyone more muscular than—' She broke off and he watched the delightful flush of colour creep into her cheeks as she waved a dismissive hand at him. 'Just more.'

'Another roundabout compliment?' He laughed deeper, happy to have her focus off the swarm still buzzing outside. 'Don't worry, I won't take it personally.'

'There's nothing…' She jumped at the rap on the glass beside her and spun to see Theo's face up against it, his famed grin broad, his blue eyes bright.

He gestured to the door handle and Sebastian unlocked the car. 'Follow his lead. I'll be right behind you.'

Theo pulled open the door and the shouts around them upped:

'Theo, Theo! Are you back to stay?'

'Why change your name?'

'What's the story with the estate?'

'Are the rumours about Dubois and the estate true?'

Sebastian cringed. 'Get her inside, Theo.'

'Oh, I'm on it.'

'What rumours?' She frowned at Theo as he helped her out of the car, his palm on her back as he urged her forward.

'Don't worry,' Theo said into her ear, 'it's us they want.'

'For now,' Sebastian grumbled under his breath as he came up behind them, ensuring she was protected from all sides.

Over his dead body would he let one of these reporters get to her. Her or Angel.

He let his brother lead the way and as soon Flick was safe inside, he turned and raised his hands to the pressing rabble.

'You'll be getting nothing more from us today.'

And with that he closed the door, ignoring the harried shouts trying to break through. He bowed his head, pressed his palm against the wood and thanked his lucky stars that his brother had arrived when he did.

'How long have they been hounding the place for?' He combed a steadying hand through his hair as he turned to face him.

'They arrived just before lunch according to the fiery skirt out front.'

'Fiery skirt?' Flick choked over the reference. 'You mean Bree?'

'Aye, that's the one.' Theo rubbed the back of his neck. 'How to make an entrance, hey? I turn up outside and that lot circle me like a pack of vultures, then one step inside and she was on me. She knows how to protect those she cares about; I'll say that for her.' He threw a wink Flick's way that had her blushing and taken aback in one. 'And before you ask, brother, I gave her my good side, best behaviour and all that jazz, Scout's honour.'

'You were never a Scout.' Flick seemed to respond on autopilot, her eyes still sporting the rabbit-caught-in-the-headlights look and chewing Sebastian up inside.

'Ooh, harsh!' Theo's grin made a return. 'But you've got me.'

'I'm going to check on Angel…and Bree,' she said quietly. 'Where are they?'

'In the kitchen, baking up a storm.'

'Thanks.'

She hurried away and Sebastian fought the urge to go with her. The need to protect her, to protect them both, burning in his veins. And this was only the beginning—the inevitable disruption to their lives in the coming days would be monumental.

And all Flick had wanted to do was protect this time for Angel and her studies…instead he'd brought this chaos to their door.

'What's up with you?' His brother eyed the fists he had unknowingly formed, his gaze devoid of the humour from seconds before.

'You don't want to know.'

Theo folded his arms, the crease between his brows deepening as he leaned against the wall, his blond hair flopping over his right eye and doing its best to ruin any attempt he had at looking serious. 'Oh, I most definitely *do* want to know. Why do you think I'm here a day earlier than planned?'

He eyed his brother. In the light of the hall and without the distraction of his impish grin and the frenzied press, Sebastian could see his brother was tired. His eyes were red-ringed, his skin lacking the lustre of its usual tan. Something was up, and that something had sent his brother driving through the night from Paris. 'I think that has more to do with whatever you're running from.'

Theo didn't even flinch. 'This isn't about me; this is about you. Now spill.'

'Mum! It's about time!'

Angel grabbed the remote and muted the TV, tossing it on the kitchen side as she rushed towards her and came to an abrupt holt.

'I can't believe who he is!'

Oh, God, did Angel already know? But how?

She looked to Bree as if she would have the answer… which was madness because even Bree didn't know that Sebastian was Angel's father.

She couldn't know but, oh, God, her head was spinning.

It had all happened so fast. Arriving in the car, taking in the flurry of activity outside her quiet B & B. One second, she was stepping out to the shouts and cries of the local media—national even—the next she was being ushered in through the rear door of her own home, the brothers providing an effective and much-needed shield.

She should have seen this coming. Of course, the media would be hot on the sudden return of the heirs of Ferrington. She'd downplayed it in the car to make him feel better, but seriously…

She should have anticipated it. Prepared for it.

As for his fatherhood status…

'He's the heir to the Ferrington Estate, Mum!' Angel rushed out when Felicity failed to speak. '*And* the boss of the Dubois hotel chain! He's a billionaire, Mum. A real live billionaire staying under our roof. This is insane.'

Felicity's shoulders eased away from her ears as relief set in. Angel didn't know he was her father, not yet anyway, that was—

'Wait. What?' She stared at her daughter's flushed face. Had she *heard* Angel right?

'He's a *billionaire*, Mum.'

'No…' Her head was shaking even as the truth settled in her gut. Of course he was. It explained everything. His car. His clothing. His whole successful charisma that seemed effortless…cut from money. Which of course he had been but not on *that* scale.

And that had been old money. His wealth now…that was his own doing, his and his brother's, but a *billionaire*?

'Uh-huh!' Angel was nodding, her eyes wide. 'And staying here, too! Like why? Is he crazy?'

'Yeah, crazy,' she said numbly, trying to keep her cool as she walked into the kitchen and reached for the kettle. She needed a tea. Alcohol was no longer the answer, not when she needed to think clearly—*which you knew earlier, but that didn't stop you*…

'It's gonna be weird having a high-class hotel on our doorstep,' Bree piped up. 'I can't work out whether it's a good weird or a bad weird, but I—'

'Wait!' She slammed the kettle on and turned to face Bree. 'What did you just say?'

Bree gave a shrug. 'The hotel—the estate—it's going to be weird when it gets converted into some luxury spa resort.'

'Who said anything about converting it?'

'It's all over the news. The heirs to the estate are the

world-renowned hoteliers, the Dubois brothers…' she did little finger quotes '…and they are back to take ownership and convert it into an exclusive spa resort. The village are already up in arms about it, as you can imagine, but then no one likes change here so it's no surprise.'

Pins and needles came alive all over her skin. *Dubois. Thee Dubois hotel chain.*

Bree frowned. 'You didn't know?'

Her head was shaking again. Why hadn't she twigged? Why hadn't she put two and two together before now and realised who he was? Why hadn't he told her?

Why would he? It's not like you asked.

No, she hadn't. But then how could she have begun to imagine Sebastian and the worldwide hotel chain was one and the same?

No wonder the reporters were milling outside.

Reporters who would kill for the kind of scoop Angel represented.

Oh, God.

'But he's famous, Mum, like proper famous, and he's *here*. Maybe he'll attract some extra business our way after the hols are over. It'll take the pressure off financially and—' Angel abruptly stopped talking and frowned. 'Mum, you look grey, are you okay?'

Her ears were ringing, her head was spinning, words were impossible to form. No, no, she wasn't okay.

The TV was playing the local news, with an emboldened headline across the bottom: *Billionaire recluse Sebastian Dubois comes out of hiding…staking his claim over the Ferrington empire and expanding the Dubois presence to Yorkshire.*

Blindly, she reached for the remote control and turned up the volume, listening to the news report and feeling as though she were having some weird out-of-body experience, observing, not living it.

Like a dream. Only it wasn't a dream. It was very, very real.

A picture they must have captured of Sebastian very recently was on the screen while the man himself was in the room next to her.

But he wasn't back to live, he was here to take his family home and turn it into…into… Her stomach rolled.

Did this mean he would do what needed to be done and head back to France, or wherever home was for him now, as if nothing had changed?

Walking into their lives and out again, as he had before.

No, not quite as he had before, but…

'Are you all right, Flick?' Bree was by her side, her hand gentle on her shoulder. 'You look like you need to sit down.'

She sank into a stool at the centre island and felt both Angel's and Bree's eyes upon her. She needed to get a grip, if not for herself, for Angel. Only…

'Flick, can I speak to you for a second?'

Her spine straightened, eyes darting to the doorway and the man now filling it—one very apprehensive and definitely unsure of himself billionaire.

Well, that had to be an act.

As had the connection she'd felt budding between them the past twenty-four hours.

It was something to start falling for him all over again when he'd been a runaway heir returning to his home. But a billionaire, wholly in control of his life, his future? A man that didn't need his inheritance and had designs on transforming the village landscape in such a way as to negatively impact her own business, her livelihood?

How could she have been so foolish?

A ridiculous laugh erupted and she cut it off with an abrupt swallow, spying the concern in all the eyes pinned on her. 'I'm a little busy right now.'

Busy trying to take stock of everything—my life, our mess, the future.

'Don't worry about things here, honey,' Bree piped up. 'The O'Briens are out for the day, no one expects the front to be open with that rabble outside and I'm happy to keep an eye on the place.'

'But I'm back now and it's your day off, Bree.'

'Precisely, and I'd already planned to spend it here. That lot out there don't change a thing. Besides, Angel and I are working on some new recipe ideas. Aren't we, love?'

Angel nodded as Felicity tried to come up with an excuse, any excuse that didn't leave her alone with Sebastian again so soon. 'But—'

'Hush! You've helped me enough in the past, now I get to return the favour.' Her friend pulled mugs out of the cupboard, ignoring Felicity's pleading stare. 'Why don't you both go through to the front, and I'll bring you a cuppa when it's ready?'

Felicity looked at Angel, who was eyeing her as if she were mad, her elevated eyebrows screaming, *Come on, Mum, he's a billionaire! A hot billionaire! And he wants to talk to you! Get out there!*

'We don't want no poncy hotel on our doorstep...'

Felicity stiffened as the TV filled the silence—it was Tim the butcher, a microphone stuffed under his nose, the B & B in the background. 'We're quite happy just the way things are. Back in my day, the estate was a huge part of our community, our traditions. It would have been good to see some of that return. Not this...this...'

'Luxury spa?' the reporter provided as an artist's impression of what it could like appeared on the screen and Felicity's stomach rolled anew.

'Aye. It's a disgrace. His grandfather was a disgrace and now he's—'

She snatched the remote and slammed the off button, her eyes finding Sebastian of their own accord. His mouth was set in a grim line, his brow furrowed, his pallor making him less bronze God and more the English aristocrat he was by blood.

The shrill ring of the oven timer cut through the air and Bree came alive, her hands clapping together.

'That'll be the muffins, Angel.' Relief filled her friend's chipper tone to the brim. 'An experimental batch of mojito muffins—I'll bring one out with your tea, so long as they taste good enough.'

'Someone say muffins?' Theo appeared alongside his brother, his muscles straining the fabric of his pale blue T-shirt as he leaned into the doorframe. 'If you need a guinea pig to taste test, I'm all yours.'

Angel laughed and Bree choked, her cheeks oddly aglow, but Felicity had bigger problems occupying her thoughts.

Like why Sebastian had led her to believe he was moving back when clearly that wasn't the case…and worse, it seemed she was the last person on earth to know.

And why did that hurt so very much?

They weren't together, they weren't even friends…not really. He owed her nothing.

Angel, on the other hand…

CHAPTER NINE

SEBASTIAN LET HER walk out ahead of him, following on her tail as she entered the bar area, and watched as she surveyed the entire room.

'Don't worry, it's definitely clear.'

She acted as if she hadn't heard him, checking and re-checking the locks on the front door and making sure the lace that fell over the front windows didn't let anyone peep in. She leapt when a woman's face appeared on the other side, pressed up against the glass as she sought to get a glimpse of something.

He cursed under his breath. 'They'll tire soon enough.'

Her eyes widened as they shot to him. 'You reckon?'

'We have some people on their way. They'll see them gone for today at least.'

'Some people?'

A brief nod.

'Right, because you're a billionaire now and money solves everything.'

He caught the bitterness, the resentment, and tried to ignore it. 'It has its advantages.'

Her throat bobbed. 'I bet.'

'Look, Flick…' He stepped forward and she backed up, the move small but no less painful, and he stopped.

'Why didn't you tell me?' Her blue eyes glittered, bright and accusatory.

'Tell you what, exactly?'

She shook her head, gave a choked scoff. 'Isn't it obvious?'

'Not particularly.'

He blew out a breath when she said nothing, turning on the spot, head shaking.

'What did you expect me to say?' He threw his hands towards her, palms out. '"Hey, Flick, I don't know whether you know but I co-own one of the world's leading hotel chains. I'm on the world's rich list even. Fancy that, hey?"'

His gut writhed. Sickened by the importance she was placing on his wealth, sickened by the distaste he could see in her eye. 'I wasn't aware I needed to sell myself to you.'

'I don't care about your money, Sebastian,' she whispered. 'I meant your intentions for the estate. The fact that you're not moving back, that you're going to convert it into some, some soulless hotel…' She flapped an unsteady hand about her. 'Why didn't you tell me? How could you let me believe you were coming home?'

Her voice cracked and the air shuddered out of him— she wanted him home. *Him*. After everything he'd done…

The pang in his chest was too much to bear and he pressed a fist to it. 'I was hardly thinking straight, Flick. I would have told you, but when you…' He looked to the hallway, checking for eavesdroppers, wondering how far his voice would travel, and decided to close the distance between them to be sure they wouldn't be overheard. 'When you told me your news, it's all I've been able to think about.'

She didn't move away, neither did she encourage him closer, her arms wrapping around herself.

'Is that what this is, Flick? You're upset I'm not moving back to the village?'

'I thought…' She shook her head, bit her lip and he lifted his hand, slow enough that she could choose to back away, soft enough that he wouldn't scare her.

He palmed her cheek, holding her gaze that swam with unshed tears, tears that he felt resonate within him. 'You thought what?'

What *had* she thought? That he would return to the estate to live there, and they would be a fully fledged family of sorts? No, she couldn't have. But then, she'd never had one. She'd only ever had her grandmother. Was she craving one now? Did she think it possible? With him?

He could barely breathe for it. The idea. The impossibility.

'I'm sorry, Flick, it wasn't my intent to hurt you, but I could never live there again, not after everything.'

'It was your home.'

'It was also my hell.'

Her lashes fluttered with her sharp inhalation, her brows drawing together.

'Look…' He lifted his other palm and ran his thumbs along her cheekbones. 'Just because I'm not moving back, doesn't mean I'm abandoning you again.'

'That's not… I…' She shook her head, broke away from his touch as she straightened and raised her chin. 'This isn't about me, it's about Angel.'

He knew there was some truth to it, he also knew it wasn't the whole truth.

The noise outside built again and she stepped further away, peering through the lace.

He ignored the way his body ached to close the distance she'd created. 'More news crews arriving?'

She nodded. 'Looks that way.'

He cursed and knew what he had to do. He also knew

how much she'd hate it. But Theo had suggested it and now he knew his brother was right. 'You're not going to like this, Flick, but hear me out.'

Her gaze snapped to his. 'Not going to like what? It can't get much worse than this, can it?'

He stared back at her—could she not see what this meant? For her, for Angel and the time she'd asked of him?

'Theo and I think it's best if you come and stay at the estate with me…just until the media frenzy dies down.'

She choked on a laugh, eyes wide. 'You're joking, right?'

'No.'

'I have *guests* staying, a *business* to run, Angel has school starting back up next week, I can't *leave*.'

'Theo will keep the B & B ticking over. You can trust him. As for Angel, she'll have space to study, away from all of this, and I can drive her to school easy enough. The commute isn't an issue.'

'I can drive her myself. *That* isn't the issue…' She was shaking her head, her ponytail sashaying, freed strands getting caught in her damp lashes. 'This is crazy. This whole situation. I can't *move in* with you.'

'A minute ago, you were worried I was running away again, now you don't want to be under the same roof?'

'Moving in together for the short term and having you in our lives for the long are completely different things.'

'Think about it, Flick. It's not going to take much for the press to uncover our history and to start speculating about Angel. You think the story of the missing heirs returning is big? Just think what the headlines will be like when they piece the rest together. "Missing heir abandons pregnant girlfriend." "Reclusive Billionaire discovers he's a father sixteen years after the fact." Or worse, so much worse, however they decide to play it, but all variations on the same.'

She was getting paler and paler, her head shaking rapidly now, and his palms itched to reach for her; he wanted to convince her everything would be okay.

And then she stilled. 'We're going to have to tell her.'

'We are. But let's take control of the situation first and get out of here. You can trust Theo. He knows what he's doing. I promise.'

She ran her teeth over her bottom lip, gripped her middle tighter as she stared at him, the internal debate flittering across her face. But he knew this was the only answer that made sense and he knew she'd realise it, too.

The Ferrington Estate was vast and well protected. He could keep the press away and they could stay ahead of the situation, they could tell Angel on their own terms.

'Okay.'

Her agreement was quiet but definite and his pulse gave the tiniest leap.

'You're sure?' Guilt had him foolishly pressing.

'No, I'm not sure, Sebastian.' She started to stride away. 'But what choice do we have?'

'Where are you going?'

'To pack…and to work out how we explain this to Angel.'

'Okay. I'll get packed too.' Only he couldn't move. Reality had him rooted to the spot. They were moving in together. Him, Flick, and their daughter, living on the estate… no matter how temporarily.

Something shifted deep inside his chest, something impossible to acknowledge, even harder to ignore.

What was he doing?

Laughter trickled through from the kitchen as Felicity approached the stairs, her daughter blissfully unaware of the trouble ahead.

Trouble is a bit extreme, her brain tried to reason.

But was it?

They were about to leave the B & B, her home, for some unknown stint on the Ferrington Estate. A place that harboured as many bad memories as good for Sebastian.

And they were going to have to break the news to Angel.

She wasn't ready. Angel wasn't. Not with her exams on the horizon too.

As for the way he made Felicity feel…

A simple look and her heart took off inside her chest. A touch and her entire body came alive. She'd thought he was coming home. That he'd be a short drive away and Angel would have them both in her life.

But no, he wasn't coming home.

And did that mean he was leaving again soon? Would Angel want to go with him? She'd had sixteen years with her mum, would she see it as only fair that she spent some real time—quality time—with her father?

Sebastian could give Angel so much. Opportunity, life experience, the wealth to travel the world until she found her feet and knew what she wanted.

None of which required her…

Felicity refused to be needy; she wouldn't stop Angel doing what she wanted, and she wouldn't stop Sebastian forming a bond with her.

But where did that leave them? Mother and daughter?

'Hey!' Bree swept into the hall, a loaded tea tray in her hands, a frown on her face as she absorbed Felicity's frozen state. 'You okay?'

How many times had she been asked that since his return?

She shook her head and Bree slid the tea tray onto the sideboard. 'Want to talk about it?'

'I thought you were busy baking?'

'I have them mixing up a different recipe. It'll keep them occupied for a while.'

Angel's laugh reached them along with Theo's deep rumble. 'She clearly likes him.'

Bree rolled her eyes. 'Well, he *was* on the cover of that teen mag she buys just last month.'

'He was?' Felicity gave a weak laugh, feeling even more out of the loop, but then it wasn't as if she had time for magazines, TV, gossip...

It explained why Angel was so excited though.

'Yup. The man has an ego the size of a small planet. I think he thinks everyone likes him.'

'Not you though, hey?'

'I'm admitting nothing... Come on, let's talk this out upstairs. Whatever it is, I'm sure offloading will help—as will the mojito recipe I was perfecting this morning.'

'You were perfecting mojitos *this morning*?'

'Well, duh! I had to have something to compare the muffins to, and something tells me this tea isn't going to cut it... Not driving anywhere, are you?'

Was she? Or would Sebastian drive? Shouldn't she take her own car to at least keep some independence? Though the idea of driving when her hands still shook from the press encounter...

'No, I'm not driving.'

'Excellent, you go on up. I'll take the tray through to the front and get the jug I prepared earlier.'

'The *jug*?'

'Oh, yes!'

A little while later they were sitting together on Felicity's bed; a very enthralled Bree waved a half-drunk mojito at her. 'Okay, so let me get this straight... Sebastian is Angel's dad, he ran away because of evil grandfather, now he's a billionaire back to reclaim the estate, only he's not keeping the estate, he's turning it into a flash resort and then…'

'I've no idea.'

And she needed to get an idea, fast. For her and for Angel.

'He wants to be a father to Angel though, yeah?'

'I think so.'

Bree squinted, and she realised her response had been far too wishy-washy, but she felt as if the rug had been pulled out from under her and it still felt strange telling Bree when Angel didn't know. But she'd needed to speak to someone to stop herself going crazy.

Someone who wasn't Sebastian.

'We've not had chance to talk about it properly, but yes, I believe he does.'

'Well, that's a good thing, right?'

She nodded, telling herself the same as she sipped her drink, wincing at the strength. 'How much alcohol did you put in this, Bree?'

'Hey, don't curse the maker. I followed the instructions to the letter and this one has *all* the alcohol…with a smidgen of soda and juice. Beats tea, though, right?'

A laugh hiccupped out of her. 'I guess.'

'So why the long face? He's back in your life and he wants to be in Angel's and he's about to whisk you off to his private estate…which sounds like a grand palace complete with an *enormous* swimming pool. Total holiday material.'

'Because we're going to have to tell Angel, like *now*, and I'd wanted to wait.'

'You'd only be putting off the inevitable and she's gonna want to know.'

'I know, but I was hoping we'd get her exams out of the way first.'

Her friend gave her a sympathetic smile. 'She'll be fine, honey. She will. It'll be a shock, of course it will, but she's strong, determined and has her head screwed on right.'

'I know.'

'And she has you. You'll get through it together.'

She wished she shared her friend's optimism. 'I hope so.'

'No hope about it, you will!'

She tried for a smile.

'And look on the bright side, he's one hot stud muffin. Which is, of course, irrelevant. More of a bonus.'

'Bree.' She gave her friend a shove.

'Sorry. Couldn't resist. But on a serious note…' she reached over to squeeze Felicity's fingers '…it *will* be okay. From what you've said he's a good man, so it stands to reason he'll make a good father. And now he's back you can get to know one another again… Who knows what might happen?'

The twinkle was back in her friend's eye and Felicity cocked a brow. 'Nothing's going to happen. We're going to tell Angel and take it from there.'

'And it's the taking it from there I'm talking about…'

She couldn't stop the laugh from erupting; even if Bree was way off, it was hard to be frazzled for long in her friend's upbeat presence.

'And you must admit, you've not been serious about any man since him. Don't you think that tells you something?'

'It tells me I was ruined for anyone else a long time ago and if you think I'm going to fall into that trap and be ruined some more, you're even more crazy than I thought.'

'Geez, you're no fun when you're like this.'

'I'm sorry, Bree. My life has been upended in the space of forty-eight hours and I'm playing catch up. Getting it on with my childhood sweetheart, who abandoned me pregnant at sixteen, is not high on my list of priorities.'

Her skin suddenly prickled, heat spreading through her middle.

Oh, my God, they weren't alone.

Her eyes flew to the door to catch Sebastian backing away. 'Sorry, Flick, I'll come back.'

'No—no, it's fine.' Her cheeks burned, but Bree was positively glowing—her eyes and smile wide as though that would somehow make up for what he'd overheard. 'We're done.'

'Indeed, we are!' Bree launched to her feet, her black waves tumbling down her back as she ran a hand through them. 'And don't you worry about this place, *Flick.*' The way she used Sebastian's pet name for her, the twinkle persisting in her eye, wasn't lost on Felicity. 'I'm only next door. Theo can bring any problems my way.'

She bent down to pull Felicity into an embrace, careful not to spill either of their drinks as she whispered in her ear, 'Now, get that down you and start looking to the future. No fear, okay?'

'Uh-huh. Thank you.'

Her friend squished her to her bosom, unconcerned that she was suffocating Felicity's face in her generous assets. 'Any time.'

She picked up the almost empty jug of mojito and made for the door. 'I'd offer you some, Mr Billionaire-With-Big-Plans-For-This-Village, but you're driving.'

Sebastian gave a tentative smile. 'Maybe next time.'

'If you play your cards right, sure.' She smiled serenely. 'You get my drift?'

A little wink and a cheeky nudge with the elbow and she was off, leaving Felicity staring after her openmouthed and unsure whether she should apologise or run for the hills. How could her life have changed so much in less than a week and how could she even begin to pick up the pieces?

'Are they your bags?' He gestured to the pile behind her on the bed and she nodded, getting to her feet.

She eyed the bags, but her mind was on the conversation ahead. 'How do we tell Angel we're moving out for a bit without telling her the truth?'

'You tell her you're moving out while the press attention dies down.'

'But she knows we never leave. Not even—not even for a holiday. She's hardly going to put the press attention on you as something to run away from, especially when she sees it as being *"great for business"*.'

The creases around his eyes eased a little. 'Does she, now?'

'She's excited about the whole thing, Sebastian. It's a nightmare, a real-life nightmare! How can we hope to keep a lid on it? What if she—? What if they—?' She could feel her body start to shake, her lips trembling as she pressed a hand to them.

'Hey!' He strode forward and cupped her arms, gently rubbing her skin, which was all too willing to warm to his touch. 'One step at a time, Flick. Tell her what you need to and once we're home, we can tell her togeth—'

'Home?' She frowned up at him, his own brow furrowing. 'You said home?'

'Sorry...' He shook his head, and she could visibly see

him regathering his wits. Had it shocked him as much as her? 'I mean when we're on the estate we can tell her. Or you can tell her on your own. Whichever you—'

'Tell who what?'

Oh, God, Angel!

CHAPTER TEN

SEBASTIAN SPUN ON his heel, heart in throat, his hands snapping back to his sides.

Angel was in the doorway, arms folded, her sharpened gaze not missing a beat.

The intimacy of his touch, their closeness...

He opened his mouth, but nothing would come.

For the first time in his life, he was struck dumb, but then he'd never had a secret so big, so momentous that he wanted to shout it from the rooftops and keep it trapped in one.

He looked back at Flick.

'You might want to come and sit down, love.' She was white as a sheet, her eyes flitting between them as she sank into the mattress and patted the space beside her.

He backed away, giving her room, giving them both room as he sensed it wasn't just the temporary move Flick was about to tell her.

Angel closed the door slowly, her eyes wary as she watched him and crossed the room.

'Okay. You're freaking me out, Mum.' She lowered herself onto the bed and looked to Flick, her lips pressing together and deepening the dimples in her cheeks. Dimples that were so like... His chest spasmed, his heart too. 'You wanna just come out with it?'

Flick reached over and touched her knee. 'There's no easy way to tell you this, and with the press outside, there isn't the time to wait either…'

She looked at him and he tried to give her a smile of encouragement but feared it looked more of a grimace.

How he wished they could hit fast forward and be coming out the other side of this, in a good place…with a fresh start.

'Mum…?'

Flick dragged her eyes from his to their daughter's and blew out a breath.

'Sebastian and I used to be together, a very long time ago. We were—we were in love…'

A soft smile touched her lips, reaching inside him, the past and the love they'd shared resonating in his bones. His knees felt weak but there was nowhere else to perch that was close enough but not too close. He'd never felt more of an outsider, an outsider who was supposed to be very much a part of this unit. This family.

The ache was back, deep within his chest, choking up his throat, fogging up his brain.

'Okay, you were an item. No biggie. Can't see the press being all that interested, though, but it's cool. Reckon my mates will think it's kinda cool, too. Not sure why you're making such a big deal of it though… No offence,' she added, looking at him.

'None taken.'

'But it's not that simple, honey.'

'Not that simple?' She frowned at her. 'Why? Oh, hang on, are you…' she pointed at him, pointed at Flick, her mouth curving up '…getting together again? Are you dating, is that what this is? Cos that's cool, too. It's about time you got out there, Mum, and it's not like you need to run it by me. I'm not your keep…' Her voice trailed off, her mouth falling open as her eyes darted between them before landing squarely on him.

He clenched his jaw, his body poised.

'Hang on, when you say you used to be together, like how long ago?'

'Sebastian is your father, Angel.'

The air in the room seemed to still. Angel blinked. Blinked again. Her throat bobbed and she opened her mouth. Closed it. Opened it again. *'You?'*

He nodded, felt the strangest prick behind his eyes as his jaw throbbed.

'When did you find out?'

He was grateful for an easy question to answer. 'Last night.'

She looked back at her mum. 'But I thought you couldn't reach him. I thought that's why he didn't know; you didn't know where he was to tell him. That he'd vanished.'

'That's all true.'

'But he's *famous*, Mum! How could you not know how to reach him?'

'He's not famous in the traditional sense. You could hand me the world's rich list and, though I might recognise a name to two, I couldn't identify their faces.'

She shook her head, staring at her mother in angry disbelief. 'But Theo… Everyone knows who Theo is! He's on the TV, in magazines…he's in the top ten fittest…'

Her voice trailed off as her head continued to shake, her anger unabating as she refused to accept it.

'I'm not in the public eye, Angel.' He couldn't hold quiet any longer. 'Theo is, and he's unrecognisable now. He was so young when we left.'

She looked at her mother. 'I can't believe it. How could you not…?'

'It wasn't your mum's fault.' It scraped out of him, raw; he was desperate for her to understand. To put the blame where it belonged. He cleared his throat as he looked into his daughter's eyes that were so like her mother's, especially when they blazed as they did now. 'I left her with no word, no forwarding address, no way to reach me. We changed our names. Your mother knew me as Ferrington, not Dubois. Even if she'd caught a glimpse of me on the TV, I'm not sure she'd have recognised me.'

Flick made a slight noise and he looked at her, saw the denial in her gaze. She'd have known. Just as he would have known. The connection that pulled them together in their teens persisting even now.

'Right…so now what? You're back? Not to stay though, if the press is to be believed. You're going to build some fancy spa on our doorstep and then clear off again?'

'Angel!'

'*What*, Mum? He abandoned you, abandoned us, don't I get to be angry about it?'

'He didn't know about you.'

'So? He still left you, Mum, broke your heart. Gran told me how it was after he'd left, she told me how much you'd loved him—*you* told me, and he would have known it, too.'

'It's not as simple as that. He had his reasons for leaving.'

'Good enough reasons to break my mother's heart and walk away?' His daughter's gaze speared him now. 'Did you even love her?'

'Yes.' He didn't hesitate as the answer pulsed right through him.

'Yes, to which?'

'I loved her.'

'Angel, please.' Flick touched her daughter's shoulder. 'There are things we need to explain but right now we need to pack up and get away for a bit. You have your revision to focus on and staying here with the press camped outside isn't going to help with that. Not to mention…' Flick looked his way, her smile small '…it'll be an opportunity for you to get to know one another.'

'What are you suggesting? That we go away *together*? You know the press will follow him, right? If he leaves— *alone*—the problem's solved.'

That hurt. Hurt a lot. So much he couldn't speak.

'Again, it's not that simple. Everyone in the village knows our history. It won't take long for the media to get wind of you, of my—my teen pregnancy—and put two and two together.'

'*So?* They won't know anything for sure.'

'And since when has that stopped the press?'

'They won't stop until they have you hemmed into a corner, applying the pressure, drilling you.' He spoke up, his need to protect them overriding all else. 'And frankly, I want you and your mother protected from their tenacious and insensitive tongues, and the Ferrington Estate can give you that.'

'The *Ferrington* Estate,' she spat, her laugh harsh. 'What? Live like one big happy family?'

He winced.

'Wow!' She looked from him to Flick, her eyes wild and wide. 'Is he for real? Pulling out all the stops to protect us now. Well, newsflash, *Dad*…' She shot to her feet, her cheeks blazing as she thundered up to him, her eyes pinning him as tears formed at their corners. 'You're sixteen years too late. We've done all right without you up until now, and we'll carry on doing all right without you.'

'Please, Angel.' Flick came up behind her, reaching out to touch her shoulder once more. 'Listen to—'

'No! I've heard enough.' She spun away and stormed from the room, slamming the door closed behind her.

He scrubbed his face, his hair, let out a breath he hadn't known he'd been holding. 'That could've gone better.'

Flick caught her lip in her teeth, stared at the door and back at him. 'I'm sorry, she'll come around. She's in shock, but when she understands why you left, why you stayed away, she'll be okay.'

He searched her gaze. 'You sure about that?'

Because he wasn't.

Didn't he agree with his daughter on some level? If he'd loved Flick so much, couldn't he have come back when he was older, wiser, and wholly in control of his life?

What did that truly say about him and his so-called love for Flick?

'Sebastian?'

He couldn't look her in the eye. 'I'll take your bags downstairs and clear out my room. You should go and talk to her, make sure she's on board because she's right about one thing—I don't get a say in whether you come with me or not. That has to be a decision you both make.'

'And if we decide not to?'

'I will go and hope they leave with me.'

She hesitated on the threshold and a part of him, a part that wasn't so different from the boy he'd been before he'd fled, wanted her to say something, anything, to suggest she didn't want to be separated from him again.

What he got was silence.

To say the quiet in the car was unbearable would have been an understatement.

Felicity glanced at Angel in the back. She was fixated on the passing world outside, avoiding her mother's eye.

Sebastian was much the same, his eyes set straight ahead, his knuckles white around the gear stick and the wheel. Everyone was avoiding her...

She let out a trapped breath and tried to ease into her seat.

It would all be okay. She'd explained Sebastian's reasons for leaving to Angel, she'd explained why he'd stayed away as best she could, but her daughter's mutinous expression hadn't lifted.

There was no joy in having found her father. No joy in the possibility of what the future held.

Oh, she'd agreed to leave the B & B, to pack up her books and wardrobe and get in the car, but Felicity knew her daughter well enough to know she wasn't happy about any of it.

And maybe Felicity should take a leaf out of her daughter's book.

She watched Sebastian out of the corner of her eye. He emanated strength, wealth, confidence...a confidence that had been knocked by their situation that had understandably thrown him. But why hadn't he come back? Faced his grandfather and returned to her.

His eyes slid her way, a second's connection as they narrowed and her breath caught, her stomach coming alive with a thousand flutters, and she pressed her palm to it. How dared he still make her feel like this?

She blamed their kiss the other night, the intense reconnection and reignited passion, and the continued thrill in the air whenever he was around...but she knew she was fooling herself. It went much deeper than that.

She'd wanted to come between him and Angel when their daughter had gone at him. She'd wanted to stand by his side and defend him when their daughter had thrown the cold hard truth at him: that he'd left without a backward glance.

Left and failed to return even when he'd clearly been empowered to do so.

It hurt. Too much. And she needed to stop dwelling on how it made her feel and focus on Angel and him, the relationship they needed to form.

To think she'd been worried about Angel sailing off into the sunset with her billionaire father. Instead, Angel had been fuming. Far too livid, far too hateful of all he had done and now she felt guilty. Guilty that she'd been a little relieved when her daughter had demonstrated her loyalty so clearly.

She knew it wasn't fair.

She needed to help pave the way for them to form a relationship, and she needed to have the fight over her own feelings herself.

It wasn't her daughter's place to have that fight for her.

'You okay?' His voice was low enough for Angel to miss and she nodded, fighting the urge to touch his hand, the desire to unite them burning despite the pain.

Would he have shown her half as much interest if Angel hadn't existed? Would he have walked into the B & B and back out again when his business was done?

No, that wasn't fair.

He'd kissed her before he'd known, the connection between them burning as strong as ever. The memory alone made her lips tingle now and she pressed her fingers to them, snatching them away as she caught his eyes follow the move.

'You sure?'

She nodded, unable to trust her voice as she clutched her hands in her lap.

She was still wrangling with it all when they arrived at the gates. Only they weren't unmanned any more. Two security guards stood to attention, clocking the number plate and giving a respectful nod to Sebastian as the gates swung seamlessly open.

'When did you…?' She turned to look at him.

'I called ahead. The house is fully staffed now, the rooms are ready and there are enough cameras to ensure the press don't get past the boundary.'

'You managed all that in a few hours?'

'The cameras were always here.'

That wasn't what she meant, and he knew it.

Money. This was what money bought you. People jumping to attention at a moment's notice, smoothing the path, making life easy.

She snuck another look at Angel. Her dark hair was braided over her shoulder, her denim shorts, far too short, her skinny-strapped T far too skimpy. Her daughter had her wardrobe moments and, though they were experiencing something of an unexpected heatwave, Felicity knew this outfit was about something else entirely.

Day one and she was determined to test her father. Sebastian had said nothing when they'd come downstairs, bags in hand, silently loading up the car with the aid of Theo. Frank and Bill had fashioned off a little barricade to keep the car park free of prying eyes and lenses, and they'd managed to escape relatively interference free.

Now they were through the estate gates, the outside world seemed miles away. She wasn't naive, she knew many, if not all the journalists would be hot on their tail, that some would've already been turned away from the estate by the team that Sebastian had put in place. But she felt safe here. She trusted him to keep them that way.

Her heart, not so much.

She refocused on Angel, who was busy taking it all in. Even her daughter in her moodiness couldn't hide the widening to her eyes.

'What do you think?'

Angel looked at her and forced a shrug. 'It's an old house.'

'I always thought it looked more like a castle.'

Angel's mouth flickered at the corners. 'It does have a Sleeping Beauty vibe—*"Sleeping Beauty meets Yorkshire Spa"*.'

She added air quotes around the latter, her eyes rolling.

'It was built by the Ferringtons two centuries ago,' Sebastian explained, purposefully ignoring their daughter's dig as he tried to steer the conversation into safer territory. 'Your ancestors fell in love with the land and all it could offer. The design was very much led by your fifth-great-grandmother, who was said to be something of a romantic and her husband loved her enough to oblige. She wanted a fairy-tale castle for her children to grow up in and her children's children and so on.'

'And you want to make it into a swanky spa?' She shook her head. 'Despite fifth-great-grandmother's dreams for her children's children to live here?'

His hands flexed around the wheel, his brows drawing together. Felicity felt a flicker of sympathy, but then, Angel did have a point.

His ancestors—Angel's ancestors—had dreamed of keeping this home in the family—a fairy-tale castle for generations to come. Did he seriously think converting it into some fancy spa owned by his company was one and the same?

'What will happen to the deer?' Angel asked, catching sight of them in the distance.

'They'll stay,' he assured her quietly. 'The herd has been here longer than the house itself. This is their home.'

'*Lucky deer...* I'm sure they'll love getting their legs waxed and being gawped at daily.'

The strained silence returned, no one saying a word until they pulled up outside the house and the front door opened. A smartly dressed woman, hair pinned back and greying at the temples, appeared in the entrance.

'I'll introduce you to Madelaine.' He cut the engine. 'She'll be looking after the house and your needs while we're here.'

'Ooh, goodie—do we get a butler too?'

'Angel!'

But Sebastian only smiled. 'Would you like a butler?'

To which Angel could say nothing and instead shoved open her door and jumped out of the car.

Felicity opened her mouth to apologise on her daughter's behalf, but Sebastian raised a hand to stop her.

'Don't.' Grimacing as the rear door slammed shut, he added, 'You need to stop apologising for her. She has every right to be angry and upset. This is going to take time.'

And how much time did they have? she wanted to ask.

How much time before he packed up and left for wherever home was now, and then where would they be?

With a luxury spa on her doorstep, a potential threat not only to her livelihood but the calm normality of their village, too, and a heart left raw once more.

CHAPTER ELEVEN

'WINE?'

Sebastian offered up the bottle, taking in Flick's distracted frown as she chewed on her thumbnail, a nervous habit she'd had all those years ago. She nodded and looked to the hallway, to the stairs that led up to Angel's bedroom where their daughter had taken herself off to straight after dinner.

To his mind, the day could've gone better but it also could've gone a whole lot worse. And the optimist in him was trying to label that a win.

He filled her glass before filling his own. 'Want to take it outside? It's a nice evening.'

She gave him a small smile. 'Why not?'

He led the way into the garden, this time bypassing the table they'd sat at when the message had come in from Theo and choosing the cushioned sun loungers instead. Maybe their softness would ease some of the tension holding Flick's body taut.

Unlikely but…

It was the perfect evening. The heat of the day had faded to a comfortable warmth. The amber glow of the setting sun turned everything it touched to gold—the trees, the pool, the fields. And it was so peaceful, the only sound that of the pool gently lapping and the wildlife surrounding them. A sound he hadn't appreciated in a long time.

'I can't believe you'd want to give this up,' she said softly, leaning back into a lounger. 'It's so beautiful here.'

Yes, the grounds were beautiful, but Flick…skin aglow, her lashes lowered as she let the rays of the disappearing sun caress her skin, her lips glossy from her recent sip of wine…

He dropped onto the edge of the lounger beside her. 'Why is it so hard to believe when you know what happened here?'

The question rasped with the swell of need he couldn't dampen, and he took a drink, hoping it would ease the longing.

'Are you simply wiping out the good?' She turned her head, her eyes finding his as a surprising smile touched her lips. 'Do you not remember all the firsts that happened here too?'

Swallow. 'The firsts?'

Her eyes sparkled. 'You taught me to swim, to dive even…to ride a horse…to stand on my head while humming the theme tune to *Star Wars*.'

He chuckled. 'That I did.'

Though they weren't the firsts he was thinking of when she'd said it…

'And you taught me to kiss…' Her lashes lowered as she relaxed back, her white shirt revealing much of the perfect silhouette beneath—did she know how captivating she was? 'You taught me the kind of pleasure I hadn't known was possible.'

Fire ignited in his gut, the burn of that first passion, the burn of everything he wanted to do now and knew she wouldn't welcome.

Or would she?

Was she doing this on purpose to tease him? To provoke him? Was this some strange game she was playing? Because the last time they'd been alone, he'd been getting different signals altogether.

But she'd been in shock. They both had.

He took another sip of wine. 'You taught me that, too.'

She laughed softly, a hand running through her hair, which she'd freed from its tie. Another added tease as his fingers itched to join hers, to lose themselves in the glossy strands and hold her close as they relived as much of the old as possible.

'I mean it, Flick. There was never anyone but you.'

The air caught with the rawness of his confession and her eyes locked with his. 'Why are you telling me this?'

He gave a choked chuckle, an awkward shrug. 'I don't know. I want you to know, I guess.'

'Why?'

He shook his head. 'Do I have to give a reason other than wanting you to know?'

She worried her bottom lip, her vulnerability killing him, and he leaned forward, slid a finger beneath her chin, his thumb beneath her lip. 'You *were* special to me, Flick, you will always be special to me.'

'Because of Angel.'

'Not just because of Angel.'

'Then why didn't you come back?' She sucked in a breath, her lashes fluttering. 'Like Angel said, you could have come back a long time ago. You'd earned your independence. You were strong enough to face off your grandfather and yet you stayed away.'

Ice gripped his heart. 'I couldn't.'

Gently, she pushed his hand away and sat up, putting distance between them as she sipped her wine. 'Why couldn't you?'

'I've told y—'

'No. You've told me why you left, not why you stayed away.'

The ice spread through his veins, his laugh cold, awkward. 'Isn't it enough?'

She didn't reply; her narrowed gaze all the answer he needed.

'I hated the place as much as I hated him, why would I come back to that?'

Her eyes flared, the pain he'd inflicted swimming there. Her point made. Angel's too. That if he'd loved her as he claimed to, his hatred wouldn't have stopped him.

He swallowed the rising nausea, gripped his wine glass in both hands as his jaw pulsed. He saw the night unfold in his mind's eye, the blood, the scream, his fist...

'What is it you're not telling me, Sebastian?'

She said it so quietly he almost missed it above the roaring in his ears. He lifted his gaze to hers to find so much sympathy. He'd hurt her and still she looked at him like that. With compassion, with care, with...*love*?

No, she could never love him again.

'I'm not the man I was, Flick.'

'Of course, you're not. Life changes us.'

'You don't understand.'

'Then help me understand.'

He stared at her, hard, savouring the look in her eye that would surely die the second the truth was out. The truth that he knew he had to give. That he owed her.

She reached to touch his knee and he moved away, shut himself off as he let it out. 'I hurt him.'

Her brows drew together, her body stilled. 'Who?'

He swallowed. 'That night, the fight that broke out. It wasn't just my mum who got hurt.'

He dragged his eyes away, watched the amber light

playing in the ripples of the pool and wished himself on the bottom of it, safe from the past, present and the future.

'I saw red,' he admitted quietly. 'Mum was on the floor, her lip bleeding, he was standing over her, his fist still shaking, his cane raised and I… I didn't know whether he would strike her again, I wasn't even thinking…' Another swallow. 'I lost it. He hit his head on the way down, there was…there was blood, so much blood and he…he…'

'Oh, Sebastian.' She was reaching for him as his voice cracked and he flinched away, his head shaking as he tried to rid himself of the sickness, the image, his grandfather's shrill laughter as he'd clutched his bloodied head.

He stared at his hands, his head back in time. 'I didn't think I was capable of it.'

'You were defending—'

'It's no excuse.' His eyes speared hers in his vehemence. 'My grandfather was laughing; can you believe it? There he was lying on the floor, a bloodied nose, head, and he was laughing. Telling me I was a chip off the old block. Like father, like son.'

'What? But your father…'

A chilling smile touched his lips. 'Abused my mother.'

'No.' She shook her head. 'I thought… No, you were…'

'Happy. So did I. Turns out my childhood was a lie. That my father wasn't the man I thought he was. He was careful. Only hurt her where we wouldn't see. But my grandfather knew, and he took great delight in telling us. Me and Theo. My mother tried to stop him, but…'

'Oh, God, Sebastian.'

'I was standing there, blood on my hands, Mum was sobbing, Theo was raging, and my childhood was a lie. He threatened me with charges, told me to see sense, to see my mother for the weak link she was, that he knew this would happen. That it was her fault. That he should have stepped in sooner, seen her gone sooner...'

His entire body vibrated with the memory, and he squeezed his eyes shut, shook his head.

'I'm so sorry,' she whispered, and his eyes slammed open.

'Don't be, Flick. I don't deserve your sympathy. I'm telling you this so you can see the truth, see the real me, see why I stayed away, why I don't deserve you—your...'

'But it wasn't your fault, Sebastian. You were a boy defending his family. You were angry. It doesn't make you—'

'A monster?'

She choked. 'God, no.'

'Doesn't it?'

'You're not your father, or your grandfather. You're you, Sebastian. You're the boy who became a man to take care of his mother and brother. Who fled to France to keep them safe.'

'To keep myself safe, you mean. It wasn't just the threat to Mum, his cruelty to Theo, he threatened me with charges.'

'But he'd hurt her first, and he was likely going to hurt Theo too.'

'So?'

'You were a minor.'

She was desperate to make him feel better, desperate to try and rewrite the way he saw his own past. He should have known his confession would have the opposite effect. 'It doesn't matter now, Flick. Don't you see? I was broken, damaged; you and Angel were better off without me.'

'I don't believe that.'

'I do, Flick. I'm here now, but...but I'm still broken.' There, he'd said it. 'I shut off my ability to love a long time ago, the passion that drove the violence… I won't be that man, the animal out of control, angry…'

Her frown deepened. 'You're a good man, Sebastian.'

'I thought my father was a good man, too, Flick.'

She shook her head, choked out, 'It wasn't your fault, you didn't know. It doesn't make you the same.'

'Doesn't it?'

'You had every right to feel the way you did, to do what you did even. You were hurting, you were angry, you were young.'

'It doesn't excuse it.'

'No, but neither does it mean you should hate yourself for it, that you should shut yourself off from loving…' she swallowed '…from loving someone again.'

He didn't respond. Couldn't.

'It's not like we get a say in it anyway.'

His eyes snapped to hers.

'What? You think we get to choose who we fall in love with, when we fall in love, even?' She shook her head, gave a harsh laugh as she threw back some wine, looked away. 'I admire your confidence in your own ability, even if it's misplaced.'

He stared at her. Was she serious? After everything he'd told her, she wanted to encourage him to open himself up all over again.

'Come on, Sebastian. You loved your mother, your brother… You loved me once, too.'

He scanned her face, felt that nostalgic warmth creep unbidden through his middle. 'I did.'

'Are you truly saying you can't love anyone now? Not even Angel?'

His heart pulsed. 'She's different.'

'Because she's your daughter.'

He nodded.

'And Theo's your brother?'

Another nod and he watched her throat bob, her eyes glisten as they willed him to see things differently. 'You're as capable of love as you ever were.'

'And I think you're—'

'Mum!'

Their heads snapped to the right, to the open kitchen door, where Angel now stood in her PJs.

'What is it, love?'

'Can you come here?'

Flick looked at him. The fight to stay, to have it out with him burning in her depths.

'You should go.'

Yes, please go. He didn't think he could take much more of this conversation, not without belying his words. Because Flick did something to him. She stirred things up so deep within that he couldn't trust his ability to control his thoughts, let alone his actions, and that was a warning in itself.

But as he watched her join their daughter, it wasn't the cold taking hold, the courage of his conviction, it was a warmth. A warmth he struggled to gauge. A warmth that had nothing to do with nostalgia now...

From this distance they were practically identical, save for the extra inch to Flick's height. Their long brown hair falling well below their shoulders, creamy skin, and slender frames.

He couldn't hear what they were saying, but he could see Angel wasn't happy. Flick was placating her, her hand gentle on her daughter's shoulders as she encouraged her back inside. His chest tightened and he ignored the desire to follow, to fix whatever the issue was even though he knew he *was* the issue. He needed to afford Angel the space she needed to adjust. Flick, too.

Still, his chest ached, the warmth persisting. He understood the need to protect them; he was well versed in it thanks to his mum and Theo. His grandfather, too. But love, the kind of love he and Flick had once shared... the kind of love he could almost see shimmering in her gaze... His gut twisted.

He couldn't be that vulnerable again.

You reckon?

Flick's words came back to taunt him:

You think we get to choose who we fall in love with—when we fall in love, even?

'Is she okay?'

Felicity sank into the edge of the sun lounger and took up her wine glass, grateful to find the drink still cool on the tongue. 'She will be.'

He nodded, his eyes dark and glittering with the light of the moon. Had he been lying there thinking it all over while she'd been gone? The past? The future? Did he really think he was incapable of love now?

Did he really think a man who had spent the last sixteen years putting his family first could no longer put his own heart first?

'What was it?'

She bit back the words—*aside from the obvious?*—that wanted to erupt. 'She doesn't like the toothpaste.'

He gave a soft laugh. 'The toothpaste?'

'Yup.'

'That can easily be fixed. Just let Maddie know what brand she prefers, and she'll see it sourced tomorrow.'

Just let Maddie know... Oh, how the other half lived. She sipped her wine, trying to swallow the weirdness of it.

'Anything else?'

'She asked if she could have her friend come and stay tomorrow; they're studying together.'

'No problem. I'll send a car to collect her.'

Her eyes widened. 'You'll send a car?'

'Or I'll drive.' He frowned as her eyes continued to widen. 'Or you can go and collect her if you'd rather, I'm assuming it's a her—or is the issue more that it's...?'

'No, no...it's a her. But first off, I told her maybe we should leave it a week or so, get used to *us* being around one another first before introducing a friend into our midst.'

'Sensible.'

'And second, I don't have my car so I couldn't drive anyway, but I think I should go and get it. I should've driven myself today but the idea of getting past all the press with everything going on...'

Heat rose to her cheeks as she toyed with the stem of her wine glass. Why hadn't she been able to pull herself together? She'd been through so much over the years and managed to keep her cool, but Sebastian's return had shaken her so completely.

And now that she knew the truth about that night... how he saw himself...she shuddered.

'You don't need to worry about getting your car.'

'Huh?' It took her a moment to catch up with what he was saying, another to realise he thought she was upset about the car. 'No, I do. I would prefer to be able to come and go on my own steam.'

'And you can, there's a car in the garage for you.'

'You have a spare one?'

'Not as such. It's for you. Call it a gift. I trust you'll approve; if not, tell me what you'd prefer, and I'll see it—'

'You bought me a *car*?'

'Yes.' His frown returned. 'Is that a problem?'

'You can't just buy me a car, Sebastian,' she spluttered.

'The wheels in the garage prove otherwise.'

'Sebastian.' She choked out his name, the excited flutter of a new car contending with the refusal to accept it.

'What, Flick?' He swung his feet to the floor as he faced her head-on, his body hunched forward, his wine glass cupped in his fingers between his knees.

'I don't *need* you to buy me a car.'

'You're still driving that rusty old Beetle.'

'Which I love.'

'Which is a death trap. I'm surprised it's still roadworthy. It was barely that when Annie bought it.'

She flinched as pain reared up within her. Grief doing its thing. One minute life was fine and the next, its crushing force made you want to curl up and cry until you were too exhausted to cry any more.

'Sorry, I didn't mean to upset you…'

His palm was soft upon her knee, his warmth permeating her jeans and she eased away before she did something stupid, like grabbed both of his hands and tugged him to her. To hell with the consequences, his tainted view of the world, and the risk that Angel might return. Anything to rid her of the grief.

'I get that you're sentimental about the car, Flick,' he said quietly. 'I remember when she bought it for you, you couldn't even drive yet but there she was handing you the keys.'

She risked a glance his way, loving that he remembered, loving how he looked even more. The emotion blazing in his eyes, their darkened depths enhanced by the deep blue of his shirt, his slightly ruffled hair.

She took a long sip of her drink as she waited for the tears to recede. 'She had her reasons.'

'Oh, yes, I remember.' He laughed softly. 'The poor car had looked ever so lonely sat on the forecourt.'

He had her gran's reasoning word perfect, and so did she: 'Lonely and desperate for someone to love it.'

Her laugh was just as soft, even as she acknowledged the strange affinity that existed between her car then, and her now. Was that why she was so shaken by his return? So susceptible to him? The only man she had ever fallen for and been loved by in return.

Was it either Sebastian—the man who claimed he was now incapable of loving anyone—or no one at all?

'To give it a whole new engine, more like.' His gaze held hers, the intensity in his eyes at odds with his jest.

'New engine or not, she said it suited my personality.'

'All sunshine and flowers.' His smile lifted to one side, a familiar glint in his eyes. 'I remember.'

She wanted to kiss him. Kiss him for remembering. Kiss him for loving her. Kiss him until he forgot the monster he believed was inside him and saw all that was good.

Her lips thrummed with it; her body fired with it.

'You'd been here that day,' he continued. 'We'd taken a picnic down to the lake.'

'You'd had the cook bake my favourite cookies.'

'And you'd worn my favourite dress.'

'If you liked it so much, maybe you should've kept it on me longer.'

His laugh was much lower now, the fire in his eyes deeper. 'And spoil the fun we had?'

'Fun that we had in these grounds,' she reminded him as she leaned forward, unable to stop herself. She was so close she could breathe in his cologne, see the dark shadow of stubble along his jaw... 'Maybe you need to create some new memories here to fall in love with it again.'

Fall in love with me...

She swallowed down the impulsive thought.

'You think?'

She took his glass from his unresisting fingers and placed it on the ground with her own. She came back to him, smoothed her palms along his thighs that flexed beneath her, grateful that he hadn't moved away, rejected her.

'I do.'

'Flick...' it rasped out of him '...don't tease me.'

'I'm not.' She brought her lips to his, looked into his eyes that were both confused and blazing. 'I'm teaching you to feel again.'

She captured his mouth with hers before he could stop her, before she could lose the nerve, too, and bow down to the warning in her head telling her this was madness, that it could only end in more pain, more heartache.

He growled low in his throat, his hands reaching for her hips as he lifted her over him, their kiss unbroken, their bodies melding together. She ran her hands through his hair, angled his head so she could kiss him deeper and deeper still.

'Tell me you feel it?' she urged against his lips, her body rocking over him.

'Of course, I feel it.'

'You think this is just sex, desire...?'

She didn't stop kissing him, didn't stop moving over him, and he bucked beneath her, met her move for move, his hands rough in her hair.

'Isn't it, Flick?'

How could she answer that without giving too much of her heart away? And how could she stop this now when every bit of her felt so alive, more alive than she had in years?

'Maybe we should have fewer words?'

His laugh was strained, his head bowing forward as he

sucked in a breath. 'We can't do this. Not here. If Angel comes back and finds us like this…those questions on top of everything else…'

Oh, God, Angel. She scrambled back as though burnt. A curse was on her lips as she buried her head in her hands, felt her cheeks burn through her palms.

He was right. Some parent she was, getting her rocks off while her daughter was grappling with the enormity of their situation. How *could* she?

'Hey.' He reached out to touch her shoulder, but she shot to her feet, her brain in freefall. For sixteen years she'd been a good mum, a good role model, thoughtful and empathetic, now look at her. Out of control, desperate, wanton.

And it was only going to get worse the more she was around him.

Whereas he…even mussed up by her hand, he looked so measured and in control, emanating the kind of strength she felt she was losing.

'It's not that I don't—'

'I'm going to bed.' She couldn't bear to listen to what he was about to say. To know he'd been able to put Angel first when she'd—she'd…

He thrust himself off the lounger. 'But it's only nine o'clock… I thought we could make some plans for the next few days while Angel is still off school.'

She sucked in a breath, refusing to look at him. 'We can do it in the morning.'

'But, Flick…'

She was already heading to the house, her wine glass left behind, and her heart…

'Flick?'

She paused and looked back over her shoulder, a spark of hope fluttering to life. Not that she knew what she was hoping for. A sign that he was as affected as her, a hint of the feelings he'd once had for her and now claimed were impossible.

'About the car…'

'What about it?'

'Please accept it.'

She was too stunned to respond.

'Please. I'd feel happier knowing you were driving around in something that's up to modern safety standards.'

She gave a soft scoff. 'For a man who claims he can't care for another, you sure know how to contradict yourself.'

She left him staring after her, wishing she could take pleasure from his sudden pallor, but it only made her feel worse. More frustrated. Frustrated at him but frustrated at her heart more.

She was trying to tell herself he couldn't love her again. She was trying to listen to all he had told her, but actions spoke louder than words and the way he looked at her, the way he looked out for her…

Never mind her heart, she was going to lose her mind if she continued to let him in.

Distance. She needed distance and lots of it.

One thing the Ferrington Estate could offer in abundance.

CHAPTER TWELVE

SEBASTIAN WAS STUNNED to see Angel in the kitchen before him the next morning. Stunned even more to see her reading from her textbooks as she ate her cereal.

Studious and up early, she was going against everything he knew—or rather assumed—about teenagers.

She looked up as he entered, and he smiled. 'Morning, I hope you slept well?'

She shrugged, gave a non-committal sound, and went back to her book.

Okay, so she wasn't going against *everything* he knew... the mood was still on display, along with a healthy dose of obstinance.

But in a weird way, it impressed him. He liked that she was defending her mother, he liked that she wasn't giving him an easy ride... If she had been he'd feel even more off kilter.

'Ah, Mr Dubois, what can I make you for breakfast?'

He dragged his eyes from Angel to see his housekeeper already at the stove. 'It's okay, Maddie, I'll grab some toast and coffee. I have a meeting with the architect shortly.'

'Some toast?' She eyed him with open disapproval, something he wouldn't tolerate from any other member of staff, but this was Maddie. '*Sacré bleu!* First Angel and now you. It is the most important meal of the day and neither of you want me to cook anything.' She threw her hands up. 'I might as well go back to Paris.'

'I did tell you I'd get someone else to cover here so you could stay.'

'And leave you to eat toast? No, no, no. Besides, Pierre is away with his classic car rally and the children are all working abroad—it's too quiet. I'd much rather be here in England, keeping busy. *So*…keep me busy.'

He laughed. 'How about packing up a picnic?' He sensed Angel's ears prick up. 'It's another glorious day. I thought I'd take Felicity and Angel down to the stream for lunch. We spent a lot of time there as kids.'

'A *picnic*?' Angel lifted one sardonic brow. 'How old do you think I am? *Five?*'

'Angel!'

He turned to see Flick behind him, and his heart leapt into his throat, guilt quick to rise—her hair was scraped back, exposing the paleness to her cheeks, the dark smudges beneath her eyes, her vibrant summer dress the only colourful thing about her.

'What?' Angel pouted. '*You* want to go for a picnic, that's fine, but count me out. I have studying to do.' She slid off the bar stool, gathering up her books and making to leave. 'Have *fun*.'

'Don't leave your bowl—'

'I'll get it.' Maddie swept it up before Flick could say anything else and Angel left, the frosty atmosphere settling in her wake.

'Thank you, Maddie, but she shouldn't be treating the place like a hotel. She doesn't get to leave stuff lying around at home, and I prefer she didn't here either.'

'Of course. *Pardon.*'

Flick nipped her lip, cheeks flushing. 'Sorry, I don't mean for you to apologise. I—' She sent him a strange look that he couldn't decipher. 'Not everyone has the luxury of a housekeeper.'

'I understand.' Maddie nodded swiftly and backed away. 'I have laundry to take care of and a picnic to prep…unless you would like me to cook you something for breakfast?'

'No, no, I'm fine. Thank you.'

Flick watched her go and then turned to him. 'Laundry? Already?'

'Code for "I'm going to give you both some space", I think.'

She nodded but didn't smile.

'Coffee?'

'Please.'

He headed to the machine, pulling out two mugs and filling them as she slid onto the stool their daughter had vacated. When he turned back, her arms were folded on the counter, her head bowed.

'Rough night?' He set the coffee down before her and she looked up, those tired eyes tugging at his chest.

'Restless.' She lifted the mug and breathed in the aroma. 'What I would give to have all the answers.'

'How about not trying to tackle all the questions at once?'

She tilted her head to the side. 'I kind of feel like they're all related to one big one.'

He nodded, wishing he could magically fix everything.

'How are we gonna make this work, Sebastian?'

'We take it one day at a time.'

'Is that what your picnic idea was, taking it one day at a time?'

He grimaced. 'Yeah. Full of great ideas, me.'

'It was a nice idea. And we should do it. I'll talk to her.'

'If you keep doing the talking, I'm never going to stand a chance.'

'I just mean I'll talk her round.' She gave him a sudden smile, a light creeping into her captivating blues that had looked far too dull until now.

'Fair enough.' He returned her smile, feeling his chest ease with her mood. 'What can I get you for breakfast?'

'From what I overheard it's a coffee and toast kind of day.'

'I have time to make you something more if you want... just don't tell Maddie.'

She gave a laugh and shook her head. 'Toast is fine... I have a picnic to save myself for.'

So much for using the estate to gain distance between them.

She'd joined him for breakfast, which had been too cosy by far, even with the frosty opening courtesy of Angel. And then she'd gone and agreed to a picnic.

But she'd agreed to a picnic with their daughter and that was the biggest distance creator there was.

And she'd spent the morning post-breakfast away from him. She'd taken to the grounds, had a leisurely swim, then felt so guilty and on edge at relaxing that she'd rung Theo at the B & B. Bree, too. Making doubly sure that everything was okay back home.

It seemed to be. In fact, it seemed that Sebastian's brother was not only adept at charming the guests and playing the perfect host, but he could also bake, too. And though he clearly had the power to wind Bree up, even wound-up Bree couldn't deny she was impressed by his skills.

Felicity felt her lips quirk into a smile and Angel chose that exact moment to open her bedroom door.

'What's got you looking so happy?' She held a swift hand up to her mother's face. 'Actually, don't tell me, I don't think I want to know.'

'What's that supposed to mean?'

Angel rolled her eyes as she strode back to her bed and pulled her hoody and her latest read off it. 'I'm sixteen, Mum, not a child.'

'And?' She followed Angel to the stairs, her frown as quick as her pace.

'Don't worry about it.'

'Angel, what are you—?'

'It's nothing, Mum.' She turned to face her, the crease between her brows at odds with the smile she gave. 'Honest. Let's just get this picnic over with and I can go back to studying. Okay?'

'Okay.'

She moved off and then stopped, blowing out a breath. 'Just…you know…' she looked back over her shoulder '…be careful, yeah.'

She scanned the empty stairwell, the deserted hallway below and turned to face her properly, her frown fully formed. 'I see the way you look at him and the way he looks at you, but I don't trust him. There's nothing to keep him here. He's converting this whole place into a hotel and then he'll be gone again.'

When did her daughter get so serious and why did she think her mother was the one that needed protecting? And what was with the whole role reversal?

'You're wrong, Angel. He has you to keep him here, or at least to come back for.'

She gave a disgruntled snort.

'He's a good man, love. Give him a chance.'

'A good man who left you when you needed him most.'

'We've been through all this.'

'Yeah, well, I can't let it go. Not yet. He has to earn it and I don't want you getting hurt again.' Angel shoved her hoody and book under one arm and gave her a quick squeeze. 'You've looked after me for sixteen years, can't I look after you just a little?'

Felicity gave a soft laugh. 'Who are you and what have you done with my Angel?'

'Hey.' Her daughter gave her a soft punch. 'I always cared.'

'I know, sweetheart, but I'm the grown-up and I can take care of myself, okay?'

'If you say so... Right, come on, let's get this *family time* out of the way.'

And she was off, seemingly unaware that she'd left a shell-shocked mum in her wake.

'You ready to go?' Sebastian said as she entered the kitchen a few soul-steadying minutes later. Maddie was there, too, a traditional picnic hamper in her arms while her daughter stood on the sidelines playing with her nails.

'Sure am.'

Sebastian's smile was strained and she cringed inwardly. Had he heard some of their conversation on the stairs? Oh, Lord, she hoped not. It was bad enough her daughter seemed to think her emotionally incapable of handling this situation, she didn't need him thinking it too.

Well, maybe you should stop with all the kissing, then.

'Right, let's go.' She clapped her hands together, her voice pitched with her thoughts, and they all eyed her.

Way to go in acting normal.

'Thank you for the food, Maddie.' She reached out to take the hamper with a smile that nearly split her face in two.

'You're welcome. I went with the white chocolate chip cookies you suggested.' Maddie's eyes slid to Angel. Felicity had told her that they were her daughter's favourite but the girl in question was still projecting the *I'm not five* look.

'Even better.' She hooked her free arm in Angel's and took her with her as she headed out into the garden. 'Let's go have some fun.'

'I'm not going to run off, Mum.' It came from the corner of Angel's mouth as she tried to tug her arm back.

'I didn't say you would.'

'Then you can let go of me.'

'Oh, right, yeah, sure.' She released her but she didn't want to. She needed Angel to anchor her, to stop her dwelling on all the other times she'd done this walk, nearly all with her fingers entwined with Sebastian's.

She glanced at him as he caught them up. 'How did your meeting with the architect go?'

It wasn't as if she wanted the reminder of his intentions for the place, but she was desperate for conversation. Normal, everyday conversation. And she wanted to show Angel she wasn't worried, so her daughter shouldn't be either.

'It was good. Pretty much as I expected.'

'Are you planning a lot of work?'

'Mainly internal stuff.' He shoved his hands in his pockets, kept his eyes ahead. 'A few rooms will need knocking through, some of the upstairs rooms will need modernising, there'll be health and safety changes, too.'

She nodded, quiet for a beat. Two.

He cleared his throat. 'Theo tells me everything's running smoothly back at the B & B.'

'Yes. Him and Bree make a good team.'

He chuckled and her eyes narrowed as she looked up at him. 'What?'

'That's one way to put it.'

'What's that supposed to mean?'

He looked at Angel ahead of them, who was somehow managing to text and walk at the same time. 'You know what I mean.'

'You got that impression too?'

'Oh, yeah.'

'Your poor brother won't know what hit him.'

He chuckled further. 'I was more worried about Bree.'

'Oh, *she'll* be fine. Believe me.'

He gave her a bemused grin before turning his focus back to their daughter. 'Your mum says you'd like to have a friend come and stay, Angel?'

She hummed without looking up from her phone.

'Is she a study buddy?'

Felicity could sense her daughter rolling her eyes. 'She's a friend who I study with, yes.'

'How does the weekend sound? Before you go back to school next week.'

She spun on her heel. 'For real?'

'Yeah, why not?'

The weekend was a couple of days away, hardly time for them to acclimatise to one another, and she'd already told him it was too soon. But as she took in Angel's unrestrained grin, she knew exactly why he'd done it. An easy win.

And she got it, she only wished he'd consulted with her first.

She made a mental note to discuss it with him later and parked it. She wanted this picnic to be a success and that meant doing all she could to keep the atmosphere relaxed and easy.

But relaxed and easy soon became stilted and awkward.

She could sense the cogs straining in Sebastian's brain as he exhausted it for things to say, questions to ask and

Angel didn't help, giving monosyllabic answers where possible and keeping her mouth busy with Maddie's food.

'Your mum says you like rock music. Do you have a favourite band?' Sebastian was leaning back on one elbow, his body stretched out on the picnic rug as Felicity sat next to him and Angel sat cross-legged opposite, the food spread out in the middle.

Angel gave a one-shouldered shrug. 'Not really, though Bon Jovi is pretty cool.'

'Good choice.' She sent him a death stare and popped a cookie in her mouth.

'Nice to know we're not completely out of touch, hey?' Felicity said to him, her smile sympathetic as she wondered what he would try next. They'd done school, favourite subjects, hobbies, friends...

'Is there anything you'd like to do this weekend when your friend comes to stay?'

She raised her brows at him. 'Do?'

'Yes. Like shopping, a movie, bowling...?'

She nibbled on her cookie. 'I figured most of that was off the cards with us in hiding.'

He shrugged. 'So long as you don't mind a protective escort you can do whatever you wish.'

Her eyes lit up. 'For real?'

'Is that one of your favourite phrases?'

Her lips quirked. 'Maybe.'

'Then yes, for real. My treat.'

Angel looked to her mum and Felicity realised she wanted her approval. She nodded. If Sebastian thought it was safe then she trusted him to make it so.

'Cool! Wait until I tell Iona! Can I go call her?'

She was already grabbing her phone from the picnic rug and getting to her feet.

'Sure, just don't be too long.' Felicity watched her

daughter walk off, adding for Sebastian's benefit, 'You may live to regret that.'

'Nah, how bad can it be? Besides, she'll be going out of her mind come the weekend having only had us for company. I may be past it, but I'm not so old that I don't remember what it's like being cooped up on the estate with no friend around.'

'Poor, poor you,' she teased, elbowing him gently. 'With your stables and your swimming pool and your games room, how tedious it must have been.'

'Why do you think I snuck you in at every opportunity?'

'You mean you were just *using* me?' She pressed an affronted palm to her chest and bit back a laugh. But his eyes weren't dancing as they met with hers, they were intense, dark…hungry. She swallowed.

'I never used you, Flick.'

She gave a shaky laugh, ran her hand through her hair. 'I know, I was teasing.'

'You sure about that?'

She looked away, her eyes lighting on Angel in the distance and seeking safer terrain. 'You should have consulted with me first.'

'Consulted with you? On what?'

'On having a friend come and stay. We should have agreed it together before putting it to Angel and I told you before, I thought it was too soon.'

He grimaced. 'You did, I'm sorry. I guess I'm finding it hard to find some common ground and I figured it might help if she had someone familiar with her here.'

'And I'm not familiar enough?'

'You know what I mean, someone unrelated to us. I'm hoping it will help her relax, give her someone to talk to, and I know you said you wanted us to have time together first but...'

'You were desperate.'

His laugh was tight. 'Guilty as charged.'

She studied his profile, his eyes that tracked Angel as she wandered between the tall pine trees, carefully picking her way through the carpet of wild bluebells. It would make the most beautiful photograph, a stunning keepsake...

What would it look like when the hotel transformation was complete? Would they be able to come back here? Would he?

'Where will you go? After the work is done, I mean?'

His eyes came back to her. 'I don't know. I haven't figured that far ahead... I'd like to stay close.'

How close? she wanted to ask but fear kept it trapped inside and she let her eyes drift back to Angel.

'I'm back in your life for good, Flick.' His eyes hadn't left her, and his intensity, sincerity, had her heart fluttering up in her chest. 'Don't doubt it.'

'I wasn't.'

'No?'

She turned to him. 'It's going to take some getting used to, that's all.'

Some getting used to, and some major rebuilding of her defences. Because the longer he was around, the deeper she would fall and then where would she be?

With a plush hotel on her doorstep, a village up in arms and a B & B whose trade could suffer, her independence with it.

'Well, you best hurry up, because I'm not going anywhere. Regardless of where I settle, you and Angel will always have me to depend on.'

Heart and mind at war, she nodded. 'Good.'

Only she didn't want to be dependent on him; she didn't want to depend on anyone.

And just how did the future look when it wasn't only the two of them any more—her and Angel—a safe and trusty duo? How did it look when he wanted to make more decisions that affected them? Yes, he'd been desperate enough to go against her wishes and invite Angel's friend to stay. But was it just the tip of the iceberg? Would it happen more and more? Him making parental decisions that had always been her own to make.

'You say good, but you don't look like it's good.'

She tried for a smile. 'Of course, it's good.'

'Then why are you gripping your knees to your chest like a life preserve.'

'What? I'm n—' She was. There was no use denying it. She forced herself to let go and gave him an apologetic smile. 'Sorry, this isn't easy.'

'I know, Flick.' He reached out to comb her hair behind her ear and her breath caught at the look in his eye. They shone with so much…so much… Why did he have to look as if he cared so much? 'I know.'

He leaned towards her ever so slightly, and she blinked, panicked, broke away.

No. No more kissing. No more thinking about kissing. No more of any of it.

He cleared his throat and she swallowed, her gaze returning to Angel chatting animatedly in the woods, everything about her far more relaxed than she'd been the whole time on the blanket. Would there come a time when she would be like that with him? Her father? It was a strange thought, triggering an even stranger sensation in her stomach as she imagined it.

'Have you thought about what you want to do?'

'Hmm?' Slowly she turned to look at him. 'About what?'

'The future? The B & B?'

'What about it?'

'Have you thought about selling it?'

She laughed abruptly. 'And why would I do that?'

'It's a hard life, Flick, for anybody. And you've worked there for ever—don't you sometimes wonder how life would be if you didn't have it weighing over you?'

'It isn't weighing over me, it's our home.'

His expression didn't change. 'And it's a lot of work for not a lot of reward. You could go back to school, study…'

'And how exactly would I do that?' No sooner had she asked than the pieces fell into place. 'No, Sebastian. Just no.'

'Why not? I'm not suggesting you'd be a kept woman, Flick, I'd never—'

'Only you are.' She was disgusted, her gut writhing even as she registered the softening of his eyes, the compassion and understanding.

'I'm telling you that I can help you fulfil those dreams you once had. People go back to school all the time. You could study anything you wanted. You wouldn't even need to sell the B & B, not if you didn't want to. I can get my management company to take it on. Get that roof done while we're at it, replace the boiler too. We could look at—'

'Stop, Sebastian, just stop.'

She shot to her feet, desperate for the distance she'd craved the night before. Desperate to rewind the past week even and have life return to how it was. Calm, orderly, all within her control.

'Just think about it, Flick.'

'I don't need to think about it, and I don't need your help.' Her spine stiffened, her body strengthening with her heart as she stared him down. 'I didn't need it sixteen years ago. And I don't need it now.'

And now she sounded exactly like her daughter...but maybe that was a good thing.

A very good thing.

CHAPTER THIRTEEN

SEBASTIAN UNDID HIS seat belt and pushed open his door, telling Angel and Iona, who were chatting away in the back seat, that he'd only be a couple of minutes. He nodded to his security team in the car behind and crossed the B & B car park.

It was early Saturday evening, the end of a long day shopping with the girls, and as he pushed open the rear door he almost walked straight into the chest of his brother, who was dusting down his grey T-shirt…was that flour?

'Enjoying a bit of baking?'

'Maybe.' Was it his imagination or did his brother look a little flushed, too?

'Is Bree here?'

'Maybe.'

'What's with the evasive answers?'

'What's with all the questions?'

'You're covered in flour.' He brushed off a patch his brother had missed. 'It's not a sight I've witnessed in a while.'

Theo shrugged. 'I'd forgotten how therapeutic it is.'

Sebastian fought back a grin. 'The baking?'

'Yes, the baking, what else?' The grin broke free and Theo punched his arm. 'I'll have you know I've been showing Bree some of the techniques I picked up in Paris.'

Sebastian raised his brows. 'I bet you have.'

'That's not— Why are you here, anyway?'

'I was in the area so wanted to check in. Everything going okay?'

'Absolutely, it's all in hand. What about you? Any idea how long you're going to stay at the estate for?'

'I don't know.' He didn't like being pressured into thinking about it, let alone giving an answer. 'It's not been a week yet.'

'True, but the press is behaving, the village too. It seems the villagers are doing everything to protect Felicity and Angel's privacy. Don't get me wrong, when it comes to us and our plans for the estate, they're far from quiet. But the second questions get asked about your personal history with her they all clam up.'

He gave a one-sided smile. 'Good.'

'It's nice to see such loyalty exists.'

'It's nice to have earned it.'

They met each other's gaze, the unsaid passing between them. They had that loyalty in Paris, in their firm, across the globe even. But in this sleepy Yorkshire village, where they'd been born and bred, it was non-existent and who could blame the village when their first move upon returning was to be at odds with its population?

He ran his finger under his collar, felt the unease rise. Unease over what they were planning. Unease over the imminent end to Flick and Angel's time with him. Unease over the way they'd both crept beneath his carefully crafted exterior and made his heart beat again.

Theo's eyes narrowed, his perceptive gaze seeing far too much. 'You know, we could keep the estate, if that's what you wanted?'

He shook his head, though his outright refusal wouldn't come. 'What makes you say that?'

'Oh, I don't know, maybe that strange wistful look you got going on there.' He twirled a finger at him, and Sebastian cringed.

'That bad?'

'Just a little.'

He raked a hand through his hair, blew out a breath. 'The idea has more appeal than I would have expected, that's all. But it makes good business sense to fold it into the company.'

'Good business, sense? Right, cos we need the money, yeah?'

'All right. All right.'

'Hey, I'm only reminding you that there are options. We're not so far down the line that we can't go back. And besides, maybe having a base here isn't such a bad thing. I'd forgotten how nice the Dales are, not to mention the fact that you *need* a base here.'

He gave his brother a grim smile. 'I'll think about it.'

'Don't think too hard, bro. Those lines on your forehead are getting worse.'

He laughed. 'You know, you can be really annoying at times.'

'Funny you say that; Bree says the same.'

'She has good taste.'

'Impeccable.'

The laughter dissipated as a niggle wormed its way in—should he be worried? There was clearly something going on between them and with his brother's playboy rep and Bree being Flick's best friend…maybe he should say something.

And maybe you should leave well alone.

Especially if Bree was helping his brother deal with whatever had sent him running from Paris. Theo hadn't told Sebastian about it, but then they rarely got serious when it came to the personal stuff. Which was what made his brother's interfering now so disconcerting.

'What are your plans once the B & B guests check out?'

'I don't know. I haven't thought that far ahead.'

'Well, let me know what you decide. You're welcome at the estate any time, not that you need an open invitation.'

'I should hope not. It's my home, too.'

'It's not our home, Theo.'

'But it could be. Maybe this is the excuse you need to set down roots, bro.'

'Forgive me if I'm not quite ready to take life advice from my delinquent younger brother.'

'Hey, less of the delinquent.' His brother punched him in the arm. 'It's just good to see that spark back in your eye. I was beginning to worry you'd never get a life.'

'And on that note...' he turned to leave '... I'll be seeing you.'

His brother's trademark grin followed him out. 'Bye, bro! Pass on my regards to Flick, won't you?'

This is the life...

Felicity trailed one hand through the water, the other holding a delicious fruit cocktail courtesy of Maddie as she lay back on the inflatable pink flamingo Sebastian had purchased for Angel.

She felt her lips curve up, her cheeks nudging her sunglasses.

Yes, this really was the life. The spring heatwave was showing no sign of abating and normally she'd be a hot mess—rushing around the B & B, cooking, cleaning, maintaining...

And though she'd have to go back to it soon enough, for now she had this.

She eyed the house glowing in the early evening sun,

almost too stunning to believe it was real, and sipped her drink. Sweet, tangy, refreshing. Heavenly.

Much like her surroundings that would, in the not-too-distant future, be filled with guests rather than family. A shiver ran through her core. How could Sebastian go through with it?

Yes, she understood the darkness that haunted him, but to strip away the ancestry of his home—its heart—to create a soulless hotel.

Her B & B might be a guest house, but, above all, it was still a home. It had her heart, it was loved…

She stiffened as the unmistakable sound of tyres on gravel reached her and knew it had to be Sebastian and the girls returning. They'd been gone since ten that morning, a full day of Angel and Iona with their buzzing enthusiasm for the shops.

Had it been cruel sending him off alone? Payback for his insensitive suggestion that she give up the B & B and accept his handouts like some charity case. Not a living, breathing woman with a heart that was far too soft where he was concerned.

Her mood darkening with her thoughts, she frowned. Play time was over. It was time to get out. Gone was the heat of the sun on her skin, the pleasure of the drink, the ease of some R & R…

She was still trying to paddle the giant flamingo to the edge when the girls appeared in the kitchen doorway. 'Hey, Mum, check it out!'

Arms raised to the sky, both girls were laden with more bags than she could count and grins the size of the Cheshire Cat's. She was about to respond when the inflatable went out from beneath her and just managed to plant her cocktail on the side before she went under.

When she spluttered back to the surface it was to find

that Sebastian had joined her mini audience and, judging by the spark in his eyes, caught her delightful mishap.

'Enjoying the inflatables?'

Her belly flip-flopped at the husky edge to his voice as she swept her hair out of her face, aware that, aside from the water at waist height, her bikini didn't hide much.

'Don't knock it until you try it.'

'Me, on a pink flamingo?'

'Now there's a sight I'd love to see.' She couldn't stop the grin from lifting her entire face or her insides coming alive with the pressing heat.

Oh, how quickly he can make you forget your displeasure...

She switched her focus to the girls, who were watching their interplay with far too much interest. 'Any incidents with the press?'

Angel rolled her eyes. 'No. But we drew plenty of attention thanks to the presence of Tweedledee and Tweedledum.' She sent her father an unimpressed look, which seemed to roll off him. 'It's hardly subtle when you have two big burly men on your tail.'

'Attracting attention is one thing, reporters in your face another.' Felicity pushed herself up and out of the pool, feeling Sebastian's eyes graze over her skin. How could a look feel like a caress? A caress that had an unwelcome but no less thrilling current running through her. She grabbed up her towel and pointedly kept her attention on Angel. 'Definitely the lesser of two evils, wouldn't you agree, sweetheart?'

'I s'pose.'

'And you have to admit,' Iona piped up, tossing her blonde hair over her shoulder, 'it was kinda cool that they could help carry everything.'

'I'm sure they loved that.' Felicity sent an apologetic

smile Sebastian's way, but she needn't have bothered, he looked quite…happy. Slightly ruffled around the edges, his black polo shirt untucked and hair a little mussed, but happy.

She gestured to the shopping bag in his hand with its designer name in block letters across the middle. 'Treated yourself, too?'

A hint of colour slashed his cheeks. 'Not quite. I saw it and thought…' he offered it out '…well, I thought you might like it.'

Nervous excitement fluttered through her middle, crashing back down with caution. 'You bought me clothes?'

He gave a shrug. 'It's no big deal.'

She dried her face as she tried to compose how she felt. *No big deal.* Yet it felt like a big deal. Too big a deal. And she didn't know how to respond…other than with the obvious.

'Thank you.' She wrapped the towel around her and took the bag from him, still absorbing the designer label and wanting to look grateful, especially in front of the girls. 'Maddie says she's doing dinner for seven; I'll go get ready.'

'Wait until you see what we got for the party next week, Mum.' Angel stalled her, drawing Felicity's eye to the obscene number of bags again.

'Party?' she asked dumbly, wondering how much he'd spent. 'What party?'

'You know, Iona's birthday party next Saturday.' She gestured to her friend. 'I'm sleeping over?'

'Oh, yes, of course, sorry.'

'A sleepover?' Sebastian stiffened. 'I'm not sure that's a good idea.'

'You're kidding, right?' Angel rounded on him. 'We've been planning it for months!'

Felicity eyed him. Was it really such a risk? Surely, now the excitement of his return was over, it wouldn't hurt for their daughter to get back to her life. Her *normal* life. Just as she needed to, but… 'Let's see how things are this week, love, okay?'

'But, Mum, there's no way I'm missing this party. *Everyone* will be there.'

'Let's just wait and see.' Her daughter opened her mouth to say something else and Felicity beat her to it. 'Or do you want to return all those lovely things your father bought you?'

'But, Mum—'

'We're not saying no, Angel.' Sebastian's tone brooked no argument. 'Just that we'll see how this week pans out, see how the return to school goes.'

Angel's eyes flitted between them, wide, disbelieving, and then she blew out a breath and spun away. 'Right. Fine. Come on, Iona. I feel the need for chocolate before dinner.'

Felicity watched the girls go and then looked to Sebastian, took in his dazed expression. 'Don't worry, she'll get over it.'

He nodded, raking his fingers through his hair. 'Aside from that, I think the day went rather well.'

'Good.' She dipped to pick up her almost finished drink, her eyes averted now as she headed for the kitchen wishing to put distance between them as soon as possible. He was far too attractive, and she was far too naked to be anywhere near him. Especially alone.

She placed her glass on the side and was about to tell him she'd see him at dinner when an almighty squeal broke out from upstairs.

'Angel!' She started running, Sebastian hot on her tail.

She took the stairs two at a time, which was no mean feat with the towel, damp legs and a bag clutched in her hand.

'Oh, my God, Mum, you've got to see this!'

She burst into her daughter's bedroom and halted two strides in. There, on the antique dresser, was a state-of-the-art TV and sound system wrapped in a giant bow. Her mouth fell open—he had to be kidding!

She looked behind her to see the man himself in the doorway and arched her brows.

'She mentioned in passing that she didn't have one…' he looked decidedly sheepish '…figured it would double up as a music system.'

'It's immense. Like utterly cool!' Angel grabbed the remote and turned it on. 'Is it for keeps?'

'Sure is.'

'Wow!' Angel's eyes were still wide with awe, her rage over potentially missing the party all but forgotten in the face of his gift. 'Thanks, Sebastian.'

Like mother like daughter—fickle where this man was concerned.

Felicity wasn't rolling over on this one though.

'Isn't it cool, Mum? I've been saving for one for, like, for ever, but I would never have been able to get one like this.'

'Yeah. Cool.'

Though her tone said something else entirely. Her gaze drifted from the TV to the flushed face of their daughter, to the bags upon bags on the bed.

She left the room, her eyes lifting to Sebastian's as she passed. 'Being a father isn't about spoiling your children twenty-four-seven. At some point you need to learn the art of saying no.'

He frowned, quick to follow her. 'She didn't ask, it was a gift.'

'Right, like this is a gift?' She raised the bag in her hand but didn't stop moving. 'And the car?'

'Yes! And if you don't like them, they can easily be exchanged for something else.'

'It's not about me liking them, Sebastian.'

'Then what is it?' He was right behind her now, muttering to avoid being overheard. 'Is it the money, because if it's the money then you don't need to think about it. Not when I owe you years and years of maintenance. Not to mention the physical hours spent raising our daughter—'

She gave a pitched laugh as she pushed open her bedroom door. 'Of course, it's the blasted money!'

'Why can't I spend money on you? On you both.'

She strode into the middle of the room and spun to face him. 'What exactly are you trying to achieve?'

He pushed the door closed, folded his arms as he leaned back against it. Frustratingly calm. 'What do you mean?'

'All this spending, buying her things—' she shook the bag in her hand '—buying *us* things.'

'I just want to make you happy.'

'You can't *buy* happiness, Sebastian.'

She threw the bag and her towel on the bed and strode to the dressing table. She reached for her hair-conditioning spray, needing something to do, *anything* to stop her hands from shaking. She squirted it onto her hair, her scowl for him but directed at the mirror as she took in the flush to her skin, her blue eyes bright with anger...

Anger that he was spoiling them, anger that he wasn't listening to her, anger that he was putting her B & B at risk with his fancy hotel, anger that he was breaking into their mother-daughter duo that had always been...

'What's this about, Flick?'

Everything.

The fact a mere glimpse of him had her entire body lighting up—eager, hot, wanton.

Didn't matter that her head told her no. That her heart felt threatened. That the safe life she had built for her and Angel was over.

She wanted to cry and jump him in one.

'*Please*, talk to me.'

She speared him with her gaze through the mirror. 'Why, when you don't listen?'

'I do listen, I'm just—I'm trying to make things better.'

'Like when you told Angel she could have her friend over after I explicitly told you not yet.'

'I'm sorry for that, I told you, I was—'

'Desperate, I know. But think how that made me feel. I'm her mum, I've cared for her alone all this time, the buck began and stopped with me and now you saunter in taking over, making her every wish a reality.'

'I'm sorry.' He started to walk towards her, but then stopped. 'I'm not trying to take over, and I'm not trying to buy your happiness, Flick.'

His grey eyes pleaded with her as he raked a hand through his hair, mussing it up more, making him appeal more, making her belly tighten with the need to cross the room and kiss him more.

'Okay.' He blew out a breath, threw his palms out. 'Maybe I am, on some level, but why can't I? I have the money and if anyone deserves to benefit from that, it's you two.'

She snatched her brush, started yanking it through her hair. It would be so easy to say yes and take all that he was offering. Take it all, be spoilt, so easy, only…it wasn't his money she wanted. Her stomach turned over and she fought the urge to press her hand to it.

Focus on the fight you can openly have…not your heart.

'We're not some charity case, Sebastian.'

His eyes flashed and before she knew what he was about, he was across the room and grabbing the brush from her hand. 'You think that's how I see you, Flick?' He tossed the brush to the side as he spun her to face him. 'As charity?'

Her breath caught in her lungs at the fire in his eyes, her mind emptying. He was far too close, and she was far too naked. And he smelt… *Oh, God*, he smelt so good.

She couldn't speak, couldn't breathe as her breasts crushed up against his shirt, the intoxicating mix of anger and lust in her blood sending her dizzy.

'Does this feel like charity, Flick?'

And before she could say anything, his lips were upon hers, their force a punishment, a reward, an absolute shot of ecstasy straight to her core. His tongue parted her lips, twisted with her own, and she revelled in it, relished it, gave as good as she got. Her hands lifted to his hair as she clung to him, her body closing every gap, bare skin against clothed hard heat.

'This isn't charity, Flick,' he growled against her lips, the sound vibrating through his chest into hers. 'This is desire, need, a want to protect you, to take care of you, to lose myself in you.'

His words were like music to her soul—*to lose myself in you.*

Wasn't that what she wanted, too? To lose herself in the pleasure she knew he could provide. To forget the past, present, future in the blissful heat of this.

'God, how I want you.' He forked his fingers through her hair, his eyes searing hers. 'Tell me you want me too.'

'I do.' She clawed his shoulders, held him tighter, her

vision misting as the lustful heat spread within, making her ache, making her throb. 'I want you.'

He growled anew, kissing her hard—her mouth, her jaw, her throat. He nipped the sensitised flesh and pleasure tore through her.

'It's like a pain deep inside me, Flick. An ache, an emptiness...'

Her breath hitched. Did he even know what he was saying?

'Only you can fill it. Only you.'

She whimpered, willing him on. More words, more kisses—more, just more.

'What are we even doing?' He sounded agonised, desperate, his touch no less urgent, even as his voice betrayed the continued fight within.

'I don't know.'

It was honest, it was breathless, it was raw.

His gaze found hers, searching. His hands cupped her face. His touch turning gentle, his breathing deep, steadying...and then he kissed her again, his eyes locked on hers, making her insides clench, her heart pulse, her soul want to cry and sing in one.

Oh, God. She loved him. Drowning in his blazing greys as she kissed him with her all, it was as obvious as the need racing through her veins. She truly loved him.

'Tell me to stop, Flick,' he urged against her lips, lifting her against him. 'Tell me to stop and I will.'

But she wasn't. She was showing him the opposite, her fingers trembling as she worked his shirt over his head, her legs wrapping around his hips.

'I want you, Sebastian.'

I love you, Sebastian were the words so desperate to

erupt, and she clamped her eyes shut as she kissed him, praying he wouldn't see it, knowing he would run.

And if he ran in that moment, it would break her all over again.

CHAPTER FOURTEEN

FEAR WARRED WITH NEED, desperation. A crazy fight he couldn't win.

'I want you, Sebastian.'

The look in her eyes, the words she'd breathed seconds before she'd slammed her eyes shut—why did he feel as if she was telling him so much more?

It should have had the fear winning out. It should have stopped him. He'd *begged* her to stop him. Pleaded to put her in control and put an end to the madness. Knowing he couldn't give her what that look demanded in return, what it deserved in return.

Instead, she'd gifted him everything.

'I want you, Sebastian.'

The words fired through his blood, his soul…

He didn't know what they were doing, what tomorrow would bring, but the connection he'd found, that they'd found…he craved it, he needed it. He felt as if he'd been fumbling around in the dark for so long and she'd brought him the light. Made him feel alive again. And like a man starved for sixteen years, he was ravenous for it all.

Even that look in her eye.

'Look at me, Flick.'

Her legs pulsed around him, her body urging him on, but her eyes…still, she hid.

He carried her to the bed, laid her down, and she trembled as she hit the cool sheets.

'Look at me, Flick.'

She raised her hands to his hair, her lashes fluttering open and there it was, swimming in her blues, so much… so much *love*. He couldn't breathe. Couldn't speak. He stroked her hair from her face, refused to listen to the panicked beat of his heart as he absorbed the warmth of it.

'You want this?'

She nipped her bottom lip, the smallest of nods. Down the hall, music blared, the girls were testing out the new sound system, they weren't about to walk in, but…

He pushed up off the bed and her eyes flared, panic firing in their depths. 'Where are you going?'

'Better safe than sorry.'

Better safe than sorry—who are you trying to kid? You do this there's no going back…

He locked the door, sealing them in, sealing their fates, too. But as he turned back, the sight of her on the bed, the slip of a bikini all that protected her modesty from his hungry gaze, silenced any warning.

Heart in his mouth, his blood roaring with his need for her, he joined her on the bed, his fingers forking through her hair as he raised her head to him. He kissed her softly, savouring her lips, her taste, her whimper…his Flick.

'I've never wanted anyone like I want you.' There was so much more he wanted to say, so much more he wanted to be able to give, to feel… 'You do something to me, Flick.'

'And you, me.'

It was a whisper and all those missing years…they tortured him with the unknown. Had there been other men? Other men that had meant something to her?

Jealousy tore through him. A jealousy he had no right to feel.

And are you sure it's just jealousy?

His gut rolled.

'Sebastian?' She lifted her hands to palm his cheeks, a crease forming between her brows as she searched his gaze... 'Kiss me.'

She was giving him a get-out.

Kiss me and forget.

Kiss me and let go.

Kiss me with no promises, no regrets.

And so he did.

He kissed her as though his life depended on it, kissed her as deeply as she was kissing him. She arched against him, her breasts teasing against his chest, her nipples pressing through the damp triangles of fabric.

Like a man possessed, he let his instincts take over... hungry to see her, to have all of her. He found the tie at the nape of her neck, at her back too and tugged them free, tossed the fabric aside, fingers trembling, eyes disbelieving.

God, she was beautiful.

He traced a hand over her front, around one flushed breast. Treasured how she shivered and whimpered and bit into her lip. He bowed his head to tease it free, to trail sweet kisses from her mouth to her throat, her collarbone, dipping lower as his thumb rolled over one eager bud. She cried out, the sound shielded by the music blaring, and a smile tugged at his lips.

He wanted more. More cries, more passion, more of everything she could give.

He surrounded the peak with his mouth, sucked her in deep and her hands flew to his hair, his name a cry on her lips. Another as he ran his teeth over her. He breathed her in, savoured her bare skin, her scent, the way she moved against his arousal, the way she panted and clung to him.

He took his time, etching it all to memory…what she liked, what she loved. Remembering, relearning, eager to take her to the brink and himself with her.

'*Please*, Sebastian. I need you.'

God, he needed her, too. So much it hurt.

'Are you on the pill?'

'Yes!' She reached for his trousers, caressing him through the fabric, and he gritted his teeth, the rush of pleasure too much.

He gripped her hand and tugged it above her head.

'Soon,' he promised, kissing her pout away, his fingers trailing down her arm, down her side and hooking into her bottoms.

He continued down, his eyes locked in her hooded gaze as he tugged her bottoms free, watched her bite her lip as he pressed her thighs apart.

Brazenly he took her in, positioned his knees between hers and rose over her. 'You are beautiful.'

The colour in her cheeks deepened, her hands moving to cover her stomach and the silvery trace of her long-ago pregnancy. A pang of all he'd missed caught at his chest, his breath a gentle rush as he dropped forward and lifted her palms away, replaced their touch with his kiss. 'Don't hide from me.'

Her breath shuddered through her, stalling as he shifted lower. Telling her with every flick of his tongue, every press of his lips, how beautiful she was, and how sorry he was.

'You are stunning,' he whispered over her wetness, his body contracting as he parted her with his fingers and dipped to taste her, her scent almost his undoing, her sudden cry making him spasm.

'That's it, baby,' he murmured, feeling her climax build with the rising tension in her limbs as he circled her, teased her, his palms pressing into her thighs that threatened to close around him. Aroused by her every response, he drove her higher, wilder, and just when he thought she could take no more, she shot up.

'Sebastian, please.' She pressed him away, sucked in a breath. 'I want you with me. I want you inside me.'

He didn't hesitate. Shucking his clothing, he climbed over her and she hooked her legs around his hips. Clung to his shoulders as he eased forward. He had to fight to keep his eyes open as she moved to meet him, her inviting warmth surrounding him, welcoming him, threatening to tip him over.

She was perfect. Oh, so perfect.

And he was drowning in her.

'Sebastian... Sebastian...'

They moved in tune, their moans interspersed with their shortened breaths and heady pants. He let her set the tempo until she was tensing around him, her mounting climax spurring his own. He wanted to savour it, he wanted to draw it out, he didn't want it to end...*never to end*.

He tried to tame the pace, to stave it off, to...to...

His cry was guttural, he was fighting for the impossible.

'Be mine, Flick. Be mine.' Desperation kept his eyes locked on hers, words pouring out of him without thought. 'Be mine. Always mine.'

Her eyes glistened, confusion and ecstasy swirling in her depths as she gripped him tighter, fingernails digging into his skin as her climax ripped through her.

Yes, baby, yes.

He roared as he let go.

Let go of everything, the past, the pain, the emptiness…
and prayed he wasn't more broken than before.

Inside, she was shaken.

Outside, she was the picture of calm.

She knew this because even Angel had commented on
how serene she looked. *Serene?*

She blamed Sebastian. Blamed him for the outward
calm, which was courtesy of the floral jumpsuit he'd
bought her. It was stunning—the fabric, delicate and light,
felt so good against the skin. The style, wide leg trousers
with a halter neck that draped into a crossover front, was
subtly sexy. She *felt* sexy.

Even more so when she caught his eye and the banked
desire still there.

Which brought her to the inner frenzy, the panicked
beat of her heart…her head-over-heels, against-her-bet-
ter-judgement love.

But then, she'd never stopped loving him—wasn't that
the truth of it?

Wasn't that why no one had been able to make her feel
the way he did in all the time they'd been apart?

Didn't matter that he was the one who'd put those walls
around her heart, he'd succeeded in breaking through and
taking hold of it once more.

'Be mine, Flick. Always mine.'

He might as well have said *Love me, Flick. Always
love me.*

And she had. She'd let him in, she'd revelled in him.
The attention, the passion, the pleasure they'd drowned in.
The memory sending her toes curling inside her sandals
even now as her body contracted around a rush of heat.

But he hadn't told her that he loved her.

Yes, the connection had been all-consuming, but she'd seen the fear there, too. And those words he'd used...

In the heat of the moment, she'd thought—no, she'd wanted to believe—they spoke of love.

In her post-orgasm shivers, she'd realised the chilling truth. He was only treating her like a possession. Like all the many wondrous things his money could buy, he wanted her to be his. Only his.

She eyed him across the table and felt the blaze of his greys sear her to the core, her lips parting on another heated rush that went against every bit of sense she possessed.

But want and love weren't the same thing.

And it wasn't enough. Not for her.

'Are you going to take me, Mum? Or you can drop me at the bus stop, and I'll make my own way in?'

She frowned as she zoned in on Angel and the conversation she'd lost track of.

'Take you?' She lifted her wine glass and took a steadying sip. 'Take you where?'

'To school?' Angel frowned. 'You know, on Monday?'

'I can do it,' Sebastian offered. 'I have a meeting in the city later in the day, but I can drop—'

'No, no, it's fine,' Felicity hurried out. 'I need to call in at the B & B anyway, and I'm sure you have more important things to be doing.'

'Not at all, I'm happy to do the school run.'

'I said, I'll do it.' She softened it with a smile, hoping it would mask the bite to her words. But she wanted her routine back. Hers and Angel's. She needed it. Just as much as she needed to get out of his world of luxury and back into the reassuring comfort of her B & B.

She wanted the safety of what she knew, what was familiar and hers.

Soon. Things were calming down. At some point the news would be out about Sebastian being Angel's father and the press would gather but at least the most important people knew. Angel knew. Operation Damage Limitation was complete...well, almost.

'Do we need to speak to the school, Sebastian? Give them a heads up about potential reporters hanging about and—'

'Already done.'

Her eyes narrowed. 'When?'

'Last week.'

'But it was the Easter holidays.'

'The headmistress was happy to take my call.'

Her brows lifted. 'I bet she was.'

'What does that mean?'

'How much?'

'How much what?'

'How much did you donate to the PTA?' She clutched her wine glass tighter. 'The school?'

'I—' He closed his mouth on the denial she could see he wanted to give but couldn't. 'What does it matter?'

The girls' eyes dashed back and forth between them as though watching a riveting tennis match and Felicity bit her tongue. Now wasn't the time or the place.

And was it really so bad when she thought about it? Hadn't the school been desperate for funds following the latest government cuts? Wouldn't it benefit not only Angel but also the other children of the village and surrounding areas?

'It doesn't.' Though she said it quietly. 'I'd like to have talked about it first, that's all.'

She took up her cutlery and eyed the perfectly prepared steak and chips, another of Angel's favourites, but her appetite was non-existent. She also knew she hadn't fooled Sebastian. Under his watchful eye, she purposefully focused on her food and the girls, keeping the anger simmering down low.

This wasn't a fight to have in front of the children; perhaps it wasn't a fight she should be having at all. Perhaps her reaction was fuelled more by the knowledge that her heart was only one beat away from being torn in two again.

And she only had herself to blame.

CHAPTER FIFTEEN

'I STILL DON'T get it.'

He looked over his daughter's bent head at the equation she was trying to solve. 'Here, let me show you.'

And as he had many times over the past week, he helped her.

And treasured helping her.

Every time he found her like this, hunched over her books in the kitchen, grumbling about some piece of work, he'd try and lend a hand. It made him feel like a father, one capable of doing some good...the kind of good he didn't feel when Flick was around.

He'd worried that succumbing to the desire between them would break him further...and it had. But only because it had pushed her away so completely, destroying whatever gains they'd made since his return.

She could scarcely stand being in the same room as him now.

At breakfast she would grab something and run, barely letting out a 'morning' before escaping with Angel on the school run, and she rarely came home during the day. At dinner, she would arrive with Angel, and leave with Angel, making their daughter a persistent chaperone.

Her walls had erected so fast he felt something akin to whiplash. Whiplash with a healthy dose of panic. Because he was panicking. Panicking that she would be leaving soon. Panicking that she would never look at him as she had that day again. Panicking that the connection they'd shared was broken for ever.

'You see, if you move this...' he dragged himself out of his stupor and pointed to the numbers on the page '... you must reverse the method.'

'But what if...? Oh, hi, Mum.'

His heart flipped inside his chest. Flick stood in the doorway, her eyes on them, her body frozen. She came alive the second his eyes collided with hers, an awkward smile on her lips as she walked in. 'You ready for school?'

'Sure.' Angel started gathering up her books, shoving them into her bag. 'Thanks, Sebastian, maybe we can go through it tonight.'

'Sure, kiddo.'

'The post is here.' Maddie came bustling into the kitchen, placing it down on the centre island and sliding the top envelope across to Angel. 'And there's something for you, Miss Gardner.'

'Really?' Angel picked it up.

The morning scene was unfolding before him but all he could think about was Flick. Flick and what they'd had, what he wanted to get back to but didn't know how.

'Oh, my God, Mum!'

Angel's cry speared his thoughts, his eyes falling to the envelope in her fluttering hands...the envelope that—

'Wait!' He moved to take it from her, but she was already dancing on the spot, her squeal making Flick jump. *Oh, God.*

He shot her a panicked look.

Apologise, say something, anything, before...

'Thank you, Sebastian!' Angel's arms were around his

neck, squeezing him so tight she was cutting off his air supply. 'Thank you, thank you, thank you.'

'What is it?' Flick's voice was strained, her eyes on Angel's back where the lanyards were swinging, the sharp edge of tickets digging in his ear.

'Mum! Just look!' She spun to face her, the damning items in her outstretched hands. 'Tickets for Bon Jovi in the summer *and* backstage passes. I can't believe it. I can't.'

He wanted to explain, he wanted to tell Flick he'd asked his PA to organise it the day of the picnic, before she'd made her feelings clear on his spending, before he knew what a bad move it was, but the shutters were already down, the walls within erecting ever higher.

She gave Angel a weak smile.

'Isn't it great, Mum? I have to go call Iona, she can be my plus one, right?' She spun to Sebastian, her eyes earnest, hopeful.

'Of course, unless your mum wants to…or I can sort more tickets.'

'No.' Flick seemed to catch herself, softening her expression and her words as she added, 'No, of course Iona should go with you.'

'Yes! This is so *cool*!'

She snatched her packed bag off the table, pulled out her phone and was already dialling as she left. Maddie had made herself scarce, too. It was just him and the woman he so desperately wanted in his life but didn't know how to keep.

'I'm—'

'Save it, Sebastian. I thought I'd made my thoughts clear, but you clearly don't get it. Or you just don't care.'

'Of course, I care, Flick. And I *do* get it. I listened and

I'm sorry. I'd forgotten about the tickets. I'd asked my PA to arrange it after the picnic, before you…'

She was shaking her head, refusing to listen. 'Why don't you get it? We don't need you to buy us stuff. Gifts don't make up for the lack of you the past sixteen years. Gifts don't make us trust that you'll stick around now, that you'll still be here in a month, or a year.'

'I'm not going anywhere, Flick, I told you. I *promise* you.'

'Not right now, you have this house to transform.' She waved her hands around her. 'But when you're done, what then? Have you even thought about what might happen to my B & B, my livelihood, when this becomes a Dubois?'

He frowned. 'What do you mean?'

She was shaking, tears spiking in her eyes that looked so pained and angry. 'You planting a swanky hotel on our doorstep. Don't tell me you haven't considered the impact it'll have on my trade?'

'It should help it.' His frown deepened with his confusion. 'It'll bring more people to the area, raise Elmdale's profile and give you more potential guests.'

She gave a cold laugh. 'You reckon?'

'Yes! Do you honestly think I would do it if I thought it would hurt you?'

Her eyes flared, her lips parted, and he heard the words repeat back at him, his blunder cutting right through him. He'd hurt her plenty. They had the history to prove it.

'God, I'm sorry, Flick.' He wet his lips, his breath shuddering through him as he closed the distance between them. 'Look, I'm not even sure I'm going ahead with the hotel.'

She coughed out another laugh. 'Oh, that's right, say that now when—'

'No, no, I mean it, Flick. I've been thinking about it.'

He reached out to cup her arms. 'Please listen to me. I'm not ready to leave. I want to be here. I want us *all* to be here.'

'I can't—' her head was shaking, her eyes closed to him '—I can't do this any more.'

'What do you mean?'

'*This*, Sebastian!' she flung at him, stepping out of his hold. 'The whole playing at happy families. Seeing you and Angel together, studying, laughing, joking, as though the last sixteen years didn't exist. I can't live in this…this fantasy world, where you snap your fingers and things appear.'

'I'm sorry about the tickets, I—'

'It's not about the tickets. It's about *everything*. It's too much. I feel suffocated. I need to go home. I need my own space, away from you, from us, from this place!'

'Please, Flick, don't do this.'

'The B & B has been quiet this past week, the press seems to have lost interest. There's no reason for us to stay here any longer.'

'There is if you want to stay, if you want to give us a chance.'

'*Us?*' She stared at him, wide-eyed, incredulous. 'There isn't an us, Sebastian! There hasn't been an us for sixteen years. Last weekend was a huge mistake. It shouldn't have happened. It's because we're living on top of each other, getting caught up in it all when we need space.' She reached for her bag on the centre island, thrust it over her shoulder. 'We should proceed as we mean to go on. Separate homes. You can visit Angel as much as you like, and she can stay with you, too. But I'm out.'

She moved to leave and he grabbed her arm.

'Don't go.'

She tugged herself free, strode away. 'I have to.'

'Marry me, Flick!'

It burst out of him and she froze, a shocked silence descending. He took hold of her hand, slowly pulled her back to face him.

'Marry me?'

She was so pale. 'You don't know what you're saying.'

'Don't I?' Softer, more sincere. The realisation that he wanted it more than anything steadying his voice, his heart. He had to make her realise he was here to stay. He had to make her realise he wanted this to work. He was trying to be a good father, he was learning. He could learn to be a good partner, too…if she just gave him the chance.

'Don't tease me, Sebastian.'

'I'm not.' He took up her other hand, held them both, stared into her eyes. 'This life of mine is no fantasy and I want you and Angel at the heart of it. Marry me, be mine, let me look after you, let me give you this.'

He gestured to the roof above their heads, released her hands to caress her arms through her fluffy pink sweater—the same sweater she'd worn that very first day two weeks ago, when his life had been so very different, when he'd been so very different. Lost. Broken. 'Please, Flick.'

Her breath shuddered through her. 'Do you love me?'

'What?'

'You heard me. Tell me that you love me, and you can have me.'

'But…' He tried to swallow, tried to speak.

'You can't, can you?'

Her words speared him. Every syllable hammering an icy nail through his chest.

'So, what is this? A proposal born of obligation? Desperation?'

'It's more than that; you know it is. We work well together, last weekend proved how good we can be, and I know you still want me, just as I want you.'

'I do want you.' Her laugh killed him, her eyes ablaze with something so much worse than love as she mustered the strength to face him off. 'To my own detriment, I'll always want you. But marriage, on that alone, hell no. I'd rather take my chances back at the B & B with your luxury resort on our doorstep, than share your bed in a loveless marriage. Goodbye, Sebastian.'

Helplessly, he watched her go, the weight in his chest making it impossible to draw breath. He had all the money in the world, he could buy anything but the one thing he wanted above all…

And Flick had proven it so spectacularly.

'Mum?'

Angel reached across the front seat as Felicity kept her sights fixed ahead, refusing to let the tears fall. It was bad enough that she was driving the car he'd bought her. A very nice, very sensible hatchback that could drive itself if she was so inclined. And one that would be going straight back to him as soon as she could see it done.

She wanted nothing from him.

Save for the one thing he couldn't give—his love.

She swiped the back of her hand across one cheek, whisking away a betraying tear before her daughter could see it.

'Mum?' Angel gave her leg a gentle squeeze.

'Yes, love?' She didn't turn her head. She couldn't. She was afraid Angel would see everything—the hurt, the panic, the pain.

'Are you—are you and Dad okay?'

Dad. Hearing her say it so readily made Felicity's chest

ache, knowing what it would mean to Sebastian and cherishing it all the same.

'Why wouldn't we be?'

'Oh, I don't know,' her daughter said softly, 'maybe because you're crying.'

Silently, she cursed. 'We're fine, or at least we will be. It's been a strange couple of weeks, that's all. A shock to the system.'

Angel nodded. 'I know.'

'But it'll be good for us to get back to the B & B, back to a bit of normality, and you have your party tomorrow, that's gonna be fun, right?'

'Yeah, but if you'd rather I stayed with you, I can cancel. I don't like the idea of—'

'No.' She flicked her a quick look. 'No. I'm fine. It'll be good for you to go and it'll be good for me to get back in my own bed. A decent night's sleep will work wonders.'

'Only if you're sure though, Mum. I honestly wouldn't mind staying with you...' She hesitated, nipped her lip. 'He was only trying to make us happy, you know. His heart was in the right place.'

Felicity gave her a sad smile, feeling her love and pride for her daughter swell as she acknowledged how far she'd come in her road to healing. 'I know.'

It just wasn't in the right place for him to return her love...

'Oh, is that Uncle Theo?'

A Porsche came tearing down the drive towards them, roof down, Theo's blond hair wild in the breeze. Thankfully, he was alone. No would-be inquisitive Bree in tow. The two seemed inseparable of late. 'Yes.'

'Such a cool car.'

Felicity made a non-committal sound and gave him a wave, an attempted smile and kept on going. She wasn't in any fit state for pausing and enduring small talk. The sooner she could get away from the Ferringtons and their home, the better.

Her heart was too exposed; it had been the second she'd succumbed to him last weekend. And the more she'd witnessed him with Angel, the more she'd yearned for it to be real—all of it. The home, the father, the husband. A family.

And for one idiotic second, she'd thought he was offering it all, his proposal driven by the same love she felt.

But no, it had all been about duty.

A duty to look after them…*hell*, a duty to see his libido satisfied on a nightly basis too.

'I know you still want me, just as I want you…'

How could she have got it so wrong? Her knuckles whitened around the wheel. Well, he could take his money and his sexual prowess and shove them where the sun didn't shine.

Whether he stayed on the estate or changed his mind, it didn't matter so long as he remained in Angel's life. As for Felicity, she would just have to deal with the fallout… for the B & B and her heart.

It was far better that than tying herself to a man who could never love her back.

CHAPTER SIXTEEN

'RIGHT, ARE YOU going to cheer up, or am I cracking open the hard stuff?'

Sebastian glared at his brother.

'Good God, bro! I came here to spend time with you before I head to Paris. If I'd known you'd be like this...' He waved a hand at him across the living room, the fire flickering in his blue eyes that half laughed, half despaired with him. 'The hard stuff it is.'

'Throw another log on while you're up.'

He was cold. The heatwave was over, and it was back to being dark and grey, the house chilling with it. Or was that just the way it felt now that Flick and Angel were gone?

Empty and soulless, no longer a home without the presence of the two women who had sparked the desire to stay.

His brother pushed out of his seat, stoked the fire, and strode across the room to the freshly stocked liquor cabinet. He didn't ask, only poured.

'This will see you right.' He shoved something amber into his hand. 'Cheers.'

'Cheers.' He threw back a swig. Grimaced. Warm. Hearty. Should be satisfying. Yet it couldn't hit the spot. Nothing could.

'Are you finally going to tell me what's going on?' His brother sank back into his seat. 'You've slept on it, you've had another day to stew on it, you might as well accept that I won't leave until—'

'I asked her to marry me.'

'You did *what*?' The drink in his brother's hand almost escaped as he swung the glass down.

'You heard me.'

'Why would you…?' His brother visibly paled. 'You haven't— She's not…pregnant, again?'

'No, God, no. Why would you even—?' He shook out the thought, saw his brother's shoulders drop as he visibly calmed. 'It would be too soon to even… God, I don't even know why I'm talking about it.'

Or why his gut danced to life with something close to excitement at the possibility.

'So, if she's not pregnant, what in God's name were you thinking?'

'I was losing her, Theo, I was desperate. I needed to convince her I was here to stay.'

'And you thought *proposing* was the way to go?' Theo was looking at him as if he was crazy. Hell, he *was* crazy. 'After two weeks?'

He shook his head. 'I know how it looks.'

'Do you? Because from where I'm sitting, you either need your head examined or…' Theo's eyes narrowed on him, his lips twitching. 'What am I missing?'

'What do you mean?'

'Bree's pretty convinced Felicity never got over you, so if that's the case, why'd she run? I mean, I get that maybe she wouldn't be keen on skipping up the aisle with you just yet, but running at that speed… And she didn't look like a woman who had just been proposed to, she looked distraught and keen to avoid the third degree from the younger brother who really picked his moment to arrive… so, what aren't you telling me?'

He shook his head, stared into the flames of the fire as his mind replayed his proposal in all its nightmare glory, twisting up his heart, stealing his voice.

Tell me that you love me, and you can have me.

'She accused me of proposing out of duty.'

'That's not so horrendous…'

His smile was cold. 'I didn't think so either…'

'But still she—'

'She wanted me to admit that I—' he clenched his jaw '—that I loved her.'

It scraped out of him, raw in his chest, his throat.

'And you couldn't?'

He shook his head, couldn't breathe as the tightness inside swelled.

'But you do? Love her, I mean.'

His nod was stiff, his mouth a tight line. Acceptance of his love cutting as deep as her rejection. Of course, he loved her. Loved her even though he shouldn't, even though he'd sworn he couldn't.

His brother leaned forward, both hands wrapped around his glass as he stared down into it, the room falling silent save for the fire crackling in the grate. 'What is it you're so afraid of, Sebastian?'

Theo rarely used his name, rarely used the grave tone he set on him now either and he knew it was the past talking. That night, his grandfather's words, the anger that had filled the room, fired in his veins.

'You can talk to me, brother. Don't forget I was here, in this very room. I saw your face when the old man threw all that at you, at us, the horror as you stared at your fists, the way you shut yourself down after. You've been different these past two weeks though. I thought you'd put it to bed…'

'I don't trust myself.' It rushed out of him then, hoarse, quiet; he was so afraid that admitting it gave weight to it.

'Trust yourself to what?'

'To let go…' He met his brother's gaze. 'To love her as she deserves, without fear of…of…' He looked away, threw back his whiskey, wishing the burn could take out the chill, the sickness.

'You're not our father, Sebastian,' Theo said quietly. 'You're not our grandfather even. You'd never hurt her. Not in that way.'

'How can you possibly…?'

'Because I know you.' Theo's smile was sad. 'Because you're a good man.'

'Now you sound like Flick.'

'And you should've listened to her.'

His jaw pulsed. 'I don't… I don't deserve it. I don't deserve her.'

'Rubbish! I'm the screw-up, not you.' Sebastian went to interject, and Theo raised his hand to silence him. 'It's not open to debate. I wouldn't be here now if it wasn't for you. What you did for Mum, for me, you did it out of love. It wasn't pretty. We all wanted to forget. And we buried it for a time, but we can't outrun our past. Neither of us can. I thought you were done with it, seeing you in this house, this *room* even…you seemed over it. Miserable as sin since my arrival yesterday, but over it.'

Sebastian gave a soft scoff, his fist flexing around the glass.

'It's time to accept the past and move on, bro, before you lose the best thing that ever happened to you.' A hint of his brother's infamous grin returned, its warmth traversing the room. 'And just for clarification, that's Flick. You owe that woman the truth. Heaven knows she's waited long enough to hear it.'

His mouth quirked as the warmth of his brother's words seeped into his soul. 'When did you get—?'

The shrill ring of his phone cut him off and he slipped it out of his pocket, stared at the caller ID and felt his heart turn over.

'I need to get this…' He already had the phone to his ear. 'Hey, Angel, what's up?'

Felicity filled the kettle and turned it on. She wasn't tired enough for bed, her brain was far too active and her heart…well, her heart was a mess.

She'd hoped being back in her B & B would bring a sense of calm, of familiarity, a reminder of how content her life had been before Sebastian had returned.

Instead, it only served to highlight how empty it felt without him.

Had she made a terrible mistake? Would it have been better to accept his offer? To have lived like a family… even if he couldn't love her in return.

No. She couldn't bear it, not when she'd known his unconstrained love once before. She couldn't settle for less now.

And she had to focus on the positive—Angel had her father in her life and, as her mother, Felicity would keep her distance while encouraging their relationship. She would protect her heart, while helping her daughter heal hers.

It wouldn't always hurt like this. Time had dulled her pain before, it would do so again…even if it had to happen in his presence this time.

The kettle clicked off and she reached for a night-time tea bag, pausing as her ears pricked to the sound of the rear door opening. It was a bit late for unexpected visitors and only a select few had a key.

Frowning, she headed out into the hallway and gasped. 'Angel!'

She slammed on the light, took in her daughter's tear-

and mascara-streaked face and her gut turned over, her arms opening as she rushed forward. 'What's happened?'

'It's okay, Mum.' Her daughter sank into her embrace. 'I'm okay now.'

'But…' She pressed her lips to the top of her head, her questioning gaze lifting to see Sebastian in the doorway. She met his eye, took in the grim set to his jaw, the tight smile he gave her. 'Well, you've certainly picked your moment, love. I've just boiled the kettle.'

Angel gave a snotty laugh against her. 'Perfect timing.'

'How about you tell me all about it over a brew?'

'I'll leave you to it.' Sebastian turned to leave.

'No, Dad.'

He froze, his eyes shimmering in the lights of the hall as he glanced back at them. *Dad.* He was most definitely Dad now. And her heart warmed even as pain echoed around it.

'Please, don't go.' Still in Felicity's arms, Angel looked up at her. 'He doesn't have to go, does he, Mum?'

'No.' She gave her a small, reassuring smile. 'No, of course he can stay. I think I'm going to need the moral support for whatever this is.'

'Thanks, Mum… I'll just go get changed.'

'Of course. You happy with tea, or would you prefer a hot chocolate?'

'Chocolate, definitely the chocolate.'

Easing out of her grasp, Angel walked up to Sebastian and wrapped him into a hug. 'I'm sorry, Dad. I didn't mean to… I thought… I thought he was just being nice. I don't think I told him much.'

'Shh! You don't need apologise to me. I'm sorry it happened at all.'

'It's not your fault. I should have been more careful… more aware. I should have…'

'Shh, honey, it's okay, everything will be okay.' He stroked his daughter's hair, but the guilt was written in his face. His daughter might not blame him for whatever had gone down, but he certainly blamed himself.

'I'm sorry to drag you out in the middle of the night, too.'

'Don't be silly, Angel. I love you, you're my daughter. You can come to me, any time—day or night—and I'll be there for you, okay?'

She nodded against his chest and he looked up, his eyes colliding with Felicity's, and her heart tripped over itself. 'Why don't you go and get those PJs on? I have it on good authority that everything feels better in PJs…'

She gave a soft laugh. 'It so does.'

Felicity watched her go before heading back into the kitchen. 'Can I get you a tea, chocolate, coffee?'

She couldn't bring herself to look at him now Angel had gone.

'Whatever you're having is fine.'

She dropped two tea bags into mugs followed by hot water, poured milk into a jug and set it going in the microwave, all the while her head and pulse racing. What had happened? Who was this guy that had made her daughter cry? Why was Sebastian the one bringing her home? And why wasn't he saying anything?

She was about to prompt when he said, 'Angel called me.'

She nodded, swallowed the rising lump in her throat as she stirred the tea. 'I take it something went wrong at the party.'

Silence.

She let go of the spoon, turned to look at his immobile form. 'Sebastian?'

He raked his fingers through his hair and moved into the room. 'There was a guy there. A guy she didn't know.'

He shrugged off his jacket and tossed it onto the back of a stool, his hands gripping its back, his eyes avoiding hers.

'He was a little older than her and she was—she was flattered. Turned out he was—' He cleared his throat, his eyes almost lifting to hers as she pressed her back into the counter and folded her arms tight. 'He was a reporter, Flick, looking for a story, an inside scoop.'

She'd expected it. She'd known it was only a matter of time. But still…she raised a hand to her neck, clutched it as she fought back a shiver. 'What happened?'

'Thanks to our daughter's quick thinking and her fierce friends, not a lot. The moment she figured it out, she and her friends saw him off, but she was—she was pretty shaken up.'

Her gut clenched. 'I bet she was. Why didn't she call me?'

'She didn't want to worry you.'

'But I'm her mother.'

'She was scared it would cause more problems.'

She frowned. 'What do you mean?'

'She feared it would put even more distance between us.'

She gave a soft scoff. 'Well, she's not wrong.'

He winced and she fought the urge to take it back, to cross the room and hug him. Give him the support his broken form was begging for.

'I'm sorry, Flick. I wish I could have prevented it.'

'You and me both.' She took an unsteady breath, realising as she did so that she was being unfair. Her heartbreak getting in the way of her rationality. 'But Angel's right, it wasn't your fault.'

'Wasn't it?' He looked devastated; his eyes were shadowed, his skin sallow. 'I should have stayed away. I never should have come back. I never should have...'

He shuddered and she couldn't bear it. Throwing caution to the wind and with a strength she didn't know she possessed, she crossed the room to cup his face in her hands, stared up into his pain. 'You can't be accountable for the lack of human decency in others, Sebastian. We'll get through this. We'll deal with the news as and when we must. Given a choice, Angel would choose to have you in her life, regardless of the trouble it brings.'

'I wish it could be different.'

'You and me both,' she repeated. 'But it's not and we'll get through it.'

He gave her a wry smile, his stubble teasing at her palms and making her belly flutter. She snatched her hands back as the microwave pinged, a timely reminder to focus on the drinks and keep her hands to herself.

'I have to admit, this wasn't the reaction I expected.' He spoke to her back as she took out the jug, his laugh strained. 'Not that I expected you to take a swing at me, but...'

'She called you Dad.' Her fingers trembled as she picked up the cocoa and scooped it into Angel's *No 1 Daughter* mug. 'Famous or not, it's who you are.'

'She did, didn't she?' His voice cracked as she lowered the spoon into the cup and she sent him a small smile, her vision blurring with unshed tears.

'I think you've earned a place in her heart.'

His eyes wavered over her face. 'And you, Flick, could I earn a place in yours again?'

Her breath stuttered out of her. 'Don't, Sebastian...' she raised her palm to him '...don't start this again. I'm happy you're back in our lives, I'm happy that Angel now has her father, but...'

She couldn't say any more, it hurt too much.

'Flick.' He took a tentative step towards her. 'I need to tell you something. I should have told you yesterday, but I was a mess...so confused and afraid. So very afraid.'

She frowned. 'Afraid of what?'

'Afraid of my feelings for you.'

Her heart leapt.

It's not what you're thinking. Don't get your hopes up. Don't let him—

'I love you, Flick.'

The very air stilled, her heart too. 'What did you say?'

'I love you. God, how I love you.' His hands were clenched in fists at his sides, his steps bringing him closer and closer. 'I know you probably don't want to hear it, but I do. I can stop spending money on you, I can stop spoiling Angel, but I can't stop loving you.'

He was so close now, the warmth of his body, his scent, washed over her, but she was paralysed by the words coming out of his mouth.

'Yes, I want us to be a family. Yes, I want you to live with me so I can protect you, care for you, look after you. But above all, I want you to marry me because I am in love with you.'

'It's been two weeks...' It was barely audible. 'How can you say that after two weeks?'

'It's been most of my life, Flick. I loved you before I left. I loved you when I was gone. No one has ever been able to take your place in my heart.'

'But you said, you *told* me, you couldn't.'

'I know, and I was a fool. A broken, damaged fool, who didn't realise what was staring him in the face all along.'

'Which is?'

'That I'm only broken when I'm without you. That I want to look out for you, care for you, protect you *be-*

cause I love you. That I am not my father, I could never
hurt you. Though this pain…' he covered his heart '…the
pain of being apart…this *hurts.*'

'It does.' She wet her lips, her heart fluttering out of her
control, tears making her vision blur anew as she placed
her hand over his. 'You *really* love me?'

'*Yes.* If I'm honest with myself, I've never stopped loving you. And I understand I need to give you time, I need
to earn your trust, I need to…'

He broke off, a crease forming between his brows as
he took in her head shake, her fingers soft as she reached
up to palm his cheeks.

'You don't need any of that, Sebastian.'

'I don't?' he choked out.

'No, because I love you, too.'

'You do?'

'Yes!' She gave a watery laugh. 'I didn't want to. I was
so scared that everything you were doing was out of obligation that I wanted to run the other way. But I couldn't
stamp out my feelings for you, any more than I could turn
you away just now.'

'God, I'm such an idiot!' He pulled her to him, kissed
her and kissed her again. 'Theo was right.'

'What does Theo have to do with this?'

'I'll explain all later, but for now, just to be clear, you
will marry me?'

'Yes, Sebastian.' She laughed wholeheartedly, planted
a kiss on his lips. 'Yes!'

'Bagsy bridesmaid!' They sprang apart, their eyes darting to the open doorway and a grinning, fresh-faced Angel
complete with fluffy PJs.

'Angel! We were…your father and I…we were…'

God, what were they doing?

'Quit with the blushes, Mum! You're old enough to

get married, you know.' She laughed and raced over, her arms encompassing them both. 'Worst night ever becomes best night ever.'

'You can say that again.' Sebastian hugged them to his chest, kissed the tops of their heads. 'I don't know what I did to deserve you two, but I'm going to spend the—'

'Less of the spending!' they both blurted up at him and he chuckled.

'I meant it figuratively!'

They rolled their eyes.

'As I was saying, I'm going to *spend* the rest of my life making sure I'm worthy of you both.'

'You already are, Dad.'

Flick reached up on her tiptoes and pressed a kiss to his cheek. 'What our daughter just said.'

EPILOGUE

Three years later

'It's PERFECT, MUM.'

Angel hooked her arm in her mother's as they both stared up at the building that had always been their home. 'Isn't it just.'

'I think Frank did a great job on the sign too.'

'Yeah, he did.'

She felt her stomach tighten and winced, her hand cupping beneath her very round bump.

'You okay?'

'Don't you start.'

'Dad's just worried about you—you *and* my baby brother; he doesn't mean to nag.'

'I know.' She pressed a kiss to her daughter's cheek. 'And we're fine. I think your little brother is impatient to make his grand entrance into the world.'

'Yeah, well, he needs to hold on for twenty-four hours at least. We have a launch party to enjoy first.'

'I'm not sure it quite works like—'

'Hey, do I get one of those kisses?' Sebastian came up behind them, his arms hooking beneath Flick's bump as he lowered his head over her shoulder, cheek to cheek.

'Of course.' She curved her hand around the back of

his neck and kissed him with all the love she felt brimming over inside.

'Are you all set?'

She nodded, the chatter behind them building as the village turned out in force to watch the relaunch of the Gardner Guest House in its new guise. 'Thank you.'

'What for?'

'For making this possible.'

'It's all you, Flick. Your idea, your dream and it will help so many.'

'It feels right.' She leaned back into him and took her daughter's hand. 'Frank did do a great job.'

They all looked up at the beautiful sign he had made, much like the old but with its new purpose woven in.

'I'm so proud of you,' Sebastian murmured.

'Me too, Mum.' Angel squeezed her hand. 'And I'm going to help out every chance I get.'

'You, my love, are concentrating on your degree and your travels. You've given enough time to this place as it is.'

'Because I love it here and, besides, I can do it all. The world is my oyster, isn't that what you and Dad are always telling me?'

She laughed softly. 'True.'

'You ladies ready to cut the ribbon?'

Felicity nodded and he slipped the scissors out of his back pocket to hand them to her as she turned to face the crowd. Drinks had already been handed out and they were all waiting for her. Sebastian passed her an orange juice and Angel a champagne, taking one up for himself too.

'Thank you all so much for coming.' Her smile swept over the audience. 'As you all know, the Gardner Guest House has been in my family for generations and my grandmother Annie cherished this building. She taught me to cherish it, too, not just for the memories but for the roof it kept over my head when I needed it most.'

She turned to pull Angel to her side and leaned into Sebastian's hold.

'Unfortunate circumstances broke our little family apart before it had chance to grow, but we're united again, and together we are stronger and happier, and in a position to give back what was once given to me. A roof to those who may need it, a haven for mothers and babies alike, a place to feel cared for and safe. So, without further ado…'

Sebastian stepped away as Angel tugged the ribbon between the gateposts tight and Felicity positioned the scissors.

'I declare the Gardner Guest House for Single Mothers now open.'

With an efficient snip, the ribbon fell and the crowd cheered. Happiness erupted within her, tears too…along with another, very definite contraction.

'Sebastian?'

'Yes, darling.' He was immediately by her side once more, his hand gentle on her lower back, his grey eyes soft with love, concern, and everything in between.

'I love you.'

'I love you, too.' He was frowning now. 'What is it?'

'I think it's time.'

'Time?'

She nodded and watched as his eyes widened.

'Oh, my God! Now? But you're not due for another two weeks.'

'And I thought girls were meant to be the impatient ones,' Angel remarked. 'Way to go, little bro.' They all laughed as Angel shooed them to the car park. 'Go! I have the party in hand.'

'You sure you'll be okay?' Sebastian asked their daughter.

'Are you trying to offend me, Dad?'

'Never. I love you.'

'I love you both. Now, go!'

* * * * *

SECOND CHANCE
IN SRI LANKA

NINA MILNE

MILLS & BOON

To my family—you are all amazing!

CHAPTER ONE

ZOE STARED OUT of the villa window, focused on the scene, the peaceful, idyllic scene, focused so hard the vista blurred as she desperately tried to summon up a corresponding tranquillity.

After all, how hard could that be? Sand curved in a crescent of different-hued tones: honey and amber and the haze of absorbed sunlight. The blue of the ocean, a glorious swirl of azure and teal that stretched to the horizon, blended with the light turquoise of the sky. Palm trees fringed the landscape and the only sound was the caw and coo of the exotic birds that plumed this gorgeous bit of Sri Lanka.

But none of it made an iota of difference to the turbulence that had taken hold of her nerves. All because in the next hour or so she would see Matt again. The idea churned her stomach, accelerated her heart rate and turned the view from her window into an anodyne tawdry souvenir postcard vista.

Get over it, Zoe.

This was not about her. It was about Beth, her much-loved older sister. Zoe was here in Sri Lanka to celebrate Beth's wedding to Dylan. It was simply unfortunate that Dylan's best friend and best man happened to be Matt Sutherland. Of course, if Matt and Dylan weren't friends

Zoe would never have met Matt. Five years ago she had agreed to let her sister arrange a date, a single mojito; she had met Matt, the mojito had been followed by dinner and she'd fallen for him. Six months later she'd fallen pregnant and fallen into a hasty marriage.

Remembered pain struck, her miscarriage and the aftermath. She'd only been ten weeks pregnant, had known she wasn't 'safe' yet, but it hadn't made a difference to the pain she'd felt, at the loss of the potential life, the son or daughter she'd never now hold or know, or even feel kick in her womb.

'No particular reason,' the doctor had said in an attempt to reassure her. 'No reason not to try again.'

And Zoe had known that was what she wanted to do—she might not have planned to have a baby, but her pregnancy had given her a bone-deep knowledge that she wanted a family, wanted to be a parent, wanted the family life she'd never had herself.

But then she'd told Matt how she felt and that was when he'd dropped the bomb that had blown their short, ill-fated marriage up. Words that were etched on her brain, burnt there for ever.

I don't feel the same way, Zoe. I would have done the best I could to be a good father. But I don't want children.

The words had devastated her, made her feel as though everything was a lie.

Why didn't you say?

Because there wasn't any point. You were pregnant and I...

Thought you'd have to make the best of it.

Her voice had been small and tight as the cold hand of grief had touched her again.

I thought you wanted our baby, I thought...

I did.

He'd made a helpless gesture with his hand.

And I am devastated we lost the baby. I swear it.

And she'd known he spoke truth; had witnessed the white face, the set expression, the storm of grief in his brown eyes.

But that doesn't mean I want to try for another one.

Zoe had known she couldn't live with a man who didn't want a family and so she'd left. Packed a bag, taken off travelling, decided to spend a few years honing her cooking skills abroad, before fulfilling her dream to open her own restaurant. So she'd taken jobs as waitress, kitchen assistant, worked her way up to chef status, and had just completed a six-month contract managing a restaurant in Switzerland to cover maternity leave.

She had put Matt out of her mind, a small sliver of her past, a blip, no more. After all, in truth, as his words had proved with such bleak clarity, they had barely known each other, their marriage a mistake. Even if she hadn't lost the baby, what real chance had they had? With hindsight the wedding had been a foolhardy venture, and yet, looking back, Zoe could recall the heady rush that had carried her away. Being with Matt had made her feel alive for the first time since Tom's death. Tom, her first doomed love. Together they had spun off the rails so far they hadn't seen tragedy bearing down on them. Tom had been so vital and alive and then he'd died, aged eighteen, of an accidental overdose.

So with Matt it had seemed almost as though fate had given her a chance to make up for the tragedy she felt responsible for. Had gifted her an opportunity, to have a baby, have a real family, and she'd snatched at that chance. She'd wanted to give her baby a father who wanted to be there, and Matt's instant insistence on marriage had seemed proof of exactly that. And so she'd believed in the fairy-tale ending—oh, he'd never claimed to love her but that hadn't mattered. In truth she'd believed they could live happily ever after, had been carried away on a sweeping tide of attraction and illusory optimism, headed towards the dream where she would give her baby the perfect family she'd craved for herself. Well, that hadn't happened, and Matt had been consigned to history. A sliver of history.

Until today. When she had to acknowledge that the idea of seeing him had sent her into an out of proportion spin. She closed her eyes and started reciting spices in alphabetical order in her head. It would all be fine. It had to be. Beth had always been there for her and no way would she spoil the next few days that her sister had planned with such care.

Dylan's mum was from Sri Lanka and, though she had not been back for many years, she had always wanted Dylan to know and understand his heritage and so Beth and Dylan had decided to get married here, combine their wedding and honeymoon with the chance to spend time on Lavantivu, an island where his family had once lived.

They also decided they only wanted a small wedding with just close family and Matt in attendance and that they would like to spend time together before the ceremony. So they'd booked a few adjoining holiday houses on a beautiful small resort on Lavantivu for a week prior to the wedding and planned an itinerary of activities. Then the party would move to the city of Burati for the actual wedding, to be held in a luxurious hotel.

Today was arrival day and everyone was about to congregate for lunch in the central building that housed a large kitchen and dining area. Everyone except their parents. The all too familiar sense of anger, frustration and sadness ran through her. Neil and Joanna Trewallen had missed nearly every single one of their daughters' important life events, their lives dominated by the number of charitable causes they supported, one of which always needed them. In this case they had decided at the last minute not to attend as it would be hypocritical, given they were about to march for climate change.

So you see, darling, getting on a plane to Sri Lanka wouldn't look good.

I understand, and I agree, but don't you think you could miss this one protest to be at your daughter's wedding? Zoe had asked.

No, because, as we've told you all your life, you can't put individuals first. Even when they're your family.

But...

Zoe had stopped herself, because she'd long since learnt anger, discussion, spectacular gestures... Nothing pierced her parents' devotion to a plethora of causes. Zoe had tried everything and it had resulted in tragedy. Tragedy that had taught her the only way forward was to abandon all attempts to win her parents' attention, to stand on her own two feet and live the best life she could.

I know Beth will understand. Much love, darling. Bye.

Back in the present Zoe gritted her teeth—she would not let it get to her. She welcomed the knock on the door with relief, smiled as her sister entered.

'Hey,' Beth said. 'Just came to check if you were ready.' She paused and said with overstudied casualness, 'And tell you that Matt is here.'

'I'm ready.' Zoe gestured downward. 'And that's fine.' Even if her heart had chosen this moment to hammer her ribcage and she could feel nerves twist and strum inside her. At least whatever happened she looked good; one last glance in the mirror confirmed that.

Her dress was both elegant and eye-catching, a vivid

bold floral mix of red and orange that would complement the red of her auburn hair. High-heeled sandals
completed the ensemble, and she'd clipped her hair back
with barrettes on both sides in a 'casual, but I've made
an effort' style.

The whole hopefully conveyed insouciance, verve and
flair and concealed the fact that inside she was a wreck.

'You sure you're OK with this?' Beth asked.

'Of course. Why wouldn't I be?' From somewhere she
manufactured a light laugh. 'Matt and I were such a long
time ago now—there is no reason for there to be any awkwardness.' Beth didn't know about the miscarriage—she
and Matt had told no one about the pregnancy, had been
waiting until the 'safe' date. The date that had never come.
Then when she'd miscarried the grief and pain had been
too raw and Zoe had retreated inside herself, and once her
marriage had detonated, she'd run for the hills. So Beth
believed that the marriage had been a foolish whim, a
mistake soon realised and moved on from without hard
feelings. 'It will be good to catch up.'

Liar, liar.

But the words achieved their aim, erased the look of
concern in Beth's blue eyes. 'So let's go. This is all going
to be fabulous. But… I am sorry Mum and Dad aren't
here.'

'Don't be. I don't think I even thought they would be.
They have said they'll attend by video link so that's something. I need Mum there for some of the ceremony. Some
of the rituals involve the mother-daughter relationship
and she does have a role to play. At least she's agreed to
do that.'

Beth and Dylan were incorporating both Sri Lankan
and Western traditions in their marriage and Zoe knew

they'd put a lot of thought into making it feel right, a balanced mix.

'I'm so happy how close you are to Dylan's parents.' David and Manisha had taken Beth into their family and Zoe was glad, hoped it made up for their own chaotic parents.

'Me too.' Beth grinned. 'Come on, little sis, let's go and get this party started.'

Matt Sutherland surveyed the room, forced himself not to look at the doorway, told himself to stop scanning for Zoe. It wasn't as though he even wanted to see her; he would certainly never have solicited a meeting of his own free will. But needs must—this was Dylan and Beth's wedding—and there was no way to avoid Zoe. Especially given how small the guest list and the fact the itinerary necessitated spending masses of time together. His eyes returned to the doorway.

Perhaps it was simply a desire to get it over with, the requisite awkwardness of the initial meeting. How did one greet the woman who had turned one's life upside down, then walked out with no warning or discussion?

He'd returned home to find their penthouse flat purged of her belongings. She'd even left the windows open as if to cleanse the very air. That had oddly hurt more than anything else, the way she had so completely erased herself from their home as if showing him that she had erased him from her life.

Just as his parents had done, just as so many foster carers had done. To the latter he'd been one of many, a revolving door of troubled, traumatised, unwanted kids. Some homes he'd only been there a day or a week. But he'd nearly always arrived to a room with open windows, opened to rid the air of the child before.

But that was then and this was now. And if he had re-learnt one thing from Zoe it was to never put himself in the position of expecting loyalty or, dare he say it, love. That was how he'd survived childhood, teenage years… life. Play the game, get along, survive—but rely only on yourself, not others. That way you wouldn't get let down.

He figured he must have worked out a survival strat-egy from the moment he opened his eyes or perhaps even in the womb itself. His parents had been alcoholics who had pretty much ignored his existence, the first five years of his life spent in a state of criminal neglect. The only saving grace was that he couldn't actually remember it, though things would trigger panic in him even now. Hun-ger, or certain smells… And sometimes the nightmares still came, strange, distorted visions, faces he couldn't quite remember in the morning. Yet he'd eked out a way to survive. But his baby brother hadn't, perhaps hadn't cried loud or hard enough, had relied on a trust in his parents. Matt closed his eyes, opened them again. Now wasn't the time or the place to think about the baby brother whose life had been so brief, a brother who had fallen ill and died.

That had alerted social services and Matt had been saved. Guilt panged through him—along with a deep yearning that he could have saved Peter.

But wishes didn't change anything; they couldn't turn the clock back. Bottom line was he hadn't. Had done noth-ing, couldn't even recall his brother's existence. What sort of person did that make him?

Enough. That was then, this was now.

Now he was here, on the beautiful island of Lavantivu, to celebrate his best friend's wedding. He would never for-get his baby brother, but equally he had learnt to carry the memory and the guilt within him, a memory he had shared with no one—not Dylan, not Zoe, not anyone.

As if on cue his eyes roved to the doorway once again; Beth entered, and his heart lurched as Zoe came in behind her.

Any pretence of calm was a sham; it took every ounce of his iron will to keep himself still as his lungs constricted, the twisting, seething emotions becoming an uncontrollable blur. Memories filtered and streamed his consciousness in vivid images, laughter, pain, grief, anger, joy. Confusion, discomfort, failure.

Matt braced himself and focused.

He would not let Zoe back under his skin, would not give her that power.

Luckily he knew how to neutralise power—had perfected the technique in childhood. A time where he had spent so much time feeling powerless. Social workers had been in control of his life, his destiny. Their reports had influenced which foster family he would end up with and that had filled him with fear, enough so that at first he'd lashed out in panic. And so he'd been labelled as disturbed, problematic, in need of help. Matt hadn't wanted the label or the help, so he'd figured out what to do.

All he'd had to do was play the right part, be an easy placement, and so he'd submerged all his fears, anxieties, anger and confusion and he'd developed the persona they'd wanted. Well behaved, quiet but not too quiet. He'd practised a fake smile and even a fake laugh—one that sounded genuine. He'd learnt the right words to use and by doing so he'd neutralised their power. He'd been in charge.

Same with his foster families; he'd learnt how to arrive, assess the situation and the people and play his part accordingly. If they were the sort of family who preferred to treat him as a lodger he'd kept himself to himself, if they were the sort who'd wanted to believe he was 'part of the family' he'd 'muck in'. Whatever it took.

So now he would do the same, submerge the emotion and play the part of a mature, civilised man. He would cross the room and speak to her, utter platitudes and exude nonchalance with a smile on his face. He focused on putting one foot in front of the other, aware his smile did not come as easy as usual, felt tight and forced.

Beth stepped forward to greet him first. 'Matt, thank you so much for coming. Dylan has just gone up to get his parents—they should be back any minute.'

'I wouldn't miss it for the world, and it's an amazing idea to spend a few days together.'

He turned towards Zoe—*Keep it smooth, Sutherland*—but before he could say anything a staff member approached and gestured to Beth. 'Could I speak with you, Beth?'

'Of course.' Beth turned back to Matt. 'I'll be back soon—it's probably about the lunch. I'll be right back.'

Which left him with Zoe. He turned towards her, and his rehearsed words withered and died an early death, destined to never be uttered.

She looked so familiar and yet so different.

The hair the same vibrant red hue, but longer now, falling in glossy vivid waves past her shoulders. To his own horror his fingers tingled with a need to run through the silky smoothness; he recalled doing just that. She wore heels that brought her up to his shoulder height, her head tilted up at the angle that showed off the slender column of her neck, and his gaze lingered on the spot he used to kiss. He remembered her purr of desire, the shiver that would run through her body.

Oh, hell. This had to stop. But as he met her gaze, saw the slight flush to her cheeks, the darkening of her eyes as they lingered on him, he knew she was having the same reaction. The attraction was mutual and as absolute as it had been all those years ago. But they'd learnt the hard way that attraction wasn't enough.

And still they stood rooted to the cool marble floor tiles, simply looking at each other; he needed to say something. Anything.

Seemed as if she had the same idea.

'Long time, no sex.' Her eyes widened in sheer horror, and her intake of breath spoke volumes. 'See… Long time, no *see*.'

Perhaps he should be a gentleman and go with it, pretend he hadn't heard the slip. But… 'True on both counts,' he said instead and now there was a silence, a silence fraught with tension and…and an edge, a sizzle and fizz that he truly hadn't anticipated.

And then she laughed, the gurgle of laughter he remembered, oh, so well; it lilted with sweetness and the tension dissolved and he laughed too. Then the silence returned, only this time it was spread tauter.

'So,' he said.

'So,' she said.

'So how have you been?'

'Good. Fine. How about you?'

'Good and fine as well.'

'Great.'

'Great.'

This wasn't going to go down as the world's most scintillating conversation, yet the words were meaningless. They might as well have been saying 'Blah, blah, blah'. Because the real conversation going on here was in their body language, which translated into a simmering undercurrent that he'd swear was trying to pull him towards her, encouraging him to sweep her into his arms.

This was ridiculous. Zoe had abandoned him, and, hell, he got it, even if he abhorred how she'd done it. He couldn't be the man she'd needed him to be. It had been the one part he couldn't play, couldn't pull off. But to still be attracted to her was humiliating.

'Well, now we've got that over I'll leave you to continue to circulate.' The words were foolish—as he glanced round the room he realised they were its only occupants. This was a small intimate gathering, immediate family and close friends only. Dylan's parents, Beth and Zoe's parents, Beth and Dylan and Zoe and Matt.

'That might be a bit hard,' she said.

Her gaze dropped, before flying back up to his, her cheeks flushed with embarrassment even as he said, 'Looks like we're stuck together,' and an image filled his mind of the literal meaning of the phrase. 'Until everyone else gets here,' he said hurriedly. 'Um…have your parents arrived yet?'

The question at least deflated the tension; her expression tightened. 'Unfortunately they won't be able to make it.'

For their daughter's wedding? He bit the words back, changed them to, 'That's a shame. I hope everything is all right.' During their brief ill-fated marriage he hadn't even met Zoe's parents—they had been away, had moved abroad for a six-month period, to settle in a camp of protestors who were dedicated to saving wildlife. Zoe hadn't been keen to speak about them, and when she had her words had sounded like a rehearsed spiel, a tactic he recognised because he used it himself.

Her parents were 'committed to a lifetime of causes', 'cared deeply about the world and its many issues', had 'a lovely home in the heart of Kent', went on 'lots of protest marches' and that had been it.

And he'd respected her wish to not talk family, because he'd had no desire to discuss his background or childhood either. His spiel ran along the lines of, *My parents died when I was little; they were both only children, whose parents had died, so I had no family to go to and I ended up in care. Luckily I had good foster carers.*

'The past doesn't matter,' she'd said fiercely to him once. 'I want the present and the future to count.'

A sentiment he agreed with completely.

Only their present and future hadn't worked out. Even before the miscarriage that had precipitated Zoe's departure, their marriage had been in trouble. He'd married her, wanted to prove he would never do any wrong to his baby. How could he do any different after the way his own parents had treated him? But the sheer intimacy of it all had spooked him, the closeness made worse because for once he hadn't been able to figure out how to play the role right. The role of husband and prospective father. Because the idea of fatherhood terrified him, provoked an underlay of fear, shadowy memories that sprawled his brain and caused a pervading terror that he would be a bad parent, was genetically programmed as such.

So he'd thrown himself into work, decided to play the role of provider. Because the one thing he was definitely good at was making money. Not for nothing was he known as Midas Matt—he was a top hedge-fund manager, had been described as having an 'uncanny instinct for the markets, provided by a brilliant statistical, analytical mind'. So at least his baby would want for nothing, never feel that gnaw of hunger in his belly, have every luxury money could buy. So he'd barely seen Zoe, had escaped the emotions by avoiding their cause. And then when they'd lost the baby his emotions had escalated into a horrible churn of grief and guilt.

A black echo of how he felt about the loss of the brother he'd never known. And it had solidified a knowledge he'd had already—that it was somehow wrong for him to be a father, just as he had been unfit to be a brother.

But that had been then and this was now.

'Beth must be disappointed,' he continued.

'Of course, but it can't be helped.' Her voice was flat. 'But it does mean it's crucial that we make sure there isn't any awkwardness between us. I want this to be perfect for Beth.'

He shrugged, hoped he could carry off nonchalance even as sudden anger sparked in him. 'Awkward. Why would it be awkward?' But he could hear the edge to his voice. 'You ran out on me and our marriage. But there's no need for awkwardness—after all, you left a note. A whole paragraph.'

Two sentences, nice and easy to remember.

Dear Matt
I'm sorry to leave like this but we both know it isn't working out. The present isn't working, and I can't see a future.
Zoe

'That is not fair.' Anger blazed in her green eyes and he realised his attempt at lightness had fallen flatter than the proverbial pancake.

The hell with it. 'But it is accurate. You can't deny that.'

CHAPTER TWO

ZOE CLOSED HER EYES. It had all been going so well…or had it? The past half an hour had been a see-saw of emotion. Instant attraction—one she'd foolishly assumed had been eradicated. Foolish because their attraction had always been there, an instant, physical, chemical reaction that had only fizzled out at the very end of their marriage, subsumed by grief and confusion.

But now…hell, she'd taken one look at him, and she'd almost combusted, the shock like a lightning bolt that had still jolted her body and for a few glorious moments it had felt so good, her body alive in a way it hadn't been since their split.

Over the years she'd had a couple of brief relationships, but nothing that counted, and she'd known it wouldn't have been fair to either guy to pretend something that wasn't there.

But now anger superseded desire. How dare Matt blame her for her actions? He might be accurate in that, yes, she had left and, yes, she'd left a note, but…

'I think you may be forgetting the preceding events,' she stated. 'You had done a runner in all but name. You may have been physically present, but you had checked out of our marriage from the day I lost the baby…' Or even from the day they'd returned from their honeymoon. The words flew out as though there had been no intervening years. The past she had been running from had caught up with her and was biting her with a vengeance.

'This was a bad idea,' she said on a gasp. On all levels. She'd learnt long ago that if you were going to run, the most important thing was to not go back. She'd tried running as a child, had been the serial runaway. Back then it had been partly a bid for attention, partly a need to see if her parents truly loved her, whether they even wanted her back.

In all honesty she'd never figured out the answer. Quite often it seemed to Zoe she'd been returned, spotted by a neighbour or friend, or once by a police woman, rather than actively found by her parents.

Then, after Tom died, she'd decided the answer was to run and never look back.

His death was one Zoe felt morally responsible for— she'd taken him to the party, not knowing then how out of hand it would get. Once she'd realised there were hard drugs circulating she'd gone to find Tom, had known this was too far. She'd found him kissing another girl and she'd flipped, refused to listen or accept the excuse that he was drunk, that the girl had kissed him.

She'd stormed out. The next day she'd found out he'd accidentally overdosed, found out too that he'd been telling the truth about the girl, and the if-onlys haunted her to this day. If only she'd listened to him, forgiven him, not told him it was over, made him come with her... If only, if only, if only.

But she couldn't change history and so she'd taken her grief and guilt and tried to learn from it. Had given up her dangerous rebellious lifestyle, accepted that no amount of rebellion would attract her parents' attention, let alone their love.

And she'd run, run to university in Scotland, got a degree and after that she'd travelled, three years living out of a suitcase. Then on a trip home she'd met Matt—and life had taken on a fairy-tale quality. Somehow a first date had led to a one-night stand that had led to another date and another and they'd coasted along for months. She'd got a room and a job in London and had steadfastly refused to be carried away by his wealth or lifestyle. Had insisted on only going to places where she could pay half, and soon instead of going out they were cooking together, concocting meals, getting closer in some ways, though they never discussed the past or the future except in the most superficial terms.

Those months had felt like a bubble, a pause on her journey away from her past. But then she'd fallen pregnant, they'd got married and the bubble had slowly deflated until eventually it had collapsed along with their marriage. But he had no right to blame the way it had ended on her.

He was the one who had led her so far up the garden path she'd been embedded in a flower bed that had turned out to be illusory. She'd been smelling the roses when she should have been scenting the coffee.

Because it had turned out the man who had stepped up to fatherhood didn't actually want a child. She'd questioned whether it was that he didn't want a child with her, asked him why.

Could still remember how his expression had closed, shadowed, and then had come the next revelation. 'I don't want to be a parent. But I do want to help children—one day I want to set up a foundation to help children in care.'

The irony had hit her with a clang. Matt was like her parents—he was a man with a cause. But clearly he recognised that meant he couldn't also be a good parent. And

Zoe honoured that but knew she couldn't live with it. But how she wished he'd told the truth from the start—because otherwise she would have watched her dreams of a family fade into a repeat of her own childhood. Being put in second place for 'the greater good'.

So she'd left; maybe it had been the coward's way out, maybe she should have tried to explain, but there hadn't seemed to be a point. Bottom line was they weren't right for each other and never had been, the whole marriage an ill-fated, poorly-thought-out venture from the start.

She glared at him now; she wouldn't back down. 'Look, if I had a choice we wouldn't both be here—but there is no choice and I really do not want to make a scene and ruin Beth and Dylan's wedding.'

He inhaled deeply and rubbed his right temple in a brief, all too familiar gesture. 'Agreed. My bad. I was attempting humour and it came out wrong. As you said, we don't want any awkwardness so let's leave the past in the past. At least no one witnessed our conversation.' He glanced round, a small frown on his face. 'I wonder where they are though?'

Worry touched Zoe. 'Actually, it is a bit strange.' She was sure that leaving Zoe alone with Matt for so long had not been part of her sister's plan. She looked at her watch. 'Plus, it's supposed to be the lunch in five minutes.'

They glanced at each other. 'Come on,' Matt said. 'Let's go and see what's happening.'

They headed towards the doorway and Zoe sucked in a breath as they collided, the brush of his skin sent desire surging through her, and she was rocked back in time to delicious, incandescent memories. The simplest of touches from Matt had always been enough to ignite desire, the reaction instant and welcome. Back then.

Right now it was not welcome at all. Stepping back hurriedly, she gestured for him to go first, all too aware of her flushed face and his ability to read her body's reactions as easily as he could his own. He always had, right from that first tumultuous date. It was as if she was an open book to him and he to her, both knowing exactly what the other wanted by some basic primal instinct.

She took a deep breath in an attempt at calm and followed him, tried not to allow her gaze to linger on the breadth of his back; she'd always loved its scope, the strength of his shoulders, the assured lithe power of his walk. *Stop.* This was not helping matters at all.

But then she saw his body tense and as he quickened his step she did too and then they were both running towards the scene ahead.

Zoe gasped as she saw Dylan bent over a prone body on the floor, saw Beth in urgent conversation with a member of the catering staff, saw Dylan's mother white-faced on the sofa.

'What happened?' Zoe asked.

'It's Dylan's dad. He collapsed suddenly—we think it may be a heart attack.'

'What can I do to help?' Zoe thought quickly and then turned to the hotel staff member. 'When will the ambulance arrive?' She wasn't sure how Sri Lanka's health system worked.

'It should not be too long. Our service is relatively new but very good in this part. He will be taken to a private hospital in the city, but it is some way from here.'

'Is there anything you can do to quicken it up?'

The man thought and then his face cleared. 'I can't, but I know the hotel ten minutes away has a doctor staying; my sister works there and she served her table.'

He raced away and a minute later returned. 'She is on her way.'

True to his word, a few minutes later a petite lady raced in and moments later was stooped over David.

Beth squeezed her sister's hand. 'Thank you. Good thinking. I just can't think straight. David is…'

'I know.' And Zoe did understand. David was like a father to Beth, in truth a better one than their real dad.

'I'm so glad you're here. Both of you.' Beth nodded at Matt, who was sitting next to Manisha, had her hand in his.

Zoe nodded again—Beth had told her how much David and Manisha liked Matt. Had done ever since Matt had stepped in to protect Dylan from bullies. Dylan was dyslexic and had been small for his age. Matt had stopped the bullies in their tracks and had then taken Dylan under his wing, had encouraged him to go to the gym and learn to defend himself. Looking at Dylan now, it was hard to believe he had ever been anything other than strong, but Dylan's parents had been very grateful to Matt, and Matt in turn was fond of them.

Beth blinked back tears. 'You won't go, will you?'

Zoe's heart twisted. Beth never asked anything of her, had always been the calm one, the one who got on with things in the background. 'Of course not.'

As she spoke, Matt and Dylan came towards them.

Matt spoke quickly, his voice deep and calm. 'The ambulance is here. Dylan and his mum are going with them, but there won't be room for Beth so I've sorted out a car and a driver and Zoe and I can come with you.'

Beth nodded. 'Thank you. But…' She reached for Dylan's hand. 'There is so much to do. I'll need to cancel the wedding, sort out—'

'I'll do it,' Zoe said. 'Truly, Beth. You need to be with Dylan and the family right now. Matt can go to the hospital with you, I'll sort everything else out.'

Beth sniffed and wiped her eyes. 'Thank you. And thank you both for agreeing to stay—it means a lot to us knowing you are here.'

'It's fine.'

Zoe realised that Beth was clearly too distraught to realise that she hadn't even asked Matt to stay. But it didn't matter. This was the sister who had always been there for her, from their childhood when it had been Beth who worked out how to cook pasta, how to manoeuvre a tin opener, how to make baked beans on toast. How to coax Zoe into being a 'good girl' when they were dumped on a succession of long-suffering family friends or neighbours.

In the darkest days after Tom's death, it had been Beth's shoulder she'd cried on.

So, 'It's no problem at all. Is it, Matt?'

The slightest indication of a jaw clench, the only tell that he'd probably rather shoot himself in the foot. Otherwise his expression was the perfect blend of acquiescence.

'Of course it isn't. The priority here is David. Anything I can do to help, I will. Now let's go.'

Hours later Matt let out a sigh as he approached Zoe's villa, felt soothed by the early evening breeze with its scent of carnations that blew away the sterile antiseptic hospital smell that had seeped into his skin.

The front door was on the latch and he pushed it open, walked down the wide marble-floored hallway and into the lounge area, where Zoe was at the lacquered desk, her laptop open. She turned as he entered and rose to her feet, anxiety in her green eyes.

'It's OK,' he said. 'David is OK.'

'Beth called to say that, but she still sounded frantic.'

'It was all a bit touch-and-go at times, but he is now stable and in one of the best private hospitals in Sri Lanka.

And the doctors are cautiously optimistic. There's a chance they may have to do a bypass, but the surgeon has got an amazing reputation and the fact that David looks after his health is a big plus.'

She let out a breath. 'I hope, and I believe that he will pull through. Anything else is unthinkable.' She folded her arms round her midriff and he could see the tiredness in her stance, the worry around her eyes, and suddenly an urge gripped him to reach out and put his arm around her and pull her close. An urge he knew he should shut down. 'I can't bear what losing David would do to Beth; she adores him and Manisha. They welcomed her in from the start, treated her like a daughter. He was there for Beth with advice, helped her when she was looking to retrain, gave her real support. She will be devasted if...'

She broke off and he could see the concern in her face, wondered now about Zoe and Beth's real father, who clearly did not provide any support at all. Realised too how close the sisters were and he couldn't help but wonder what would have happened if his baby brother had survived. Would they have been close? Of course they would; he would have looked out for him, had his back. Or would he?

Guilt twisted inside him as the unanswered questions drummed his brain. Why couldn't he remember his brother? Why hadn't he tried to help him? Why had he survived and Peter hadn't? Even his brother's name was only gleaned from a conversation with a foster carer, who had assumed he knew he had a brother. The remembered shock still reverberated through his body, as his childhood self had processed the stark facts. His brother had been called Peter, had always been sickly, and had died of pneumonia aged five months. Though if he'd been treated sooner, perhaps he would have survived. If only Matt had got help; instead it had been through the intervention of a neighbour that social services had been called in.

Sadness for the past mingled with a sadness for the day's events, the threat of death that had ruined a day that should have been a happy one. Now, seeing Zoe's distress, he couldn't help himself, he did move closer, though he held his arms by his side. 'I truly think David will be OK—he is definitely in good hands. So let's focus on doing all we can do to help Beth and Dylan.'

She nodded and now a small rueful smile tipped her lips. 'Including staying here. Together.' Now the atmosphere subtly shifted, an awareness of their proximity pervading the air. 'I suppose at least we're in separate villas, so we won't be on top of each other.'

The words fell from her lips and they both froze, as the whole atmosphere changed, just like that. He knew she was replaying the same memory stream as he was, that their hormones had picked up on the words and decided to spin them into literal images.

Her cheeks flushed as she gazed at him. 'I...' She closed her eyes as though to block him out, then opened them again, gave a small shaky laugh. 'I'm sorry. I don't know why I keep opening my mouth and things like that emerge. I—'

'You do know why, Zoe.' He would not let her hide behind disingenuity; he wanted this attraction as little as she did, but he wouldn't pretend it didn't exist.

'Why?' The syllable was breathless, the chemistry so hot and vivid and alive he figured he could take a university degree in it on the spot. And somehow, right now, all the emotions, the anger, the trauma, the sadness of the past hours made it seem imperative to seize this moment and damn the consequences.

'Because all I have wanted to do since I saw you is this.'

As he stepped towards her she moved towards him; he could see the pulse pound in her throat, saw the taut neediness of her body, knew her every nerve end was tingling just as his were.

She gave a small sigh. The familiarity of her scent spun his head, and he glanced down as she laid a hand against his chest and looked up at him, her eyes wide, flecked with green glints of desire. Reaching up, she ran her fingers, oh, so gently down his jawline, the touch soft and sensuous, and he cupped her face in his hand. Her lips parted, and now he was no more capable of stopping this momentum. It would be simpler to stop breathing altogether.

One kiss—there could be no harm in that. A bittersweet reminder of the past.

Then he did kiss her, and it felt gloriously familiar and yet, oh, so new. And as she moaned a fierce satisfaction rocketed through him and he deepened the intensity of the kiss, wanted to plunder the sweetness of her lips. She pressed against him, and his fingers tangled in the glossy silk of her hair.

Then the sound of a bird, an echoing, haunting cry, permeated the fugue of desire and they sprang apart, stood, their ragged breaths mingling as they stared at each other in mirrored horror.

What the hell was he doing? Had he no pride? This woman had left him, he hadn't seen or heard from her in four years, and now what? A few hours and he had given in to the still-present humiliating attraction.

Zoe looked as appalled as he felt. Panic widened her eyes, her cheeks were still flushed, her lips slightly swollen, her hair dishevelled. Turning, she said in a low voice, 'That shouldn't have happened. I suggest we make sure we minimise any contact at all from now on. And we erase that kiss from our memory banks.'

With that she turned and headed for the door.

'Wait.' For a moment he thought she'd ignore him, then she turned back.

'What?'

'Where are you going?'

'Anywhere but here.'

Irrational anger touched him at her need to get away from him. 'The Zoe Trewallen trademark reaction. If the going gets tough, run away.'

'Excuse me? I am not running away. I am leaving an awkward, embarrassing situation.'

He took a deep breath, knew he shouldn't let anger dominate. This was his fault and he wouldn't take it out on Zoe. 'You're right, awkward and embarrassing sums it up, but I don't think pretending it didn't happen or walking away from it will help.'

'So what do you think will help?' The question was asked with a heavy dose of sarcasm, for which he could hardly blame her.

'Well...' He paused, tried to gather his thoughts. 'I didn't expect this attraction to still exist. I thought we were over and done with and the attraction was dead.'

'Me too.'

'Well, clearly it isn't. So we have a problem. Because this will keep on happening. If the end of our marriage and four years apart hasn't doused it, we need to work out what will. We are going to keep seeing each other because of Dylan and Beth—complete avoidance isn't possible. In the next days, or hours even, they will need us. In the years to come there will be birthdays, family occasions. If they have children, they will most likely want us to be godparents. So whatever is going on here—' he gestured between them '—I'd like to kill it off now.'

'And exactly how do you propose to do that?'

It was an excellent question and one he wasn't sure he had the right answer to. 'Spend time together. Remind each other exactly why we can't work. That should have the knock-on effect of eradicating attraction as well.' In theory. 'What do you think?'

CHAPTER THREE

WHAT DID SHE THINK? In this precise moment Zoe wasn't sure she could think at all— everything seemed too overwhelming. Her lips still tingled, her head still spun from the impact of a kiss that had left her shivery with desire, frustration still churned in her gut in a seething yearning for more. Even as her common sense uttered outrage at her body's stupidity in succumbing to the lure of attraction.

Was that what Matt meant—that they needed to somehow allow common sense and sanity the upper hand, use them to quell the primal hormonal surge and the seething emotions? Because he was right. This didn't feel like a lapse of four years since the day she'd walked out. This felt as if they'd picked up right from where they'd left off. And that wasn't going to work, not as long as Dylan and Beth factored in their lives.

Plus, if she didn't get rid of this…this…'Matt effect', then she would never meet Mr Right, would always be haunted by this man, and then how would she ever have the family she was determined to have?

So whilst all her instincts told her to run, whilst she kept her eye on the open door, she forced herself to stay still, to consider his words. Came to the reluctant conclusion he was right: running was not a viable option. As if sensing her hesitation, he continued, 'Let's go and have dinner. Have a sensible conversation to demonstrate how wrong we are for each other and that should knock attraction on the head.'

Danger! Danger! Danger! called a klaxon in her brain. Yet perhaps if she spent time with him she would recall all the excessively good reasons why she'd left. Optimism made a surge forward; perhaps over dinner she'd remember she'd built him up into something he wasn't, see that all they'd ever had was attraction and a desire to force things to work for the sake of the baby.

'OK,' she said. 'Let's do it. After all, we do need to eat.' Her stomach growled as if to underline the fact. 'I just need five minutes to freshen up.' Any more than that and she would chicken out, would run clucking over the horizon. 'Then there is a list of recommended restaurants in the kitchen—we can go to the closest.'

Ten minutes later she glanced sideways at Matt and her tummy lurched. He looked gorgeous—the shower-spiked damp hair, the lithe swell of his sun-kissed forearm that caught her breath, the jut of his jaw, the firm mouth that had wreaked havoc with her senses mere minutes before. The whole damn package.

It occurred to her that, five minutes in, the plan was *already* not working, so the quicker they got to the restaurant, the better. Yet she could hardly march there and as they walked it was impossible not to be affected by the sultry evening breeze, the scent of the flowers that mingled with the puffs of red dust from the path, the shriek of birds, the dusky cobalt blue of the sky against the sweep of the palm trees, their fronds waving gently in the breeze.

It all fuzzed her brain, as did his sheer male proximity, the tantalising scent of the shower gel that was, oh, so familiar, signature Matt—and he smelled so good—

the confident stride, the way he was always so focused on the moment.

Gritting her teeth, Zoe tried to ground herself, remind herself that this was not a first date with potential—this was a closure meeting, with the view of achieving civil indifference.

'Here we are.'

'Oh.' Zoe came to a halt. This was beautiful.

Fairy lights cascaded down, twinkled in the dusky scent-laden air. The outside dining area was arranged under a thatched bamboo roof, the tables simple wooden squares surrounded by benches. Candlelight flickered on each table and the tantalising smell of spices rode the air.

Fronded palm trees fluttered over the whole edifice and flowering plants laced the roof and supporting posts in a froth of green spiky leaves and white blooms that added a fresh sweetness to the air.

A waiter approached and soon they were sitting at one of the tables, the candlelight pooling a circle of illumination that complemented the starlight that twinkled down.

She studied the menu, with both professional and personal interest, then looked up to see Matt watching her.

'What are you going to have?' she asked, knowing how much he enjoyed his food. It was something they had in common—food was an important part of their lives. For Zoe it was because she'd never been sure where the next meal would come from. Her parents would get distracted sometimes and simply assumed Zoe and Beth would learn to fend for themselves. After all, 'You need to realise how lucky you are, darlings, living here with so much to eat.'

And Zoe understood that, she really did, but it did seem that sometimes their parents didn't realise that the plentiful food supplies were in the shops and Zoe and Beth were unable to access them. Or if there were supplies it wasn't always easy to work out exactly how to cook them.

Zoe had tried to get these points across, yelled and screamed when simple discussion hadn't prevailed, but she hadn't been able to permeate her parents' dense shield of protection. Sometimes she wondered if they simply didn't see her or had some sort of filter that retranslated her words and actions. Beth had taken a different route, accepted her parents would never change and had worked out how to cook pasta, how to access what there was.

But to Zoe that had been giving in. She'd wanted her mum to cook her dinner, to have family meals, wanted to have friends round and have a mum or dad who made sausages and mash, and then took them to the park for ice cream.

But, sweetheart, there are so many more important things to do. Maybe your friends could help us leaflet drop.

She shook off the thoughts, reminded herself that she too had accepted that her parents would never change. But one day, when she had kids, they would have proper home-cooked meals, and she would never miss a single sports day or school concert. And she would listen to them and…

'You OK, Zoe?'

'Yes. Sorry.' She turned her attention back to the menu. 'I was thinking of asking if they would do a taster plate so I can sample everything—that way…'

'It takes away the need to choose,' he said with a sudden smile.

And for a minute she was transported back in time to the halcyon weeks they'd spent together when they weren't married, she wasn't pregnant, and they'd just been happy. They'd visited a restaurant from a different country every week, bought cookbooks, experimented with recipes. Hand in hand, talking about food and spices, arguing over the merits of paprika and cayenne—what had happened to them?

His face softened as if he too was revisiting happy memories.

Once they'd ordered he leant back, picked up his bottle of beer and took a sip. 'So, Dylan told me you've spent the past years working your way round the world.'

'Maybe not the world, but as much of it as I can. I wanted to learn as much as I could about cooking in different countries—I've got a plan.' At first all she'd wanted was to run, to get away from the sadness and the grief and the sense of betrayal and stupidity. So she'd done literally that, run away, started travelling again, but this time she'd decided to instil her travel with a purpose. Because after the miscarriage she'd known that, no matter what, she wanted a family. And in order to have that she needed security, a job, a career.

'Tell me.'

She hesitated and he smiled. 'I'm really interested.'

'I want to open a restaurant and I want it to offer cuisine from round the world. I would either do theme nights, or theme months. So a country a night or a month.'

'It sounds a bit like what we used to do,' he said. 'When we picked a country every week and chose a recipe to cook.' His words arrested her; she hadn't even realised that fact, but he was right, and she wasn't sure how that made her feel. As if he sensed her ambiguity, he gestured. 'Anyway, go on.'

'So I've spent the last few years working my way around different restaurants—I've tried to do different roles so I understand the business side of it as well as the actual cooking. I've had in-depth discussions with accountants, chefs, managers, waiting staff…everyone. I've just finished a contract, covering maternity leave in a restaurant in Switzerland, and after Sri Lanka my plan is to return to the UK and get started. I'll give myself a year or so to get up and running and then I can get on with the next part of the plan.'

'Which is?'

'I want a family, to settle down. I want to have children and I don't want to leave it too late.' She met his gaze full on, realised she was holding her breath. Ridiculous. What was she hoping? That he'd say, *What a good idea. By coincidence, me too. I've changed my mind and become a family guy.*

'So you're in a relationship?'

Had she imagined it or had his body tensed as he'd asked the question? Was there a fleeting clench of his jaw?

Before she could respond the waiter approached with their food.

Matt focused on the ensuing conversation, entered into the discussion on 'turmeric, lime leaves…wine should complement it, but so would tea…vanilla pods, cardamom…' with an enthusiasm aimed to deflect the sense of edginess inspired by the idea that Zoe had found someone to settle down with.

He should, he knew, be pleased if she had, or at least indifferent, but… No buts. No way would he acknowledge even a tremor of jealousy. What was wrong with him? Envy or jealousy were not his style—he'd realised long ago there was no point. When he'd seen families that worked, parents who looked after and cared for their kids, who hugged them, *loved* them, of course he'd been jealous until he'd figured out jealousy changed nothing. It couldn't give him a different past—the facts were his parents hadn't looked after him, or cared, and hadn't loved him. Had seen nothing in him worthy of love. That was the truth and no amount of jealousy could alter that fact. The emotion did nothing but cause him pain. In truth, he'd come to that conclusion about most emotions, and so he'd learnt to cut them off. Just as he would now.

And so he would not show undue curiosity, or allow even a tinge of negative emotion, and when the waiter finally departed, he gestured to the food. 'You go first.' Waited as Zoe helped herself to some of the aromatic curry, tore off a piece of *roti* and dipped it in.

'This is incredible,' she said. 'Try it. I think it's the *kukul mas* curry, which is chicken curry but not as we know it.'

He took a spoonful and tasted it and for a second was genuinely diverted from thoughts of Zoe's relationship status. 'Fennel seeds. Coconut milk.'

'Definitely. And *pandan* leaves. I came across them in Thai cooking as well. They are long spiky leaves and you can use them to wrap food in before cooking it. Or you boil them up for the juice and add them to curries.'

He waited a few more minutes whilst they both sampled the *wambatu moju*, a delicious aubergine pickle, and the *gotu kola sambol*, a salad made from a shredded green vegetable, pennywort, combined with chillies, shallots and freshly grated coconut.

Then, finally, with exactly the right degree of nonchalance, he said, 'So where were we? Oh, yes. You're planning on settling down. Does that mean you're in a relationship?'

'No!' She put down her piece of coconut *roti* and stared at him. 'Obviously I wouldn't have kissed you if I was with someone. So, no, I'm not in a relationship yet but I'm working on it.'

'How?' The edginess increased. Was she out there dating a variety of men? Was she using dating apps? Why the hell did he even care? The dog-in-the-manger attitude was not one he was comfortable with. This was all about getting rid of the attraction between them and making sure they could move on without baggage. So the fact she had a plan to settle down was a good thing—made it crystal clear that any lingering attraction was pointless.

'It's a work in progress. I've devised a system—I just haven't tested it out yet.'

Relief tempered the unease and now curiosity surfaced. 'What sort of system?'

'Well, in the past few years I've dated a couple of guys…but they didn't work out. One of them was a great guy, we got on, we had shared interests…blah, blah, blah. But there was no spark at all and I didn't think that was fair.'

'And the other one?' Guilt twinged inside him that he was happy to hear about these strangers' shortcomings.

'He was too…serious. I couldn't imagine falling about laughing with him and that kind of ruined it. Sometimes I wanted to have a frivolous conversation about silly things. So I guess there was no real spark there either.'

It occurred to him that miraculously he and Zoe had managed to laugh earlier that day—despite the anger and the awkwardness, they had still managed to laugh.

'So the system doesn't seem to be working.'

She shook her head. 'No, they were why I devised a system. I realised the "seems like a good guy…let's see what happens" approach wasn't working. So now I have put together a tick list, a questionnaire. So the deal-breaker is whether or not he wants a family. If not, that's it—we go no further. If he does, I work out his test score in the remaining areas, analyse the data. If they tick enough boxes, I'll try a second date.'

'Assuming anyone wants a second date. I've spotted the flaw. Don't you feel the questionnaire may be a little off-putting?' he pointed out.

She grinned at him. 'Ha-ha! I'm not going to actually sit there with a pen and paper or hand them a questionnaire. It'll be more *subtle* than that.'

Raising his eyebrows, he gestured with one hand. 'Give me an example.'

She tilted her head to one side as she considered. 'OK. For example, if I need to know if we share a sense of humour, I'll tell a joke or a funny story and see if he gets it or not.'

'Let me guess—you've already compiled a list.'

'How did you know that?'

'Because I know you. I remember the spreadsheets and lists and research you used to do. Go on, try me with a joke and I'll tell you if it sounds natural.'

'OK. So let's say we're chatting about work and you've told me what you do. So you tell me you're an investment manager, or that you own an investment company. Then I say how interesting that is, ask a couple of intelligent questions to ascertain your ethics and then I go, "Hey, I've got a joke you may like. Why is a skateboard a good investment?"'

Matt stared at her. He knew he should focus on the answer, but he couldn't. Her expression was animated in the candlelight, her green eyes bright, her lips upturned as she waited for him to reply. Damn it. All he wanted to do was kiss her. Instead he was helping her prep for a first date.

'Do you give up?' she asked.

'I give up. Why is a skateboard a good investment?'

'Because you can flip it.' Her smile widened into a grin and the sheer absurdity brought an answering smile to his face, followed by a chuckle.

'That is a terrible joke,' he said when the laughter subsided.

'I know, right? But it is still funny.'

'I don't think you can slate a guy for not having a sense of humour if he doesn't laugh at that quality of joke.'

'You laughed…' There was a silence and something shimmered in the air. Hurriedly he helped himself to another helping of *dal* and rice.

'Which proves my point. Because I am definitely not the kind of guy you're looking for. But I get that a sense of humour is important. What else will you be vetting for?'

'Spark,' she said, and the very word seemed to alight the connection.

'So how do you figure out if there's a spark or not?' He could hear the tightness in his voice, her gulp audible before she replied.

'I thought I'd orchestrate an accidental brush of our hands.' She picked up one of the small bowls and held it out. 'Like this.'

He held his hand out over the candle, knew he was literally playing with fire, and took one of the fritters and as he did so allowed his hand to brush against hers. The lightest of contacts yet it sent a fierce jolt through him.

'Then,' she continued, her eyes wide now, 'I could offer to read their fortune. Tell them I'm interested in palmistry.'

Now he held his hand out palm up and she took it in hers. Jeez, his whole body tautened as she, oh, so slowly ran a finger over his hand, along the grooves and lines. He heard her breath catch in her throat and desire rocked through him at the sound, at the sensation of her touch.

'I…' She blinked and dropped his hand. 'I'm sorry. That was not supposed to happen.'

'Or at least not with me,' he said.

'No.' She sat back, picked up her water glass and

gulped, then took a sip of wine. 'Definitely not with you. But actually I don't want that to happen with anyone. It's too much. I want a tingle. A *faint* tingle.'

'Why? I thought you were looking for spark.'

'Spark, not forest fire. Attraction is important but it's not the be-all and end-all. Too much attraction complicates things, masks other flaws. We're proof of that.'

Maybe she was right. Attraction had caught them up in a vortex and propelled them into a pregnancy, a marriage, a disaster.

'It also distracts from problems because you solve them with sex. That's what we did. And when we didn't have that any more it turned out we didn't have anything. We were so blinded by attraction we didn't really get to know each other. I won't risk that again. Because the most important thing for me, the deal-breaker, is whether he wants a family. He needs to be decent and hard-working, willing to put his family first, be a hands-on dad and be able to give our children love and fun and attention and support.'

Her voice was fervent and Matt suddenly realised how very far short he had fallen from what she wanted and needed. He was decent and hard-working, but the ticks stopped there. The rest of it was out of his zone of experience. The idea of being hands-on brought him out in a clammy sweat—what if he got it wrong? What if he hurt his own child, or messed up in some way? The best he could have done, would have done if they hadn't lost the baby, was provide—his child would never have gone hungry, never wanted for anything money could buy.

But that life path had closed and couldn't be reopened, and he understood exactly why Zoe was looking for a Mr Right so different from him. Yet...

'That all sounds grand, but what about you?'

'What do you mean?'

'Surely he needs to be a good husband as well, be there for you when you need him.' Guilt suddenly twinged inside him in the knowledge that he hadn't been there for her, in her grief. His own grief, so intense, the echo of the loss of his baby brother, the fear that somehow it was all his fault, that he should have looked after Zoe better, had somehow rendered him unable to do anything. The harder he'd tried to do the right thing, the more he hadn't been able to because the one thing she'd wanted to make it better he couldn't give her—the promise of a family.

But his flaws didn't mean she should settle. 'I get your Mr Right has to be proper dad material, but he has to be right for you on a personal level as well.'

'Of course, and any decent man with a sense of humour who loves his kids will be right for me.'

'But he needs to care...to love you too.' The idea didn't sit well with him. If he was honest his prime desire right now was to take the mythical Mr Right and shake him by the scruff of his neck before hurling him superhero-style up to a planet far, far away. But that wasn't the point.

'I don't think that matters; I'm not looking for grand romantic love. I don't want us to be so wrapped up in each other that our kids lose out. They need to come first.' The certainty in her voice was absolute. 'I want to be a happy family. I think that means I need to have a partner who has the same outlook on family.'

'I understand that. But your relationship is important as well—after all, once the children have left and as they grow up it is that man who you will spend your life with. That's the man you'll wake up to every day.'

Memories filtered through again, of waking up with Zoe in the crook of his arm, warm and secure, tendrils of her soft red hair tickling his chest. And then other memories, of the last few weeks when his nightmares had returned and he'd slip from the room, not wanting to disturb her, or even admit to having those night terrors he'd thought he'd licked in childhood.

Yet another reason why he wasn't programmed for family life.

'I understand that, and I know what I'm doing.'

'So what happens if you can't find a Mr Right? Will you settle for Mr Nearly Right? Or Mr I Only Tick One Box or—'

'If I can't find a man I want to settle down with, a man I believe will provide a happy family life, then I will become a single mother. Simple.'

'Is it that simple?'

'It is still possible to use a donor, but it is much more complicated now legally. So perhaps I would ask a friend or perhaps I would adopt. But, one way or another, I know I want to be a mum. I'd way prefer my child to have a hands-on dad, but if that's truly not possible I won't give up being a parent.'

He saw the fervour in her eyes, could see how important a family was to her, and guilt pierced him once again that he'd let her down so badly. Guilt and a renewed sadness that they'd lost the baby—what would have happened if their child had been born? Would he have managed to be the hands-on dad she wanted? Would he have been able to love the baby as he presumably hadn't loved his brother? Or would he have felt nothing? Would he have spent years faking emotion? The questions all unanswerable. Pointless.

'I truly hope you achieve your dreams,' he said softly. 'However you do it.' The one thing for sure, he wouldn't be part of them. So there was little point allowing emotions to the table. Time to change tack, however abruptly.

'So now how about we get dessert?' he suggested.

'Good idea,' she said. 'We've talked about me, so once we've ordered we can talk about you.'

Marvellous.

CHAPTER FOUR

ZOE WAITED UNTIL the waiter had deposited the *halapa* in front of them, explained that the dessert was made from a *kanda* leaf filled with honey, flour and sugar mixture.

'You will definitely want another one.'

'I am sure we will.' A sentiment she knew was correct as she bit into the tangy green concoction.

Placing the parcel down, she then looked across at Matt, his dark eyes slightly wary, his six o'clock shadow more pronounced, and somehow the prospect of her Mr Right seemed to fuzz around the edges.

No!

That was attraction speaking and exactly why spark was so dangerous and unwanted.

'So, your turn,' she said. 'Tell me what you've been doing the past four years. Moving towards domination of the financial world?' she quipped, trying to keep her voice light, to not rekindle the confusion and resentment she'd felt about his work. She'd loved that he loved his job, but she'd hated the hours he devoted to it, the ever-increasing time away from her.

He'd told her he was doing it 'for the baby'. But she hadn't got it; when she'd met him he was already an uber-successful hedge-fund manager, he'd worked for a prestigious investment company, owned a swish London apartment, had a fridge stocked with food and drink, luxurious furniture, an expensive car. He hadn't flaunted any of it, had seemed content with simple ownership, but he surely hadn't needed to work even harder.

But he'd claimed he did. Had wanted to set up his own business. 'That way I'll be in control. It'll be down to me how well we live and how much security I can provide.'

Which begged the question: How much security did any one family need?

'But we can budget, economise. Plus, I'll be earning as well and I don't need luxury.' Then she'd seen the set of his lips and had wondered if maybe he did.

'I know that. But I want my child to have the best I can give him.'

'But...' She'd trailed off. 'The best you can give him is yourself.'

He'd glanced away and then back at her. 'Sure, I get that.'

But he hadn't. In actual fact, it turned out that Matt had quite simply never wanted the baby, didn't want a family, had only married Zoe as a matter of honour and principle. The idea still sent a sheen of humiliation over her, along with a knowledge that his work ethic had simply been a means of escaping her, the reminder of the responsibility he hadn't wanted. Yet it seemed that he had done what he had wanted to do—

'Beth told me you've set up by yourself.'

'I have. I set up Sutherland Investments two years ago.'

'And you're doing pretty well.' Before coming to Sri Lanka she'd done what she hadn't done for four years—an Internet search on Matt—and discovered exactly how well he was doing. His investment company had won coveted business awards and, whilst small and niche, it was exclusive and had a more than enviable track record.

'Yes. I've got a growing client base. I've taken on a few employees, including an excellent second in command. So I can juggle my time however I want.'

'So you get more free time? To do what? Race fast cars, spend time on a luxury yacht?'

Somehow that was hard to picture. It was something she'd never worked out about Matt—he owned the requisite trappings of wealth, but she was pretty sure he didn't need them. She wasn't even sure he liked them—he'd barely driven the fast car in his garage, didn't seem to pay a lot of attention to shopping, though all his clothes were super expensive.

'No. I do have a couple of flash cars and a fancy apartment, but most of my spare time and money is spent on my foundation. The one I told you about.'

'That's great.' She could hear the flatness in her voice and the guardedness in his, loathed herself for it.

But she couldn't help it. The echo of her parents jarred on her. The knowledge Matt had decided to prioritise a cause over a family still…hurt.

'Tell me about it,' she said now, knowing this was the best way to kill attraction stone-cold dead.

He shook his head. 'It's OK. I can be very boring when I get on my hobby horse.'

'That's a good thing. We're reminding each other why we're bad for each other, remember? So the more tedious, the better.' Only somehow she suspected Matt couldn't be tedious however hard he tried.

She watched as he marshalled his thoughts, the slight crease to his brow, the intensity in his dark eyes. 'I started out with simple donations, but since my company took off I've been able to do more. I knew it was bad, but I hadn't realised how widespread the problem is. So many kids in care, so many youngsters caught up in a life where crime seems to be the only option, so many without a family to look out for them and care for them. Some of them trapped in families who patently don't care for them. My foundation aims to help as many as possible.'

It was a fervour she recognised all too well, the clarion call of a man who had a cause. She understood too that Matt had a reason for his fervour; he himself had been in care, though he had hardly ever spoken about it. Only to say that he had been one of the lucky ones who'd had good carers who had provided all he'd needed.

'We do a lot of different things, from organising food banks to a programme of activities, career advice, private tuition at centres throughout the UK. We also offer counselling and therapy. I've got great dedicated managers and I try to be as hands-on as possible as well.'

'That sounds incredible.' And it did. 'And like a second job.'

'Yes, it is—it all certainly keeps me busy. But it's fun as well, and really rewarding. Some of the kids blow my mind.'

Zoe frowned, realised she'd never heard her parents call what they did fun or rewarding—to them it was a mission, a road strewn with obstacles. 'It must be frustrating sometimes too.'

'Sure, but whilst I realise whatever I do there's more to be done, I have to believe I am making a difference.'

'It sounds like what you do makes an enormous difference.' And it did, yet she knew her voice still lacked the enthusiasm he deserved, and Matt had noticed; she could see from his face that he was perplexed, and she ploughed on hurriedly. 'What about relationships? How do you find the time?'

'I don't. As we both figured out, I am not relationship material; to be honest, I don't want to be. My life works how it is now. I've got the right balance. I'm not planning a life of celibacy, but I am happy with short-term and uncomplicated. The type of relationship where you kick back and relax for a while, have fun in and out of bed, and then resume normal life.'

'So a bit like recharging your batteries?' She knew she sounded snarky, but somehow she couldn't help it.

'Exactly and what's wrong with that?'

'Don't you think it's a bit shallow?'

'No, I don't. And even if it is, what's wrong with shallow? In this part of my life shallow is exactly what I want if it means avoiding getting out of my depth.'

'Or you could learn to swim?'

'I tried that, Zoe. With you and it didn't work.'

He was right, but he'd only tried it because he'd felt he had to; perhaps it would be different if it was the right woman. 'Perhaps your Ms Right will come along and change your mind.'

'I'm not on the market for a Ms Right.'

'Unless she is Ms Shallow,' Zoe said, and then shook her head. 'Sorry. That's not fair.'

'No, it's not,' he agreed. 'Or not if you mean it as an insult. There's nothing wrong with paddling in the shallows—not everyone wants to swim in the deep end. I'm always honest with my partners and I do my best to make sure they are being honest with me. It works.' He gave a sudden smile. 'The shallow end can be a whole lot of fun.'

The smile sent a shiver through her; she knew he spoke nothing more than absolute truth, knew just how much fun Matt could be. But that wasn't enough—not for her. So...

'I guess we really do know now that this attraction has nowhere to go. You want shallow relationships and no family. I want Mr Right and children. That really is a never the twain shall meet. So let's hope attraction gets the picture and fades away. We have both moved on.'

'Exactly,' he said. 'I'll drink to that.'

Yet somehow the brightness of their voices sounded forced and once they had clinked bottles a silence weighted with awkwardness descended.

It was almost a relief when her phone rang. 'It's Beth,' she said, and relief morphed to anxiety. *Please let David be all right.*

Matt watched, as Zoe's face relaxed and she did a thumbs up to let him know it was OK, or at least not the worst news. She listened for a while and her expression lightened and a small smile touched her lips as she nodded.

'I think that's a wonderful idea and I'll sort it all out.' More words from Beth, and Zoe shook her head. 'I don't mind at all. Leave it all to me, and you and Dylan focus on being with David.'

She disconnected and looked across at him. 'David is OK, but they are doing the bypass surgery the day after tomorrow. Just in case anything goes wrong Beth and Dylan want to get married before the operation, so I am going to organise a hospital wedding for the morning of the op.'

'*We* are going to organise a hospital wedding.' The words fell from his lips without thought. 'Dylan is my best friend—I want to be part of trying to make this as good as it can be in the circumstances. Plus, it makes sense— it's a lot to organise in a day. It will be easier.' He raised his eyebrows. 'Why the look of surprise?'

She shrugged. 'As you're a non-believer in deep and meaningful relationships, I didn't think you'd want to organise a wedding.'

'I believe in them for other people—just not for me. I

truly want to help make this as special and precious as we can. For Dylan and Beth and Dylan's parents.'

'Then I guess we should get back to the resort and come up with a plan of action.' She hesitated. 'As long as it won't be awkward.'

'Absolutely not,' he stated. 'Project wedding will keep us focused and busy—there won't be time to be awkward.'

The theory was sound, he assured himself as they started the walk back to the resort. 'So how do we go about organising a wedding in a hospital in Sri Lanka?'

'Well, Beth has discovered that it is definitely possible to do. Lavantivu has various laws surrounding "overseas weddings" and it is allowed, but there is paperwork that needs to be done.'

'I'll get on to that. I spent time in the hospital so I spoke to people there already.'

'Perfect. I'll contact the celebrant who was going to officiate if the wedding had gone ahead next week as planned. She sounded lovely—I really hope she'll be able to carry out the ceremony here. I know Beth and Dylan had in-depth conversations with her as to how they wanted it to be.' She thought for a minute. 'I'll need to call my parents to make sure they can still attend by video; Mum in particular has a part to play. Oh, and we'll need to go shopping for clothes.'

Matt slowed down. 'Clothes?'

'Beth and I were going to go and find her a dress here. She didn't want the hassle of bringing a dress over here, so we were going to make a day of it, have lunch, go to a spa and shop. Dylan and his dad and you the same.' She glanced at him. 'I take it he didn't mention it.'

'Nope. He was probably going to surprise me.'

She grinned. 'You mean he didn't want to give you a chance to wriggle out of it.'

'Something like that. But that's OK—add shopping to the list.'

They approached the garden of the villa and she paused. 'Good idea—I will make an actual list. I've got pen and paper here.' She perched on the wall that bordered the lushness of the garden and began to write and his breath hitched. Silhouetted in the starlight, Zoe looked almost ethereally beautiful. The moonbeams illuminated and highlighted the red of her hair, which rippled in the gentle balm of the breeze, emphasised the length of her eyelashes, the sweep of her cheekbones.

And it seemed as though dinner had cleared the air, and the idea of a shared goal had allowed them to walk back together, bouncing ideas off each other with no sense of awkwardness. Could it be that simple to sort out the past? Doubt touched him—they hadn't discussed the past at all—but that was OK. Why revisit pain and angst, why rake up hurt, or regurgitate arguments and mistakes?

Much better to focus on the here and now and the wedding.

She looked up and smiled and now his heart beat a little bit faster. 'So we have a plan.'

'We do.'

Perhaps she saw something in his eyes, but now everything seemed to hush, to maze around them into a haze of sweet-smelling aromas, the gentle caw of a nightbird and himself and Zoe in a timeless moment.

'I'm…glad we're doing this together,' she said softly.

'Me too.' The words sounded strangled as she rose, stepped towards him and, oh, so gently kissed his cheek, the brush of her lips sending a bittersweet thrill of desire through him along with a sense of warmth. She stood back and he could see it in her eyes, the same yearning to close the gap and this time share a different sort of kiss. He forced his feet to adhere to the ground, reminded himself that they must not succumb to attraction. Because they knew it could get them nowhere.

'Goodnight,' she said, her voice breathless, infused with panic, before she turned and left.

Matt opened his eyes, heard the sound of birds drifting in on the balmy breeze, smelt the tang of coffee in the air mixed with a heady smell of warmth and sunshine. He swung his legs out of bed, stretched and headed for the welcome cool of the shower, emerging from his villa fifteen minutes later to find Zoe sitting in the shaded garden area outside the building that housed the kitchen and eating area.

'Good morning.' Her voice was brisk and she couldn't quite meet his eye. 'I thought we could call the hospital and the celebrant and then eat. The caterers have left an amazing breakfast inside for us.'

'Sounds like a plan,' he replied, careful to keep his voice as businesslike as hers. Her hair was held up in a messy bun, she was dressed in simple, flowing, wide-bottomed trousers and a sleeveless top, her face make-up-free, and she *still* looked beautiful.

He sat down and quickly pulled out his phone to call the hospital, saw that she was doing likewise.

Ten minutes later, he hung up, just as she said, 'Thank you, we'll see you then.' He raised his eyebrows in question. 'We decided it was best for Edwina to come here to discuss the arrangements. Obviously she's already met with Beth and Dylan but we need to discuss how it will work in the hospital.' She gestured to his phone. 'What did they say?'

'It will all be OK. Beth and Dylan have already done all the paperwork allowing foreign nationals to get mar-

ried here. They've presented their passports, birth certificates and certified certificates to show they are both
single. The hospital would like to see the copies. David's
consultant will also provide a letter confirming David is
unable to leave the hospital, and that means I can get the
necessary letter of permission.'

'Perfect. Now let's eat. It's going to be a busy day and
I'm not going anywhere with you if you're hungry.'

'Why not?'

'Because I know you get grumpy when you don't eat.'

He blinked. 'How do you know…?' He stopped, an-
noyed with himself for the giveaway admission. Zoe was
dead right, but he truly hadn't registered that she knew.
Thought he'd long since learnt to master or at least hide
his reaction to hunger. As a child, once he'd been taken
from his parents his relationship with food had been problematic.

Piecing together his early years, he now knew food
had been something he'd had to scavenge, probably from
bins, and any person he could appeal to. With hindsight
he understood that to his five-year-old's mind the sudden
availability of food must have blown every nerve cell. The
whole thing had sent him into a tailspin, unable to work
out whether to eat the food, hide the food or assume it
was some sort of trick.

A social worker had once explained to a foster carer,
'It is vitally important to keep him regulated with food.
Without it he goes almost feral. His mood dips and he
turns angry.'

He'd been too young to fully understand the words,
but as he'd grown older he'd learnt to regulate himself,
learnt that hunger triggered panic so it was best to make
sure he stayed fed. That he controlled food and never let
food control him.

Now Zoe looked at him in puzzlement. 'I don't know how I know. I just always thought you got a bit edgy when we'd skipped a meal.' She dipped her head to one side and contemplated him. 'Your jaw clenches. You rock back on your heels.' She gurgled with laughter. *Call me Holmes... Zoe Holmes.* 'Because I'm right, aren't I?'

He shrugged and she frowned.

'Hey, I didn't mean to upset you. Lots of people get irritable when their blood sugar levels drop. I do. Maybe that's why I recognise the signs in you.'

'It's fine. No big deal.' And it wasn't, but he loathed that his first years still had an impact on him. All he wanted was to erase them, wipe them out. Ironic the one thing he did want to remember, he couldn't—his brother. 'Let's get breakfast.'

'They've set it up inside—it is amazing. Truly. I'll take you through everything—one of the caterers explained it all and I took notes.'

He followed Zoe inside and his eyes widened at the array of food. 'Wow.'

'I know, right? So these here are hoppers. These ones are called string hoppers and they are rice noodles, pressed into flat spirals, or you can have egg hoppers. Look.' She glanced at him. 'I don't mean look at me, I mean look at the food.'

But he couldn't help it. Her face was so animated, so pretty, so full of enthusiasm it was hard not to look at her. 'Sorry. It's just...good to see you happy.' There was a silence and then he turned to the table. 'Anyway, tell me about egg hoppers.'

'Right. So instead of making noodles you fry the batter into a pancake and then you put an egg in the middle. Then you garnish it with chillies, onions and lemon juice.' She paused for breath. 'Then over here you have a kind of porridge-like dish. It's called *kiribath* and it's made of coconut milk, rice and bananas.'

'Well, it all looks incredible.' There were other dishes, as well as bowls of fruit, and *roti*, *dal* and pots of chutneys and pickles.

She piled her plate high as he did the same and they went to sit back outside.

'So what else did the hospital say?' she asked.

'They were great; we can use a room overlooking the garden so it can look pretty, and we can take photos out there after the ceremony. They are happy for us to take in flowers and decorate the room however we like.'

'Perfect.' She glanced up and, following her gaze, he saw a grey-haired woman approach. Slim and svelte, she smiled as she approached. A woman with dark brown eyes that spoke of an inner peace.

'Good morning. I'm Edwina Storrington, the celebrant. Apologies, I am here early. Please finish your breakfast.'

'Or why don't you join us?' Zoe offered. 'There is plenty inside.'

'That is most kind.' A few minutes later she sat down opposite them. 'Thank you so much for agreeing to meet with me. I thought it would be easier to sort out the details in person. First, though, is there any flexibility on the time of the wedding? I do have a prior commitment that day. I work with the local orphanage, and I have plans to take the kids out that day. These kids are let down time and again—I prefer not to add to that burden.'

'Because of the operation I don't think we can change the date.' Zoe's face fell. 'But we could do the ceremony as early as you like?'

'If the hospital can accommodate an early morning ceremony, then I should still be able to zoom off to get the minibus, to collect the kids.'

'That would work fine,' Matt said.

Edwina nodded. 'Then I am happy to go ahead. Beth, Dylan and I spoke at length about the ceremony and how they wish to have a mix of Sri Lankan and Western traditions. Can we just go through the details and see how to accommodate everything in a shorter ceremony in a hospital?'

Matt sat back and watched the two women discuss the details, free now to admire Zoe, the way she gestured with her hands, the way she gave one hundred per cent to the conversation, the gurgle of her laugh, the charm of her smile. And how much she cared about getting this right for Beth. Twenty minutes later Edwina pushed her cup away and smiled.

'I think we've covered everything. Thank you both very much for the breakfast.'

'Would it help if we pack up the rest of the food and drop it to the orphanage?' Matt offered.

Edwina smiled. 'That would be marvellous. But no need for you to drop it. I can take it there now. I pop in whenever I can anyway.'

Zoe rose. 'I'll get started. I'll go and see if I can rustle up some Tupperware.'

'Tell me about the orphanage,' Matt asked Edwina.

'It's a residential place I helped set up a few years ago. It houses up to fifteen kids up to the age of eighteen at any one time. Their backgrounds vary. There are some pretty sad stories there, yet they really all are great kids—I do my best for them and we raise as much money as we can, but it's tough. So every little bit helps.'

'So what have you got planned for them?'

'It's not a lot—I'm taking them on a picnic and they'll have a chance to run off some steam and have some fun.'

Zoe returned as they continued to speak and soon they

were all packing away the food. But Matt sensed that Zoe's mood had changed, her previous enthusiasm and exuberance muted; she seemed to have distanced herself from the conversation and he wondered why. Continued to wonder as he walked Edwina to her car.

CHAPTER FIVE

ZOE WATCHED MATT walk away with Edwina, could tell their conversation was an important one by the way Matt bent his head towards the older woman, the way he moved his hands as he talked, the nod and bob of his head… She just knew. Knew too that the orphanage had sparked his interest, and to her own shame a sense of dread weighted her stomach.

She knew what would happen next: Matt would abandon their plans to shop in favour of a visit to the orphanage. She knew too that helping orphans was of course more important than shopping, and she could easily shop on her own. Knew it was not on a par with her parents' behaviour and yet…yet anger still roiled inside her. An anger she knew she had to hide, an anger she disliked herself for.

As he approached the table he looked down at her with a slightly puzzled look on his face.

'Is everything OK?'

'Of course.'

'Good. Then are you ready to go?'

Huh?

Now his frown deepened. 'We've got shopping to do, or have I missed something?'

Oh.

Perhaps she'd overreacted and she was aware of a small

smile on her face as she stood up. Told herself it shouldn't matter, but it did and, like it or not, she was glad that Matt was coming shopping. Was glad that he hadn't acted as her parents would have.

'Let me grab my stuff and we'll go. I thought we'd do the dress first. I've done some research and I think I've found an ideal shop.'

'Sure. I've hired a car and a driver. That way we don't need to work out parking or worry about directions.'

'Great.'

Once in the car she turned to him. 'I really want to make this perfect for everyone.'

He nodded. 'I know you do, and I really think you will.'

'Beth told me that they are doing this as an affirmation of life, of hope and joy and to give David a sense of happiness before his operation.'

He nodded. 'I spoke with Dylan yesterday. They told David that and he said he appreciated that, but he *knows* he may not survive and he wants to see them married before the operation. David is a realist—and a statistician. He'll know there is a chance he won't make it, but that will make it even more important to him that he sees Dylan get married. If it were me, even if I were terrified, or knew my chances were low, I'd want to see my son happy, to know I'd seen him married and, yes, I'd want it to be a proper celebration, not muted by thoughts of my death.'

The words caught her and she couldn't help it—his discussion of a hypothetical son when he'd decided so categorically not to have children. Decided to put his foundation and his work first and prioritise those. A niggle touched her—Matt wasn't a man who didn't believe he could do it all. Yet he'd decided he wouldn't have children of his own.

Enough—it was no longer her business, and she was relieved when the car glided to a halt outside a row of shops.

Five minutes later they entered the welcome air-conditioned temperature. She glanced round and her eyes widened at the sheer extent of choice. The clothes on display were truly amazing, an exotic burst of colour and style… dresses, saris, cashmere shawls all draped over tables in an array that made her eye dart from piece to piece.

A smiling assistant came forward, introduced herself as Anesha, and Zoe explained what they were looking for. 'I am hoping to find something celebratory that somehow combines Sri Lankan and Western tradition and is something my sister would love.'

'I understand,' Anesha said. 'Sri Lankan brides often wear a wedding sari, known as a Kandyan sari.'

'I think Beth would feel that wasn't quite the right thing to do as she isn't actually Sri Lankan and doesn't live here.'

'Then how about a sari? Not a wedding one, but a beautiful one none the less.'

'I think Beth and Manisha would like that, and, as it is a small wedding, I don't believe it could offend anyone.'

Anesha nodded. 'To me it is a compliment to my culture that your sister wishes to include Sri Lankan traditions.'

Zoe nodded. 'Thank you, Anesha.'

'What sort of colours would your sister like?'

A discussion commenced and ended with, 'Give me five minutes and I'll have a selection for you.' Calling for help, Anesha walked away.

True to her word, she arrived back a few minutes later and Zoe gave a small gasp. 'They are all utterly beautiful.' The eclectic mix of colour and whites, the delicacy of the beading and intricacy of the patterns whirled in her head as she tried to work out what her sister would like most. Turning to Matt, who had been silent throughout, she said, 'What do you think?'

'They are all beautiful; it's hard to say.' His tone was a little short and, as if he realised it, he smiled at Anesha. 'You have done such a good job it makes ours harder.'

'Perhaps you would like to try them on?'

Temptation beckoned and then Zoe shook her head. 'It wouldn't feel right—I don't want Beth to wear something I've actually worn. I know Beth will prefer something not too bright, so I think it's between this one and this one.' She pointed to two of them.

'I understand.' Anesha thought for a moment. 'If you like I can put them onto mannequins and then perhaps you will be able to see how each one will look and then you can choose.'

'That would be perfect.'

'And whilst I do that why don't you choose something for yourself?'

'I've got a dress that will probably work with either of the saris.'

To her surprise Matt shook his head. 'I agree with Anesha—you should choose something new, something chosen to complement Beth's dress. For the photos, for your memories… I think it's important.' He looked round the shop. 'It doesn't have to be a sari—or perhaps it should be.'

Anesha gestured to another shop assistant. 'Leela will help you, if you like.'

Ten minutes later Zoe surveyed herself in the mirror. 'I love it,' she breathed. The sari was a shimmering grey material shot through with threads of silver, and it made her feel almost magical. She liked too that it was both subtle and special—

'Would you like to show your partner?'

'No. I mean, he isn't my partner. He's the best man and I'm the bride's sister. So he doesn't need to see it.'

But it was more than that. She didn't want him to see it now—because, truth be told, Zoe wanted to knock Matt's socks off the next day.

Back in her normal clothes, Zoe followed Leela out and gave a small gasp when she saw the mannequins. 'Oh. They're both beautiful.' She looked at Matt. 'How are we going to decide?' After she had walked round five times Matt came over and gestured to a chair. 'OK. Close your eyes and picture tomorrow. What do you see?'

'Beth in the dress on the left.'

'Then that's the one we get.'

'Thank you.'

As they walked out of the shop Zoe glanced at Matt. 'You were very quiet in there.'

'There wasn't any need for me to say anything. So where are we going now?'

'To try and sort out the cake. I spoke to the bakery who were going to do it and they said we could pop in and they'd see what they can do. I'm pretty sure we can walk from here.'

'Sure.'

Zoe glanced at him, sure she could see trouble in his eyes.

'Is something wrong?' She halted. 'Didn't you like the sari? You should have said. If you think Dylan won't like it or Beth or—'

'Whoa. It's not that. That sari is perfect.'

'Then what is it?'

His steps slowed. 'It's just. I was just…' He rocked backwards on his heels. 'I'm sorry,' he said.

'Sorry about what?'

'That you didn't have a proper wedding day. A chance

to choose a dress with your sister. A chance to choose a dress at all. I should have thought at the time, instead of rushing you into it.'

She could hear genuine regret in his voice and she laid a hand on his arm.

'Please don't feel bad. If I'd wanted any of those things I would have said so. I was there, remember? But it wouldn't have felt right to have gone for a traditional wedding. We were getting married for the baby's sake. We barely knew each other. With hindsight we were fools to do it.' Only it hadn't felt like that—it had felt magical, as though she could finally put tragedy behind her, lay the ghosts of the past down and start a new chapter of her life. With a man she'd believed had wanted the baby as much as she had, welcomed the idea of family. 'But it was our decision, foolish or not,' she said. Though, really, if anyone had been the fool it had been her. She'd heard what she wanted to hear, seen what she'd wanted to see.

'In the end it doesn't really matter. Our marriage was brief and ill-fated, so what we wore on the day of our wedding doesn't really matter.'

'You wore a floral dress with daisies on it,' he said. 'And you tucked a carnation in your hair.'

'You remember.'

'Every minute of it and, for what it's worth, you looked stunning.' He hesitated. 'It may not have been conventional, or traditional, but we were happy.'

In that moment Zoe was no longer standing in the shade of trees on a Sri Lankan island… Instead she was back to her wedding day four and a half years ago.

'Do you remember our wedding lunch?'

'You said you had a craving for proper fish and chips.'

'So after the register office you drove us down to Brighton.' She inhaled and it was almost as though she could smell the tang of salt, hear the cries and shouts from Brighton pier. 'We had proper fish and chips on the beach.' Her tastebuds tingled with the remembered tang of the salt, the vinegar, the crisp, cooked-to-perfection batter. She could hear the swish of the waves and see the soar of the seagulls. Feel the smooth bumpiness of the pebbles under her toes.

After lunch they'd paddled in the sea and then wandered round the city hand in hand, bought each other silly souvenirs from the shops, ended up starting their honeymoon in Brighton.

'No matter what happened after, that day was magical.'

And so had the night been. Memories cascaded over her, her body shivered with remembered pleasure and a bittersweet desire that culminated in an unstoppable urge to step forward now, to place her hand on his chest, to feel his strength under her fingertips, to stretch up on tiptoe and brush her lips against his...and then she was lost.

Lost in him, in his smell, his taste...in the glorious escape of his lips as they locked onto hers in an inevitable, wonderful kiss that wove a sensory magic that engulfed her in a sheer maelstrom of pleasure that sent a surge of desire through her body, that twisted and clenched her tummy with a yearning for more as his hand slid down her back and she pressed against him.

It was the caw of a bird that brought her to her senses. *Whoa.* What the hell was she doing? How much of an idiot was she? Somehow from somewhere she found the strength to pull away, and stared up at him aghast. Anger—with herself, with him—caused her already ragged breathing to catch further and she stepped backwards.

'Zoe.' His voice was jagged, almost hoarse. 'I—'

'Don't say anything. That was stupid, triggered by

something that was never real. Our wedding day wasn't magical or, if it was, it was an illusion.'

'That isn't true. It was real, Zoe. All of it.'

Anger deepened as she shook her head in disbelief. 'How can you say that? You didn't want to get married. You didn't want a family. You didn't want the baby. You married me because you thought it was the right thing to do.'

'Yes, I did. But I wanted it to work. I believed we could make it work. I believed we could be happy together.' Now he stepped towards her. 'You are right—I hadn't planned to have a baby… *We* hadn't planned that. But I wanted to be a good father.'

'But you would just have been making the best of it—it wasn't what you wanted to do with your life.'

'It wasn't what I planned to do with my life—but sometimes plans change. You can't always control what happens, but you can try and control what happens next. I had no regrets about the baby, Zoe. From the minute I knew you were pregnant I wanted to do right by him or her and I won't apologise for that. That is what I wanted to do with my life.'

Zoe looked up at him, saw sincerity in his dark eyes, but saw a darkness as well, a shadow that made her want to reach out to him, to soothe the demon she could see there.

She knew he spoke truth. It had been Matt who had urged the marriage—why would he have done that if he hadn't wanted to be part of the baby's life? He could have offered maintenance and weekend visitation rights, but he'd wanted to be there properly. Wanted to give the baby exactly what she had wanted to—a family. He'd also been willing to sacrifice his own dreams, his own plans, and had been willing to do that without complaint. So perhaps she should let her anger go.

She shook her head. 'I understand that,' she said. 'But I feel stupid. I believed you wanted what I wanted.'

'I did. I wanted us to be a family.' His voice was taut with sadness now.

'But not enough to try for another baby.' That was the bottom line and that was unanswerable.

'I...' Now the shadows darkened his eyes further and she could see the depth of pain there, one she couldn't fathom or understand. Then it was gone, like the clichéd shutter clanging down. 'No. Not enough for that. But I swear to you, Zoe, I would have done all I could to be a good father if life had turned out that way. And... I swear to you that I grieved for our baby.'

Again, she heard sincerity, knew that again he spoke truth, and she felt the last vestiges of rancour dissipate. 'I know you did,' she said softly, and now she did step closer to him and gently placed her hand on his arm, took comfort when he covered it with his own. 'But it was a long time ago.' Her glance caught the dial of his watch. 'And now we have a cake and flowers to sort out.' She hesitated. 'Unless you think we shouldn't do this together after what happened.' The kiss, the aftermath of which was still buzzing inside her. But... 'I promise you it won't happen again. It was a moment of stupidity.'

'Agreed. And we shouldn't let that moment stop Project Wedding. Not when we have so little time left.'

'OK. Let's go. The cake shop isn't far, then we'll go to the bazaar for the flowers.'

Half an hour later, cake sorted, they entered the bazaar and Matt gazed around, tried not to get swept away by the hustle and bustle of the crowds of shoppers, the mishmash of stalls selling an assortment of wares, from brightly co-loured fruits and vegetables to exotic swathes of materials.

A chaos that matched his thoughts; he was still knocked for six by the kiss they'd shared, his body still alive from the zing of desire. But he was also fazed by the conversation, loathed the idea that Zoe believed their marriage had been based on a foundation of lies.

Perhaps hated more the shades of grey that meant he couldn't explain the truth to her. That the reason he didn't want a baby was his own inadequacies, that his greatest fear in their marriage was that he would let them down. That when she'd lost the baby, the grief had dredged up an older grief, had mixed and swirled with the loss of his baby brother until he couldn't think straight.

All he knew was that he couldn't go through that sort of loss again, that he couldn't risk that sort of responsibility. After all, why hadn't he done something to save his brother? Why couldn't he even remember him? Why hadn't he raised an alarm? Told someone. Run out on the street and proclaimed it. Maybe because he'd been too busy looking out for himself.

Enough. He couldn't change the past. Not what he'd done aged five or aged twenty-six. Telling Zoe wouldn't change the past either. Nothing could.

'Matt? Are you OK?'

'I'm fine. Just getting my bearings.' A sensation alien to him; he was always in control. It was a defining feature of his character. Perhaps with that control came a certain emptiness, but that was fine with him. So he had to be careful, careful not to let Zoe in. So there could be no more kisses.

Zoe glanced down at her phone. 'I think the flower stall I want is over that way.' She pointed and he nodded.

'If we get separated, let's meet up back at the entrance. But in the meantime maybe hang on to the loop of my jeans. Or...' He held out his hand. 'It makes sense to hold hands. That way we won't get separated and waste time having to fight our way back to the entrance.'

She looked at his hand for a while, then nodded, placed her hand in his, and he tried not to react to the sheer familiarity of it. The memories of times gone by when holding Zoe's hand was as natural as breathing. But now it was simply for efficiency as they wended their way through the bazaar. Efficiency. Efficiency. Efficiency. A mantra on repeat until they reached the flower stall.

Scent and colours exploded onto his sensory fields; heaps and piles of exotic blooms and greens exuded a medley of fragrance. The smiling owner stepped forward.

'How can I help you?' he asked, his English accented but fluent.

'My sister is getting married tomorrow, at the hospital. I'd like to decorate the room with flowers and create a floral arch that they can stand under for the actual ceremony. They need to smell enough to mask the hospital smell but not be too overwhelming. I also need a bouquet for the bride to hold and I want the whole thing to be full of life and vibrancy and happiness.'

'OK. Then this is what you need.' The man took a quick glance round the stall and tables and then, with impressive speed, he gathered together a sample of flowers. 'For the arch. And then these for the bouquet. And what about for the bride's hair and your own?'

'I don't think I'd know how to arrange flowers in someone's hair.'

'It's easy. Do you have a phone?'

'Well, yes…'

'Then I will instruct your man how to do it, my son will video it and tomorrow you will know how to do it.'

'I…' Matt saw the frantic look she cast at him and man did he sympathise.

'Your sister—she will look amazing.'

'If that's OK with you, Matt?'

It was almost comical. *Almost.* The fact that two adults were both in a spin at the prospect of him braiding her hair. This wasn't personal. Hairdressers did it all the time— and he would not admit to anyone that he was loth to do something so simple. 'Of course,' he said.

'OK. I will do it for my daughter and you will follow what I do. My son will video us and tomorrow you simply need to follow the video. It is easy. Really easy.'

Easy. Really easy. Matt tried to keep the words in the forefront of his mind for the next twenty minutes, all too aware that his expression, her expression, were being captured on screen. But, damn it, it wasn't easy.

As he separated her hair into three parts, his fingers skimmed the nape of her neck and he felt the shiver run through her body, tried not to recall exactly how sensitive her neck was, how much she'd loved him to trail kisses…

Easy. Really easy, Matt.

As his fingers twined in the silken tresses of her hair, memories awakened of all the other times he'd run his fingers through her hair, washed it for her when they'd shared a shower, the times when he'd woken to have it tickle his nose…

It was a sort of exquisite torture for both of them. The tautness of her body gave her away. Until finally it was over and he stepped back, managed a smile at the approving nod of the stall owner.

'Very fine job,' he said. 'Tomorrow the bride will look beautiful and so too will her sister. Come early and all the flowers you need will be ready.'

Zoe rose to her feet and he saw her sway slightly as though perhaps her legs were trembling in sheer desire, saw her pull herself together. 'Thank you very much. For everything. You have been wonderful.'

'It is our pleasure.' The man beamed at them. 'My great-grandfather started this stall many, many years ago, and his motto was always that happy customers make a happy business.'

As they walked away she raised her hand to touch her hair. 'I'm sorry if it was uncomfortable.'

'It wasn't.'

Zoe came to an abrupt stop and half turned, gave a gasp of surprise.

'What's wrong?' Matt, wrong-footed, stopped.

'I saw your pants catch fire,' she quipped, and he couldn't help it—he laughed.

'OK. Maybe I lied. Maybe it was a little awkward.'

'Just a bit, right?' Now she laughed too and as they started walking again he felt a pit-pat in his chest as he watched the grace of her walk, inhaled the sweet fragrance of the flowers woven into the vivid red of her hair.

'What next?' he asked.

'I want to pick up some material from one of the stalls to decorate the walls with, and I thought I'd pick up some food and we could make dinner tonight? That way we can go over the preparations for tomorrow and make sure we haven't forgotten anything.'

'Sounds good.'

Memories of the first heady months of their relationship, before Zoe had discovered she was pregnant, before he'd rushed her into marriage, before the miscarriage, popped into his head. Memories he hadn't thought of for years—the good ones submerged by the dark shadows of the final weeks of their marriage and the jagged pain of its end.

The days when she'd come round to his flat armed

with various ingredients, when they'd taken it in turns to pick new recipes and cooked together, the laughter, the fun, the times the cooking had been abandoned halfway through as attraction had simmered alongside the meal.

But that was then, and this was now. This dinner had an agenda of a different sort. Yet as they chose the vegetables…the jackfruit and sweet potatoes…anticipation grew inside him, even as he told himself it was pointless, dangerous, stupid…

CHAPTER SIX

ZOE LOOKED ROUND the kitchen and tried to quell the sense of excitement, knew it was stupid and inappropriate. They'd spent the whole of the previous evening figuring out how wrong they were for each other. A conclusion that was supposed to have knocked attraction on the head.

So why wasn't it working? Matt was one hundred per cent not her Mr Right. Wouldn't even make it to first-date status. But…her body hadn't got the memo. Worse, though, was the fact that she'd enjoyed today, enjoyed his company, enjoyed being with him. She closed her eyes, knew that she had to be careful; she would not tread the same road as before. Couldn't let attraction and liking con her into believing they had a future. It hadn't worked last time and there was no way it could work now—not when she knew he didn't want a long-term relationship or a family. So to fall for the illusion this time would be beyond foolish—she had a plan, a life plan, and she wouldn't let Matt derail it.

But no amount of common sense could stop her heart from giving a hop, skip and a jump when he entered the kitchen. Shirtsleeves rolled up, hair spiky, his brown eyes warm and relaxed, and the way he looked at her brokered memories of the past.

No, no, no!

'Perfect timing,' she said brightly. 'I've got all the in-gredients together. Do you want to chop or cook?'

'I'm at your service. I'm happy to do either.'

'You chop.' That way she could concentrate on the cooking and noting down the recipe to see if it was wor-thy of adding to her restaurant list.

Though soon enough she figured she'd got it wrong. There was something so goddamn sexy about a man chop-ping up vegetables, especially the way Matt was. Deft, competent, quick, and now she couldn't drag her eyes away from the lithe strength of his fingers, the sturdi-ness of his wrists, the smooth sculpture of his forearm.

'Ouch…' That was what happened when you got dis-tracted—she'd completely taken her attention off the pan and it spat oil at her.

Quickly she turned the heat down and turned to find him next to her. 'Hey, are you OK?'

'I… I'm fine. Honestly. I had the heat on too high and I…' The words shrivelled on her lips because right now all she could focus on were his lips, his face, the way he had taken her hand and stretched the palm out to look at it. Heat flushed her whole body and she was pretty sure it had nothing to do with the spicy scent of the chillies 'I'm fine.'

Hell and damnation. She had to stop this now. Using every effort of will, she gently pulled her hand away and turned towards the oven and Matt stepped back hurriedly as if he too realised the danger proximity brought.

'Good. Well, here are the first of the ingredients.'

And soon the kitchen was imbued with the scent of gar-lic and onions, the sizzle of chilli and ginger.

'Smells amazing,' she managed, but knew too that she wasn't only talking about the food. Because as they worked together, adding the ingredients with care, the pumpkin, beans, the raw banana and the coconut milk, it was impossible not to occasionally brush against each other, not possible not to be close enough that she could smell him, that elusive whiff of expensive soap and sheer Matt. That made her want to move closer, move in, snuggle against the hardness of his chest, feel his arms around her…

'I… Sorry, you'll need to chop some extra ingredients—we need to temper the curry. It's like the final step. It adds that extra layer of spice and intensity of taste.' But now the words took on a different meaning, and she wanted, craved, something more than food, a different type of spice, another type of intensity.

'No problem,' he said, his voice deep, and she could feel heat flush her body.

So it was almost a relief when her phone rang…a relief moderated by anxiety when she saw that it was her mum. *It's OK.* Of course they would be able to spend a few hours on a video call. For Beth's wedding. No way could this be a cancellation call. Not when her mum knew she needed to be there.

'Hi, Mum. Thank you for calling me back. I just wanted to go through the timings for tomorrow and what you need to do.'

'Actually, darling, there's been a bit of a problem.'

'What sort of a problem?' Zoe moved into the corner of the kitchen, turned slightly away from Matt as she listened.

'Your dad's been asked to make a speech at the start of the protest march. It's a great honour and of course a great responsibility and it means that we'll be on the road at the time of the ceremony.'

'But…surely someone else could make the speech? Perhaps Dad could write it and—'

'That wouldn't feel right, darling. This may even be televised, garner a lot of press—he can't shirk that duty. He has a chance to make a real difference.'

'But what about Beth? It will make a huge difference to her whether you are there. Or maybe Dad could go and you could be there.'

'No, your dad needs me by his side. And we know too that we brought you girls up to put others before yourselves. If your dad's speech can potentially change the mind of people about the climate, then it could make a difference that actually impacts on the planet. If Emmeline Pankhurst had stayed at home to attend to family matters women wouldn't have the vote today.'

As always, a sense of hopelessness prevailed, a sense that actually she was being selfish, that Zoe was a bad person to expect her parents to put family above the greater good.

Her mum said, 'There. I knew you wouldn't disappoint us. Please explain to your sister and send us photos. Love to everyone and your dad sends love as well.'

Zoe put the phone down and tried to quell the rage inside her. What she now wanted to do was break things, anything. But she wouldn't, couldn't. She'd vowed all those years ago after Tom's death to turn her life around and not let her parents get to her.

But right now that was hard, when it was Beth who would be hurt.

'Hey. Is everything OK?' She could hear the concern in his voice and she forced her face into neutral with a hint of bright.

'Absolutely fine. Sorry about that. I'll put the rice on and then we can eat.'

'Zoe. Don't.'

'Don't what?'

'Don't pretend you're OK. I can tell you're not.'

'I said I'm fine.'

'And I can see that you're not. I'd like to help.'

'I don't want to talk about it.' Somehow she needed to get the anger under control, the anger and frustration and disappointment and confusion.

'Fair enough.' He glanced round the room, walked over to a sofa and picked up a cushion, walked back and held it up.

'What are you doing?'

'You look like you'd like to hit something. Why not this? Seeing as I don't think there is a punchbag handy. It's OK to be angry—whatever it is you're angry about. Take it out on the cushion.'

Her mother's voice echoed in her ears, the time-worn excuses she'd heard time and again, and perhaps *she* could accept them, but not when they were going to hurt her sister. Lovely, kind, loving Beth, who never asked anyone for anything, who had been the perfect daughter whilst Zoe had run amok. She deserved more. The anger roiled.

Matt moved out to the centre of the room and held the pillow up. 'Go for it.'

Zoe eyed the cushion; at first she felt stupid, as though she was making a colossal fool of herself, but as he stood there, his face neutral, no judgement and not even a hint of a smile on his lips, the pillow held straight out, she shrugged. Stepped forward and lashed out.

Her first attempt was soft, still fuelled by the idea of ridicule.

'That's it, but you can hit it as hard as you like. Don't worry about feeling silly— channel the feelings, the anger, the frustration, the lack of control…whatever it is that's making you mad. Take it out on the cushion, then it doesn't have to be inside you.'

Zoe nodded. The hell with it. *Wham-wham-wham.* She slammed her fist into the cushion time and again. Each thud reverberated and for a few minutes she was lost in the sensation; the satisfaction of venting and focusing her anger did help, and finally she stopped, dropped her hands to her sides and looked at him, her breath still coming fast.

'That really did work. I feel…better, though I'm not sure why. It hasn't changed anything.' He dropped the pillow onto the sofa. 'Why do I get the feeling you've done this before?'

'I have. I'm not a counsellor, but sometimes I do work with the kids at the foundation, only under guidance, of course. Some of the kids are so angry and they can't or won't or just don't want to talk about it. That anger can lead to them punching walls and hurting themselves. So we try to help them by telling them it's OK to be angry and finding a different way to let it out. Sometimes we take them somewhere outdoors so they can scream and shout and swear. Some people like obstacle courses or massive ball pits and throwing things. Others prefer punchbags. But a cushion works too. It's a physical outlet so the anger doesn't fester so much inside you, because that's the worst of it, isn't it? It feels like you can't change it, can't control it, can't do a damn thing.'

The way he spoke the words showed an understanding that ran deep on personal levels—she knew it and the question tumbled from her lips: 'You've felt it, haven't you? Punched walls, been angry.'

He hesitated, then nodded. 'Yes. It's a long time ago, but, yes, I've punched a wall or two.' On impulse she reached out and took his hands in hers, turned them over and saw the light scars on his knuckles, ran a finger gently over them. Wondered what had triggered his anger. 'The wall won,' he said, his smile rueful. 'That's why cushions

are better. They put up less resistance. And once you've released the anger that then frees you to try and consider the
situation from a different perspective. Sometimes there's a
solution you couldn't see before, sometimes there's nothing you can do but accept it and move on.'

'I thought I had accepted it,' Zoe said with a sigh. She
walked over to the counter and stirred the curry. Saw that
he had started the rice.

'Do you want to talk about it?' he asked. 'You don't
have to, but if you think it would help?'

'I...' As she looked at him Zoe realised she did want
to. After all, it was hardly a secret—she would have to
tell him anyway. Perhaps telling him would make it easier to break the news to Beth. 'That was my mum. They
aren't going to be able to attend the ceremony tomorrow
even by video.'

'Why not?' His tone was non-judgemental.

'For the same reason they couldn't get on a flight. A
cause. They are in the midst of participating in an en-
vironmental protest, a proper organised march through
London, various sit-ins, et cetera. Dad's now been asked
to make a speech in central London and he feels it's his
duty to do it.' She shook her head. 'Actually, no, that's not
true. He wants to do it.'

'Instead of being there for his daughter?'

Zoe nodded. 'They believe the cause is more important
than the individual. It's always been like that and I know
it's wrong but sometimes it makes me angry. I used to be
angry for myself—I wanted them to come to sports days,
to concerts, even to parent-teacher evenings. But this time
I wanted them to be there for Beth, to put Beth first and
stuff the cause. Which probably makes me a bad person.'
Or an even worse person than she already was. Her attitude, her behaviour, her neediness to win her parents over,

had cost a life. She had been the one to take Tom to the dark side and then she'd left him there. And she couldn't blame her parents for that.

'Of course it doesn't. You are not a bad person, Zoe. Your parents have a duty to you and Beth. More than a duty—they should want to be there for her.'

'They do. But they believe what they want is less important than doing what is right.'

'To me, that doesn't make sense. They could do both. Someone else could make the speech. They chose to have a family—that means their family should come first. They should have come to your school sports events, your graduation and everything else.'

His words were a reminder of his own decision—to not have a family. Because he knew he couldn't put them first, that his foundation came first. The way he'd spoken about the kids and their anger, the way he empathised with them, showed her how much they mattered to him. And she couldn't help but wonder what had sparked that. He'd told her so little about his childhood, other than his parents had died when he was young and he had gone into care. That he'd had good carers and been lucky. Now she wondered, realised that they'd both drawn veils over their childhoods, relegated the past to the past. Maybe that had been a mistake.

'And I'm sorry they didn't, sorry they aren't going to be part of Beth and Dylan's wedding. But…perhaps Beth won't be as hurt as you think. It sounds as though it won't be a surprise.'

'I know. But some of the Sri Lankan traditions do centre around the mother- daughter relationship and…' Frustration wobbled her voice. 'Just once I wanted Mum to come through.'

'Can you take your mum's place?'

'No. I'm the younger sister—but it's not even that. Beth has always been the one who looked after me. It was Beth who worked out how to cook pasta, how to push a chair over to the stove. Beth worked out how to use a tin opener so we could have baked beans on toast or spaghetti hoops. Beth looked after me.' Whilst all she'd done was shout and rage and seek attention.

'Beth did what any good older sibling would do.' There was an edge to his voice and she studied his expression, saw the grim set of his lips. 'But I bet you were there for her too.'

'I…' Zoe stopped and said slowly, 'I tried. But I wasn't very good at acceptance and getting on with it. I tended to shout and scream and yell and I suppose that did sometimes achieve something. It did sometimes jolt Mum and Dad into doing things they would simply have forgotten otherwise. And I did look out for her at school.'

'Sometimes you have to scream. It sounds like you and Beth worked as a team.'

Zoe nodded. 'We did. We did everything together even if we did it differently. Until…' She broke off. Until she'd decided to go a step further for her parents' attention, until she'd taken rebellion several steps too far. 'Until we got older. But we are still really, really close.'

'Then the most important person for Beth tomorrow is you. And you will be there and you have done her proud— really you have. It's sad that your parents are as they are, but you can't change that. But what you have done is make tomorrow special for your sister. So do not beat yourself up that your parents won't be there. That's on them, not you. OK?'

'OK.' She hesitated. 'And thank you. For helping me put it all in perspective.' Reaching out, she touched his hand. 'And I'm sorry—for whatever made you punch walls.'

She allowed a hint of a question to imbue the words, but wasn't surprised when his face closed off, as though perhaps he regretted his earlier admission.

'It's OK. It was all a long time ago. Water under the bridge.' But Zoe wondered, wondered if their belief that the past didn't matter was truly valid. Gently he pulled his hand away. 'Now how about we eat and make sure we're ready for tomorrow?'

'Good plan.'

CHAPTER SEVEN

EARLY THE NEXT MORNING, Matt entered the kitchen to find Zoe already up and ready. Her hair pulled back in a pony-tail, dressed in cut-off trousers and a T-shirt, she looked ridiculously pretty, silhouetted against the beauty of the Sri Lankan sunrise.

'We can pick up breakfast at the market,' she said. 'I really fancy a freshly made egg hopper. If you don't mind going straight away.'

'Perfect.' And it was—Matt had something he wanted to do at the bazaar, an idea that had come to him the pre-vious night after their conversation. He studied her ex-pression, saw anxiety in her eyes. 'Hey. Don't look so worried. You've got this. We've got this. Beth and Dylan are going to have a happy wedding. Truly. And we're in this together, OK? Now let's get the flowers and then go and transform the hospital room.' He moved closer, tried not to be distracted by her proximity. 'Beth is lucky to have a sister like you.'

For a moment sadness panged through him as he won-dered what would have happened if his baby brother had survived—would they have formed a bond, or would Matt quite simply have felt nothing? Did the fact his parents hadn't bonded with him mean he had no abil-ity to bond with others? How he wished he had done for

Peter what Beth had done for Zoe—worked out a way to look after him.

'Right. Let's go.'

Fifteen minutes later the driver dropped them at the bazaar and they climbed out. 'You head to the flower stall. I need to go and get something. I'll explain later.'

Twenty minutes later he returned to find the car brimming with sweetly scented delicate blooms creating a veritable blaze of colour.

'Wow.'

'They're beautiful, aren't they?' Zoe said. 'But now spill. Where did you go?'

As the car drew away Matt had a sudden qualm. Maybe he shouldn't have gone off and done this without consulting Zoe.

'Matt?'

'I had an idea. I looked up some Sri Lankan wedding traditions and there's one where the brother of the groom gives the bride a necklace to welcome her into the family. I realise Dylan hasn't got a brother, but I thought maybe David could do it, and I thought maybe as Beth's sister you could do the same and give Dylan something. That way you as a sister are performing a ceremony even if your mother isn't.'

He paused for breath and studied her face, saw tears sheen her eyes. 'That is…' She sniffed. 'It's made me want to cry. It's a perfect idea.'

He shifted on the seat, a mixture of pleasure that he'd got it right mixed with a sense of embarrassment at the praise.

'I'm glad you're pleased, but it's no big deal. I hope you approve of what I got as well.' He reached into the bag and pulled out two boxes. 'I didn't want it to be too personal, more symbolic, so this is what I settled on.' He showed her the cufflinks, a simple circular design made of white gold and onyx, for Dylan, and the brooch he'd chosen for Beth, a delicate leaf design of gold.

'They will love them and they are beautiful.' She picked up her phone. 'I'll call Edwina and slot this bit into the ceremony as well.' She glanced at him. 'She's been great.'

'Yes. She is a lovely person.' Matt wondered if he should mention he'd been in touch with Edwina about the orphanage and decided not to. He understood now Zoe's reluctance to get involved with or engage in any sort of cause. Now he knew more about her parents so much more made sense. Especially her need to find a man who was a good father, who would put his family first. The box Matt could most emphatically never tick, but what he could do was be here now and make this wedding a success. 'Let's get this show on the road,' he said.

A lovely nurse greeted them at the hospital and showed them to the room where the ceremony would take place. 'I'm sorry it's so sterile, but it truly is the best room.'

'There is no need to apologise. We are so grateful the hospital agreed to the ceremony at all. And Beth and Dylan would like everyone to come and have cake later on.'

Matt turned to Zoe. 'I am in your hands. Instruct me and I will do whatever you ask.'

In truth he had no idea how to transform the clean but sterile room into anything approaching festive.

An hour later Matt looked round the room, hardly able to believe the transformation. The window was now the focal point with an arch of flowers skilfully arranged in a riotous, glorious assembly of colour and scent. Red mingled with white and twisted together to create the perfect backdrop. Drapes of gauzy material toned down the institution-coloured walls and added a touch of magic, and a trestle table in the corner held a beautifully decorated chocolate cake atop a snowy-white tablecloth covered in gold foil wedding bells.

'This is beautiful; I cannot believe you managed to make it this…magical.'

'We did it,' she said. 'I couldn't have done this on my own.'

'But it's your creation. I was just the…'

'Muscle…' she said and suddenly flushed as her gaze lingered on his shoulders and then she looked away. 'Now I'll go and help Beth get ready.' Her eyes widened in sudden anxiety.

'What's wrong?'

'How will I know how to do it? I mean, we saw it on the mannequin but—'

'Hey. Don't panic. I videoed Anesha putting the saris on the mannequins. I'll send you the video.'

'I take it back. You're not the muscle—you're the brains. Thank you.' Moving over to him, she brushed her lips against his cheek and the feeling of warmth that trickled through him was bittersweet. The urge to simply take her in his arms and hold her, to feel her head rest on his chest, was nigh on overwhelming. But he resisted, knew he needed to be careful, that he could not, would not, get involved with Zoe again. He couldn't give her what she wanted most in life and he mustn't forget that. Mustn't let her ignite the swirl and whirl of emotion that had sent him into a spin that had ended in pain and hurt and disillusionment four years before. Stepping back, she waved. 'I'll see you at the ceremony.'

Zoe smiled as Beth headed towards her, pushed all thoughts of Matt from her mind and moved forward to hug her older sister.

'Happy wedding day! I am sorry it's not how it was meant to be but—'

'It doesn't matter. Truly. We are so grateful David is alive and with us and the doctors are optimistic about his prognosis. And we are so happy to be getting married.' She stepped back, held Zoe's hands in hers. 'And thank you, Zo, with all my heart. For organising this.'

'You're welcome. I hope, really hope, I've got it right.'

'It couldn't be wrong.'

'And it wasn't just me. I couldn't have done it anywhere near as well without Matt.'

To her own annoyance she could feel heat touch her face as Beth studied her expression. 'Is there anything I should know?' her sister asked.

'Absolutely not. Definitely not. No.'

Beth raised her eyebrows. 'What was that quote again? Something about people who protest too much?'

'Not applicable here. All that has happened is that we had a proper talk, and we have decided to put the past behind us and focus on being civilised and polite so there is no awkwardness now or in the future.'

Aware of how stilted her words sounded, she frowned. 'Anyway, this is your wedding day. We don't have time to discuss Matt of all people.'

'OK. But…' Beth hesitated. 'Putting the past behind you is all well and good provided you've faced it and actually discussed it. You did, didn't you?'

'Um…sort of. But not really. You can't change the past. The past is gone, Beth. I don't want to revisit it.'

'Revisit or face?' Her sister's voice was gentle with no judgement.

'Same difference. But the most important thing is Matt and I have agreed to be civil.' Time to close this down. Beth looked way too dubious and way too interested.

'Anyhoo… It's time for you to get ready.' She pushed the door open. 'Ta-da.'

Beth's eyes widened and she raised her hand to her mouth on an intake of breath. 'It is gorgeous. Beyond beautiful.'

'And it will look even better on you. Matt videoed the shop assistant putting it on a mannequin so we should be able to figure it out. And we got a video of Matt braiding flowers into my hair, so I know how to do yours.'

'So you and Matt really did everything together.'

'Yes. He wanted to be part of it. We both wanted this to be special for you and Dylan. That's all.'

'Sure.' Beth nodded. 'And it will be, because you're here.'

'I am so sorry Mum and Dad aren't.'

'Don't be. It's not really that surprising and I'd rather they weren't here than they came grudgingly. Mum and Dad are who they are and the best thing to do is simply have no expectations of them. Because you know what? *They* miss out—they miss out on us and being a family. That's what Dylan's family have shown me. What it's supposed to be like. They all look out for each other, but they are all good people as well. They do good things, but they believe family comes first. And for me you come first. I've got your back and you've got mine and nothing can change that.'

'Nothing,' Zoe agreed and hugged her sister. 'Now, let's get you ready.'

'Let's get us ready.'

Half an hour later they looked at each other in satisfaction. 'You look stunning,' Zoe said. The cream sari flowed in elegant waves of silken material, and Beth wore it with a grace and fluidity Zoe could only hope she emulated.

'So do you.' Beth smiled mistily as there was a knock on the door and seconds later Manisha entered.

'I came to see if I could help. And to thank you, Zoe, for all you have done.'

'I enjoyed every minute,' Zoe assured her.

'And you have done a wonderful job. Beth, you look...' the older woman's eyes filled with tears and she blinked fiercely '...very beautiful. I am so grateful to you. David is thrilled that the wedding is going ahead before his operation. As am I. I know he will go into the operation more at peace.'

Beth moved forward to hug her mother- in-law-to-be. 'He is going to be all right.'

'I know, but I also know, whatever happens, I have been so lucky to have been married to the love of my life.'

'Manisha and David got married three weeks after they met,' Beth told her sister.

'Yup.' Manisha smiled. 'It is hard to believe now, but back then we were young and we knew... I can't explain it, but we knew that what we had was real. And now here we are all these years later with a wonderful son who is about to marry a wonderful woman. And I believe that David will come through this. But whatever happens I am glad that we have spent every possible moment with each other.'

Zoe blinked back tears, rose and hugged the diminutive woman.

'If anything will help bring him through, it is the knowledge that you are here.'

'Thank you.' The older woman smiled. 'Now let's go. You are such a beautiful bride, Beth, inside and out, and my son is lucky.'

Zoe smiled, filled with genuine happiness for her sister, not only that she had found the man she loved, but

that she had also been welcomed in by his family, was
secure in the knowledge that she was truly loved. Would
anyone ever feel like that about her? Did she even want
them to? It didn't matter. Soon she would start her search
for Mr Right and that was the right way forward for her.
Her first step towards a family.

Matt stood next to Dylan, saw the expression on his best
friend's face, the love as he looked at his father. David
smiled. 'Look at the door, son,' he said. 'This is a moment
you'll remember for the rest of your life.'

Matt glanced at the older man, relieved to see that, al-
though he had shadows under his eyes, his skin held some
colour and his voice was strong. He'd insisted on wearing
a shirt and tie and he was seated to the side of the window,
love and pride on his face, his wife's hand securely in his.

The love in the room, the sense of family solidarity,
was palpable and Matt felt a searing sadness that he'd
never experience this, never feel that bond. That for some
reason his parents hadn't had that basic primal love for
their children.

Then all such thoughts fled as the door opened and Zoe
and Beth came in. Perhaps he should be focused on his
best mate, on the bride, but he wasn't. All he could see
was Zoe, dressed in a shimmering grey sari shot through
with silver; the glimpse of bare shoulder and the elegant
flow of the material all complemented her natural beauty.

But it wasn't just the attire. It was the way she looked at
Beth, the grace with which she walked, the brightness of
her green eyes, flecked with happiness for her sister. Her
glance went to Matt, snagged there; her focus was fully
on him, and he hoped she saw the admiration in his eyes,
admiration and desire and the fact that she had knocked
his socks off.

And something lit in her eyes too, desire and also… perhaps a hint of wistfulness, for the memories, for the might-have-beens. For the fact that once they had embarked on this same journey and fallen at the first hurdle.

Seeing David's gaze rest on him, he pushed the thoughts away as futile and focused on the ceremony itself.

Edwina did an incredible job and everything went without a hitch. The whole ceremony was both seamless and moving, the mix of Western and Sri Lankan perfect, every vow and ritual conducted with love and meaning as Beth and Dylan promised to love each other for the rest of their days. The whole unleashed so many thoughts and in these beautiful moments Matt had a sudden wish that he could be different, could offer this rich deep relationship, and a sadness that his start in life, his own parentage, meant he couldn't.

Pushing away the thoughts, he tried to focus only on happiness for his friend. Reminded himself that he had turned his own life around, was a success, had wealth, a job he loved, a lifestyle he enjoyed, a foundation he believed in. His life was good and, as he'd told Zoe, he was perfectly content with shallow relationships full of fun.

So now he'd focus on the cake cutting, watching Beth and Dylan pose for a photo, radiant smiles on their faces.

Matt found himself next to Edwina and smiled at the celebrant. 'You did an incredible job. Thank you.'

'It is I who should be thanking you. What you are doing for the orphanage is wonderful.'

Matt shook his head. 'I want to show my appreciation to those kids that they were kind enough to release you for the morning. Organising a day out and donating some cricket gear isn't that big a deal.'

'It is to them. Half of them are cricket- obsessed.'

'I'd like to do something for the other half too. But

we can discuss that tomorrow when I come to see the orphanage.'

'We're all looking forward to it.' Edwina forked up the last bit of her cake. 'Now I need to shoot off to collect the minibus.'

As she headed off Matt caught a glimpse of silver out of the corner of his eye and turned to see Zoe, her gaze fixed on his face, and he wondered if she'd overheard the conversation. A question that was soon answered.

'That is kind of you. To donate cricket gear and organise a day out. When is it?'

'I'm not sure yet. I'm hoping to get a couple of the national cricket team to come along for a couple of hours. One of my clients is a big Sri Lankan cricket fan and sponsor so I'm hoping that will make a difference.'

'And you're visiting the orphanage too?'

'Yes, I want to thank the kids personally. And I want to see if my foundation can help the orphanage on a permanent basis. To do that I need to see for myself how the orphanage works before I commit any money to it.'

'What will it depend on?'

'Whether the whole organisation is legitimate—a lot of charities start out with excellent intent but then somehow paperwork, bureaucracy and downright dishonesty can take over. I know it sounds a bit ruthless, but I like to know the money I donate and raise genuinely helps the people who need it. Otherwise what's the point? I may feel good for being generous but that's not what it is all about.'

This he knew. There had been times as a child when he'd heard the praise heaped on his foster carers, when in fact he'd known they were in it for the money. Because he'd been the one given the cheap meals, the hand-me-down clothes, the room with the radiator turned off. Yet those carers had genuinely believed they were being good people to take him in at all.

'It doesn't sound ruthless at all,' she said. 'It sounds like the exact right thing to do. And I can hear how much you genuinely care.' She hesitated. 'Why didn't you tell me about all this?'

'I didn't want to distract you from the wedding preparations and I wasn't sure you'd want to hear about it. After what you told me about your parents, I can see that people with a big interest in a charitable cause must be problematic.'

She bit her lip and he could see trouble reflected in the green of her eyes as she shook her head. 'I do have mixed feelings about people with causes, but you're different. Everything you've just said shows me that. You're different from my parents—you've decided not to have a family because you want to prioritise your foundation.'

Matt focused on keeping his expression completely neutral as he processed her words. Zoe believed he didn't want a family because he believed his foundation was more important.

He was tempted to set the record straight, to say he fully believed you could do both, that her parents could have balanced their causes with their responsibilities as parents. After all, if they hadn't lost the baby that was exactly what Matt would have done. Again a glimpse of that future materialised and an ache for what could have been tugged inside him.

But that hadn't happened and wouldn't happen. In all consciousness he couldn't risk parenthood, yet, standing here next to Zoe, regret seeped through him. Regret and a sense of sadness. *Enough.* It was easiest to let Zoe believe what she believed. Best to focus now on helping the children he could help.

'I'll keep you posted on the orphanage from now on.'

'Actually, I was wondering if I could come with you when you visit. I'd like to thank the kids too. Without them all of this wouldn't have happened and that means a lot.'

'I'd like that.' Problem was, he suspected he liked it for all the wrong reasons: because it gave him another legitimate reason to spend time with Zoe.

At that moment Dylan rang a bell. 'Time for the speeches,' he said.

Zoe listened to the speeches, Matt's a perfect mix of serious and humour, David's short through necessity, but his words displayed dignity and a dry wit. Once he had finished Manisha stepped forward and Zoe saw Beth and Dylan exchange a look of surprise.

'My husband has asked that I also say a few more words,' Manisha said. 'We both wish to say thank you to Zoe and Matt for everything they have done. And we would like to give them a gift. Three days in Burati during the annual festival—it is a time of joy and significance and we think you will enjoy yourselves there. Have a holiday.'

Next to her David nodded and then spoke. 'It is important to me, to us, that you accept this gift.'

Zoe tried to think, her brain clouded with the sheer unexpectedness of the gesture. David and Manisha knew that she and Matt were divorced—so why on earth would they do this? A quick glance at Beth and Dylan indicated they were as taken aback as Zoe was. But what she could also see was that, for whatever reason, this was important to David. A man who was about to go into potentially life-threatening surgery.

So she wasn't surprised when Matt moved next to her. 'We need to accept,' he murmured. 'And sort it out later.'

With that he stepped forward.

'That is a very kind gift and we thank you both very much.'

Soon after that the nurses and hospital staff dispersed back to duties and, after a chat with David and Manisha, Beth and Dylan headed towards Zoe and Matt.

'We had no idea they were going to do that,' Beth said.

'I know. But the point is, what are we supposed to do?'

Dylan sighed. 'I've just spoken to Dad. I'm not sure if it's the medication, or something to do with the operation, but he is adamant he wants you to go. Says he owes it to Matt.'

Matt raised his eyebrows. 'He does remember Zoe and I are divorced?'

'Yup.' Dylan shook his head. 'I genuinely don't get it, but he got quite agitated when we tried to explain it may be awkward for you both.'

'I hope you told him we'll go,' Zoe said. 'The whole point of today was for everyone to be happy and for David to be at peace before the operation.' Manisha's face when she'd spoken of her husband filled her mind and on impulse she left the group as a nurse was getting ready to wheel David from the room.

'I wanted to thank you both for the gift,' she said. 'And tell David that we will go.'

'Is that a promise?' His voice was dry, held a hint of scepticism.

'It's a promise.' Looking up, Zoe saw that Matt was behind her, his voice deep and full of reassurance.

'Good.' The older man smiled, a smile that lit up his face. 'Then I'll see you on the other side.'

As he was wheeled from the room followed by his family Zoe looked at Matt. 'What are we going to do?'

Matt held her gaze. 'What do you want to do?' he asked softly.

His gaze held hers and she gulped, wanted to shy away

from the truth. Because she wanted to go with him. Knew it was foolish, knew that in truth she couldn't even justify it. But that didn't mean she wasn't going to give it a damn good go.

'I think we have no choice. We have to go. We promised him, a man about to have a life-threatening operation. I don't think we can lie to him or renege.' She frowned. 'I just wish I understood why it mattered so much to him.'

Matt frowned. 'I don't know. Perhaps it *is* something to do with his medication, or perhaps it is simply a nagging feeling he owes me a debt for rescuing Dylan all those years ago. Whatever his reasoning, I think you're right. We'll have to go.'

Zoe tried to stem the stupid anticipation that welled up inside her. It was only a few days, one day at the orphanage and three in Burati. They had no choice; they couldn't refuse the wishes of a man about to enter the operating theatre for a bypass operation. Four days. It was nothing in the scheme of things.

'OK. It'll be fine,' she said brightly. 'It may even be fun.'

CHAPTER EIGHT

THE FOLLOWING DAY as the car travelled towards the orphanage Zoe watched the lush landscape whizz past and contemplated the day ahead. She was glad of the chance to thank the kids who'd helped make Beth's wedding possible. But she was also glad of this trip for other reasons.

She wanted to see Matt in action, physical proof that he had chosen this cause above family. A much-needed reminder of why Matt was not and could not be Mr Right. Because that was the best way to kill off any burgeoning feelings before they could take root. And she sensed if they were to spend more time together, then that was a must for her.

So today was the perfect way of showing common sense the futility of attraction to a man who had a cause.

As the car glided to a halt Zoe looked around at the group of houses in a large fenced area. The whole area looked welcoming and well kept. Curtains fluttered in the windows and plants were dotted around the doors in big heavy pots, the yard was well swept and there was a fenced-off garden that boasted a healthy-looking vegetable patch.

As they climbed out of the car Edwina came to greet them, a wide smile on her face. 'Thank you so much for coming.'

'It's no problem. I'm very happy to be here.'

'I thought you'd maybe like to look around, and then perhaps you'd join the kids for lunch.'

'That sounds perfect.'

The tour of the houses showed small but well-kept rooms. The rooms were shared but each child had their own designated area.

'I like that,' Matt said to Edwina. 'That everyone clearly has their own personal space.'

She nodded. 'I believe that is important. They need stability and as much as possible they need to know this is their home. Once here we do everything to make each child settle in and know that this is where they can stay until they are adults. When they do have to leave, I try, I really do, to help them to their next place. It is not as if they wake up on their eighteenth birthday and can look after themselves without support. But transitioning is difficult.' She glanced at her watch. 'I am sorry but I will need to hand you over to Prisha now. She runs the kitchens. My shift at the local hospital starts soon. Any questions, please ask and I'll do my best to help. This is a good place—I hope your foundation will help.'

They followed Edwina to the kitchen. 'This is Prisha. She is in charge of the kitchens and cooking.' Zoe smiled at the young woman, who was holding a toddler by the hand and an infant in a sling. She hoped she kept the expression of surprise from her face, but the young woman gave a soft laugh.

'I am young, but I am very good at what I do and I am also very grateful for the job. It is all thanks to Edwina.' She met Zoe's gaze. 'My story, I believe, is common throughout the world. My family are poor. They also believe in some traditions and customs that I do not. I was married off and my marriage was not a happy one.' A shadow crossed her face and made Zoe want to reach

out and hold her, and next to her she saw Matt's fists
clench. 'In the end I left—I couldn't let anything happen
to my children. The first time he hit Tomas I knew I had
to leave. I was pregnant and terrified. If my husband had
caught me he would have killed me—I managed to hide
aboard a cart. But Tomas cried. I was lucky. The driver
did not take me back to my husband—instead he brought
me here. I will be grateful to that man until my dying day.
Now my babies will have a good life, without pain and
fear. Edwina heard my story and she gave me sanctuary
and offered me this job.'

Matt's body tensed beside her and she heard his intake of breath, knew he must be as moved as she was by
this story.

The young woman shook her head. 'Do not look so sad.
My story is a happy one, with a good ending. But now let
me show you the kitchens. Tomas and I will show you.
But first would you also like to see Adam?'

She tugged the sling open and Zoe saw the beauty of
the baby and felt a profound gratitude that this one's in-
nocence would be intact, hoped that Tomas couldn't and
didn't carry any memories of his start, blessed the courage
of this woman and the man who had helped her.

As they went round the kitchen, which was clean and
organised, listening to Prisha explain how she devised
the menu and encouraged the children to help, Zoe asked
questions, impressed by how versatile the young woman
was.

'But I would like more varied recipes.'

'Perhaps I can help. I'd love to come up with some new
stuff for you to try.'

'I'd like that.' Prisha smiled.

It was only then that it occurred to Zoe how quiet Matt
had been on this part of the tour; she really hoped he

wasn't questioning Prisha's capabilities to do the job. An anxiety that increased as she saw how closed his face was. Perhaps Prisha shared her concern as at the end she turned to Matt. 'I hope you like what you've seen?'

'Absolutely. I think you are doing a wonderful job. My only concern is whether two children and this is too much for you.'

'No. Truly it isn't. I still have plenty of time with Tomas and Adam. The kids all help out as well. Tomas sees them all as family. Truly, it is not too much at all.'

'I'm glad and, as I said, I think you are doing a fantastic job.'

His smile was warm, yet Zoe sensed his tension, saw that his hands were slightly clenched, watched his fingers unfurl as they made their way from the kitchen towards the dining area, where two large trestle tables were surrounded by benches where about twenty children ranging in age from about seven to seventeen sat, eyeing their arrival with curiosity.

Matt moved to the head of the table, once again completely at ease, and Zoe wondered what it had been about Prisha that had caused him to tense up.

'I won't do a big speech. Zoe and I just wanted to thank you for the loan of Edwina yesterday. My friend and his fiancée were able to get married thanks to your kindness and I'd like a way to say a big thank you. For the cricket lovers amongst you I've arranged a trip to a match, and you'll get to meet the national team afterwards and have a knock around with them.'

There was a general outcry of sheer joy and Zoe couldn't help but smile as she saw the dazed happiness on the faces of most of the tables' occupants. Most but not all, and Matt continued.

'Now, I know that there may be among you a few who

are not cricket fans—if so, please feel free to come and have a chat to me and I can work out another way to thank you.'

The lunch was delicious, fresh and aromatic and the talk round the table was mostly cheerful, though she noticed Matt was involved in a conversation with one of the older boys, his face sullen and brooding.

There was a tug on her sleeve. 'Did he mean it?' Zoe smiled at the girl of about twelve, her hair in two tight plaits, a serious look on her face. 'Did the man mean it? That if we don't like cricket we can truly ask for something else?'

'Yes, he did.'

'Oh.'

The girl lapsed into silence and Zoe looked down at her. 'So I take it you don't like cricket?'

She shook her head emphatically.

'So what would you like to do?'

'I would like to go shopping and buy books. I've read all the books here. I love them. But I'd love some new books. One day I'm going to write a book. That's my dream. Ravima says there is no point to dreaming, but I think there is.'

A girl Zoe estimated to be sixteen or so turned. 'I didn't exactly say that, Nimali. I said some dreams have no chance of coming true.'

'But you still have to try,' Nimali persisted.

'Why bother? There is no point trying if you know there is no chance of success. Much better to accept your fate.' There was a bitterness in her voice.

Zoe wasn't sure if Ravima was aware, but the surrounding conversations had tapered away and everyone was listening to the girl.

'Ravima is right. This is the life we were born to, and

nothing can change that.' This came from the youth sitting next to Matt and there was no mistaking the harshness in his voice. 'Certainly not some stupid day out—it achieves nothing except to make you feel better about yourselves. Then you'll disappear and not give us another thought.'

'That is not what I meant, Chaneth,' Ravima said. 'It is kind of them to organise a day. But dreams bring only misery.'

Matt rose to his feet and Zoe saw the darkness shadow his eyes before he blinked the demons away.

'I believe there is nothing wrong with dreaming as long as you also keep yourself grounded in reality. My background is similar to some of yours. I ended up without parents, in care. I dreamt of success, of making it, and those dreams did help me escape from reality for a while. I dreamt of being a famous footballer, a world-famous chef… In the end my dream was to be successful. In the end I did make it.' He turned to Ravima. 'If you—' he gestured around '—if any of you want to come and tell me your dreams, your ambitions, I will give you advice. Some dreams may not be realistic, but you should all dare to dream. One day they may be possible.'

'Rubbish! You're wrong to say this stuff—you're just raising false hope.' Chaneth picked up his plate and smashed it on the floor before striding from the room.

Matt turned to everyone else, his voice even. 'The offer stands. Zoe and I will be in the office for a few hours this afternoon.'

With that he turned and left the room and Zoe followed him, half running to keep up as he strode down the hallway towards the office.

'Matt?'

But before he could reply they heard footsteps behind them and Ravima and Nimali came into the room.

'We wanted to say sorry and ask you not to be angry with Chaneth. He isn't a bad person and please don't take away the day out because of what he said.'

'Whoa.' Matt stepped forward. 'I am sure Chaneth is not a bad person. You have nothing to apologise for and of course I won't take the day away. But I would like to know what your dream is, Ravima. If you want to tell me.'

The teenager shrugged, her chin jutting out as if daring them to laugh. 'I want to be a lawyer.' She glanced away. 'I know it's stupid. I could barely read when I got here a few years ago.'

'But you can read way better now and you learnt English really quickly and I think there must be a way,' Nimali said.

Matt looked at them and his face softened. 'I think there is a way. I can't guarantee you will become a lawyer, Ravima, but I can look into a way to provide you with more educational opportunities that would put you on the path to achieving it.'

'Really? You would do that?'

'I promise I will try. I don't know how the Sri Lankan educational system works but I will at least see what may be possible.'

'And you will help Chaneth too?'

'If I can.'

The girls left the room and Zoe studied Matt's face, saw a sudden tiredness there, could guess its cause.

'Chaneth's outburst wasn't true.'

'Wasn't it?' he asked. 'Perhaps I shouldn't have said what I said about dreams; perhaps all I did do was give false hope.'

'I don't believe that.' Her voice was gentle now. 'You didn't tell everyone you could make all their dreams come true, you offered advice and told them to dare to dream. And that is right.'

'Morally yes, but practically… I don't know.' He rose to his feet. 'Would you hold the fort here whilst I go and see if I can find Chaneth?'

'Of course.'

Two hours later Matt walked slowly down the corridor, trying to school his expression into one of neutrality, wanting to hide the effect of the past few hours. He was used to meeting kids who'd been through a lot, but it didn't really get easier. Each story harrowed him, even as he took a deep satisfaction in being able to help. But sometimes even that couldn't erase the sadness or the pain he felt for each child for what they had gone through.

Of course, some stories affected him more than others, triggered memories of his own and highlighted his own past. Chaneth's was one of those. So too was Prisha's. When he'd seen her with her two children, something had twisted inside him. Once he and his brother would have been like those two, endangered by a parent. Or, in their case, both parents. And in their case there had been no rescue for Peter, just for Matt.

He pushed the door open and paused on the threshold. Zoe was sitting at the desk, notebook open, pen in hand.

'Did you find Chaneth?'

'Yes.'

'Is he OK?' She shook her head. 'Stupid question. He obviously wasn't. But did you talk to him?'

'Yes.'

'You look upset. Do you want to talk about it?'

For a moment he almost did. But that wasn't the way he worked. Better to lock the emotion down, focus on work, focus on anything other than feelings. Plus, talking to Zoe was pointless—in a few days they would part ways. He didn't want to get used to having her around, could still remember the sheer depth, the dark ravine of pain of missing her the first time round. So distance was important.

'I'm good. I need to look at the books and records now and then we can head back.'

Hurt flitted across her face before she nodded. 'I'll go and see if I can help Prisha with dinner. Let me know when you're ready to leave.'

'Sure.'

To his relief all the paperwork showed that the orphanage was run well, with the residents' well-being clearly being the priority. Once done, he locked everything away and went in search of Zoe, halting on the threshold to the kitchen.

Zoe was holding the baby, looking down at him with such an expression of tenderness that something twisted in Matt's chest. This was how she would have looked at their baby. This was how his own mother had never looked at him.

Zoe looked up. 'Isn't he beautiful?' she said softly. 'Why don't you hold him?'

His heart hammered his ribcage even as he told himself not to be foolish. Forcing himself forward, he managed a smile, looked down at Adam and a memory zinged across his mind. Someone, some fuzzy figure, holding a baby out to him. 'Would you like to hold him?' The voice harsh, abrasive, with a mocking tone to it.

He stepped backwards, tried not to flinch. Was it a real memory or a fabrication of his imagination? 'He's gorgeous.' He forced the words out. 'But now we need to leave.'

CHAPTER NINE

ZOE GLANCED ACROSS at Matt as the car carried them back to the resort. He was looking down at his laptop, had apologised but said he wanted to get on with the work whilst it was all fresh in his mind.

Which Zoe knew to be nonsense. Put simply, Matt didn't want to talk to her. And, exactly as he had done in their marriage, he was using work as an excuse. The car pulled up at the resort and they climbed out. 'I'd better get on with this,' he said. 'But I'll be ready to leave bright and early tomorrow.'

'Cool,' she said, even as hurt touched her.

She bit her lip, aware that she'd simply assumed she and Matt would eat together, discuss the day's events, plan for the next few days.

Entering her villa, she opened the well-stocked fridge and stared at the contents. Closed the door and drummed her fingers on the worktop. Matt had been hurting, she knew that, had seen it and, damn it, she wanted to help him. Just as he had helped her. So this time she wasn't going to let him push her away.

Before she could change her mind she got up and headed to the door, exited her villa and walked down the path to his and knocked loudly on the door.

A couple of minutes and he answered.

'I'm going to cook an omelette and I wondered if you want some.'

'Thanks, Zoe, but I'm not hungry.'

He looked as though he was going to shut the door and she jumped in. 'OK. I lied. I'm not here about omelettes really. I thought you may want to talk. Or if you don't want to talk maybe you could use some company. Maybe I could hold the pillow and you could punch it. Or... I could sit in a corner and have a cup of cocoa.' She could see reluctance on his face. 'I opened up to you and it helped me. I'd like to return the favour.'

'You don't have to do that. I don't really do talking.'

'Fine, we won't talk. How about we go for a walk or a run? Along the beach. Perhaps a run would help.'

He looked down at her and then gave the smallest of smiles. 'You're not going to go away, are you?'

'Nope.'

'OK. Actually, a run sounds good.'

'Good.'

Five minutes later, both changed into shorts and T-shirts, they were jogging down to the beach, the evening temperature perfect, a breeze that countered the remaining heat from the day.

It didn't take long to settle into a rhythm, to work out how to run at the same pace. A sideways glance saw how easily he ran, each stride even and unlaboured as he pounded down the sand, and soon they were caught in the moment, the adrenalin of the exercise, the lap of the waves and the golden glint of the moonlight on the sand.

'Is it OK if we sprint the final bit?' he asked, and she nodded, sensed he needed to let go, to pound out his feelings and his emotions.

Soon the sand flew under their feet and she watched as he headed away from her, running as though there were demons at his back, and she wondered if in fact there were exactly that. Couldn't help but admire the beauty of him in action, the strength of his back, the muscular strength of his legs, the ripple of thigh muscle, the movement of his arms.

She shivered as he eventually slowed down into a jog and she caught up with him as he came to a stop and sank down onto the sand. She dropped down next to him and he turned.

'Thank you,' he said. 'I needed that.'

'I'm not surprised.' She drew a pattern in the sand. 'I didn't expect it, but, spending time at the orphanage, I liked those kids. A lot. Enough that I care.'

'It happens,' he said.

'But it must be exhausting, if you care about all the kids you meet.'

'You learn to manage it, but some cases hit home more than others.'

'Like Chaneth? I'm not asking you to break his confidence, but if I can help in any way I'd like to.'

'His story isn't a secret, but it is a traumatic one. His parents were criminals, caught up in gang warfare. Chaneth was brought up to follow in their footsteps. Pickpocketing, drug running, the works. Then when he was fourteen his parents were gunned down. He took to the streets and ended up headed to prison. Edwina heard about his case, stepped in and brought him to the orphanage. But he says he doesn't know any other life, is convinced it is in his blood, that once he goes he'll go back to a life of crime. That his family will make him. He believes he can't fight his genes, his blood.'

'But that's not true.'

Matt shrugged. 'But it's what he feels, Zoe. The pull of the life he knows, the tug of family, the knowledge that his parents did bad things.' His voice was grim, his eyes were shadowed and she sensed how much he cared for this young man's plight. 'I took him to a boxing gym and he exhausted himself. But that's not a long-term solution.'

'It's all so sad,' she said fiercely. 'So many of their stories are tragic.'

'Yes. But that doesn't mean they need pity.'

She glanced at him. 'There is a difference between pity and sympathy.'

'I know that, but it's a fine line. Those children need practical help—Chaneth needs a home and a job.'

'They need emotional help too.'

'I know. Chaneth punched a bag harder than I've ever seen anyone hit anything. After that we talked.' He raised a hand. 'I realise that's not enough. I'm going to look into finding a counsellor.'

Zoe hesitated. 'Did you ever have counselling?' she asked. 'After your parents died?'

'No. The social workers tried but I wasn't receptive. I accept and believe counselling is effective and useful...'

'But not for you?'

'Not for me.' He smiled. 'I managed fine without it.'

'It must have been awful though. I was speaking to Nimali. She told me about her background—she actually came from a fairly wealthy family and her parents sounded amazing. Loving, kind and wanted the best for her. But they died in a flood when Nimali was seven. She had no family willing to take her in and so she ended up in the orphanage.' Zoe shook her head. 'She is so brave; she told me, though, that what helps her are memories of her parents. She knows she was loved and she can still talk to them, even if she has to imagine their answers. It made me think of you—I guess it does help to have good memories.'

'Yes.' His voice was oddly colourless. 'I think it also helps that the orphanage offers the chance of moving into an extended family. The care system in the UK doesn't work like that. They place individual children into families who are paid to foster them. The problem with that for a child is he feels he's there because he is a job, and that however much the foster family appears to care for him, and may really care for him, he's a commodity. Or at least I did. It's a cost-benefit thing—is the child worth the money you're being paid?'

'That's horrible.' Zoe's heart ached at the thought of the serious dark-haired little boy estimating his own value.

'Yes and no. At the end of the day the system ensures you have a roof over your head and are fed and watered. And its aim is to make you feel part of the family, but that doesn't really work, because obviously you aren't. One of my families was great—I was there four years, but then the woman's mum got ill and needed to come to live with them. They needed my room so that was that. I was moved on. That won't happen to Nimali and I'm glad of that, because you can see how close they all are and how they look out for each other.' He leant back, rested on his arms as he looked out to sea. 'Perhaps I should also think of a way for them to stay in touch.'

'You could build or rent homes—they could move into them when they were eighteen, maybe flatshare. They would still need to pay rent and bills, but they could learn slowly rather than be catapulted to independence. Then those who wanted to stay local and stay in touch could do so more easily. It could be like a two-year transitional thing.'

He sat up straighter and looked directly into her eyes. 'That is an excellent idea. You do really care.'

'Yes. I do. I didn't expect to—I mean, I never once felt

like this about any of my parents' causes. Maybe because they felt so abstract. This is real—I've seen it, met the people and I want to make a difference to their lives. My parents never made anything personal—they are activists. They organise marches, write letters, protest, and I get that that all has a place and is important, but it never fired me up.' She leant forward in the dusk. 'So I'm sorry if I ever was negative about your foundation or your cause. You are making a massive difference, not just here, but in all the work you do. Nimali told me that she hoped to make her parents proud of her. I know your parents would have been proud of you.'

The reaction was instant and unmistakeable.

The light in his eyes snuffed out and his gaze shadowed, and she could feel the tension stiffen his body; his lips twisted into a grimace and now palpable anger etched his features.

'I'm sorry.' Damn it. The man had made it clear he didn't want to discuss his parents; it was clearly a grief he kept close to himself and didn't want to air. He'd barely mentioned them during their marriage and earlier he'd closed down rather than speak of them. 'I didn't mean to bring back painful memories. I just wanted to show you what an amazing job you are doing, what a difference you are making. But I shouldn't have brought your parents into it. I can't imagine how much you would have grieved and…' Oh, God. Why couldn't she shut up?

'I didn't grieve.' He sounded as if the words were torn out of him.

'I don't understand.' She shifted on the sand so she could see him more clearly, the pain on his face more jagged now. 'You don't have to tell me if you don't want to.'

'I do have to tell you, because hearing you speak of them as though they were good people who cared about

me is wrong. They weren't. In truth I don't know if they
are alive or dead or rotting in prison.'

A chill ran through her and she reached out and covered
his hand, unsure if he even noticed the touch.

'They weren't good parents. They weren't good people.
When social services intervened I was half-starved, dirty,
and I could barely speak—I was five years old. I don't really remember those years. My parents are hazy figures,
the sound of a rough voice, the smell of cigarette smoke,
a hazy, fuzzy outline. From what I can gather I survived
mostly because of other people. Friends or neighbours
who would see me hanging around and give me scraps,
and I think I used to scavenge in bins. So, no, my parents
weren't people I wish to remember and I certainly don't
want them to be proud of me.'

Zoe blinked back tears fiercely, knew how little Matt
would appreciate them, knew he would see it simply as
pity. And what she felt was compassion along with a mol-
ten jolt of fury at the thought of his parents.

'I am beyond sorry for what you went through. There
are no words that can encompass the anger I feel towards
your parents and I know that my anger must be a drop in
the ocean compared to your own. But...' She shifted forward now, looked directly at him, took in the dark hair
lit by moonlight, the cragginess of his features, the jut of
his jaw, saw the shadows in his eyes. Reaching up, she
cupped his jaw. The stubble made her skin tingle and for
some reason made her want to cry. 'You...you are amazing. I am filled with such admiration for you. For that five-
year-old who somehow negotiated that terrible beginning
and foster care.' Her voice wobbled. 'I don't know how
you came to terms with it all, but you did and then you
grew into a good, caring person who helps others. So you
should be proud of you.'

She shifted forward and, oh, so lightly brushed her lips across his, felt the shiver that ran through them both and then he shifted backwards.

She narrowed her eyes, knew what he was thinking. 'That wasn't a pity kiss, Matt Sutherland. It was a kiss of sheer desire for a man who I admire and fancy the pants off. It was a kiss to say thank you for sharing that with me. A kiss to say you are absolutely incredible. Got it?'

For a moment he simply glowered at her and then a small reluctant smile tipped his lips up. 'Got it.'

She rose to her feet, knew it was important now to keep things light, instinctively knew he wouldn't want an in-depth discussion of what he'd shared. 'So how does that omelette sound now? We can eat and talk about the next few days.'

'Sounds like a plan.'

'Good. I'm excited about the festival in Burati—it sounds beyond amazing. And so does the train journey.'

CHAPTER TEN

ZOE WAS RIGHT, Matt reflected the next day as they boarded the bright blue train that would take them to Burati. The open carriages were busy but not too busy and he saw food vendors climb aboard alongside them holding trays of food that made his mouth water and lit Zoe's eyes with interest.

No doubt in his mind that she would somehow find a way to communicate with at least one vendor and get a recipe for the street food on offer.

Warmth trickled over his chest and he knew the smile on his face would hold a hint of goofiness, but somehow the previous day had lightened him in some way. Sharing the truth about his parents had made him feel…lighter. *Careful, Matt.* Light was good, but he didn't need to get carried away towards goofiness. He and Zoe had trod that path, he'd let her in and in the end she'd left, moved on. Proving the dangers of getting involved, forming connections. They never lasted, just as none of his foster placements had. This time with Zoe was finite and he'd better not forget it.

But that didn't mean he couldn't enjoy her company for the next few days. Zoe looked round the train. 'This is so cool. I looked it up and we can even stand in the open doorways if we're careful. And the views are meant to be incredible.'

They absolutely were. As the journey continued they sat and watched, mesmerised by the scenery that sometimes flashed by the window or more often sauntered past as the train wound its way across the tracks. The landscape segued and morphed, the scent of the tea plantations wafting in through the windows an almost heady aroma as they saw the women in brightly coloured saris tend the fields, the sunlight glinting off the crops. Then from tea they moved to mountains and rolling hills shrouded in mist, villages where children played, then in a blink of an eye woodlands zipped past the windows.

But if he was a hundred per cent honest, despite the undeniable beauty of the landscape he found his gaze flicking to Zoe. Dressed simply in cropped trousers and a sleeveless vest top, she looked fresh, cool and ridiculously pretty. He recalled last night, the brush of her lips against his, and desire jolted through him.

It was a relief to see the food vendor enter the carriage and he grinned as Zoe turned and rose to approach him, watched the dialogue conducted mostly in gestures as she purchased a selection of the aromatic snacks and brought them over to him.

'I have no real idea what these are but they smell incredible. So I need you to taste them and try and figure out what's in them. I think this is a *vadai*—it's like a savoury doughnut made of lentils—and then these are mini samosas, and I'm not sure what this is—a kind of roll. Imagine if… No, imagine *when* I can make these. They will make the most amazing starters or shared platter as a dish.'

Matt took a bite and closed his eyes. 'Definitely cumin and chilli and maybe a hint of lime,' he stated.

Zoe picked one up and tasted it. 'Maybe a pinch of fennel as well.'

Again his gaze lingered on her, the lushness of her lips, the look of intense concentration as she savoured the food.

'What? Sorry, have I got crumbs all over me?' she asked.

'No. I was just thinking I'm glad we did this. Accepted David and Manisha's gift.' Though once again he wondered what David's motives had been.

'Me too.'

Now there was a silence, almost as if they were cocooned from the sounds of the other passengers, the whoosh of the breeze through the windows. Their gazes meshed and Matt couldn't help it—he smiled. 'Me too, too.'

Her answering smile lit her face. 'Good. I'm glad.' She took a deep breath. 'Over the next few days shall we try to enjoy ourselves? It is such good news that David's op went well, and the prognosis is good, and this is such a beautiful place to be... I don't want to have to keep worrying about giving out the wrong signals. We both know this can't go anywhere, whatever this is between us, so let's just relax.'

For a fraction of a moment he hesitated. The words made sense, he did know this could go nowhere, but that knowledge was fighting against a hope that somehow it could. A misguided hope that he had to shut down. And the best way to do that would be to call a halt now; he should get off at the next platform and take the train back. But he couldn't. Not when he saw how relaxed Zoe looked, the spark in her eye, the anticipation. It would be OK— it only three days; he'd take care... 'Suits me.' Yet a sense of disquiet remained for the rest of the journey to Burati, the beautiful city nestled in the hills of Sri Lanka.

They alighted from the train and looked around the bustling station, the noise and colour and sheer vibrancy

derful thing and here in this place it is authentic and clearly provides comfort and peace.'

Zoe considered his words. 'Do you think the kids at the orphanage go to temple?' she asked. 'Or church? Or do you think they've lost their faith because of what happened to them?'

Matt looked arrested. 'I don't know,' he said. 'But it's something I'll ask. See if that is something we can provide more access to—a spiritual person. Not to convert them, but perhaps to find out about that aspect of their backgrounds.' He squeezed her hand. 'Where to now? I was thinking you may want to sample some restaurants, get some ideas? So we could map out a selection. I did find one near here that we could start with. I asked one of the hotel staff, a groundsman. He says his parents own it and it's the real thing.'

'That sounds perfect.' Too perfect. Irrationally she wanted to ask him not to be so thoughtful. *Ridiculous.* Thoughtful was good and liking Matt was fine. Presumably you couldn't have a shallow relationship with someone you didn't like. The key was to remember Matt was being thoughtful and kind and relaxed *because* this was a shallow, fun relationship. Just as he'd been before she'd fallen pregnant and they'd got married. After that, yes, he'd been thoughtful in that he'd worked his butt off to provide, but he hadn't been relaxed. He'd pulled away from her because he didn't want a family or commitment. So however thoughtful he was, he was not Mr Right. But that didn't mean she couldn't enjoy the moment. The here and now.

It was a mantra she stuck to over the next days, days that passed in a haze of food and drink and sightseeing and nights filled with magic and joy. They toured the botanical gardens, visited a tea plantation and took evening walks around the central lake. And, of course, continued their tour of restaurants, spent ages researching and planning.

'I've got high hopes of this one,' Zoe said on day four of their stay as they wandered the now familiar streets, chatting or silent as the mood took them until they reached the small restaurant tucked into a meandering alleyway, crowded with a market that seemed to have sprung up from nowhere.

The restaurant itself was filled with locals and brightly lit, the inside held square plastic tables and the aroma that wafted out made Zoe pause and simply inhale in sheer appreciation.

'Lead on,' she said, and soon they were tucked into a tiny table looking down at an all-vegetarian menu. A waiter headed towards them and Zoe beamed at him. 'I'd like to have the *masala dosa*. I've had them in India but never here.'

'Ours are much better,' he said promptly. 'Here we use more *dal* and less rice in the batter and you will love our filling, though it is spicy. It also comes with coconut chutney and various sauces.'

'Perfect.'

'I'll have the *thali* and the potato *bonda*,' Matt said. He smiled at her after the waiter had gone. 'And you're welcome to try all of it—that way you'll get a wide-ranging sample.'

Zoe smiled at him. 'Thank you. Really. The *bonda* sounds yummy and you can obviously have some of my *dosa*. If you can take the spice,' she added with a teasing grin that called an answering one from him.

'As long as it's not like that curry we had on our third date.'

Zoe gurgled with laughter. 'I don't think I'll ever forget your face when you tasted it.' They had been discussing hot food and Matt had decided to try the hottest thing on the menu, a vegetarian phall.

'The worst thing was that there was a part of me thinking I should tough it out, be macho, and a sane part of me pointing out that at worst I'd die, at best I'd turn bright red and run round the restaurant with flames coming out of my mouth.' He sipped his beer and laughed. 'Thank goodness you came up with a solution.'

'Yup. I suggested we ask them to package it up and we could use it as a condiment. Not that we ever did.'

'Well, if any of the curries here are of a similar heat I'll know what to do.' He leant back slightly. 'On a serious note, though, what will you do if you open a restaurant in the UK? I mean, it is possible that the heat levels that are authentic will be too much for the British palate. You hear a lot about Asian restaurants having to trade in authenticity for realism and profit.'

She nodded. 'Of course. There is no point providing authentic food that will actually cause discomfort to your customers, or that no one will eat. I think the answer is to be honest. On the menu you say you have kept it as "real" as possible, but you've dialled down the chilli side of it. And maybe have different grade levels and I also thought, based on our experience, perhaps you provide authentic taster cups—so customers can have the tiniest taste of why I've dialled it down.' She paused for breath. 'Or I decide to appeal to a niche audience of people who really like hot food and I make my restaurant based on authentic hot food, or I have hot food on the menu. But obviously I'm not Sri Lankan or Indian so, again, I need to be honest. I kind of want it to be themed with the idea of food from my travels…' She paused again as the waiter arrived with their food. 'Sorry, I'll stop burbling on.'

'You aren't burbling at all. I'm interested.'

She popped a piece of *dosa* into her mouth and closed her eyes to savour the taste. 'This is incredible.' She sighed suddenly. 'And maybe I could create a *masala dosa* as good as this with my own spin—but I know starting a restaurant is so much more than being able to cook.' She looked at him. 'However good a cook I am, it takes more, and I know that. Just like, presumably, however good you are at investing, that's not enough to set up your own business.'

'No. I made sure I had plenty of capital saved. I also had a pretty good reputation and I started small. A few select clients. Also good publicity. And a plan—short-, medium-and long-term goals.'

She nodded. 'I thought I'd set up small—travel round the UK to various festivals and street markets—whilst I'm also working a paid job.'

'Also use social media. If you can gather a large following, or catch the eye of a prominent food critic, or get enough local interest so that a national paper interviews you, that will make a massive difference. I'd start right now—start a food blog, get yourself on YouTube.' He smiled at her. 'What about a long-term goal?'

'If I'm dreaming big I'd like to own at least three restaurants. I'd like a Michelin star. I'd like to write a bestseller cookbook. In reality, though, I would be really happy with one established, profitable restaurant that gave me job fulfilment and security to support my family.' *Family.* The word brought a sudden awkwardness to the flow of conversation, a blip.

'Perhaps your Mr Right will be in the restaurant business,' he said, and she looked at him. At first glance there was nothing but ease in his stance or expression, but she could see the slight set to his jaw and a shade of rigidity to his shoulders.

And as she studied him further it became harder and harder to even picture the fuzziest image of any 'Mr Right'. *Enough.* This was all about attraction and liking each other. That did not make Mr Right. A thrill of caution ran through her, a sudden temptation to up and run, a fear that she was getting pulled in almost without realising it. So perhaps now was a good time to focus on her future just for a while. A reminder that this was a temporary bubble on her way to her dream, a single finite layer of her life.

'Perhaps,' she said. 'But I'd rather he wasn't.'

'Why?'

'Because we would be too interdependent. I need to know that, if it comes to it, I can support my children by myself. And there is also a chance that Mr Right won't materialise. In which case I'll be having children on my own. So I need my business to be mine and I need it to generate enough income to provide my kids with a good life.' As she thought about the idea of children, the ship steadied for a moment. A small boy, dark hair mussed and spiky, brown eyes and a wide gummy smile, a replica of…of Matt.

Oh, hell and damnation.

This had to stop. Matt did not want children; there would be no mini Matts. Now she scrunched her eyes closed, determinedly conjured up a red-haired little girl and a blond boy, both of them with green eyes. That was better, much better.

'And I want to be there for my kids. So if that means toning down my business dreams in favour of my family, that's good with me. I will not miss a single important moment—I want to be there for their first smile, first tooth, first step…'

He gave an almost imperceptible flinch and she broke

off, wanted to kick herself round the restaurant and out on the street. Because Matt's parents hadn't given a damn about his first anything, hadn't cared enough to even give him enough food or clothes and that must hurt. But his gaze met hers and she knew that he would take any apology as pity, a pity that he would take as an insult.

'That is as it should be,' he said evenly. 'You will be a wonderful mother, Zoe.' He lifted his glass. 'To your future.'

'Thank you.' Yet even as she raised her glass, that dark-haired little boy flitted across her mind. She forced a smile to her face. 'But enough talk of the future.' After all, they only had a few days left before that future would be reality. 'This is meant to be about the present and the here and now.'

'The here and now,' he echoed, but she was sure she could see a strain behind his smile.

CHAPTER TWELVE

THE FOLLOWING MORNING, Matt slid carefully out of bed, breath held so as not to wake Zoe, and headed for the bathroom. Once shaved, he surveyed himself in the mirror, almost surprised to see that he didn't look different.

Because he felt different, and the knowledge grated his nerves, the feelings a throwback to when he'd met Zoe the first time round. Back then he'd let his guard slip, let Zoe get under his skin and inspire feelings that he couldn't handle and that had ultimately led to pain and abandonment. The only other time he'd done that in his life had been with foster carers who he'd lived with for four years. When he'd heard they were moving him on he'd been devastated inside—only pride had allowed him to hold it together. Outwardly at least. That had been one of the times when he'd punched walls; he'd simply done it in private and hidden the damage.

He turned away from the mirror, knew it was time to pull back—the conversation the previous night had showed him that. Zoe had a future and he wouldn't forget it. That was why he'd arranged a surprise for her this morning, something that would help her future and hopefully she'd enjoy it.

Moving back to the bedroom, he glanced down at Zoe, took in the long eyelashes, the ripple of red hair, the curve of her body under the sheet, and there it was, that trickle of warmth, the stir of emotional connection. Leaning down, he shook her gently awake, smiled as she squinted up at him through sleep-filled eyes. 'You're up,' she said.

'Very observant.' Laughter filled his voice.

'But it's not even six.' She smiled at him. 'I think you should just come back to bed.'

'That is a very tempting idea, but I've got something planned for you.'

'You do? For me?'

'Yup, so come on. Up you get.'

She rubbed her eyes and sat up. 'OK. I'm curious so I'll play along.'

Fifteen minutes later she looked around from the seat of the tuk-tuk, studied the route with a small frown of concentration. 'We're going back to the *dosa* place,' she realised. 'Will it be open yet?'

'Nope. I've booked you a culinary lesson—the owner and chef is going to show you how he makes *dosa* and various fillings. I thought it would be useful, but also something you can use on social media and to promote your food at street markets and so on. Premandi, the owner, has agreed to get his daughter-in-law to video the whole thing as well.'

'That's…' Zoe blinked back tears and then moved closer to him and kissed him '…incredibly thoughtful. Thank you, Matt.'

'You're more than welcome,' he replied as they turned into the alleyway and saw the owner wave cheerfully to them from the restaurant door. 'Enjoy and I'll be back in a few hours.'

As he walked away guilt touched him—yes, he had done it for Zoe, but he knew too it was also a reminder to himself that this time with her was finite, and he hoped some time spent without her would give him time to process and make sure his guard was firmly in place. Yet as he walked the hustle and bustle of the streets, stopped for a coffee, he missed her, missed the feel of her hand in his, her pithy commentary or the way she sometimes just walked in silence. Missed the turn of her head, her scent, her… For Pete's sake. He quickened his pace in exasperation, felt relief when his phone rang.

A relief that was short-lived.

'Matt. It's Edwina. I am so sorry to trouble you but Prisha asked me to, begged me to, because she thought maybe you could help. I am not sure what you can do but I promised her so…'

Matt could hear the panic in Edwina's voice, knew he needed to figure out what was going on even as scenarios chased through his mind. 'Are the children OK?'

'Yes. For now. But…' Edwina's voice broke. 'Her husband has found her.' Matt's blood ran cold. His head swam as Edwina continued. 'He turned up here and tried to take her by force. Thank goodness Chaneth was in the kitchen with her. He grabbed a knife and he managed to get rid of him. They called me and I called the police. But now it turns out that the husband has a lawyer—he says he is legally entitled to the children, that he wants them back, and he is also filing charges against Chaneth and…'

The world seemed to fragment. It was as though the completely unexpected words had caught him unawares, his barriers down, and for a blinding moment the stuff of his nightmares became real. The fuzzy people he could never see clearly struggled to come into focus and this time he could hear the wail of a baby and the sound of rough, raised voices, yelling at it in profanities to shut up.

He closed the images down instantly. He couldn't afford to let them in. Not now.

'Edwina, listen to me. I'm on my way. In the meantime I'll get a couple of security guards to the orphanage and I'll get on to a lawyer. Do not let anyone take Prisha away and do not let those children out of your sight.'

He hung up and then dialled Zoe's number.

'It's Matt.' He briefly explained the situation. 'I'm arranging security and getting a lawyer and I'm sorry, Zoe, I'll need to go back.'

He had to. He couldn't, wouldn't, let those children or Prisha be handed back to a violent man. Would not put them at risk of injury or death. No more children would die on his watch. Which meant he had to be there. He wouldn't desert Chaneth either. The boy did not deserve to go to jail.

'I'm sorry,' he said again. Knew that to Zoe this would be a repeat of her parents' behaviour.

There wasn't even a pause before, 'What are you on about? Why are you sorry? I'm coming too—of course we are going back. We can't stay here having fun whilst Prisha and her babies are in danger.'

'Are you sure?'

'Of course I'm sure, and I'm horrified and insulted that you would even think I would do any different. On a practical note, I'll take over the kitchens—that way Prisha can focus on being with the children or seeing a lawyer. So if possible we need to stay at or near the orphanage. Anyway, we can discuss details later. I'll head back to the hotel and meet you there.'

Even in the grip of panic Matt felt a sense of warmth, an appreciation at Zoe's words, the instant offer of help with a pragmatism to back it up.

The next few hours were caught up in getting themselves from the city back to the orphanage as fast as possible whilst keeping in touch with Edwina.

As they sat in the hire car, he tried to relax. Logic told him they couldn't get there any quicker.

'Hey.' She reached out and put her hand on his leg; the contact gave comfort. 'You have done everything you can do. You've found a lawyer and the security has arrived and it's unlikely the husband will try anything violent now.'

'I wish he would. That way we'd have something against him.' He sighed. 'The lawyer is the best we can get but the problem is, how do we prove the man is violent? And what if he even wins visitation rights or custody? Once he gets his hands on those kids...'

Worry etched Zoe's face. 'I know, and I'm worried sick too. But at least we know right now they are all safe and I know you will do everything you can do to keep them that way. And Chaneth as well.'

Damn right he would. 'I'll feel better when we get there.'

And eventually the car pulled to a stop outside the orphanage and within minutes they were inside. Matt watched as Zoe engulfed Prisha in a hug. 'I am so sorry.'

The young woman shook her head, her face pale. 'He...he said he wouldn't rest until he had us back. That the kids are his, that I deserve to be punished for depriving my kids of a father. I was so scared. And Tomas, he hasn't spoken since. He is asleep now. What am I going to do? And poor Chaneth... But if he hadn't been there...'

Hearing her panic, he knew what he needed to do, would not let even a hint of his own agitation emerge. 'Prisha, listen to me. I will not let anyone hurt a hair on your children's heads, certainly not a man who does not deserve the title of father. Or husband. You are safe. I will fix this.' And he would—he would do whatever it took, no matter what. 'You focus on Tomas and Adam.'

Tomas made a small noise, a whimper, and instantly she moved to his side.

Matt watched as the young woman carefully took the baby out of the sling and put him into the small cot that was beside the bed and something twisted in his heart. Memories, dark and shadowed, seemed to try to push up through the years. A dark contrast to this mother who loved her two children with all her heart, who would protect them from harm at any cost. Whereas his own mother hadn't given a damn, had caused harm to her children through sheer apathy and neglect.

Suddenly aware of Zoe's gaze on him, he pushed the thoughts away. This was not about him. 'We'll leave you to rest,' he said softly, and he and Zoe exited the room.

Once in the hallway, she stopped and placed a hand on his arm. 'Are you OK? I know you're worried about Prisha and I think her situation might be triggering you, reminding you of your childhood.'

Matt stared at her, realised that this was the consequence of sharing confidences, that people could read you, see into your mind and heart, and he didn't like it. Right now he couldn't afford to be triggered, couldn't afford to let emotion impact the work he needed to do. And so he did not need Zoe, or the compassion in her eyes. Zoe brought out emotion in him and that was dangerous; he'd already known that, but now the danger was magnified. He had to be on his game, in control.

'I'm fine. Truly, Zoe. Right now we need to focus on what needs to be done. Also, I spoke with Edwina. We can stay here. They've set up fold-up beds in separate rooms. I think that's more appropriate.'

'Of course.'

He nodded. 'Right, we'll meet later and I'll let you know what the lawyer says.'

Two days later Zoe stirred the enormous pan of soup she was making for the following day's lunch, glanced at the clock and saw it was past eleven. But cooking helped her, relaxed her and distracted her from the hurt she was feeling. Irrational hurt, she told herself.

Only it didn't feel that way; it just hurt. The fact that since they'd got here Matt had completely withdrawn from her. She understood he was working flat out for both Prisha and Chaneth, knew too that he was investigating the legality of Prisha's marriage, was searching for witnesses who would attest to her husband's violence. But these facts were delivered in their evening meetings with Edwina and Prisha and then he would disappear to his room, situated at the other end of the orphanage from her own.

She'd thought after their beach run, after all they'd shared in Burati, that Matt had changed, was opening up. Yet since they'd got here he'd closed down. He also looked terrible, or as terrible as it was possible for Matt to look, with dark circles under his eyes.

Zoe looked down into the orange swirl of the soup. Right. It was daft of her to think that Matt would voluntarily talk to her. And it was stupid and petty of her to be hurt that he wasn't. But what she could do was at least make sure he ate properly. She found a bowl and ladled some of the soup in. He'd worked through dinner and she had the feeling he'd skipped lunch. She quickly heated up a *roti*, placed it on a plate and found a small tray.

A few minutes later she approached his door, wondered belatedly if he might be asleep. She slowed, stopped outside the door to listen and frowned. Perhaps he was on the phone—she could hear the rumble of a voice, a mutter, a murmur that sounded distressed and then there was a cry, a cry of pain, horror, revulsion, hurt. It pierced the air and without thought she placed the tray on the floor, pushed the door open and went in. Matt was sitting up in bed, his eyes open, though she sensed he was still in the grip of his nightmare. His eyes were wide, his skin pale, his dark hair mussed. But it was his expression that tore at her heartstrings—there was fear there and she'd never once seen Matt afraid.

'Matt?' She kept her voice gentle, didn't want to spook him, even as her mind raced with questions. She perched on the bed next to him, put out a tentative hand and laid it on his shoulder, felt the clamminess of his skin, saw the twist of the sheets and wondered how long his nightmare had been. 'It's OK. It was a dream.' But clearly not any dream, not to go by the haunted look on his face. Then he blinked, a long slow blink, and she could almost see the process of pulling himself together begin.

He shifted away from her, swung his legs out of bed. 'I'm fine. I'll be back in a second.' He tugged on a pair of jeans and left the room, returned a few minutes later, towel in hand, his face and torso wet. 'That's better,' he said, remaining standing as he towelled off. 'Sorry. Did I wake you? I must have had a bad dream.' His tone was dismissive; she suspected he was aiming for nonchalance.

'You didn't wake me. I came to bring you some food.' She hesitated. 'That looked like a lot worse than just a bad dream. You were terrified.'

His expression shuttered off as he shrugged. 'That's what bad dreams can do.'

'Do you have bad dreams often?' she asked.

'No. Look, Zoe, I don't really want to talk about it.'

'I get that, but you can't expect me to walk away and pretend it didn't happen. I'm worried about you.'

'Don't be. It's Prisha and Chaneth you need to be worried about.'

'I am worried about them, but you have done everything possible to help them.'

'What if it isn't enough?' His voice was laced with a mix of frustration and fear.

'That is an unanswerable question. But the lawyer said she was cautiously optimistic—and there is nothing more you can do.'

'But maybe there is. Maybe I've missed something.'

'And maybe you are making yourself ill. You're not even eating.'

'I am…' He broke off.

'So please at least eat the soup and *roti*.' She rose and went to get the tray. 'If you get ill you won't be able to help anyone, and then what will happen?'

CHAPTER THIRTEEN

MATT MET HER GAZE, looked down at the soup and realised Zoe was right. He hadn't eaten since breakfast and he did need to eat.

'Thank you,' he said, then placed the tray on the desk and started to eat. The spicy tang of the soup, the smooth texture, offered a comfort and he realised he was in fact ravenous.

Once he'd eaten the last bite he turned, and the words of thanks died on his lips.

'What are you doing?' The question was pointless as he could quite clearly see what she was doing as she smoothed the twist of sheets on the bed, shook out the blanket and calmly climbed underneath.

'I'm staying here. I am not leaving you alone in case you have another nightmare.'

'I…' What was he supposed to do now? The only way to get Zoe to leave would be to pick her up and carry her out. He supposed he could go and sit at his desk and try to work, could read and reread the emails from the lawyer to see if there was anything he or she had missed. Problem was he'd already done that and perhaps that was what had triggered his nightmare.

He looked at the bed again. Zoe lay there, eyes closed, clearly feigning sleep, but she looked so peaceful, so calm, so right there in his bed that he shrugged. There could be no harm in simply lying next to her.

Letting out a sigh, he climbed into the bed next to her, made sure to keep a gap between them and stared up at the ceiling, felt his eyes close and wondered if he should try and stay awake. But surely the dream wouldn't recur... the same night. Not now he was properly awake.

How wrong he was—he sank back in the dream, only now the dream was muddled. Prisha's husband was there. So was Prisha, cradling her baby, Tomas by her side. The husband approached but, instead of it being Prisha, it was the fuzzy outline of a different woman who handed the baby over. And Matt was standing in a corner, power-less, watching as though it were a movie, popcorn by his side. Then he saw the baby wasn't Adam; it was Peter—he didn't know how he knew, but he did, and he let out a roar...cried out his brother's name.

And then he heard a voice...a familiar voice rife with worry but also with care, a soothing voice. 'Matt. It's a dream. It's OK now.' A tendril of hair tickled his face and the familiarity of it brought him to the present, to reality.

He opened his eyes fully and sat up, looked into Zoe's wide green eyes. 'That sounded rough,' she said.

'I'm fine.' He blinked the lingering images away.

'No. You are not fine.' Her hand was back on his arm, her touch a comfort. 'I wish you'd talk to me. I want to help.'

He stared at her face, saw such genuine compassion, and he recalled everything she'd done in the past days. 'You've already helped so much, Zoe. You've been a rock for all the kids. I've seen how much Ravima and Nimali look up to you. You've kept them occupied and you've pro-vided food and you've really been there for Prisha. I've seen how you've looked after Adam so Prisha can focus on Tomas. And she trusts you.'

'I've wanted to do everything I've done. I've got pretty attached to all these kids. But I'm not thinking about them now. I'm thinking about you. I don't even know who Peter is.' Now her other hand was on his other arm and she had shifted closer.

Looking at her, he knew he owed her an explanation. Zoe hadn't had to come here, to give him soup, hadn't had to stay. Plus, how could he not tell the truth about Peter? He wouldn't deny his brother's existence...wouldn't lie to her.

'Peter was my brother, my little brother.' Sadness, guilt, pain hoarsened his voice.

'What happened to him?' Her hand tightened round his arm.

'He died. He was five months old and he died. Apparently he was always sickly. He got pneumonia and my parents...our parents...didn't do anything. A neighbour ended up taking him into hospital. But it was too late. The neighbour told the social workers about me as well and that's when I was taken into care.' He looked at her, his whole being and soul bleak. 'He died. I lived. I should have saved him, helped him, done something.'

'No.' The word was anguished and she moved closer to him now. 'You were five years old.'

'It doesn't matter.'

'You were too young.' She moved closer to him, so close, put her arm round him, and he tried to force the rigidity of his body to relax, to accept the comfort she was offering, a comfort he knew he didn't deserve. 'You mustn't carry this responsibility, the burden of grief and guilt. It is tragic what happened to Peter, to that tiny, frail baby. But it's not your fault.'

'But if I'd acted differently he may have lived.'

'And so you wish you could turn the clock back, and you go through a litany of ifs and buts and if-onlys and what-ifs. I promise you I understand how that feels. But I know that you have no need to feel it.'

He glanced at her, knew with bone-deep knowledge the words came from empathy, not sympathy. 'But you do?'

Zoe shook her head. 'This isn't about me.'

'No. This is about us. You and me.' And the tragedy was that there was nothing more he could tell her about Peter, because he didn't remember him, saw him only in dreams. And whilst he truly appreciated Zoe's belief in him, her attempt to lift his burden of guilt, he knew no words could do that. The very fact he couldn't recall his brother's existence told him there was something wrong with him. But perhaps he could help Zoe, because he could see the pain in her eyes, a depth of guilt that mirrored his own. 'Tell me. Let me help.'

She took a deep breath and now he placed an arm on her shoulders, rested it lightly there, could feel her tension.

'I was never like Beth,' she began. 'I wanted my parents' attention and so I shouted, screamed, did anything I could to get it. At sixteen I took it up a few notches—I turned full-on rebel. I took up alcohol, started partying—I even ended up in a police cell. Even that didn't get their attention. They sent a neighbour to get me out. Then I fell in love, or thought I did.

'Tom came from a super-rich background—he was slumming it at some party I was at. But we had a bond. His parents were caught up in their own lives—they'd got him nannies and boarding schools. He said he sometimes wondered if they even remembered his name. Anyway, I took him on the path of rebellion with me. I ended up taking him to a party I'd heard about... We gatecrashed it. At first I thought it was perfect, much older kids and, oh, so cool. Then I saw there were hard drugs circulating. That was too far even for me. I went to find Tom and found him with another girl. We had a row. I told him it was over. He swore the girl had kissed him and he was drunk, told me he loved me, but I wouldn't listen. I stormed off and left him there.' Tears glistened in her green eyes now. 'I never saw him again. He took an accidental overdose and he died.'

The words were so stark they jolted through him, her pain his own as he imagined the guilt and regret that would have seared through her.

'Oh, Zoe…' He gathered her into his arms and held her. Knew and understood how impossible it was to live with a scenario where the what-ifs must saw through her brain. 'It wasn't your fault.'

'But there are so many different ways it could have played out. If I'd been more understanding—I knew Tom was drunk. I should have *made* him come with me. I shouldn't have broken up with him, then maybe he wouldn't have taken the drugs. I should have called Beth to come and get me, not a taxi. Beth would have gone and got Tom. I should never have been so pathetic as to rebel in the first place, just for my parents' attention.'

He held her tighter. 'I get it,' he said. 'I truly do. But you can't torture yourself with all those what-ifs. If you'd known what would happen, of course you would have acted differently, but none of us can predict the future— you could not have known. Tom chose to take those drugs, and of course he didn't deserve to die but it is not your fault. But I get that it seems as though it is. And I'm sorry.' He stroked her back. 'And I'm sorry for your loss. You lost your first love and even without everything else that must have been traumatic. Did you go to counselling at all? Talk to anyone about how you felt?'

Zoe shook her head. 'Beth was amazing and really there for me but somehow counselling felt too…scary. And almost self- indulgent. I mean, I didn't die, Tom did. And if I was feeling guilty, then I think I figured I deserved it.'

'Do you still think that?'

Zoe moved backwards so she could see him properly and then shifted so they were both sitting, backs against the wall, his arm still around her shoulders. 'Yes, I suppose I do.'

'No.' He shook his head. 'You don't deserve to feel guilty. Sad, of course—it is tragic that Tom died so young. Regret that you couldn't stop the tragedy. Absolutely. But not guilt.'

'Then surely the same goes for you.' Her voice was small. 'Only even more so. You were a child.'

The words arrested him and he looked at her. If he was so sure he was right about Zoe, then he couldn't refuse to look at his own tragedy through the same lens. And he tried to do just that, but how could he absolve himself? Peter had been an innocent. His baby brother had had no choice in his destiny. Tom, however, had to take some responsibility for his own tragic death. He had chosen to stay at the party, chosen to take the drugs. Zoe had done nothing wrong; she hadn't known what Tom would do… hadn't known he was in trouble. Matt would have seen his brother, must have known he needed help. At the very least he should remember Peter; the very fact he couldn't hinted that he simply hadn't cared, just as his parents hadn't.

But Zoe… He looked at her. He didn't want her to carry this burden for ever.

'I've got an idea.' It meant leaving the orphanage for a bit, but it should be OK. He knew logically Prisha's husband would not try a forced entry. Not with the amount of security that surrounded the building. Plus, there was a guard on Prisha's door. Plus, he knew Chaneth was also outside Prisha's door.

'It is always best if someone is watching the guard,' he'd explained with a serious expression on his face. 'People are corruptible. I will keep watch and so too will the others.'

Matt climbed out of bed and held out a hand to pull her up. 'Grab a jacket,' he instructed.

'Where are we going?' she asked as they emerged outside the orphanage, into the early hours of the day with dawn tiptoeing into the sky with fingers of pink and orange. The village was awakening, the clang and clatter of cooking pots, a stream of workers headed for the tea plantation, and early tea vendors plying their trade.

'To lay an offering at a shrine,' he said. 'This place is home to one of the most sacred things in Sri Lanka: an ancient tree grown from the saplings of a tree that sheltered Buddha himself. It is thousands of years old and I think… maybe if you go and lay some flowers for Tom it may help a little. It would be a chance to say sorry that things didn't work out differently.' He stopped and held her hands in his. 'I want somehow to lighten your load of guilt.'

'And what about you?'

'I'll lay some flowers for Peter as well.' Take the chance to say sorry that he hadn't saved him.

She looked up at him and he saw the slight frown in her eyes; quickly he started walking again. This was about Zoe now. He didn't want to hear any more reassurances about himself; his guilt was his to bear and could not be lightened. But he hoped, truly hoped, that Zoe's could be.

They paused at a flower seller close to the shrine and then joined the people making their way forward.

As Matt laid the flowers down he looked at the tree and sensed the awe and reverence in which it was held. He thought of Peter, his baby brother. 'I wish I had saved you, wish I had been a better brother. I'm sorry I wasn't.'

He felt a sense of comfort, hoped his brother could forgive him. Wished that he could forgive himself.

He stepped aside and watched as Zoe crouched down and put her flowers next to his, saw her close her eyes, heard her murmur, 'I'm sorry, Tom. But thank you for being there for me, for being my partner in crime, the person who understood me. I'm sorry I couldn't prevent your death. More sorry than I can ever say. But I will try and honour your memory.'

She rose, her face pale, but he thought he could see a sense of peace that hadn't been there before. Matt knew this wouldn't chase all her demons away, but he hoped it would be a start.

'Thank you,' she said as they walked away. 'That was… I'm glad we did that. I feel…lighter.'

'I'm glad.'

He smiled at her. 'We should get back in time for breakfast,' he said. 'And from now on I promise not to push you away. We're in this together.'

CHAPTER FOURTEEN

'WE WON! WE WON! We won!'

Zoe could still hardly believe it; happiness bubbled inside her along with a relief so intense she could almost cry.

A happiness shared by the entire orphanage—the past days the tension had escalated with everyone increasingly on edge. But it had been Matt who had been the calmest of them all. He'd worked indefatigably, had called in an additional lawyer, but had also promised if the case went against them it wouldn't be the end of it all.

But he had also managed to cheer people up, to keep spirits high, and Zoe had done her best to help with that.

And now Prisha was safe and so were her children. For the first time in days Tomas smiled as he watched all the orphans form a conga and dance round the table.

Zoe went to stand by Matt. 'You did it,' she whispered. 'You saved them.' She understood so much more now why he did what he did. He hadn't been able to save Peter and so now he saved as many other children as he could.

'We saved them,' he said. 'All of us. And it feels good.'

Zoe nodded. 'And now for the celebration dinner.' They'd asked the lawyer to attend as well as the local police superintendent, as Matt wanted to make sure security was maintained for a while. 'I've gone absolutely all out. I've even made sparkling pink lemonade, or something like it. And I've made jackfruit curry, which I know is Prisha's favourite, and a massive chocolate cake for dessert with cardamom ice cream.'

Edwina approached them as she spoke. 'That sounds incredible, Zoe. I just want to thank you both again for everything you've done. The past six days have felt like months. I cannot tell you how grateful we are to you—if she hadn't won this case, I don't know what would have happened to her.'

Six days. For some reason the words prompted a slight sense of panic in Zoe. Why? Her gaze flickered to Matt and the panic upped a bar. Soon it would be time to say goodbye, to move on from this layer of the present to the next. One that did not contain Matt.

One that contained her new business venture and her first step towards a family. A family. Six days. A family. Six days. Oh, Lord. Six days ago…she should have started her period.

'Zoe? Are you OK?'

She looked at Matt. 'Of course. I just remembered I've forgotten the sprinkles for the cupcakes. I'm going to pop out and get some.'

'I'm sure we can manage without sprinkles.'

'Nope. I want them to be perfect. I won't be long.'

As she left her brain raced with anxiety, panic and, she realised, a small sense of anticipation. She had to stay calm; there was no sense in second-guessing anything. The important thing now was to find a pharmacy that sold a super-sensitive pregnancy test. Mission accomplished, she bought the sprinkles she had supposedly left the orphanage for and hurried back.

She entered and forced a smile to her face as Ravima ran across the room to her. 'I've been talking to Ms Vardis, the lawyer, and she has been great. She's going to try and help me.'

Zoe's smile turned to a genuine one, and as she hugged the teenager she determined to put her potential problem from her mind for now. This was a celebration and she wanted to be part of it. 'That is brilliant news. And I know you can do this—follow your dream.' She tugged the sprinkles out of her bag. 'Now I'll just go and put the finishing touches to lunch.'

The next couple of hours passed by in a blur and Zoe was proud of herself that she genuinely enjoyed the lunch, loved seeing the happiness that pervaded the air, the laughter and jokes and, most of all, watching Tomas and Adam and knowing they were safe.

But she kept her gaze averted from Matt, the one brief glimpse she allowed herself too much. He looked so relaxed, so gorgeous, so... Matt, and her tummy swooped and dived at the possibility she was pregnant. With his baby. She closed her eyes briefly, knew with devastating clarity that part of her hoped she was. Not that she expected anything from him; this time she knew he didn't want a family, could understand why he wanted to devote his life to a cause, to helping children.

But maybe... Maybe what? He'd be a part-time father? Whoa.

She hadn't even done a test yet. But she couldn't help herself—now an impossible dream drifted into her brain like pink-tinted cotton wool. Matt being happy about the baby, saying everything was different now, that he wanted the same things Zoe wanted, that...

'Zoe?'

She blinked, aware of Edwina's concerned face. 'Are you OK?'

'I'm fine.'

She glanced round the table, realised everyone was holding up their sparkling lemonade for a toast, aware too that Matt was studying her expression. Damn, she'd been doing so well. She lifted her glass and smiled. 'To Prisha,' she echoed everyone round the table. 'And a brand-new start.' The words held an extra meaning, and she resisted the telltale urge to touch her stomach.

Two hours later, Matt approached Zoe's room, worry and disquiet churning in his chest as he knocked at the door and entered to her call of, 'Come in.'

'Hey.' Her smile was wary. 'How did it go with the police superintendent?'

'Great. Better than great.' For a second he focused on the conversation he'd just left. 'He's agreed to keep an eye on things and he's agreed to take Chaneth on.'

'You mean to work for the police force?'

'Yup. It's perfect—that way Chaneth can do good, and he'll know that he isn't born to be a criminal.' He shook his head. 'But that's not why I'm here. I'm worried because I found this.' He handed over the receipt he'd found on the floor whilst clearing up. 'One of the girls must have dropped it but I've no idea who. I wondered if perhaps you had any idea.'

She looked down at the slip of paper, a receipt from a pharmacy for a pregnancy test, then back up at him, her green eyes wide in shock and…something else.

And in that moment clarity dawned in a blinding burst of a truth so obvious he could only marvel at his own foolishness. Had he really believed the receipt had been dropped by one of the orphans?

'It's mine,' Zoe said. The words so brief and yet so massive in their impact.

'But…it can't be.'

'You mean you don't want it to be.'

Of course he didn't. Because this couldn't work. It was all wrong for Zoe, for the baby… History was repeating itself with a mocking vengeance and he couldn't keep the accusation from his tone. 'You said you were on the pill.'

'I am on the pill. I told you I went on it a year ago because I was doing a lot of travelling and it helped if my periods were more regulated.'

His eyes narrowed and suspicion raised its ugly head, spurred on by a sense of impending panic, the knowledge that for a second time he would be found wanting, the fear of failure, the fear of loss. 'Or you decided this was the way to get the family you want. Decided to dispense with Mr Right and cut straight to the chase. Was that it?' Even as the words spewed from his mouth he knew they should remain unspoken, unthought, but that dark panic drove him on. 'And I was the perfect candidate because this time you thought I'd walk away.'

Zoe sat frozen still, the pain etched on her face so raw that Matt would have done anything to take the words back.

'If that is what you believe of me, then the past weeks have been utterly meaningless,' she said. '*Completely* devoid of *any* meaning.' She rose, her face pale, her eyes dark with anger and misery. 'Get out, Matt. I don't want to see you again.'

And he didn't blame her. 'Zoe. I'm sorry. I shouldn't have said that. Any of that.'

'Damn straight you shouldn't have. I would never do that. To you, or to anyone. You knew what I wanted, what my dream is. For a family. I want my baby to have a father who wants him or her. I know that's not what you want and I respect that.' Her voice broke. 'Please leave. Now.'

'No. I can't just leave. This baby…is my baby too.'

She gazed directly into his eyes. 'It doesn't matter—I don't want my baby to have a father who resents its existence, a father who lets it down because he can't commit. So actually, Matt, this time round, this baby is mine. Of course I won't stop you from seeing him or her, but that's it. I know you don't want a family and I will not get in the way of that.' Her voice was still tight with hurt and he didn't know what to do or say to excuse himself, knew too that she was right—he couldn't give her what she wanted. Couldn't risk being a bad parent and a worse husband. 'That's even assuming there is a baby. I was about to do the test when you came in.' She rose. 'I'll let you know.'

Now a confusion of emotion hit him. There was relief that perhaps this wasn't happening, but there was also a sense of sorrow for this baby that they had discussed as if he were real. A sudden longing that things could be different, that he could be Zoe's Mr Right, that they were hoping for a positive result, wanted to welcome the baby into the world together.

But that wasn't for him. It would be selfish to risk it and yet he knew with bone-deep certainty that if Zoe was pregnant he would risk it. Because, just as it had been four years ago, he could not knowingly neglect his own flesh and blood. Even if he had to fake it to the core, even if he truly felt nothing, his child would never know it.

'I'll wait here. And, Zoe, if you are pregnant, I'm not going anywhere. I won't walk away from my baby. I won't be guilty of neglect.'

Her face softened. 'I understand that. But I won't be trapped in a fake family scenario—we will work out the best way forward. That allows you to carry on your foundation work and gives me a chance to work out how to be a single-parent family.'

'No.'

'Yes. You have made it perfectly clear that you want to prioritise your foundation over a family.'

'That is not the reason I don't want a family.'

Her forehead creased in a frown of scepticism. 'I don't understand.'

'I don't want a family because I can't risk it. I can't risk that I am like my parents, genetically programmed to be a bad father.' The words were imbued with both bitterness and sorrow.

Now sorrow touched her features, and her mouth was a circle of shock as she shook her head so vigorously her ponytail weaved and bobbed. 'You are nothing like your parents—I've seen you with all these kids—you are nothing like them. You care.'

'But I didn't care about Peter.'

'Of course you did. Maybe you couldn't save him, but that's because you were a child.'

'Then why can't I even remember him?' The question was wrenched from him as pain and guilt twisted his insides. 'I only know he existed because a foster carer asked me about him, and I didn't know what she was talking about. I don't remember anything about him, seeing him, hearing him, holding him, trying to feed him, nothing. And there's every chance that's because I didn't bother, didn't care. Just like my parents.'

'Or perhaps your brain has blocked those years out because of how bad they were. To protect you. The blame for what happened to Peter lies squarely with your parents.' The fierceness in her voice was rock solid.

'With the two human beings who made me. Their genes run rife inside me and maybe all I can do is control them. What if I have a baby and I feel nothing for him or her? That's too big a risk for me to knowingly take. But if you are pregnant, then I will not walk away, and the baby will emotions had all surged together and merged into a bleak sense of loss. For an imaginary future that would now not come to pass.

'That's g...' His tongue stumbled on the word and he forced it out. 'Good news.'

'It doesn't feel like good news.' She took a deep breath, stepped towards him. 'For either of us. I know you would be a good dad. This would have been your chance to see that, to see I'm right. I understand why you're scared—I would be too, but you need to believe in yourself.'

'I do believe in myself.' Only the words sounded hollow, as hollow as he felt inside. 'I believe in my company, in my skill set, in my foundation.' And he had the money in the bank, the trappings of wealth, the awards and, most important, a record of the good his foundation had done to prove it.

She shook her head. 'I don't mean any of that. I mean believe in your ability to love and be loved. You have that in you.'

Only he didn't. He looked down into her beautiful green eyes and he wanted to weep. He wished, wished with all his heart, that he could be her Mr Right, give her everything she wanted in life, what she most wanted in life. A family. But he couldn't—he was a bad risk. A husk of a man, empty inside. And she deserved her happy ending. He wouldn't stand in the way of that.

'Only I don't. You need to start your quest for a real Mr Right, a man who you know will be a great dad, whose dream is a family. So it is good news.' It had to be. 'This way you...we can resume our normal lives as planned.' The words were leaden and he tried for some form of uplift. 'The next layer. That's a good thing.'

'Yes.' She gave a small laugh, the sound an almost strangled gurgle, a travesty of her true laugh. 'Funnily enough today is the last day of the festival, the day the relic is returned to its golden box in the temple. I suppose that's fitting.' She met his gaze directly. 'But it doesn't feel like that. Is this how your relationships work? Because this doesn't feel fun or uncomplicated.'

She was right. It didn't. It felt desolating.

'No, it doesn't. My type of relationship didn't work for us. Maybe it couldn't between us, maybe we had too much history, but somewhere along the way we ended up drifting from the shallow end to the deep and we need to get out now before we both drown.'

Pain touched her face and then she nodded. 'You're right.' She paused. 'I don't want the children to feel there's anything wrong so I suggest I leave tomorrow—I'll explain my sister needs me.' Another deep breath. 'When we see each other next I truly hope it won't be awkward.'

He wished he could think of something—anything—to say. But there was nothing...zip, *nada*. So he turned and walked slowly from the room.

One month later

Matt tried to keep his heart from pounding his ribcage as he entered the building that housed social services in the area of London where he'd been born. He walked to the reception desk and announced his name and was told to take a seat. Five minutes later a young woman entered the waiting room.

'Matt? Hi, I'm Janine. We spoke on the phone. It's good to meet you.'

'And you.'

'Come through to my office.'

Once seated, he glanced around, appreciated the

touches to the institutionalised room—the row of cacti on the windowsill, the personalised mug on the desk.

'Before I give you the files, can I check that you are sure this is what you want to do?'

'Yes, it is. I've spoken with the counsellor and I do want to go ahead.'

'You understand these files detail the circumstances around your being taken into care.'

'Yes. I understand.'

'OK.' She unlocked a drawer and pulled out a pile of files. 'You can't take these away, but you can take notes and obviously you can come back on later dates. Take your time. If you need a break, give me a call and I'll lock the files up. I've booked the room for the whole day as you requested.'

'Thank you.' Once Janine had gone Matt looked at the files. This was the right thing to do. His whole life, he'd believed the past didn't matter. Or so he'd said. But it did. The past affected the present and the future. And now he needed to try and understand it. Why he couldn't remember those early years, why he couldn't remember his brother, what those years had been like.

He could taste the bitter tang of fear in his mouth, but he knew this was important. Knew he had to face his past to have any hope of a future. The future he wanted.

Skin clammy, heart pounding, he opened the top file and started to read.

Zoe looked up from unpacking boxes in her newly rented London apartment and smiled at her sister.

'I came to see how you were settling in.' Beth watched as Zoe rose to her feet and indicated round the room.

'I'm not settled yet. Once I get everything unpacked, I'm sure it will be OK.'

Only she wasn't. Nothing felt OK. She missed Matt, more than she thought it possible to miss anyone. She missed the feel of his hand around hers, his smell, his smile, the sound of his voice. She missed telling him things, trivial and important, she missed waking up next to him, safely cocooned in his arms. She missed all of him; worst of all, it didn't seem to be getting any better. However hard she worked.

Oh, she wouldn't give up; she'd spent the last few nights going over her business plans, contacting street-market organisers but any sense of excitement felt dulled.

But it would pass.

'Actually,' Beth said, 'I came here to talk to you, and Dylan has gone to see Matt.'

'Is he OK?' What if he'd stopped eating again? What if the nightmares were back? What if something had happened to one of the kids he cared about or there'd been a stock market crash or…?

'No. I don't think he is. And I don't think you are either, so I wanted to say sorry. From Dylan and me. We should never have let David give you that gift. It wasn't fair on either of you.'

'I don't think you had any choice in the matter. And what happened between Matt and me is not your fault. It's ours and we'll both get over it. I need to put it behind me and move on.'

'Why?' Beth frowned. 'I don't mean to pry but I don't get it. You're both miserable.'

'It doesn't matter.'

Her sister's frown deepened. 'Do you love him, Zoe?'

'Yes.' The word was a wail. 'But I don't want to. Matt doesn't do love.'

'Are you sure? Maybe he hasn't said the words, but how has he acted?'

Zoe thought about the answer to that. Recalled the time he'd held the cushion for her to punch, then listened to her talk about her family. The way he'd listened to her talk about Tom, taken her to the shrine. The things he'd shared with her. The way he'd held her close and safe. But Matt had also cared about Prisha and Chaneth and the orphans. But that was different. Because Matt had also confided in her, shared things he had never shared before.

'But none of that matters anyway. Because Matt doesn't want a family.'

Beth frowned. 'Are you sure he doesn't?'

'Yes. But I do. In fact I had—I have—a plan. I'm going to find a man, a good, decent man to settle down with and…' She broke off as she saw Beth's face. 'OK. I get that plan isn't going to work until I'm over Matt. But I will get over him. And if not, then I'll become a single parent. I'll adopt or use a donor or…something.'

Beth stepped towards her and pulled her into a hug, before releasing her and gesturing to the sofa. 'I'm making us some tea and then I want to say a few things.'

Five minutes later, cradling the steaming mug, she looked closely at Zoe.

'I get why you want a family; you want what we never had. And I understand that. I want that too and, yes, Dylan does want a family as well. But if he didn't, it wouldn't be a deal-breaker. It never would have been. I wouldn't stop loving him. Or if one of us can't have kids we wouldn't break up. We'd figure it out. But I'd rather grow old with Dylan, with the man I love and who loves me, and not have kids than not have Dylan.' She put her mug down, reached out and covered Zoe's hand. 'I get it's different for everyone and only you know your priorities, but please promise me you'll think about what I've said.'

Zoe stared at her sister, her lovely, wise, beautiful sister. 'I promise,' she said softly. Once her sister had left she sat down, her head awhirl. Got back up and grabbed her jacket.

Twenty minutes later she was knocking at David and Manisha's door, relieved when Manisha pulled it open and smiled in welcome.

'Zoe. How lovely to see you.'

'I am so sorry to drop by unannounced. I wondered if I can have a quick word with you and David.'

'Of course. Come in.'

Having refused all offers of refreshment, Zoe sat opposite the couple, touched by how close they sat together on the sofa, the way Manisha held her husband's hand as if she needed to keep him close.

'I...well, I was wondering why you gave Matt and me the trip to Burati.'

David studied her face closely. 'Because I saw the way he looked at you, when you and Beth came into the hospital room. He couldn't hide how he felt. He may have been able to hide it from you, maybe even from himself, but that look said it all. I am a statistician. I weighed up the odds. If the two of you had gone your separate ways after the wedding he may never have figured out how he felt about you. If the two of you spent more time together he might. I was trying to help the odds. I've always had a lot of time for Matt—he's a good man who helped my son. I wanted to pay my debt in case I didn't come back.'

'I'm very glad you did,' Zoe said. 'And thank you. For everything.'

Three days later

Matt glanced down at his post and froze—amongst the bills and circulars there was a card addressed in a hand of feelings he couldn't even identify. Until it occurred to him that Zoe had put it all out there, and then he rose at rocket speed and strode over to her, giddy with happiness.

'Zoe.'

'Yes.'

'Turn around. Please.'

She did, though her eyes wouldn't meet his and gently he tipped her chin up.

'I love you too.' The words fell so naturally from his lips, felt so right, so glorious, so steeped in history and yet so unique to them. 'With all my heart. You are my bright shining star and I love you.'

'Really? I don't want you to say it because it's what I want to hear.'

'I'm saying it because I mean it. I love you.' How to prove it? 'Look.' He reached into his jacket pocket. 'I even brought this today. If it seemed right, I was going to give it to you.'

She took the paper and started to read and he saw her eyes mist over.

He'd written it with such hope in his heart, a hope that had now been answered beyond his dreams.

First Date Application:

Dear Zoe
I am writing to apply for a first date. A date where we can talk and I can try to tell you what is in my heart.
    Since I saw you last I have missed you more than I can possibly say. I know I don't deserve this, but I wonder if you can give me some time...time to become the man I want to be.
    I can wait as long as you want.
Matt

'You don't have to wait at all.' She looked at him and he could see the love glow in her eyes. 'You already are the man I want you to be. You are incredibly kind, caring and decent. You make me laugh, you listen to me, you encourage my dreams. You helped me gain perspective, on my parents, on Tom, and you showed me what charity really means. You're also incredibly gorgeous and make my heart skip a beat every time I see you. I love everything about you exactly as you are, everything.'

'And I love you, Zoe. Because you gave me the courage to face my past. I went to social services and they gave me my files to read.'

'Oh, Matt.' Instantly she was there, by his side, arms looped round him.

'It wasn't pleasant reading. But it gave me some insight into my parents' backgrounds—they had pretty awful childhoods and upbringings themselves and they used alcohol and drugs to forget. I think half the time they probably forgot I was there. It isn't an excuse but at least it makes it slightly more understandable. For those first years I simply existed; I had a primal need to survive so I did. The whole case was a mess; they have no idea how my parents managed to stay under the radar.

'Peter was never even registered. I also managed to track down the neighbour who got Peter to the hospital. He recalled the meeting; the woman had cried when she'd seen him, told him how sorry she was for turning a blind eye for so long. 'It turns out she didn't even know Peter existed. Nobody did. They must have pretty much given birth at home but who knows how or where? But on the day she called social services in she heard a pounding on the wall and she thinks it was me, because when she came in I said *baby*, but it's possible that until then I didn't really know about Peter.'

'Oh, Matt. That is awful. But if it was you, then you did try to save him.'

He nodded. 'If it was me at least there is a possibility that I tried.' He stopped. 'But even if I didn't... I have realised one day I do want to be a dad, have a baby. With you.'

'You don't have to.'

'I want to. I'm not my parents. I am capable of love—you've shown me that. I love you with all my heart and I know that is real. I love how much you care about people, your family, Prisha, Chaneth. I love how much you care about food. I love your curiosity and your ambitions. I love the way you smile, the feel of your hair, holding your hand. I love that I can talk to you about anything, and I want to have a family with you. You have made me realise I have the capacity to love, and I know I will love our baby. I want to spend the rest of my life with you, Zoe.'

'As I do with you. I love you, Matt. I didn't know it was possible to be this happy. But I am and we will be. Happy ever after in all the ways that count.'

She stepped forward into his arms, and as he kissed her he knew they would swim the shallows and the deeps together for ever and that he would love this woman until the end of his days.

* * * * *

COMING SOON!

We really hope you enjoyed reading this book.
If you're looking for more romance, be sure to
head to the shops when new books are
available on

Thursday 12th May

To see which titles are coming soon, please visit

millsandboon.co.uk/nextmonth

MILLS & BOON®

Coming next month

TEMPTATION IN ISTANBUL
Hana Sheik

"I'm not tethering you to the house," he said with a frown. "You're free to go where you want. Take Zara with you. I'd like her to see Istanbul."

"And where will you be?" She ignored the alarm bell clanging in her head and the tightening mix of panic and ire pressing down onto her thumping heart. Leaping to a conclusion wouldn't do her any good.

"As I said, I'll be busy closing this partnership deal for my company. But by tomorrow afternoon, my schedule is free." His face relaxed, his frown softer and his eyes less troubled. The dark beginnings of a beard raked his jaw and climbed to his high-boned cheeks. He palmed the lower half of his face, his nostrils twitching with an audible sigh.

Suddenly the air around him shifted.

He smiled charmingly. "I was thinking a city tour might be a good way to celebrate the closing of this deal. If that's something you'd be interested in? I'm a pretty good tour guide."

His smile unleashed a fluttering in her stomach and a rush of heady warmth over her body.

"I think Zara would like that," she said.

"And you?"

She heard the rest of his question. Would you like it? After drinking down to the dregs in her cup, Maryan placed it on the tray and watched as Faisal mirrored her with his mug. She stood and grabbed the tray handles, her eye contact with him unsevered and stronger than before. He tensed his shoulders slightly as if anticipating her rejection. Even so, his smile remained sunny on his too-handsome face.

"I've always wanted to see the Hagia Sophia."

It took a few seconds, but his bright teeth flashed at her. "Then we'll add it to the tour." He stared at her afterward, his smile edging on playful and his eyes dropping to her mouth.

"Sounds good," she agreed.

"It's a date," he added.

She couldn't unglue her tongue from the roof of her mouth to give him a comeback. So she did the next best thing. Bobbed her head, lifted the tray with their empty mugs and walked away from him before she combusted from blushing too much.

Continue reading
TEMPTATION IN ISTANBUL
Hana Sheik

Available next month
www.millsandboon.co.uk

JOIN THE
MILLS & BOON
BOOKCLUB

- ❋ **FREE** delivery direct to your door

- ❋ **EXCLUSIVE** offers every month

- ❋ **EXCITING** rewards programme

50% OF
YOUR FIRS
PARCEL

Join today at
millsandboon.co.uk/subscribe